A Magic Kiss

"Are you saying I sissy-kiss?" His dark eyes lit up at the challenge. "Now you've done it, Cynthia. I'm probably going to regret this . . . you're probably going to regret this, but I have no choice now. Nope. Dare a prince and you dare the devil. *Que sera sera.*"

P.T. was acting purely on reflex now, and his reflexes were being fueled by two zillion pounds of raging testosterone.

A sissy-kiss, huh? I'll show her. If there was one thing a Spaniard—well okay, a Puerto Rican—knew how to do, it was kiss. He put his heart and soul into his kisses. He savored them, like fine wine and good sex.

He released her hands and advised in a husky voice he scarely recognized, "Hold on tight, Cynthia."

Romances by Sandra Hill

KISS OF WRATH
THE PIRATE BRIDE
KISS OF TEMPTATION
KISS OF SURRENDER
KISS OF PRIDE
THE NORSE KING'S DAUGHTER
THE VIKING TAKES A KNIGHT
VIKING IN LOVE
HOT & HEAVY
WET & WILD
A TALE OF TWO VIKINGS
THE VERY VIRILE VIKING
THE VIKING'S CAPTIVE
(formerly MY FAIR VIKING)
THE BLUE VIKING
TRULY, MADLY VIKING
THE LOVE POTION
THE BEWITCHED VIKING
LOVE ME TENDER
THE LAST VIKING
SWEETER SAVAGE LOVE
DESPERADO
FRANKLY, MY DEAR
THE TARNISHED LADY
THE OUTLAW VIKING
THE RELUCTANT VIKING

SANDRA HILL

Love Me Tender

AVON
An Imprint of HarperCollinsPublishers

AVON BOOKS
An Imprint of HarperCollins*Publishers*
195 Broadway
New York, New York 10007

Copyright © 1998, 2014 by Sandra Hill
ISBN 978-0-06-201906-6
www.avonromance.com

First Avon Books mass market printing: November 2014

And finally, a book dedicated to my best friend . . . my sister, Flora Cluston Drapalski.

It is especially appropriate that Flora get a book which centers around dreams and a young woman's fancy. She was there when both of our dreams first sparked . . . in the old house in the poor neighborhood, in the disciplined atmosphere of St. Agnes School, along the wide Susquehanna, which swept through the center of town, in the nooks and crannies of a creaking Victorian library. Oh, the tears and laughter we shared these many years . . . over dreams!

How apropos to this book, which focuses on dreams, that Flora once wrote:

> *Snowflakes*
> *and silent tears*
> *long frozen by the howling wind*
> *sent out to lonely lovers' ears*
> *who wait.*
>
> *In dreams,*
> *my heart and soul*
> *join in a minuet*
> *and dance to the tune of time*
> *in loneliness.*

Please enjoy *Love Me Tender*, Flora, dear. There's a little bit of this Cinderella in both of us.

READER LETTER

Dear Reader:

Once upon a time, in a magic kingdom, there lived a handsome prince. Prince Charming, he was called by one and all.

And to this land came a gentle princess. You could say she was Cinderella.

Magic kingdom?

Well, okay, if you're going to be a stickler for accuracy, in this fairy tale the kingdom is Manhattan. But there's magic in the Big Apple, isn't there?

Prince Charming?

Oh, boy! You've heard the rumors, I suppose. So this fantasy calls for a little imagination. So he's Prince Not-So-Charming on occasion. So he sells shoes, not glass slippers. So he drives a pick-up truck, not a pumpkin coach. Big deal! He *is* handsome.

A gentle princess?

Picky, picky, picky! Who says a woman has to be soft and fluffy all the time? Haven't you ever heard of a royal case of PMS? And just because this princess is called "The Shark" doesn't mean she can't harbor some tender emotions inside.

Cinderella?

Geesh! Who's telling this story? She *is* Cinderella, all right . . . Wall Street Cinderella. This is the twenty-first century, people. The feminist movement, I-am-woman-hear-me-roar, and all that affirmative-action business. Remember, even Kate Middleton had a career before her prince came galloping down the castle boulevard.

And, no, no, no, my lips are sealed over the glass slipper not fitting incident. You didn't hear it from me that the princess has a corn.

Now, dear reader, if you will open your eyes and ears and heart to all the enchantment awash in this earthly realm, I hereby present to you a most fantastical story.

Elmer Presley, fairy godfather

Love Me Tender

Chapter One

Cinderella's slipper would have never made it over a corn . . .

"THE PRINCE IS A ROYAL PAIN IN THE . . . FOOT."

Prince Pedro Tomas de la Ferrama had just shimmied out of his jeans and was pulling up his gray silk Armani slacks when he glanced out the shaded side window of the limousine and saw the sign wielded by a female picketer. He did a double take.

A long-legged strawberry blonde on crutches brandished the ignominious placard. Although she leaned against a telephone pole, she was clearly the ringleader of the line of chanting women—at least a dozen—who paraded in front of the skyscraper housing his sixteenth-floor offices. They carried similar messages: FERRAMA IS ANTI-WOMAN. WHAT'S SEXY ABOUT CORNS? PRINCE FERRAMA IS A FROG. THE VAMP=CORNS. DOWN WITH

FERRAMA SHOES. CORNS, BUNIONS, CALLUSES . . . WHAT NEXT? WARTS?

"Maldito!" he muttered and leaned forward to speak into the intercom. "Circle the block, Jake." With the usual noontime traffic congestion, that could take half an hour.

"Sure thing, boss," his head designer, Jacob Beaunare, replied with childlike glee. Due to their ongoing financial crunch, Jake had been forced to double as chauffeur, but it was a role he enjoyed. The former MIT whiz kid whipped the leased stretch limo, with its detachable imperial crests, out into the bustling Manhattan street, oblivious to the honking horns and curses of cab drivers, not to mention the WBOT news van.

Oh, great! Is that Robin Roberts coming up the street, flanked by two ABC cameramen?

"What the hell's going on, Dick?" he snarled, turning to his lawyer and figurehead CEO, Enrique Alvarez, who sat beside him on the other side of the limo's wide bench seat, sipping a Scotch and perusing the file of papers in his open briefcase with calculated coolness. Dick prided himself on his smooth composure under pressure.

He was about to give Dick some *real* pressure . . . like a fist in his too-pretty face. He was sick to death of all the PR games Dick orchestrated, although, to be fair, he didn't know if Dick was responsible for this latest travesty.

Peering up at him over a pair of wire-rimmed reading spectacles, Dick smoothed a hand over his long, slicked-back hair, which was gathered into a ponytail at his nape. "Relax, P.T. I told you when I picked you up at La Guardia that we have a minor crisis. *No problema.*"

Uh-oh! Every time Dick said *no problema*, he could be sure they had lots of problems. P.T. mentally fortified himself for the worst, then said, *"No problema?* You call a herd of . . . of femi-Nazis circling my headquarters *no problema?* You call that ABC News vehicle on our tail *no problema?* You call this kind of publicity just before the Ferrama stock offering *no problema?"*

"Don't get your laces in a knot, *mi amigo.* I'll handle it."

"Carramba! Were articles of incorporation filed today with the Securities and Exchange Commission?" he asked stonily.

"Sí . . . of course. Now we have three weeks before Ferrama goes public on August sixteenth. Next starts the road show, taking our presentations to the brokerage institutions in the selling group. The lawyers are proofing the final prospectus as we speak."

"And the opening price?"

"Five dollars per unit." Dick beamed with satisfaction. He'd been afraid the initial offering would be set at a lower price; anything under five dollars smacked of penny stocks, which he'd wanted to avoid.

"So, with two million shares, we'll raise ten million in equity, as we'd hoped."

"Yep. Man oh man, we landed in a pile of gold dust when we chose Donaldson & Donaldson for the managing underwriters. The fifteen securities firms they invited into the initial selling group are primo . . . the best in the business."

"It was more of a coup that Donaldson chose us," P.T. pointed out dryly, but he couldn't help smiling at Dick's enthusiasm.

"*Dios*, I'm so anxious, I wish we could hit the boards today, but the SEC demands this twenty-one-day 'cooling off' period. I can see that you're wired, too, P.T. So, why don't you take this time to cool off. You're entirely too uptight."

P.T. realized that Dick had managed to divert his attention from the problem at hand . . . the picketers. He released a long sigh of exasperation. "Ah, Dick, you know that this is a delicate stage. News of our stock offering will surely hit the financial news by tomorrow."

"Yeah. In fact, you have an appointment this afternoon with a *Wall Street Journal* reporter. And the tombstone ads to be run in the financial pages of all the major newspapers on the big day are ready to be sent out. They just need your final stamp of approval."

P.T. groaned. "So why are those women picketing our offices?"

"We had no idea the crackpot would go this far. She and her cohorts weren't here when I left the building two hours ago."

"You *knew* there was a problem? And didn't nip it in the bud?"

"Hey, I had my hands full with your stepsisters. Those two bloodsuckers would put Cinderella's wicked stepsisters to shame."

P.T. winced. "What are Naomi and Ruth up to now?"

"Same old, same old. Money, money, money . . . they just can't get enough. They're driving everybody at the office bonkers. Wait till the accountant gets ahold of you. Naomi bought five thousand dollars' worth of power tools and fifty gallons of paint last week. And Ruth ordered three Bob Mackie sequin jumpsuits for her boyfriend, Elmer Presley, for a cool ten grand."

"Elmer Presley? He's still hanging around?" P.T. groaned, then waved a hand dismissively. "I can't deal with Naomi and Ruth now. Back to the picketers . . . what can we do to avert a disaster?"

"Don't overreact. I'm sure it's just a tiny blip in the scheme of things."

"Are you *loco?* I smell a lawsuit waiting to happen. *Any* negative publicity could deflate our opening stock price."

"I said I'd handle it, man."

That was the problem. He probably would. The question was how.

Lifting his butt off the seat, P.T. tucked his black T-shirt into the pleated slacks, then buttoned, zipped and belted himself in, the whole time scowling his displeasure at his colleague. As a final touch, and with a grimace of distaste, he draped the matching double-breasted suit jacket over his shoulders like some Italian movie star . . . or prince. Who the hell ever heard of wearing a T-shirt with a suit? But Dick proclaimed that was the hottest look in international men's couture, according to *GQ.* Dick knew about that kind of thing.

The persona finally in place, P.T. took a deep breath. "Let's cut to the chase and—"

His words were interrupted by the screech of brakes and the sound of metal abrading metal as Jake misjudged a corner and sideswiped three trash cans. A bag lady gave them the flying finger salute and a cop blew his shrill whistle. Jake could be seen in the rearview mirror shrugging sheepishly and mouthing, "Oops!"

P.T. braced his forehead with the carefully manicured fingertips of one hand—another of Dick's bright ideas . . . clear nail polish!—and closed his eyes, counting to ten. Then he leveled a withering glare at Dick, who had the good sense to put aside his booze and briefcase. "Fill me in on everything."

"She's Cynthia Sullivan."

"Who?"

"The redhead."

Oh. The babe on crutches with the Rockette legs. "That wasn't red hair. It was blond . . . well, reddish-blond," he pointed out, having no time to wonder why or how he'd noticed such an irrelevant detail.

"Oh, God!" Dick's mouth went slack-jawed with surprise before he hooted with laughter, shaking his head at him. "You dumb schmuck. That's Cynthia 'The Shark' Sullivan, and you've got the hots for her."

"Knock it off," P.T. sliced out. Dick had been a friend for more than a decade and a business associate for more than five years, but sometimes he went too damn far.

"Take my advice. You need all your wits about you the next few weeks, and it's a proven fact that testosterone is a natural I.Q. suppressant. I oughta know."

"Damn straight you oughta know." Since his divorce Dick had gone through one woman after another.

"Believe me, this *señorita* is bad news . . . a pit bull in high heels."

"I am *not* interested in the woman. I only commented on her hair," he protested. "Besides, my sex life is none of your business."

Dick just grinned at him.

P.T. inhaled deeply for calm. "What did you mean by the shark remark?"

"Didn't you see the *Business Week* article last year profiling Cynthia Sullivan, the Wall Street trader nicknamed 'The Shark'?"

P.T. rubbed his chin pensively. "I thought *shark* referred to a ruthless corporate raider or 'Black Knight.'"

"It usually does, but in her case, she earned the tag another way. She's so aggressive on the exchange floor that some brokers refer to her as 'The Irish Barracuda.'"

"Is she the kook who made network news when she told the Federal Reserve Chairman to f-off?"

"Bulls-eye! The Fed chief was giving a speech at the *Forbes* magazine luncheon when she overheard him saying something about brokers taking voluntary pay cuts to help curb inflation."

"Hmpfh! It's about time someone put that dipshit in his place." But then P.T. frowned. "I don't understand. We have a Wall Street trader leading a picket of our business? And you say *no problema?*"

"No, no, no," Dick corrected. "Her job has nothing to do with this campaign of hers . . . well, not directly. Don't you remember me telling you on the phone last week that some fruitcake had been calling customer service to complain about a corn she got from one of our shoes . . . 'The Vamp'? You told me to ignore her."

"A *corn?*" P.T. yelled. He felt a headache the size of his debit balance begin to pound behind his eyeballs.

"I thought you were talking about some old lady with blue hair, not someone quite so . . . uh, young. And wipe that smirk off your face."

"Oh, Cynthia Sullivan's not young," Dick said with a knowing snort. "She must be at least thirty."

P.T. slanted Dick a wry glance. They were both thirty-two. "That's young," he insisted. "Let me get this straight. We're being picketed because some chick allegedly got a corn on her big toe from one of our products."

"Pinky."

"What?"

"The corn's on her pinky toe, not her big toe."

"*Mierda!*" he murmured.

"She claims her profession requires her to be on her feet all day on the exchange floor. Traders are those people you see on the evening news during the daily stock reports, standing around yelling out bids, like at an auction. Anyhow, she says the pain of the corn kept her from doing her job."

"Don't make me laugh."

"Then, because she wasn't able to move quickly, one of the other traders stepped on her foot and broke that toe, along with two others. She lost her job . . . temporarily, at least. And she might have to default on the two-million-dollar apartment she recently bought in the Dakota."

"Two million dollars?" P.T.'s jaw dropped with incredulity. Then he thought of something. "The Dakota? Isn't that the place where John Lennon was shot?"

"Uh-huh. It's harder to get into that building than Fort Knox now—visitor or resident. Very ritzy place, like a castle. Believe me, she got a bargain at two million. And talk about elite occupants! Over the years it's been home to Lauren Bacall, Rudolf Nureyev, Gilda Radnor, Roberta Flack, some Arab princess, Boris Karloff. In fact, the movie *Rosemary's Baby* was filmed there."

"What are you, a walking real estate encyclopedia?" P.T. snorted with disgust. "So, we've got some Boris Karloff creature from the black Dakota lagoon, living in Rosemary's baby's co-op, about to put a curse on our company?"

"I never said she lived in those particular apartments."

"Whatever! A corn, Dick? A corn? Talk about frivolous complaints!"

"That's what everyone said about that lady who sued McDonald's over a hot cup of coffee. She got millions."

"I needed to hear that," P.T. grumbled. "Dick, our shoes sell because they're sexy, but also because they're guaranteed to be ergonomically and orthopedically correct. Is it possible our product caused her . . . injury?"

"I doubt it, but it doesn't really matter. We can't risk a court battle."

"Okay, what's our happy picketer looking for . . . fifteen minutes of fame on the TV tabloids? An easy cash settlement? Or is she just plain crazy?"

"At first I would have said crazy. Now I'm leaning toward crazy like a fox."

"Or a shark."

"Yep," Dick agreed. Then he added, "We need a plan."

"Will our liability insurance cover this kind of injury claim?"

"Probably. Even our bare-bones budget isn't skimpy in that department."

"So, the problem is publicity. We have to do everything to avoid publicity," P.T. concluded.

"Yep. The bankers say we have every reason to expect Ferrama to be hyped as a hot issue. But what we don't want is a swooner . . . a stock that's volatile . . . supersensitive to news of any kind."

"Like picketers," P.T. deduced. "Okay. You'll have to set up a meeting with Wall Street Barbie, ASAP."

Dick nodded. "And you're going to have to be her Ken. Lay on the princely charm with a trowel. Seduce her if you have to."

P.T. didn't even blink at the suggestion. They'd both done worse for the company in the five years since they'd begun the blitz to change its image in the marketplace. Now the pot of gold was almost in their grasp, the end of the rainbow no longer an impossible dream.

Besides, he'd never made it with a stockbroker before. Maybe he could learn something new.

Still, P.T. balked inwardly. "I've spent the past week dodging the Countess Ariana," he complained.

"That oversexed tart who owns a chain of European fashion mags? I read about her in the *New Yorker*."

"One and the same," P.T. said tiredly. "I gotta tell you, I'm all charmed out. Why don't you do the seducing this time?"

"Because you're so much better in the charm department. Because women, no matter how intelligent, no matter what age, still harbor this fantasy about Prince Charming coming down the pike on a white horse to carry them off into the sunset. Because the only horses I'm acquainted with are at the track," Dick answered with a grin. "Besides, it probably won't come to that. Maybe Ms. Sullivan will be reasonable."

"A reasonable shark? Somehow I doubt it."

Dick tucked his pager and cell phone into his briefcase as the limo approached the front of the building again.

P.T. slid on a Rolex watch and inserted one tiny gold loop earring—additional ostentatious props in their dog-and-pony show. On his neck, he squirted a minuscule amount of French cologne that cost an ungodly five hundred dollars an ounce. Then he wet his palms with water from a bottle of Perrier that Dick handed him and raked the fingers of both hands through his collar-length hair, pushing the long black strands back off his face in a style meant to evoke a casual cosmopolitan air—all window dressing to enhance the image of Ferrama, Inc. Thus far it had worked.

"Well?" he inquired finally.

After a quick assessment of P.T.'s appearance, Dick nodded his approval. It was a silent ritual they'd repeated too many times to count these past five years, ever since P.T. had converted his stepfather's tacky Friedman's Wholesale Shoe Factory into the elegant Ferrama, Inc.

"Lookin' good, my friend," Dick commented with a playful poke in his arm.

Dick knew how much P.T. hated this playacting scam. Well, only three more weeks. Then he could buy out the interests of his greedy stepsisters and be free, free, free. No more prince baloney. No more non-stop business pressures. He would become P. T. Ferrama, regular guy.

"How many lawyers does it take to change a light bulb?" he asked, wanting to lighten the strain between them. He'd posed the same hackneyed riddle to Dick hundreds of times, often in situations far tighter than this. Hell, some men bonded by hugging; he and Dick bandied ridiculous jokes.

"How many can you afford?" Dick shot back, bobbing his eyebrows at him.

They exchanged smiles.

"None . . . if we go belly up."

"Hey, where's the kick-ass Norman Vincent Peale attitude that's carried us this far?"

"I'm just tired, that's all." It was more than that, but this was not the time to open that can of worms.

Donning his dark sunglasses, P.T. waited for Jake to come around and open the door for him. He closed his eyes briefly, willing himself into the suave, debonair guise that should have become second nature to him by now. He'd reinvented himself so many times, he barely knew who he really was. Then, bracing himself for the gauntlet of reporters and picketers, he gave Dick one last meaningful look. They both knew the drill.

"Well, *hombre*, let's launch this boat and make some waves." As much as his friend annoyed him, they were in this together, sink or swim. "Oh, and another thing . . ." P.T. added.

Dick's lips twitched with amusement, anticipating what he was about to hear.

"Bring Ms. Sullivan up to my office," he said. "Let's show her how the big sharks play."

It takes a con man (woman) to know a con man . . .

Physical image was important, even in the business world. Therefore, Cynthia glanced quickly in the mirrored side of the elevator and adjusted the mid-thigh skirt of her Versace navy blue, pinstriped suit, making sure the white lace camisole beneath its open jacket was tucked into the waistband. On her jacket lapel was a platinum brooch from Tiffany's in the form of a bull sitting on the chest of a downed bear—animal symbols of the two extremes of the stock market. The pin had been a gift from her firm's senior partners five years ago when she'd grossed her first million in sales. Now she averaged ten million in production every year, easily.

She double-checked the lace camisole to make sure nothing unseemly was showing. Some women on Wall Street, which was still a predominantly male bastion, felt the need to hide their femininity. Cynthia worked hard to tone down her provocative curves and brassy coloring, but still she delighted in flaunting her femininity in a subtle way.

As her dear old Irish grandma used to say, "There's no need to fear the wind if your haystacks are tied down." Well, Cynthia preferred to wrap her haystacks in designer clothes and the illusion of womanly softness, which hid her hard inner core.

Cynthia had learned long ago to rely on no one but herself. She had no husband or family or significant other to lean on when the going got rough. Only herself. And that was just fine.

When she was satisfied with her appearance, despite the ugly, thick-soled sandal she was forced to wear on one foot and the open-toed, Velcro, post-op bootlet on the other, she hobbled with as much panache as possible out of the elevator on her crutches.

Waiting for her was the man who'd identified himself as Enrique "Just-Call-Me-Dick" Alvarez. He'd extended an invitation to her on behalf of his employer, Prince Ferrama, the president of the shoe company from hell—the cause of all her current problems. Apparently his highness, the shoe toad, wished to meet with her privately to clear up the "little misunderstanding."

Hah! She'd show him a "little misunderstanding." More than one trader on the exchange had been burned by underestimating her intelligence. Her grandma had been right. A sharp lass *could* beat the devil at his game.

"Are you certain you wouldn't like to lean on my arm?" Alvarez purred. His words oozed politeness, but his spider-crafty eyes said, "Step into my parlor, Ms. Fly."

As if! Cynthia reminded herself of another of Grandma's proverbs, "It's for its own good that the cat purrs."

She shook her head at Alvarez's extended elbow. She really didn't need crutches all the time, even though three of her toes had been broken a month ago and were still terribly sore. If she walked carefully, she could put her weight on the inner ball of her foot.

But she wasn't about to give the enemy that information to use against her.

And make no mistake, this Hispanic man in the ponytail and thousand-dollar Italian suit and flamboyant Bolgheri tie was her enemy.

A sly rogue is often in good dress, she cautioned herself.

Alvarez was the full-time attorney as well as the puppet CEO of Ferrama, Inc., the company she intended to take to the cleaners for all her pain and suffering. The man behind the action was the president—the prince himself, she'd discovered through research—but for some reason he preferred to maintain a mysterious, aloof presence, giving the misleading impression that he wasn't the driving force behind Ferrama, Inc.

"Are you sure I shouldn't have legal counsel present?" she asked, blinking her eyelashes. She'd once negotiated a billion-dollar takeover with just such a ploy. Men could be such idiots.

They were approaching a suite of walnut-paneled offices where an efficient-looking middle-aged secretary in a jade silk shirtwaist peered up at them from her computer. She waved them forward, announcing, "Prince Ferrama will be with you shortly."

Oh, goody! Cynthia wondered if she'd be expected to curtsy or something. Right. That would be a classic picture—her on crutches, bending, and her short skirt hiked up to her behind.

Cynthia repeated her question to Alvarez, "Perhaps I should call my attorney? I don't understand all this legal mumbo-jumbo. My lawyer might want to be here, don't you think?"

The secretary swept her with an are-you-for-real? once-over of disdain.

Alvarez snickered under his breath—the jerk!—and waited until they'd entered a large corner office—presumably the royal chamber—before answering. "No, an attorney won't be necessary, Ms. Sullivan," he assured her, flashing a dazzling smile, which reeked of utterly transparent skullduggery. Lucifer couldn't have done it better.

God, she was going to enjoy bringing this egomaniac to his knees, along with his condescending, pretentious shoe company.

"It won't be *that* kind of a meeting."

Give me a break. What kind of meeting will it be? Wham, bam, screw-you-ma'am . . . betcha that's what kind of meeting he has in mind. "Oh? Well, golly, I don't know."

"Trust me, my dear. I'm a lawyer."

"Now there's an oxymoron," she mumbled.

"Perdóneme?" he inquired as he motioned her toward a wing-back leather chair in front of the desk. He sank down into the chair facing her and stretched out his legs, ankles crossed. "What did you say?"

His posture said relaxed, his eyes said coiled like a cobra. Cynthia warned herself not to underestimate the man.

"Oh, I was merely wondering if you were the Mr. Alvarez I spoke to on three occasions last week. Or was that Mr. Everest?" She plastered a silly grin of embarrassment on her face, as if she was the most scatterbrained woman on the face of the earth. "Dear me, I can't remember." With a sigh, she propped her crutches against the side of the chair and settled back. *Come on, you dumb flounder, you. I've fed you the line. Now take the bait.*

"Yes," he said tentatively. "I believe I may have spoken with you."

"I thought so, but I wasn't sure. I've spoken to so many people in this firm the past few weeks, trying to arrange an amicable settlement. In fact"—she pulled out a small leather notebook from her side pocket and flipped it open—"in fact, I was shuffled around to seventeen different persons in your organization during the course of fifty-three calls. When they weren't laughing at me, they put me on perma-hold—"

"Perma-hold?"

"Yeah, that's the tactic known as receptionist's revenge, when they put you on hold so long you eventually hang up. The unspoken message in all this stonewalling was, 'Take a hike, lady.'" She nailed him with a level look now—the pretense of gullible dingbat dropped. "Does that about sum it up, Mr. Alvarez?"

"Ouch," he said with a grimace. "Have I just been subjected to a shark attack, Ms. Sullivan?"

"You bet your wing tips." Cynthia kept her face deliberately bland, not revealing her surprise that he was aware of her reputation. Heck, the guy probably knew the size of her mortgage, her education history, where she bought her Tampax.

Unruffled at being zapped, Alvarez grinned at her, obviously relishing the battle to come. "You're going to be difficult, aren't you?"

"In spades."

He removed his wire-rimmed spectacles and studied

her. A weaker-willed woman would have shriveled under such scrutiny, but she met his gaze and matched him with a lift of her chin.

"Bottom line, Ms. Sullivan. How much?"

"One million. And if your boss keeps me waiting much longer, the ante goes up to two million."

He laughed.

She shrugged.

"Twenty thousand if you sign the release papers right now."

Now this was interesting. She hadn't expected Ferrama to be willing to negotiate at all. Oh, twenty thousand was chump change to a corporation of its size and deep pockets, but most companies would rather spend the money in court than set a precedent for what they considered frivolous lawsuits. Not that her claim was frivolous. Not by a Big Board longshot.

"Deep six that, mister. Twenty thousand would barely cover my mortgage payments while I'm out of work." She started to rise from her seat. "We aren't even in the same ballpark, Mr. Alvarez. Remember, shut fists catch no hawks."

"Hawks, sharks . . . what is this? A zoo?"

Cynthia glared at him. "You'll be hearing from my lawyer."

He raised a halting hand. "Thirty thousand."

She tilted her head, trying to figure out what was going on.

"Fifty, and that's our final offer."

Okay, I smell a fish here. No way would this company offer me fifty thou unless there's trouble in paradise. Cynthia's intuition told her that she'd landed in the midst of opportunity. "What's the difference between a lawyer and a vulture, Mr. Alvarez?"

"*Mierda!* Another lawyer joke!" he murmured enigmatically, throwing up his arms in mock surrender.

"The wing tips are easily removed from one of them," she answered.

"Are you trying to say you don't like my shoes?" He waggled a two-tone wing tip of buttery soft leather at her that probably cost five hundred dollars.

"No, I'm trying to warn you. Never con a con man . . . or con woman, in my case. I make my living in the financial world, where bluff-and-call is the name of the game."

"I'm listening," he prodded.

"You thought I was faking. Big mistake." She gave him a self-satisfied smile, meant to irritate. "Some people think sharks never attack attorneys," she added, deciding to hit him with another lawyer joke. "Professional courtesy, dontcha know? But as you can see, that's just an old wives' tale."

"Ha, ha, ha. What's your point?"

"I probably would have accepted a fifty-thousand settlement three weeks ago . . . before your company made me mad. But now—"

"Now?"

"Now the shark is gonna gobble up you shoe guppies."

"That's where you're wrong, Ms. Sullivan," he said silkily, not at all intimidated.

"Oh?"

"There's more than one shark in the ocean. Keep that in mind before you hum the theme song to *Jaws*."

They were interrupted by a commotion outside the

office. Two men could be seen through the open door, speaking animatedly as they came down the hallway toward the secretary's desk. The tall one with a suit jacket draped foppishly over his shoulders—presumably the prince—was saying something to a guy in a chauffeur's uniform. It sounded like, "What the hell does the Pythagorean Theorem have to do with the arch of a stiletto high-heeled shoe?"

"Everything," answered the squeaky-voiced chauffeur whose curly hair resembled an orangey-red Chia Pet. Although he was probably twenty-five or so, he had the voice and appearance of a freckle-faced adolescent. Pulling a calculator from his breast pocket as they walked, he punched in some numbers and chortled, "See. The angle of the incline has to be reciprocal to the force of the impact on the ball of the feet or the shoe will pinch."

She thought she heard the prince groan and mutter an unprincely expletive.

Both men were speaking now to the secretary, who was presumably notifying them of Cynthia's presence.

Alvarez stood abruptly. She decided to stand as well. She braced herself with her hand lightly resting against the edge of the desk.

Jabbing a finger at her, Alvarez ordered, "Stay right there," then went out to speak to the two men.

A rapid spate of fluent Spanish flew back and forth between the prince and Alvarez. She guessed that the CEO was bringing his royal highness up to date on her complaint. During one of her innumerable calls to Ferrama, she'd learned that the prince was in Paris at a couture showing that included his exclusive shoe creations.

Cynthia couldn't believe she'd actually bought a pair of the frivolous Ferrama high heels. And for an ungodly two hundred and fifty dollars . . . on sale, at that. But it had been her thirtieth birthday . . . and she'd been walking down Fifth Avenue, past Saks . . . berating herself for her penny-pinching ways despite her fabulous income . . . telling herself that she deserved a gift, even if it was from herself . . . when she'd noticed the most delectable pair of blue suede high heels in the window. The sales clerk inside had assured her that Ferrama shoes were worth every penny because their unique design promised that a woman could wear them all day and never feel the discomfort of a normal high-heeled pump. Besides, the clerk had added with a wink, everyone knew how men reacted to women in high heels.

And the rest was history. Corn city. Lost job. Mortgage payments looming. Picketing. Payback time.

She narrowed her eyes at the biggest culprit of all. Prince Ferrama.

Finally, their conversation ended and the prince turned toward her. For a second he stood frozen, staring at her as if she were some incredible apparition.

But she wasn't the apparition. He was.

Oh, my God! She tried to remember a relevant bit of Grandma's wisdom, but all her short-circuited brain could come up with was, "A sly rogue can turn a saint to sin." No, that was dangerous thinking. A better one would be, "Do not mistake a goat's beard for a fine stallion's tail." Yep, much better to think of this handsome devil as a horse's ass, rather than an enticing rogue.

Even before he removed his dark glasses, Cynthia

could see that this man was the fulfillment of every little girl's dream of Prince Charming. Overlong black hair was wet-combed back off his dark Castilian face, which was enhanced, not marred, by day-old whiskers. Full, sensuous lips parted in surprise, mirroring her own stunned look. Oh, he wasn't as movie-star good-looking as Alvarez, but he was more appealing to her mind . . . the harsh edges softened a bit by a quickly masked sadness or vulnerability.

That was certainly whimsical of her . . . seeing things that she wanted to see, perhaps. Whoa! Since when did the Irish Barracuda engage in whimsy?

What's happening to me? I've never been attracted to pretty-boy celebrity types before.

But, Lordy, he is pretty.

A tiny gold hoop earring glittered in one ear. The effeminate European-style draping of his gray silk suit jacket was belied by a long, lean body that very nicely filled out a black T-shirt tucked into a pair of pleated gray silk slacks. Casual chic. It was probably the latest *look* in Paris. Or the royal polo circuit. *Geez!*

Exposed to all that debonair, born-to-the-manor elegance, Cynthia felt like a squirt of common yellow mustard in a sophisticated Grey Poupon world. No matter how far she'd come from the Chicago projects, no matter how much money she earned, no matter how designer-appropriate her clothing, no matter how proper her etiquette . . . there was a part of Cynthia that remained a poor little ghetto girl with her nose pressed against the glass window of upper society.

But Cynthia couldn't dwell on that now. The prince was striding toward her. At the same time his right arm extended to shake her hand, his left hand removed his dark glasses.

And Cynthia's mind went blank.

"*Buenos días*, Ms. Sullivan. Prince Pedro Tomas de la Ferrama, at your service," he said in a grainy bedroom-soft voice. His English was perfect, though heavily accented with the richness of his Spanish ancestry.

"Pedro?" she squeaked out, and could have bitten her tongue. What a stupid thing to say!

"Peter," he translated with a soft, I-can-melt-you-anytime-anywhere smile.

Get a grip, Cynthia. This is a business meeting. He is the enemy. I wonder if he likes to kiss. "Prince Peter?" she said with a laugh, trying to regain the upper hand in this initial encounter and failing miserably. Her brain appeared to have stalled in first gear.

"My friends call me P.T."

"Huh? Prince Petie?"

"P.T., the initials," he corrected her with a spark of irritation in his half-hooded eyes.

"Well, I'm sorry. Prince Peter sounds silly enough. I just can't call a grown man Petie, even if they are initials."

But then his long fingers closed over hers—*was it a handshake or a caress?*—and he turned her hand palm downward, raised it face level and kissed the air above her skin in the gallant Continental style. She felt the whisper of his hot breath all the way to her injured toes. The whole time, his sexy take-no-mercy eyes held hers captive. The sweeping lashes were so thick they must weigh down his lids. And the eyes—oh, God, the eyes!—they were so dark a blue that they appeared black. There were promises in those penetrating eyes . . . promises she couldn't fathom . . . and pure, unadulterated temptation.

The world narrowed in those seconds to the faint scent of some expensive, woodsy cologne, the sound of his breathing—or was it hers?—and the delicious feel of his palm pressed against hers, now in a regular handshake. Cynthia had never, ever been affected by a man in this way, especially not on a first meeting.

"It is a pleasure to meet you, Señorita Sullivan," he said with an intensity that implied meaning beyond the mere words.

"P.T. . . ." Alvarez said in a warning tone.

A snicker could be heard on the other side of the room, where a computer was being booted up by the chauffeur.

Cynthia understood the alarm in Alvarez's terse admonition, not to mention the nerd's chuckle. They were a wake-up call to her, as well. This was a business meeting, not match.com.

The prince came to his senses with a seeming jolt, glancing down with dismay at their still-clasped hands. He dropped her hand, and a remarkable slow-motion transformation rippled over his body.

His chin rose a noticeable notch with haughtiness. He adjusted his suit jacket over his shoulders and flicked a piece of lint off the sleeve with an impeccably manicured fingernail—*Is that clear nail polish he's wearing? Jeesh, I can't remember the last time I splurged on that kind of nonproductive pampering.* And the eyes that had been warmly attracted to her moments ago now gave her a cool assessment. The mirthless smile he bestowed on her was intended to be an intentional put-down—one of those chauvinistic I-know-you-want-me smirks.

Cynthia prided herself on her ability to judge people. Could she have been wrong in discerning a mutual lightning-bolt attraction between them? Could the prince be that good an actor? And why would he bother? She flinched inwardly as all her old insecurities rushed forth.

Still, she was not prepared for the mocking insult that followed.

"Your castle or mine, princess?"

Chapter Two

He'd always had a thing for strawberries, especially strawberry blondes ...

The woman ... Cynthia Sullivan ... recoiled, as if he'd slapped her. She still stood a short distance from him, stains of scarlet humiliation flooding her cheeks.

P.T. wished he could take back the suggestive remark, with its deliberately taunting edge. But he didn't.

In that split second of insanity when his fingers had grasped hers and their eyes met, he'd briefly considered ditching the seduction scheme and all his deceits. With a mere handshake, the madness of the past five years had melted away, and his blood surged with inexplicable joy. He hadn't been able to release her hand lest the wonderful, miraculous aura of rightness slip from his fingers.

Luckily, his tailspin lasted only a moment, and he'd soon been back in the driver's seat. He would steer this meeting, not her. Nothing and no one was going to interfere with his plans. Women were a dime a dozen . . . even knockout brokers with born-to-be-kissed lips. A man got only one shot at the gold ring, and he wasn't going to miss his big chance because he was distracted by a piece of tempting shark tail.

Thank God, Dick's terse warning and Jake's snicker had penetrated his trance, reminding him that this was a woman who could pull the rug out from under him and his company. Danger. She was a danger he couldn't risk . . . not now.

Not that she hadn't been equally assaulted by the same overwhelming sensations. He'd seen that in the widening of her eyes, in the parting of her naturally pink, way-too-enticing lips, in the pulse that leaped at the base of her slender neck. No question, she'd been just as stunned by the amazing chemistry flash-firing between them.

But not anymore.

Backing away from him a bit, she composed herself. Working in the male-dominated brokerage field and looking the way she did, she probably got hit on all the time. But she was a fighter; he could see that. And he suspected that she'd developed a talent, like him, for putting on a facade in self-defense. Before his eyes, she metamorphosed into a long, tall, no-nonsense wheeler-dealer.

She *did* have strawberry blond hair, as he'd observed earlier. It was pulled into a knot at the back of her head, but curly wisps had sprung free, framing a face of pure perfection . . . to him, at least. Creamy complexion, bright aquamarine eyes flashing blue fire, and that mouth . . . oh, Lord, that pouty I-dare-you mouth.

The conservatism of her pinstriped business suit was wiped out by a scoop-necked camisole of white lace, meant to draw a man's eye and turn his brain to mush—and his was oatmeal already. The hem of the skirt ended at mid-thigh, leaving about a mile of sinfully sculpted bare leg.

Cynthia Sullivan was a bewildering combination of shark and sex kitten. And he thought . . . if the time and place were different . . . he'd love nothing more than to explore those beguiling inconsistencies.

"Sorry, Prince, but the drawbridge is up."

"Wh-what?" He gave himself a mental shake. Bare seconds had passed since he'd made his outrageous comment, but it seemed like hours.

"You said, 'Your castle or mine?' And I'm telling you to take your lance and steed elsewhere. The only distress this damsel is suffering was caused by you. And, frankly, I'd never be able to get a glass slipper over this corn." She stuck her injured foot out for emphasis.

Ouch. Well, I guess she told me.

"In other words: Drop dead!"

Okay. The battle lines are drawn now. "Does that mean you don't want to come up to the palace and see my etchings?" he tried to joke.

She bared her teeth, and the result wasn't a smile. "Which part of 'drop dead' didn't you understand?"

God, I could love this woman. For a night or two, anyhow. "You misunderstood, Ms. Sullivan. I was making a jest," he prevaricated. "Perhaps my poor

English caused the problem." P.T. made sure he added just the right twist of a half-smile to disarm her . . . so she wouldn't be certain whether he was sincere.

Leaning slightly against the desk, she regarded him with sweeping revulsion. *All right, she's more perceptive than I thought.* Without words, she told him loud and clear that he was a worthless toad, not a prince. Not that he was a prince, anyhow. *Damn!*

And that was the problem. He had to continue the pretense, even with this woman. Especially with this woman. His company—all his efforts of the past years—were more important than any female. He would do anything, *anything,* to achieve his goals.

"*Por favor*, Señorita Sullivan. Please sit. I believe we have business to discuss," he said in the cool, slightly condescending tone he'd perfected. He motioned toward the wing-back chair where her crutches were propped.

She arched a brow and waved her hand at the other chair. "After you."

He'd forgotten that she was a woman comfortable in the business world and that she would want a level playing field, even down to the power positioning of bodies during a meeting. She would be fluent in the body language of high finance, knowing the disadvantage of having to peer up at an opponent when negotiating. Smart lady! In fact, he usually sat behind his desk, using the barrier as a sign of his superior placement in a room.

He tilted his head in compliance and was about to sit when he noticed Dick leaning against the far wall, arms folded over his chest, watching them with amusement. And concern.

Jake, in his own high-tech world, was pounding away at some graphics on the computer, no doubt working up a new shoe design.

"I believe you've met my lawyer, Ms. Sullivan. Enrique Alvarez."

"Oh, yeah. I've met *Dick*," she said with a snideness that made him wonder what had transpired before his arrival. He put that thought aside for now.

"And may I present my head designer, Jacob Beaunare. Jake designed 'The Vamp,' the high-heeled pump that allegedly caused your . . . ah, *la problema*." He purposely settled his gaze on her right foot, where three bruised toes peeked out from a thick-soled orthopedic-type sandal, then pursed his lips into a moue of disdain. "That's why I invited Jake to this meeting. Perhaps he can analyze the shape of your foot and tell us why you had a . . . ah, *la problema*."

I am pitiful. I'm stuttering here when I should be concentrating on my Spanish accent. Next I'll be reverting to my lower-class Spanish, instead of the pure Castilian Spanish I've worked so hard to master. And savoir faire. I'm supposed to be a suave, jet-setting prince, not a salivating, stammering, sex-crazed idiot. Sex? Where did sex come from? Oh, hell! I want to have sex with her. I do. Now.

Jake nodded toward her in acknowledgment of the introduction and flashed a gap-toothed grin at P.T., who realized, to his chagrin, that he was blushing. Dick was shaking his head with disbelief at the apparent crack in his veneer of regal civility.

Civility. I want to lay a Wall Street trader across my desk and raise her personal Dow Jones about two zillion points. Or maybe on the chair. That would be good, all that straddling and stuff. Better yet, against the wall. Yeah, a real knee-trembler . . . a wallbanger for a Wall Streeter. Oh, God!

"Your head designer is a chauffeur?" she asked scornfully. They were still standing, several feet apart, in modified battle stances.

He shrugged, not about to explain that they could barely afford the blast of air-conditioning that cooled his office, let alone the expense of another employee to drive the leased limo on the few occasions it was used. He made a mental note to tell his secretary, Maureen, to turn the air-conditioning down, even though his body felt unnaturally hot.

He'd read an article in an airline magazine recently that claimed men thought about sex every ten seconds, even in the midst of the most serious business meetings. The author had written that men could be aroused by something as innocuous as the curve of a woman's shoulder. He'd laughed skeptically at the time.

He wasn't laughing now.

Not that he was so easily aroused. Uh-uh. Just in case, though, he picked up a large pamphlet from the desk, casually holding it against his lower body.

"What is *that?*" She was gawking at his midsection.

He groaned silently and tried for an I-have-no-idea-what-you-mean look.

"That's a red herring," she accused.

"A red herring?" he choked out.

"Yeah. I know a red herring when I see one."

Well, I never heard it called by that name. Peter, my own pet name, yes. But red herring? Nope. The only animal terms I ever heard before were Crimson Bird, One-Eyed Trouser Trout, Snake in the Grass, Goose Neck . . . yikes, I'm losing my mind here. Thinking of euphemisms for the word penis *in the midst of a business meeting!*

"Sonofabitch!" Dick swore.

Before he could react, Cynthia stretched an arm toward him and Dick sprang forward, both grabbing for *it*. Holy cow! He'd thought earlier that Dick was going too far, telling him how to dress, but snatching at his genitals crossed the line. And, as for Ms. Hot Financier, he wouldn't mind her touching him *there*, but even he insisted on privacy.

Too late, he realized that it was the crimson-bordered brochure he was holding that drew their attention, not his traitorous body part. And he remembered through his fuzzy brain that red herring was the nickname given to a preliminary prospectus for an upcoming stock offering, its hallmark being the two red borders of type down the left side and across the top.

"Give that to me," he demanded. Ms. Sullivan had won the skirmish for the prized brochure.

"When I'm done reading it," she said, holding it out of reach. He wasn't about to tackle her to recover the document, though he'd like to.

"Ms. Sullivan, this is a blatant invasion of privacy," Dick asserted. "You have no legal right to—"

"Tell it to the judge, *Dick*," she snapped back, already immersed in what she was reading on the first page.

"Maybe she can advise us on that one confusing point related to unfriendly takeovers that we were discussing earlier," Jake suggested over his shoulder.

P.T. and Dick whimpered in unison. As if they would seek guidance from an adversary! Cynthia, who half-sat on the edge of the desk, didn't even hear the remark, so engrossed was she in the document.

With a sigh of surrender, P.T. sank into the chair, making sure he didn't clasp his hands or fidget with nervousness. He slumped and stretched out his long legs to indicate a blasé demeanor, just the opposite of his taut emotions.

And thus he waited for the explosion to come.

Swimming with the sharks . . .

Cynthia could almost taste victory by the time she finished reading the prospectus. Three things were clear: Ferrama, Inc., was about to go public. The company couldn't stand a breath of bad publicity. Most important, her lawsuit had to be settled very privately and very quickly.

By tomorrow, the news of Ferrama's going public would be all over Wall Street. Even now they'd probably started damage control with the news media who'd witnessed her picketing down below in the street. She wouldn't be surprised if they'd claimed it was all a joke, or that she was a publicity-hungry kook.

Still standing, she directed her attention first at the prince, who slouched nonchalantly in one of the wingbacks as he sipped Perrier—which she'd declined— from an etched crystal goblet. He even slouched with highborn elegance, darn it. The whole time he watched her with a disconcerting intensity . . . but he yawned behind the back of one hand with presumed boredom at least three times.

His attitude of lazy indifference was a ruse, she decided.

But maybe not.

Either way, the guy was a threat to her pride. His royal studliness had played her like a charm, turning her customary good sense to butter with just a clasp of his hot hands, and his hotter Spanish eyes. How he must be laughing inside!

"I feel like I've landed in a bad B-movie. *Return of the Living Snake Oil Salesmen.*"

Alvarez and the Phi Beta Chia Pet had pulled up straight-back chairs and were staring up at her, the only one still standing. They all shifted uncomfortably . . . a sure sign of guilt, to her mind. Suddenly she gave each of them a piercing assessment. "I just thought of something else . . . your names. It all fits."

"I beg your pardon," Ferrama responded with hoity-toity hauteur, smoothing out an imaginary wrinkle in his sleeve.

"Your names . . . Peter, Dick, Boner . . . they oughta call you the three shoe pricks."

The men winced . . . whether at her accurate judgment or her crudity, she wasn't sure. She often found it to her advantage in business meetings to disarm her male adversaries with an unfeminine choice of words.

Beaunare protested, "Hey, my name is pronounced bow-*nare*, not bow-*ner.*"

Ferrama set his drink aside and leaned forward, his aristocratic nostrils flaring with consternation. "Your vulgar tongue may impress your colleagues on Wall Street, but it cheapens you here. In my country only *putas*—women of the street—would speak thus. Take my advice: You don't have to act as a man in order to deal with men."

Cynthia cringed inwardly at his criticism, but only for a second. Then she took the offensive. "I'm sorry if my language offends your delicate sensibilities, but, frankly, I don't give a damn. I've been getting along very well in a man's world, vulgar tongue and all. As to your advice . . . here's a little advice back at you: My dear Irish grandma—God bless her soul!—was a *pishogue*, a wise old woman to whom the village folk would come for charms and good counsel. She—"

"And what village might that be?" Alvarez interrupted snidely. "I thought you were from Chicago."

"Chicago neighborhoods are just big villages," Cynthia said, waving aside the lawyer's remark. Then she directed her continuing explanation to the prince, who'd been the one to disparage her breeding. "As I was saying, Grandma was a great one for having the perfect adage for every occasion. In this case, Prince Ferrama, I think she'd have advised you thus: 'Sure, and you must not let your tongue cut your own throat.'"

Ferrama's eyes narrowed. "Ah, ethnic sayings abound in my country, too. In fact, I just thought of an appropriate Spanish proverb. 'There is nothing sharper than a woman's tongue.'"

"Never reach your hand farther than you can withdraw it," she tossed back.

"Don't show your teeth till you can bite." He smiled with obvious relish at their verbal sparring.

"Beware of the bull's horns, the dog's teeth and the rogue's smile."

The rogue smiled wider.

This is ridiculous. How did I allow myself to get caught up in word games? I guess it's the Irish spirit in me. There's nothing an Irishman—or Irishwoman—loves more than a good argument. Cynthia took a deep breath to control her roiling emotions. "Let's cut the song-and-dance routine, Ferrama. Your tab is increasing by the minute, and insults are a rather pricey luxury you can't afford."

"Are you threatening me, Ms. Sullivan?"

"If the shoe fits . . ."

Her inadvertent pun drew three simultaneous moans.

"Listen, Prince—"

"Call me P.T."

"Call me Ms. Sullivan, or call me your worst nightmare," she snarled. "Just know this, *Ferrama*: You need to make me happy more than I need to make you happy."

"Oh, really?" Ferrama replied with a slow, devastating smile that said in ancient masculine language that he would like nothing more than to make her happy.

She didn't think he had a financial settlement in mind.

"How do you say 'sexual harassment' in Spanish?" she inquired sweetly.

"Dios mío!" Alvarez groaned.

Undaunted, Ferrama continued to smile. "Hey, I didn't say a word. And I certainly didn't touch you." The twinkle in his eye said he'd like to, though. Touch her, that is.

Cynthia homed in on the word *touch*, and all kinds of enticing images floated through her brain. *Enough!*

she admonished herself, and prayed for self-control. Then, inclining her head toward the prospectus on the desk, she explained, "What I meant about the need for you to please me is this: Now that I know your corporation is about to raise ten million dollars with an issue of two million shares of common stock at five dollars per unit, representing seventeen percent of the company's capitalization . . . well, golly gee, that puts a whole new light on things."

All three sets of eyebrows arched at her regurgitating the salient figures, verbatim, from the complicated data she'd just read. A near photographic memory for numbers did come in handy sometimes. Ferrama was the first to recover.

"So you know that my firm is going public. Big deal, as you Americans say. That doesn't make your claim of damages any less frivolous. Unless, of course"—Ferrama crinkled his nose with distaste—"you are considering blackmail."

"Blackmail? Whoa! Back up a step. God, men are like bagpipes. No sound comes out till they're full of wind."

"Grandma again?" Ferrama asked.

Sinking down into the other wing-back chair, she inhaled deeply for patience. "Listen, the most basic rule of negotiation is to establish the areas of agreement, not disagreement. A good beginning is half the work. Now, the first given should be the fact that injuries were sustained—"

"*Are* we negotiating?" Ferrama drawled in a low, amused voice that had probably charmed the chastity belts off princesses in three or four continents. Good thing she wasn't a princess.

"You'd better hope we're negotiating; otherwise, you're going to find your ass in a legal sling." Her retort sounded crass, even to her, but the guy had an unnerving effect on her.

He regarded her with an odd disappointment, and that irritated the hell out of her. He had no right to be disappointed in her salty language.

And, *damn, damn, damn*, she had no right to be disappointed that he was disappointed. *Yep, my brain is in major hormone meltdown. If he offered me a kiss for a settlement, I'd probably hop right onto his froggie lap.*

"Cynthia . . ." he started, even though she'd specifically told him to call her Ms. Sullivan. "Cyn-thi-a . . ." He repeated her name with soft chastisement, rolling the syllables on his tongue as if he was doing something sexual to her.

He was.

"Get to the point," she snapped.

"Put your leg on my lap." He raised his behind slightly and dragged his chair closer to hers till they were almost knee to knee.

Put my leg on his lap? Oh, my goodness! Did I speak my fantasies aloud? "Are you crazy?"

"How can I ascertain the extent of your *injury* if you don't bare yourself for inspection?" he explained breezily. "Your toes, I mean."

She picked up her shoulder bag from the floor and whipped out some photographs. "That's a picture of the corn. And that's a picture of the broken toes."

"Very nice," Ferrama pronounced, examining each of the pictures carefully before passing them on to

Alvarez and Beaunare. "But how do we know those are even *your* toes?"

"Puh leeze! How many women do you know who carry around photographs of their toes?"

"Hmmm," he said, tapping his chin.

Was he seriously pondering her question? The pervert!

"I think it's interesting that she's been documenting her *alleged* injuries for some time," Alvarez told his boss.

Ferrama nodded.

"Ambilinear bipolarity," Beaunare interjected.

All eyes riveted on the chauffeur/designer.

"Her toes are perfect examples of ambilinear bipolarity," Beaunare elaborated, jabbing a forefinger at the pictures. "See the length and strut of the pinky toe."

Cynthia felt a blush creep up her neck. It felt as if they were discussing some intimate body part . . . and deeming it deformed.

"Aha!" Alvarez hooted in his best I-rest-my-case voice. "Then the corn was caused by a malformation of her foot, and not a defect in our product."

"Actually, that's incorrect," Ferrama declared, rubbing his bristly jaw and staring at her foot. "I believe all our shoe designs, including 'The Vamp,' should accommodate an ambilinear bipolarity. Isn't that right, Jake?"

"Uh-huh," Beaunare muttered distractedly and walked over to the computer, where he proceeded to scan one of the photographs onto the screen and overlay various shoe designs on the images of her foot.

"I think I know what the problem is," Ferrama concluded, still studying her foot and a whole lot of her bare leg, as well. "Like most women, you buy your shoes too small."

"Yep," Alvarez and Beaunare concurred.

"Now wait a minute—"

"Let's see. You wear about a size nine," Ferrama guessed.

"I do not. I wear a size seven and a half, and I have since I was twelve years old," she maintained indignantly. "Don't think you can lay the blame on me. Oh, why am I surprised? The losing horse always blames the saddle."

Ferrama mumbled something incoherent under his breath about horses and saddles . . . probably a sexual reference. But then he spoke aloud, "Don't be counting me as a loser yet, Ms. Irish Paragon."

"A person's shoe size changes not only over the years, but hour to hour," Beaunare commented over his shoulder. "Most people make the mistake of buying shoes early in the day when their muscles haven't yet expanded."

"I bought your blasted high-heeled pump on a Friday night, thirty-seven days ago. It was a gift—"

"Who purchased the gift for you? Was it your . . . husband?" Ferrama asked with undue curiosity.

She gave the prince a critical scrutiny. Criminey, his brain must be splintering apart, too, to ask such a personal, irrelevant question. "It was a gift for myself in honor of my thirtieth birthday. Two-hundred-and-fifty lousy dollars, they cost. *On sale*. Some gift! I lost my seven-hundred-thousand-dollar-a-year job—"

"Seven hundred thousand!" Alvarez exclaimed.

"Wow!" Beaunare sighed. "Does that include bonuses?"

"Happy birthday," Ferrama said.

"Aaargh! Would you guys stop interrupting?"

"Have you put on a few pounds lately? A weight gain can throw the whole foot equation askew," the nerd said. "And cheap hosiery can also be a contributing factor. Causes the fabric at the toes to bunch."

"It always amazes me how women can drop a couple hundred on a pair of shoes, then buy a discount panty hose special," Alvarez observed.

"Do you buy discount stockings, Cynthia?" the prince insinuated. He said *discount* as if it were a dirty word.

"Forget the pathetic blame game, boys. Let's get back to the subject at hand. Not only did I get an indefinite layoff from my very lucrative position, where I incidentally work on commission, but my physician says I won't be able to return to my regular work on the exchange floor for at least three months. I have no idea how I'll keep up the mortgage on the new apartment I just bought at the Dakota; it took my life savings for the down payment." She paused and wondered whether she was wasting her time trying to drum some sense into these three thickheaded musketeers.

Ferrama flicked his fingers imperiously, encouraging her to go on.

"This is the deal, boys. Ferrama, Inc., is going to pay the price for all my pain and inconvenience. Or suffer the consequences."

"How much?" Ferrama asked bluntly.

"Two million."

He made a scoffing sound of curt dismissal, and Alvarez objected, "It was one million an hour ago."

"That was before I had to endure this humiliating meeting."

"No, Cynthia, dear," the prince corrected, "it was before you found out that Ferrama is in the delicate stage of offering its stock on the open market."

"That, too," she agreed with a sugary smile. "Before you speak so carelessly in the future, Prince, *dear*, you might want to consider this: 'In spite of the fox's cunning, his skin is often sold.'"

"Another Irish saying?" Beaunare inquired.

"Nah. I read that on a greeting card."

Beaunare grinned at her, ignoring the glares he got from Ferrama and Alvarez.

"But you fail to realize, my dear," Ferrama added smoothly, "that if the cunning fox waits long enough at the henhouse door, eventually he will trap the chicken."

"Not if the chick knows another way out," she retorted with dry humor.

"Do you really think a mere corn, whether gained from our product or not, merits two million dollars?" Ferrama asked coolly. It was obvious from his tight jaw and clenched fists that he was angry now. "The courts are becoming increasingly intolerant of frivolous lawsuits. Perhaps you ought to rethink your claim."

"Perhaps you ought to consider placating me real soon, before my *frivolous* claim hits the legal system." She locked eyes with Ferrama, hoping to intimidate him, but to no avail. He stared back, unwavering. "I thought a prince would have more diplomatic skills. Grandma always said that a true diplomat has the ability to tell a man to go to hell so he'd look forward to the trip. Instead, you're pissing me off with all these subtle and not so subtle threats."

"You know what's pissing me off?" Ferrama shot back. "All these grandma proverbs that are nothing more than veiled insults."

"Did I mention that my lawyer is Marcia Connor?"

That got their attention. Even though Ferrama didn't move a muscle or say a word, she saw the quick look he shared with Alvarez and Beaunare.

Marcia Connor was the number one civil lawyer in the country. The year before she had won a ten-million-dollar settlement for a Las Vegas showgirl who'd been abused for years by her celebrity boyfriend.

"Marcia tells me that my claim could be a landmark case for modern women," she informed them. "Maybe even a class action suit."

"How so?" Ferrama snickered.

That snicker was going to cost him.

"For ages men have been subjugating women by controlling the fashion industry and the appearance of the female form. Consider Chinese footbinding. Then corsets. And dare I mention Wonder Bras? Don't deny for one minute that men think a woman's leg looks sexy in high heels. If men had their way, we'd still be wearing garter belts and seamed stockings."

Ferrama barely suppressed a grin at her mention of those unmentionables.

That grin was going to cost him.

"You'd create a worldwide female uproar, all over a *corn?*" Alvarez roared.

"Just watch me," she fumed, "and, by the way, do you know the difference between a lawyer and a vulture?"

Alvarez's lips turned down with disgust. "You already hit me with that one . . . his wing tips."

Ferrama laughed and offered, "Vultures don't get Frequent Flyer miles?"

"No, the vulture eventually lets go." Cynthia turned to Ferrama. "Are you ready to talk real money now?"

"Twenty thousand," he said through gritted teeth.

"I already offered her fifty," Alvarez pointed out.

Ferrama cast his lawyer a disbelieving scowl. "You did?"

"And I declined," she noted.

"I know what the problem is," Beaunare erupted with glee, continuing to enter figures into the computer keyboard.

What problem? She sensed that Ferrama had been about to up his offer, thus allowing her to avoid a lengthy court battle, not to mention a hefty attorney fee. It had been hard as hell to pass muster with the rigid co-op board at the Dakota; any whiff of scandal and she'd be booted out on her rear. Nope, she didn't need to hear about any problems.

"I betcha dollars to donuts she took the arch insert out of the shoe," Beaunare said. "That's what put pressure on her toes, rather than the ball of the foot. Remember what I was telling you earlier, P.T., about the Pythagorean theorem and the arch of the foot? Yep, she removed the insert."

All eyes bored into Cynthia, whose traitorous face heated with guilt. "I'm not admitting anything. Besides, most women remove inserts. They're uncomfortable . . . and unnecessary."

The prince and Alvarez exchanged a look of relief. Alvarez even dared to say, "Case closed!"

"Not until the fat lady sings, *Mister Legal-Eagle Sleazeball . . . in the jury, that is.*"

Without warning, Ferrama stood. "Out!" he ordered Alvarez and Beaunare, motioning toward the door. "I'll complete the negotiations with Ms. Sullivan in private."

Uh-oh.

"Now, P.T., that is not a good idea," Alvarez cautioned.

Right. Bad, bad idea. Me alone, with Prince Not-so-charming-but-I-can-have-you-with-a-look Ferrama? I'm not agreeing to a one-on-one meeting. That would be like the turkey voting for an early Thanksgiving. "Actually, I'm thinking the negotiations would be better handled with my lawyer." She stood her crutches in front of her and pulled herself upright, preparing to leave.

Ferrama ignored her protests and stalked over to the door, holding it wide for Alvarez and Beaunare to exit. The latter appeared rather bemused, then brightened. "I think I'll go get the limo and cruise around the block a few times."

"No!" Ferrama and Alvarez shouted at the same time.

Ferrama was rudely shoving them forward when the lady in the green silk shirtwaist poked her head forward. The middle-aged secretary glowered at Alvarez, who was winking at her in the oddest way, before notifying Ferrama in an overwrought voice, "Charles called a few minutes ago and wants to know if you'll be able to make his Ascot party."

Charles? Could she mean Prince Charles? Holy moley!

Ferrama blinked at his secretary as if she spoke some foreign language and muttered something like, "Hell if I know!"

"You have the underwriters meeting at two-thirty. The factory in Lisbon is in a panic over a Brazilian leather shipment and needs you to call immediately. The buyer for Bloomingdale's will be here at four. *Wall Street Journal* at five. And you have a dinner scheduled at the Algonquin at nine with *Liz*." She took a deep breath after her long-winded recitation.

Liz? Liz who? Liz the columnist? God, she must be ninety years old. Elizabeth Hurley? Oh, geez, is Queen Elizabeth in town?

"Is that all, Maureen?" Ferrama said dryly.

"Hardly," his secretary retorted. Apparently her job profile didn't include kowtowing to a prince. "Your stepsisters have been here every day since you've been gone. I'm giving you notice right now, if I have to deal with one more complaint from Naomi and Ruth, I'm resigning."

Ferrama rolled his eyes heavenward. "I'll talk to them."

"Darn right you will. They're down in the executive dining room right now, waiting for you to finish your meeting. They have a list this long of bills they want you to pay." Maureen stretched her arms wide to demonstrate.

"I'll handle the situation," Ferrama assured her in a tired voice as he started to back into his office.

"And another thing . . ." the secretary began.

He halted and tapped a foot impatiently.

Once again, Maureen and Alvarez exchanged a look, then the secretary went on. "Your masseur, Andre, wants to know if you'll be keeping your six-thirty appointment. And should he arrange a pedicure and facial this time?"

Ferrama's face bloomed a lovely shade of dusty rose, and his throat worked without any words coming out. He sliced a condemning glare at Alvarez before saying to his secretary, "Absolutely. But tell him I prefer the seaweed oil this time. That mud astringent he used last month irritated my skin."

Cynthia turned away in disgust. If being a prince meant being such a namby-pamby, she could do without a prince. Not that any had been offered to her lately. Cynthia directed her attention away from the group outside the office and, instead, decided to study her surroundings.

Colored prints of various Ferrama shoes lined one wall. "The Vamp." "Jezebel." "Naughty Nights." "Prim & Sexy." "Snake Magic." "Night & Day." "Well-Heeled." "Daddy's Girl." "Heavenly Toes." "Oh, Baby!" "Black Beauty." "Gotta Dance." "Tippy-Toe." "Ooh-la-la!"

She remembered when the first of the Ferrama shoes hit the stores about five years ago. Their biggest selling point had been that women could wear high heels and feel comfortable . . . that even working women could throw away sensible shoes and wear the same sexy pump from office to nightclub. It had something to do with their uniquely engineered design.

She moved to the next wall and studied a photograph of three men smiling widely at the camera. All were in shirtsleeves and loosened ties, standing outside a factory—the prince in the center with Alvarez and Beaunare on either side, arms looped over each other's shoulders. The plaque under the picture read:

FERRAMA, INC., THE DREAM BEGINS, 2009. Cynthia squinted to see better. Even though it was only five years ago, they all seemed much younger. And hopeful. Hmmm. Ferrama didn't look at all like a prince. He was much too relaxed and casual . . . one of the guys.

"You're smiling."

Cynthia jerked around to see Ferrama closing the door behind him with an ominous click. He walked slowly toward her, and it took all her resolve to stand her ground and not bolt in the opposite direction. Not that she could do much bolting with her sore foot. "I was smiling because you all looked so innocent then," she responded. Her voice sounded breathless to her own ears.

His shoulder brushed hers as he moved closer and glanced first at the picture, then at her. "As compared to . . . ?"

He'd taken off his suit jacket and was wearing only the black T-shirt tucked into the pleated gray pants. The small gold hoop in his right ear and the Rolex watch at his wrist caught her attention, but only briefly. He was so darn gorgeous . . . no, he was so darn compelling. For a second, she forgot that he'd posed a question. When she pulled herself together, somewhat, she answered, ". . . as compared to the slick, devious trio you've become now."

"Don't be so quick to judge," he murmured. "Appearances are sometimes deceptive." Then he reached out to tuck a strand of hair behind her ear. His hand trembled slightly before he pulled it back with seeming alarm.

Her heart skipped a beat, then thundered wildly

against her ribs. The feathery brush of his fingertips across her cheek was a clear intrusion into her zone of privacy. A virtual stranger, he violated her personal space with such an intimate gesture. It was almost as if he was giving her notice . . . a predatory animal marking his chosen mate.

Where did I get such an outlandish idea?

Why can't I find my voice to protest?

And that trembling of his fingertips . . . a good touch, that. Ferrama was either a consummate actor, trying to charm her into financial capitulation, or he was equally as rattled as she.

Is this a role he's playing to soften me up for the kill? Or is that smoldering look in his eyes real? And why should it matter? Blue-blooded princes don't get involved with red-blooded commoners.

I have no time for this. My job and my future are on the line. Get a grip, Cynthia. One slip and you could lose it all.

"What are we going to do?" he asked in a grainy voice, holding her eyes.

Yep, the man is pure temptation. That voice alone could make an intelligent woman's I.Q. slam dunk about twenty points.

"What are we going to do?" he repeated.

She couldn't have averted her face if her life depended on it. But it was a simple enough question— one she could easily answer. "We'll either settle this dispute now or in court. It's up to you." She gave herself a mental pat on the back for replying in a level tone, and not a squeak.

He shook his head. "That's not what I meant," he whispered.

"Wh-what?" She did squeak this time.

"This is the worst time for this," he said on a groan. His creased forehead bespoke genuine distress, but Cynthia was still wary.

He stood a respectable distance from her, arms crossed over his chest. He didn't try to touch her again. His words, though confusing, couldn't be construed as objectionable. Still, his dark, smoldering eyes swept her like a forbidden caress.

"I . . . I don't understand," she stammered.

"What are we going to do *about us?*" he rasped out.

Chapter Three

He had a sudden taste for shark meat . . .

P. T. Ferrama had three looks that made women melt. The vulnerable look. The smoldering look. The arrogant I-could-take-you-or-leave-you look.

The key to all of the looks was subtlety. It was all in the attitude. In his not so humble opinion, he had subtlety *and* attitude down to an art form.

He'd had lots of years to practice, of course, since the days he was a street-savvy shoeshine kid in Puerto Rico, hustling tourists outside their hotels. The services he'd offered had run the gamut from effusive compliments ("Lady, your face ees so pretty, you mus' be a move-hee star.") to errands ("Hey, meester, you want I should buy you some condoms?") to tours ("Cheapest rum on the island, I can show you, damn right."). P.T. had learned that a quick smile and a cheeky charisma, adapted to each situation, won over even the toughest target.

Survival had been the name of the game then. Survival . . . of a different sort . . . was the name of the game now.

Oh, it hadn't been that he was alone. His father had skipped the nest before he was born, later dying of an alcohol-soaked kidney, but his mother, Eva Ferrama, had worked long hours as a baccarat dealer in the island casinos, leaving her feisty, independent son to fend for himself.

All that had changed when P.T. was ten and his mother had married a mainland widower, Morton Friedman, who already had two children of his own, the eleven- and twelve-year-old girls, Ruth and Naomi, who would turn into the plagues of his life. The kindly Mort—the only father figure P.T. would ever know— had owned a Hoboken, New Jersey, cut-rate shoe factory, and he'd been eager to teach his new son the ropes. Then P.T.'s hustling had proved just as effective as he entered a new, more professional arena.

Five years ago, he and the new company lawyer, Enrique Alvarez, had come up with a plan to jumpstart the ailing shoe business by giving it an upscale face-lift, complete with the prince persona. P.T. had met Dick at Rutgers nine years before that, at freshman orientation. Before the end of the year, P.T. had been forced to drop out of college and take over the shoe factory, following Mort's sudden death.

Hiring Jake fresh out of M.I.T. had been one of the smartest moves they'd ever made, though shoe industry colleagues had scoffed at the time, "Who ever heard of an engineer designing shoes?"

All his life, despite the change in circumstance, P.T. had felt like a *picaro*—a person with no home or money . . . always hungry . . . always having to earn a living by his wits. So, any means to stay above water were legitimate in his book, as long as no one got hurt.

And some tactics had universal, timeless appeal, including the looks. It didn't matter if he was an eight-year-old gremlin hawking shoe polish with a teary eye or an eighteen-year-old shoe rep trying to break into the Wal-Mart chain with a teary eye or a thirty-two-year-old prince fighting for his company with a teary eye.

Right now, his mark was the corn princess, and he was laying on the vulnerability. The hooded, half-mast lids. The softened mouth. The needy tic in his jaw, which had taken days in front of a mirror to perfect. Sometimes, in especially tough circumstances, he even added a trembling hand.

Cynthia Sullivan didn't stand a chance.

Yep, she was staring at him as if he'd just stormed her castle and was about to whisk her up on his high horse. Her gaping mouth was a sure indicator of how overwhelmed she was. He'd lay odds that any minute now she would sigh. That would be the clincher.

Sometimes he surprised himself with his talent for this Prince Charming routine. Who would have thought a street kid from Puerto Rico could be so . . . princely? But then, women were gullible when it came to that everlasting fantasy of a perfect man to fulfill their dreams.

Cynthia Sullivan was no exception. She might be a shark in her business dealings but she undoubtedly shared womankind's basic yearning for a knight in shining armor. Why else would she have bought an overpriced apartment in the Dakota—the only building in Manhattan that resembled a castle? Yep, she pined for a prince to rescue her from her humdrum life.

And, voilà, P.T. was a prince.

When he wanted to be.

All these thoughts passed through P.T.'s mind in the brief seconds after he'd whispered his tantalizing suggestion. They were still standing face-to-face, an arm's length apart, in front of the wall of Ferrama pictures.

Pausing an additional moment, just long enough for her to register the full impact of his look, he repeated his husky question. "What are we going to do *about us?*" (Women melted when he made his voice husky, especially if he threw in a Spanish endearment or two. He decided a Spanish endearment at this point would be overkill.)

Her mouth clicked shut, and she started to laugh.

Uh-oh. Why is she laughing? Laughter was not the usual reaction to his vulnerable look. *She's probably just nervous. That's why she's laughing. Whew, that's a relief. My ego can live with that. But it's damn disconcerting.*

"You are beyond belief," she gasped out, laughing so hard that tears filled her eyes. "As my wise ol' grandma used to say, 'Sure and it's true as God created blue skies and blue-eyed rogues . . . what's got with guile will disappear with the wind.'"

"Huh?"

"In other words, don't waste your breath on dead embers."

"Oh, your embers aren't dead, *querida*. And never underestimate what a determined man can do with his mouth . . . uh, breath. Red-hot ashes are easily rekindled. Don't doubt for one minute that I could blow your ash into a bonfire."

She persisted in chuckling, even as her eyes widened at his suggestive boast. "Tell the truth and shame the devil . . . are you even a real prince?"

"Ciertemente," he said with as much dignity as he could muster in the face of her continuing laughter. "I am Prince Pedro Tomas de la Ferrama."

"Oh, geez!" She swiped at her eyes with the back of one hand, then walked over to get a tissue from her purse. "You're more like the prince of Smarm—as in smarmy—than the prince of Charm," she blathered on, dabbing at her eyes. "You and Alvarez cooked up a scheme for seducing me into dropping my claim, didn't you?"

"We did not," he lied. *Smarmy, huh? Calling me a liar, huh? You are too astute by far, babe.*

"If you're depending on your irresistible charm to win me over, I've gotta tell you it's the shakiest leg on your negotiating table."

"You're not so charming yourself, Ms. Sullivan."

"Where *is* your magic kingdom anyhow? Disneyland? Ha, ha, ha."

"I find your comments extremely offensive, Ms. Sullivan. My *principality* is in the Canary Islands."

"Really?" She appeared a little more convinced now. "Do you have a castle? And a moat, and everything?"

The Prince-Charming gleam of hope was in her eye. She was like all the other women, after all.

"Of course," he answered truthfully. Well, partially true. She didn't need to know that his castle was a moldering palace built by a railroad baron in the Catskills at the turn of the century. Mira Lago, it was not. He would have been a fool to erect a majestic royal structure on the snake-ridden, vacant, volcanic island Dick had purchased for him in the Canary Islands near Tenerife, just in case reporters checked his claims of princeliness and an actual "realm."

All right. Time to shift strategies here. She's still buying the prince garbage, but she knows I'm trying to charm her into a fast deal. He threw his hands up in mock surrender and walked over to the desk, where the nosy woman was perusing his stock prospectus again. "I admit that I hoped you would be so overwhelmed by my magnetic allure that you'd prove reasonable in the negotiations," he told her and grabbed the pamphlet from her hands, placing it out of reach.

"Be careful that the magnetism of your personality doesn't whack out that hard drive over there," she cautioned with an unattractive smirk, pointing to the still humming computer.

"Another bit of Irish wisdom?" he asked testily.

"No, that's modern woman seeing through modern man. It doesn't take a financial wizard to recognize when a woman's being hustled."

Hustled? I've got news for you, babe, when I decide to hustle you, you won't know what hit you. My looks are one thing; my hustle is invincible. You are going to be really surprised.

And pleased.

I hope.

"In my own defense, it wasn't hard at all trying to seduce you. I've always had a taste for . . . shark meat." He bobbed his eyebrows at her.

She made a tsk-ing sound of disbelief, then grinned. "And I've been known to devour creamed snake in exotic restaurants. Have you ever tried *Crème de Cobra?*"

"Touché." *I'd like to cream something, and it's not a reptile, honey.* He smiled widely at the thought.

"Aha! That's the first honest thing you've done today."

"What? Admit I like to eat shark?" *Dios, did I speak my thoughts aloud . . . that I'd like to cream her?*

"No, you dolt! Smile."

"Huh?"

"That smile was the first genuine expression to cross your face today. I probably wouldn't have noticed the difference until I saw that when you smile spontaneously, your eyes crinkle, the stress in your jaw relaxes and a tiny dimple emerges at the right side of your mouth." A slight blush crept up her neck and over her face at her inadvertent revelation.

So, she's attracted to me, after all. I knew it, I knew it. Not that I care.

Yeah, right.

He smiled again.

"Nope. That one's a fake smile. I've got your number now, Prince Ferrama; so save yourself the energy. Soft words and soft looks beguile a fool, but I'm no fool. Let's get down to brass tacks. We're two reasonable people. We should be able to come to an agreement. I'm not greedy. Really, I'm not. My grandma taught me well, 'A ha'porth of 'taties and a farthing's worth of fat will make a good dinner for an Irish Pat.' I only want what's fair."

"Oh, *mierda!* The grandma crap again!"

She narrowed her eyes at his maligning her dear ol' grandma, then glanced down at her watch. Slicing him a scowl, she said, "Listen, I've been here an hour and a half. Either make me a serious offer or I'm leaving."

The offer I have in mind would probably get me a slap on the face. "Fifty thousand dollars and all medical costs."

"No way! Five hundred thousand. And that's a gift. Take it now or the offer is off the table."

P.T. shook his head. "Fifty thousand, all medical costs and your mortgage payments till you return to work, up to six months."

"Five hundred thousand," she repeated.

"That's absurd, totally unrealistic."

She shrugged. "The devil dances in an empty pocket. And my pockets are empty, thanks to your shoe product. Five hundred thousand will settle the case. Take it or leave it," she reiterated, then seemed to think of something else, "or . . ."

"Or what?" he asked hesitantly as he followed her gaze to the stock prospectus.

". . . or twenty-five thousand shares of Ferrama stock."

P.T. clenched his fists to keep from leaping over the table and strangling the woman. "I'll see you in hell before I give you an interest in my company."

"Put a beggar on horseback and he'll ride to hell," she quipped saucily.

He told her graphically what she could do with her unwelcome Irish proverbs.

"Tsk-tsk," she tutted with an infuriating grin. "That wasn't very princely of you."

He inhaled and exhaled several times, glaring at her the whole time.

"So, do I get a piece of Ferrama?"

Oh, you're going to get a piece of me, Ms. Sullivan. When I'm ready. On my terms. "When sharks fly," he said through gritted teeth.

"Now, now, Prince Peter," she chastised, wagging a forefinger at him.

"Don't . . . call . . . me . . . Peter," he gnashed out, his face reddening oddly with embarrassment.

"Prince Peter, Prince Petie, Prince Ferrama, Prince Charming, Prince Not-so-Charming, whatever. Remember, when thy hand be in the shark's mouth, laddie, withdraw it gently."

"And you remember this, lassie," he countered icily, "even a shark can be devoured by a hungry wolf."

For emphasis, he made a low, growling sound of sexy menace.

And damned if Cynthia Sullivan didn't smile—a slow, lazy attack on his already eroticized senses—just before growling back at him.

I think I'm in love. No, I think I'm in lust. No, I think I'm in love-lust. Oh, hell, I think I'm in trouble.

When dingbats go dingier . . .

"Did you hear that?" Naomi Friedman said to her sister Ruth as they eavesdropped unabashedly on the secretary's intercom outside P.T.'s office. Maureen had gone down the hall to accounting to cut them their weekly expense checks. "First, that woman leads a picket; now she's trying to steal our company."

"Do you think P.T. would let her do that to Daddy's company?" Ruth asked, wringing her hands.

"He's probably more concerned with getting her into his bed . . . the horny toad! Our stepbrother is spoiled by all the women chasing after him. It's always been that way. Remember that time in junior high when the janitor found him in the broom closet with Brenda 'Breasts "R" Us' Bicarro? Did he care about us then . . . how everyone was laughing? No. Well, we can't let him ruin our lives again. Not now."

She hitched up her workman's coveralls and patted the small pistol hidden in her tool belt. Who would have thought the weapon she'd bought as protection on the remote family estate would prove so handy?

"I don't understand," Ruth whined. "P.T. promised all our troubles would be over in a few weeks. He promised we wouldn't have to come begging anymore every time we need money. He promised we would get our share . . . a million dollars in cash, plus our trust fund. I need that money, Naomi. I really do." Ruth glanced pointedly at her boyfriend, Elmer Presley, who was busy checking out his sideburns in a nearby wall mirror.

Naomi groaned inwardly, as she did every time she viewed the couple. Even a pair of Ferrama stiletto pumps didn't do much for Ruth's petite five-foot frame, encased in skin-tight leopard pants and a ruffled white, off-the-shoulder, Daisy Duke–style blouse. The only thing missing was the cut-off shorts.

And the Graceland parody—the current love of Ruth's life—wasn't much taller . . . about five-foot five . . . even though he wore a pair of high-heeled blue suede boots, along with an aqua sequined jumpsuit. Between Ruth's teased end-flip hairstyle, à la Ann-Margret, and Elmer's poufy pompadour with its silly lock of hair over the forehead, à la The King, Naomi figured these two must use enough hairspray to put their own hole in the ozone layer.

Gawd! All she wanted was to escape this zoo of a family. Three more weeks and her dreams were finally going to come true. No more P.T., with his Prince Charming act to the public and Prince Miserly act in private. No more forestalling her aspirations for the sake of the company. No more running into that slimeball, Enrique Alvarez, who was so sexy he practically made the epoxy in her glue gun melt just looking at him.

Every woman deserved a prince at least once in her life. Barring a prince, a castle would do, Naomi had decided long ago, when her mirror told her she was never going to be anything more than plain. She didn't care if everyone laughed. All she knew was that the first time she'd seen the rundown castle P.T. had purchased in the Catskills, she'd fallen in love. No one . . . not her domineering stepbrother, not a greedy female stockbroker . . . *no one* was going to interfere with her dream of renovating the castle, Naomi vowed.

"We've got to have a plan," she told Ruth, who was busy humming "Treat Me Nice" while watching with adoration as Elmer practiced his hip swivel before the mirror. He kept complaining, "I just can't get my hips and knees to work together." That was an understatement. He looked as if he was having a fit.

Although she'd addressed Ruth when suggesting the need for a plan, it was Elmer who responded. "I already tol' ya, Naomi darlin', I don't know no hit man from Vegas. I come from Tupelo. The most excitement we got there is watchin' the cotton grow."

"A hit man?" Ruth shivered. "Using a hit man would be so . . . so bloody."

Naomi rolled her eyes. "Geez, Louise! I didn't really mean we should wipe the woman out. But we have to find a way to get this Sullivan woman out of the public eye for three weeks." She studied Elmer with sudden interest. "I don't suppose you know how to drive a limo?"

He brightened. "Of course. Even *a fool such as I* can drive a limo. Dintja know I usta be a truck driver? That was before my first gig on 'The Milton Berle Show.' "

Elmer had delusions that he was Elvis reincarnated. Mostly, Naomi just humored him. Ruth believed anything he said.

"A truck? No limos?" Naomi sighed with regret. Well, that eliminated one option, crazy as it had been.

"Now don't go gettin' *all shook up*, sweetheart. Truck, bus, limo . . . they're all the same. Trust me." He batted his eyes at her beseechingly, then crooned, "Let me be your limo driver," to the tune of "Let me be your teddy bear."

Ruth linked her arm with his and glanced at Naomi as if to say, "Isn't he the greatest?"

These two are nuttier than a fruitcake, and I must be the biggest pecan of them all because I'm actually considering a scheme that involves the three of us. But what other choice do I have? Stand by and do nothing . . . take a chance that P.T. will let the woman ruin our company's stock offering? Or take matters into my own hands? "Well, this is the plan, then," Naomi said, and quickly filled in her two would-be accomplices.

Elmer and Ruth nodded in agreement.

"It could work if we can keep the woman restrained till we get to the mountains," Elmer concluded. "Yep, this plan is smellin' sweet as a daisy."

"More like a doozy," Naomi muttered.

"Where can we get some rope in a hurry?" Elmer asked.

"Rope? I doubt there's any rope in these offices." They didn't have much time, and Naomi was starting to panic. "Improvise . . . we've gotta improvise. What can we use instead of rope?"

Elmer tapped his fingertips against his chin, deep in thought—if that was possible. "How about those neckties that Dick keeps in his office closet?"

"Those are designer Bolgheri ties," Ruth informed them. "They cost about two hundred dollars apiece."

Elmer and Naomi gaped at Ruth.

"How do you know that, sweet thing?" Elmer beamed at Ruth as if she'd just spelled *transubstantiation* in the grade-school spelling bee.

Gawd!

"Dick said the ties were the only thing left after his divorce settlement," Ruth related, "but I think he was just ribbing me. Although, I remember distinctly him telling me that alimony is the screwing a man gets for getting screwed."

"Ruth!" Elmer exclaimed with shock.

Naomi smiled with wicked delight. "Perfect. Take about a dozen of them."

Fortunately, Enrique and Jake were holed up in the conference room with some bankers, waiting for P.T.'s meeting to end. Another stroke of luck was finding the spare set of limo keys sitting on Jake's desk.

A few minutes later, ties and keys in hand, they prepared to swing into action.

"Everyone ready?" Naomi asked from their hiding place in the supply room next to the elevator.

At the last minute, Elmer turned to Ruth, a worried frown creasing his brow. "It's gonna be a long trip, sugar. Did you pack enough fried peanut butter and banana sandwiches?"

She had a proverb for everything . . .

Now that P.T. had recovered from Cynthia's deadlier-than-sex growl, he marveled at the nerve of the woman . . . thinking he would give her a foothold in his company.

"Twenty-five thousand shares of your stock and we'll call it a done deal," she said, repeating her ludicrous offer.

"Absolutely not! First of all, that would be worth two hundred thousand on the day of initial offering and possibly three or four times that amount within a week."

"I know," she said with a self-satisfied smirk.

Don't smirk so fast, Ms. Sullivan. Overconfidence

has killed more than one . . . shark. "And secondly, it would be a clear violation of the SEC . . . insider trading."

She let out a hoot of laughter. "Insider trading is known on the exchange as the Chinese Wall . . . the biggest joke on the street. There isn't a broker alive who doesn't engage in insider trading when he has a hot advance tip."

"Regardless, I am *not* giving you stock in my company. Not even one share, let alone twenty-five thousand." *The only piece of Ferrama you're gonna get is a part of my body, babe.*

"You should learn to compromise. There's an Irish motto you could learn from, you know: Money is like manure. It's no good unless you spread it around."

"I don't give a flying fig what they do with shit in Ireland. In this country, we don't throw good money away."

"Well, then, I guess we've reached an impasse." She pulled a business card from her purse and handed it to him. "You have twenty-four hours to reconsider my offer. Just remember, ebb tides don't wait for the slow man."

"Slow?" *I can be slow, honey. Real slow.*

"I know what you're thinking."

He grinned. "No, you do not, Cynthia."

"Well, whatever," she said huffily, her face turning a becoming shade of pink under his amused gaze. "Don't think too long, Ferrama. Grandma always said, 'You'll never plow a field by turning it over in your mind.'"

"Plow?" He continued to grin.

"Twenty-four hours," she said with a disapproving sniff. "After that, I let Marcia Connor loose on the courts."

He schooled himself to show no reaction at the mention of Marcia Connor and handed her his business card. "Perhaps you'll see the fairness of my generous offer once you've had a chance to weigh all the angles, including the length of time it takes to resolve a lawsuit. With the backlog in the civil courts right now, I'd predict at least five years before we ever get to trial, wouldn't you?"

She rolled her shoulders to indicate lack of concern, but he could tell by the slight flicker of her eyelashes that he'd hit a sore spot. He'd guarantee she needed the cash, *now*.

"And I promise you," he elaborated in a silken drawl, "it would be a dirty fight. I hope you have a squeaky clean background, *my dear*." He smiled sweetly at her.

Like a true shark, Cynthia didn't back down a bit. Instead, she returned his sweet smile. "I should be offended by that sleazy threat, but I'm not. Needs must when the devil rides, *my dear*. I'd do likewise if I were in your . . . shoes."

Just before she went out the door on her crutches— *Damn, how can a woman look so sexy on crutches?*—he thought of something else. "And consider one more thing, Ms. Sullivan. When our differences are resolved, I still have a question to ask you. And I would hate to have to wait five years to get my answer."

She hesitated and glanced back at him over her shoulder. He could tell she didn't want to ask, but she did. "What question?"

"What are we going to do *about us?*"
And P.T. was serious this time.
Sort of.

Was this Manhattan or Graceland? . . .

Cynthia pressed the button, then leaned her shoulders against the back wall of the elevator. Closing her eyes with exhaustion, she waited for the doors to slide shut and the descent to begin. She knew from her earlier ascent that it was a slow elevator, running directly to the underground parking garage, unlike the other express elevator that went only to the first floor. She'd driven today, rather than take a taxi, because she'd had so many picket signs to carry.

It had been a stressful day and her corn was throbbing with a vengeance. She looked forward to a long soak in the deep, old-fashioned, claw-footed tub that had been one of the original fixtures in her hundred-and-fourteen-year-old apartment. Dreamily, she planned her evening. A little Opium bath oil, a glass of chilled Chenin Blanc, the soundtrack from *Riverdance* on the CD player, followed by some microwaved leftovers . . . Peking fried rice and lobster egg rolls. Yummm.

After that, she'd call her lawyer.

Then again, maybe she'd follow her instincts and wait till tomorrow to see if the prince came through, as she expected he might . . . at least with a counteroffer.

"Wait a minute!" a feminine voice shouted.

Cynthia's eyes flew open as a tall, thirty-something

woman in paint-spattered denim coveralls put a hand on the elevator door to prevent its closing. Martha Stewart had worn a similar outfit on "Good Morning America" last week when she'd been installing her own toilet. Maybe it was the latest fashion. After all, good ol' Martha was considered the czar of good taste.

If "Martha" made her grin, the two characters who entered the elevator next made Cynthia's mouth drop open with astonishment.

A short man in an aqua sequin-studded jumpsuit—complete with extra-wide belt and high, stand-up collar and mini cape—gave her a crooked smile as he edged to one side of her. "Thank ya verra much, ma'am, for holdin' the door," he drawled in a deep Southern twang he'd probably picked up in Nashville.

Cynthia remembered belatedly to close her mouth.

He had to be approaching forty and must be an Elvis impersonator. What had he been doing on the sixteenth floor, which housed only Ferrama offices? She looked down at his high-heeled blue suede boots, studded with rhinestones. *Maybe Ferrama is going into boot-wear now. No, those boots are too garish for the ritzy Ferrama lines.*

On the other hand, "gaudy chic" might actually be a successful ploy . . . the kind of on-the-edge type gamble an avant-garde business like Ferrama would try.

Hmmm. A stock settlement is sounding better and better.

Then her attention was drawn to the simpering woman on her other side. She was about the same age as Cynthia—thirty—or a few years older, but there the resemblance ended. Wearing skintight, leopard print pants and a ruffled, off-the-shoulder blouse that had gone out of style about thirty years ago, she teetered on a pair of stiletto high heels. The only thing keeping her in balance was the massive teased hairdo straight out of *Grease*. The woman was a living flashback to the fifties. And the eye makeup! Lordy, she'd better hope she didn't run into a horny raccoon.

Cynthia wished her grandma was still alive. She'd get a kick out of hearing about this incongruous trio. With Grandma's age-old perspective on life, she would probably have said something profound, like, "Aye and begorrah, but there never was a slipper but there was an old stocking to match it."

"I hope you're going to be cooperative, Ms. Sullivan." The coolly menacing words came from the lady in the workman's duds.

"Huh? How do you know my name? And what do you mean by *cooperative?* Are you referring to my picketing earlier . . ." Her words trailed off as "Martha" reached into her tool belt and pulled out a small handgun.

In the meantime, a pinging sound indicated that the elevator was slowing down at the tenth floor to pick up a passenger. Quick as his rock 'n' roll legs could carry him, Elmer opened the emergency panel and hit the bypass button. Immediately, the pinging stopped. The elevator didn't stop at the tenth floor.

It all happened so fast that for a moment Cynthia was stunned.

"Is this a robbery?" she asked, staring the whole time at the pistol, which was aimed at the ceiling . . . for now, anyway.

"Of course not," the Ann-Margret lookalike twittered. "It's a kidnapping."

"Oh, that's better."

"Don't you be worryin' none, darlin'," the Elvis wannabe added, patting her arm. "Consider this a little vacation."

"How little?"

"Three weeks," the blue-collar Barbie piped in.

"Three weeks! I can't go away for three weeks. I've got work to do."

"We know what kind of work you have to do. Picketing. Lawsuits. Bad publicity. All intended to bring down Ferrama, Inc. Well, we're about to put a speed bump on your highway of destruction, Ms. Sullivan." The words coming from the woman in denim were shaky with anger, but the hand that held the upraised weapon remained steady.

Suddenly a bizarre thought occurred to Cynthia. "Did Prince Ferrama hire you? Are you people hit men?" Stranger things had happened, she supposed.

"Hit men? Hit men? What is it with you women and hit men?" Elvis asked with disgust. "This is simple TCB . . . taking care of business. An old motto of Elvis's, and a good one, too."

"No, P.T. didn't *hire* us," the overall-clad female spat out. "P.T. is our stepbrother, but he has nothing to do with this. In fact, we should've kidnapped him a long time ago. Then we might still have our family company . . . Friedman's Wholesale Shoes."

"Daddy made the best beach clogs in the world," the other woman informed her.

Cynthia put a hand to her forehead, totally confused.

"I'm Naomi Friedman, and this is my sister, Ruth Friedman," the coverall babe said testily.

Ruth, the bimbo sister, smiled at her and gave a little wave in acknowledgment of the introduction.

"You're going to be our guest for the next twenty-one days," Naomi continued. "So I'd suggest you cooperate, and no one will get hurt."

A bubble of hysteria threatened to erupt inside Cynthia's head. *Twenty-one days? That's how long it will be till the Ferrama stock offering. I don't care what they say, this is a setup orchestrated by the scuzz-ball prince. Boy oh boy, am I gonna make mincemeat of him. I really am.*

"And I'm Elmer Presley," the little guy chirped brightly.

"Don't you mean Elvis?"

"Naw. I'm Elmer Presley . . . Elvis's reincarnation."

"Oh, God!" Cynthia groaned. Then she decided she'd had enough of these silly games.

She lunged for the emergency button.

Elmer grabbed her arm.

Ruth squealed with distress.

And then the gun went off, shattering the mirrored wall to her right.

Everything happened so swiftly—like fast-forward *on a DVD player*—that for a moment there was a stunned silence in the elevator as everyone, including the Clint Eastwood in coveralls, stared aghast at the broken glass surrounding them.

"Na-o-mi!" Ruth shrieked. "You didn't tell us you had real bullets in that gun."

"Now, now, sweetcakes," Elmer comforted her. "There's no real harm done."

"Is this 'Candid Camera'?" Cynthia inquired hopefully.

"Hardly," Naomi sniped, her composure reinstated. She blew on the end of the gun barrel in a manner that would have been laughable if Cynthia didn't fear the woman was a hair-trigger psycho. "*Now* are you going to be cooperative?"

"Whatever you say," Cynthia agreed. *Half the tools are missing from this gal's toolbelt.* "Where are we going anyhow? The palace? Ha, ha, ha."

"Yep," the trio answered simultaneously.

"I am *not* going to the Canary Islands," Cynthia protested. *They'd probably bury me in some dungeon there. I'd live on bread and water . . . or maybe coconuts. Do they have coconuts in the Canary Islands? No, I think it's bananas. And the rack . . . would they put me on a rack and—*

"Not *that* palace, silly," Ruth said with a laugh.

Of course not. How silly of me! "Which castle, then?"

"The one in the Catskills," Naomi informed her dryly.

"The Catskills Castle. This I gotta see."

The princess was developing a real dislike for "The King" . . .

Several hours later, they were cruising up I-87 in a stretch limo. Elmer, whose high hairstyle barely topped the steering wheel, was driving, with his girlfriend Ruth at his side. One Elvis song after another blasted out of the car stereo. If Cynthia heard "Don't Be Cruel" one more time, she swore she was going to scream. Or do something cruel.

And Elvis trivia! Who cared if recent polls found that 43 percent of Americans describe themselves as Elvis fans? Or that there were one thousand legitimate Elvis impersonators—though the distinction between legitimate and illegitimate Elvises eluded her. Good grief, she wasn't even impressed that there were 575 Elvis fan clubs, even though he'd been dead for twenty-one years.

She was sitting in the backseat with the gun moll. Her ankles and wrists were restrained with Bolgheri ties she'd learned were from Alvarez's cherished collection.

Any thoughts Cynthia might have entertained about escaping at a rest stop or restaurant were quickly squashed. Naomi made her relieve herself in the woods along the roadside. And they all ate the god-awful fried peanut butter and banana sandwiches that Ruth had packed for Elmer, washed down with Perrier from the miniature limo fridge. Cynthia was thinking about starting on the half-full bottle of Scotch real soon, especially if Elmer didn't stop puffing on his smelly cigar and singing along in his horribly off-key voice the lyrics to every bloody Elvis song ever recorded.

His castle was a dump . . .

Four hours after leaving Prince Ferrama's office, Cynthia got her first view of Prince Ferrama's palace. The Catskills Castle was not what she'd expected.

After a harrowing drive up a narrow five-mile access road through almost impenetrable, overgrown forests, Elmer finally maneuvered the vehicle into a clearing dominated by a massive crumbling mansion complete with towers and turrets, even a broken-down drawbridge over a muddy moat. A castle it might have been in another lifetime. Now it was just a sad, collapsing mass of stone.

That wasn't quite true. One side of the castle was completely restored. Its stonework had been sandblasted and repointed, the leaded windows replaced.

Cynthia stepped forward, braced on one crutch, to examine this strange phenomenon. She noticed another bizarre thing. Sand. Lots of white sand. And banana trees. Huge, *fake* banana trees.

Half a dozen guard dogs patrolled the area—though who would be interested in trespassing here, Cynthia couldn't imagine. The dogs were the sorriest-looking mutts she'd ever seen. Pit bulls, they were not. Geriatric candidates, maybe.

When she voiced that opinion aloud, Elmer gave her a wounded, blinking look and informed her, "They ain't nothin' but hound dogs, darlin'. Ain't you never seen a purebred Southern red dog, cryin' all the time?"

The only dogs Cynthia was familiar with sizzled on pushcarts on the city streets.

"Well, what do you think of my . . . our castle?" Naomi asked, her face softening for the first time as she gazed at the deplorable heap of rock. Her expression could only be described as one of love. Or obsession.

"It's . . . it's interesting."

Naomi's lips thinned at the perceived insult as her eyes bored into Cynthia and her fingers tightened on the gun.

"I can see that it must have been magnificent at one time," Cynthia backtracked.

"And it will be again," Naomi asserted. "I'm going to restore every one of its one hundred and three rooms. And the gardens. And the pool. And the stables."

One hundred and three rooms? Incredible! "But that would take a fortune," Cynthia blurted out before she had a chance to bite her tongue. She sensed, too late, that Naomi wouldn't want to hear any criticism of her beloved castle.

"Right. The fortune I'm going to gain once the Ferrama stock goes public. Provided, of course, that nothing and no one interferes with the success of that venture." The look of determination on Naomi's face bordered on the fanatical, sort of like Glenn Close in *Fatal Attraction*. Except that Naomi's obsession was with a piece of rock, while Glenn Close's had been with a piece of c . . . well, Michael Douglas. Cynthia began to reassess her opinion of the woman. Earlier she'd thought Naomi was dangerous because she was half-baked. Now she feared that Naomi might do anything, even kill a hard-nosed stock trader, to achieve her goals. Cynthia would have to be very, very careful.

As Naomi prodded her forward toward the castle entrance, Cynthia asked, "Where does the prince fit into this whole scheme?"

"Screw the prince," Naomi said.

Yep, I'll second that.

"He's all part of the TCB," Elmer hinted in contra-diction.

Screw the TCB, too.

Dusk began to settle over the mountains as the four of them trudged carefully, single file, over the rotting drawbridge. Just then, a million bats swooped out of the upper towers like black sheets fluttering on the wind, which set the hounds to wailing in long, doleful bellows.

It was not a pretty sight or sound.

What kind of castle was this, anyhow? And who was Prince Peter Ferrama if this was the best he could do for a palace?

Something is hinky in this kinky kingdom.

And where, pray tell, is the royal fink?

Chapter Four

She'd always dreamed of a fairy godmother, not a fairy godfather . . .

"Welcome to my world . . ." Elmer serenaded Cynthia later in a husky Elvis croon, then immediately amended, ". . . ah, *our* world." He threw his arms wide to encompass her new "home" for the next three weeks.

Naomi and Ruth had gone off briefly to do whatever needed to be done when establishing residence as the sole inhabitants of a hundred-and-three-room castle. Cynthia was being held in one of the forty-eight bedrooms of the castle, many of which were named after early twentieth-century moguls who'd visited the mansion built by zillionaire railroad financier Henry Fowler.

"There's the Rockefeller Suite, the Gould, the

Morgan, the Vanderbilt, the Stuyvesant . . ." Elmer explained with pride, like a tour guide. "Your . . . uh, domain is called the Frick Suite."

"How appropriate! But dontcha think the Frick 'n' Frack would be closer to the mark, considering the circumstances."

Elmer tsk-ed his disapproval of her sarcasm. "We gave you the best room in the castle."

Cynthia glanced around the huge chamber, impressed despite herself. The odd thing was that only one wall of the suite, a combination bedroom-sitting room, had been restored, just as only one side of the castle's exterior had been refurbished. Antique wallpaper so finely detailed it resembled silk damask, a beautiful Aubusson carpet in a delicate floral pattern, fine embroidered bed hangings, gilt mirrors and original oil paintings in the landscape style of the Hudson River artists: all these decorated the room, but just the one side. The remainder of the huge room sported faded, peeling wall murals, a smoke-stained, ornately carved walnut fireplace, bare inlaid wood floors and battered Empire furniture.

The same was true of the rest of the palace, or as much of it as she'd seen thus far. The entryway was spectacular, with its Italian marble floors, Doric columns, intricate ceiling plasterwork, bronze chandelier dripping a dazzling spray of crystal pendants and wide mahogany staircase, but the parlors and hallways were a mess. The castle appeared almost like a movie set . . . a facade.

But Cynthia didn't have time to think about that now. After a harrowing ride up the ancient clanking elevator to the sixth floor, not to mention Naomi shooting at a pigeon that had dared to roost in one of the hall sconces, her nerves were totally frayed.

And she had had enough of Elmer's rock 'n' roll nonsense, too. The twit was still singing, "Welcome to my world," accompanied by a laughable one-knee swivel gyration.

"The only world you're going to be in, Elmer, is prison . . . once I get out of here," Cynthia declared. She was sitting on the end of a high, canopied bed that could be reached only by climbing up three steps. "Kidnapping. Assault. Arms violation. Extortion. Yep, you're going to be doing hard time till your blue suede turns moldy, buster."

"I've done a little *jailhouse rock* in my early days, darlin'," Elmer admitted, unconcerned, as he checked out his pompadour in a mirror. He paid particular attention to the stray lock, which he arranged over his forehead, muttering something about needing to buy more gel. "Sometimes a man's gotta do what a man's gotta do."

"Go . . . get . . . me . . . some . . . clothes," she ordered, trying a different approach. She was wearing only her chemise and panties and a stretch blue suede headband wrapped twice around her one ankle. Elmer had lent her the headband from his Graceland memorabilia collection. The rest of her clothing had been removed to prevent her escape.

Not that she could escape anyhow. Reasoning that she couldn't hold a gun over Cynthia twenty-four hours a day, Naomi had whipped out an electric drill.

"Oh, my God!" Cynthia had shrieked. "You're a female Freddie Krueger. You're going to drill me to death."

Naomi had cocked her head in confusion, then let out a hoot of laughter. "You must have a corn on your brain, too." Naomi had proceeded to make quick work of installing a retractable dog chain on the wall, with one end attached to a locked chain dog collar wrapped three times around Cynthia's headband-padded ankle.

"No can do," Elmer insisted, pulling her back to the present and her demand for clothing. "Naomi's right. Nothing personal, darlin', but a *hardheaded woman* like you would be out that door like a great ball of fire."

"Aaargh! I'm chained to a wall. I'm on crutches. By the time that elevator got to the first floor, you three would be on me like gangbusters. Your guard dogs would tear me to smithereens, or lick me to death, if I managed to get that far. Incidentally, do they ever shut up? And—"

"The moon is none the worse for the dog barking at her," Elmer broke in with what sounded a whole heck of a lot like one of Grandma's proverbs.

She glared at him for interrupting her tirade, which she resumed. "Furthermore, I don't know how to drive a limo . . . assuming I were able to wrest the car keys from you. And hobbling down a dark road in the middle of nowhere is not my idea of fun." She took a deep breath and exhaled. "So, get my damn clothes."

Elmer shook his head, still studying his reflection in the mirror. "Do you think I should let my sideburns grow longer?"

Cynthia told him what he should do with his sideburns, explicitly.

Elmer winced. "You'll be thankin' me for this one day . . . once you open up your *suspicious mind* to the gift I'm givin' you."

"Thank you? Thank you? You are two strings short of a guitar. This reminds me of *One Flew Over the Cuckoo's Nest.* Yep, I've landed smack dab in the middle of *Three Flew Over the Cuckoo's Nest.*" Then she stilled. "What gift?"

"Prince Charming." Elmer beamed at her, waiting for her to express her gratitude, no doubt. When she didn't, he stepped up to the bed and sat down next to her. His short legs looked comical on the high bed, his boots barely reaching the floor.

"You're going to give me a prince? For a gift?"

Elmer nodded enthusiastically.

"Who? Jack Nicholson?" she scoffed.

"Of course not. Jack may be a prince in Hollywood, but he's not the type of prince I have in mind for you."

"Oh, no! Please don't tell me that Prince Ferrama is the gift."

A speaking blush flooded Elmer's face.

"I knew it! That louse Ferrama is behind this whole caper."

"No, no, no. You've got it all wrong." He glanced furtively toward the closed door before confiding, "Naomi and Ruth think we shanghaied you because of your picketing and threats of a lawsuit. But I got the orders to help you long before that, honey."

Oh, God! He really is nuts.

"In a way, you could say I'm family." Those momentous words were accompanied by a wink that seemed to contain some hidden message. "Your grandma—God bless her soul, the sweet angel!—put in a special request for you."

Nuttier than a Snickers bar. "My grandma put in a special request for a prince . . . for me?" she asked incredulously. The jerk apparently didn't know that her grandmother had died ten years ago. "Who *are* you?"

"I'm your fairy godfather, Cindy." He flashed a silly lopsided grin at her.

Walnuts, pecans, almonds, pistachios . . . I've landed in a peanut patch. "My name is Cynthia, not Cindy." Why she homed in on that irrelevant detail, ignoring his other, more ludicrous pronouncement, she had no idea. Maybe her corn really was moving to her brain.

"Where I come from, we like to refer to you as Cindy . . . for Cinderella."

She groaned. *Maybe all that peanut butter has clogged his brain.* "And where might that be . . . the land of fairies? You did say you were my *fairy* godfather. Ha, ha, ha!"

"Some people do call us fairies," he said, "but—"

She thought of something. "Fairies? You're a fairy? I thought you and Ruth were . . . well, involved."

Elmer make a harrumphing sound. "Not *that* kind of fairy."

"Look, whether you're a fairy or a guardian angel or a gay leprechaun doesn't matter to me."

Elmer straightened, insulted. "Are you saying I'm short?"

"Aaargh! I don't care if you're Tinkerbell." She took several deep breaths to calm down, then tried again. "I refuse to be anyone's Cinderella. I gave up believing in glass slippers and pumpkin coaches long ago."

"That's just what your grandma said: The wee lass has lost her dreams."

"Dreams? I've realized all my dreams, thank you very much. I'm one of the most successful women on Wall Street. Put that in your fairy pipe and smoke it, Elvis."

"Elmer," he corrected.

"Elmer . . . Elvis . . . the Big Bopper . . . whatever." She threw up her hands in disgust. "And stop bringing up my grandma. She's dead. Do you hear me? Dead." Tears welled in her eyes and she fought to suppress the lump in her throat. Damn, she still missed that wily old lady, even after all these years.

"I know your grandma's dead, Cindy," he said softly. "And she's worried about you. That's why she wants you to have your prince. I'm here to help you get your dreams back."

"Listen carefully, you lunkhead, because I'm only going to say this once. In the real world, a girl's got to make her own dreams come true. And today's woman knows Prince Charming doesn't exist. That's a fairy tale that's been fed to generations of females. By men. To subjugate women."

Elmer gazed at her sadly. "Is it not a lonesome thing, lassie, to grow old without a mate?"

"I'm not old. I'm only thirty."

"Autumn days come quickly, like the running of the hound on the moors."

"I am only thirty years old," she repeated.

"And a beautiful thirty years old you are, too."

"Don't try to soft-soap me, you buzzard. Soft words butter no parsnips."

"Ah, but they won't harden the heart of the cabbage, either." He beamed, finishing the old Irish saying for her.

Cynthia narrowed her eyes. He was continually quoting Grandma's favorite proverbs. Could he possibly be telling the truth about being a fairy or Elvis reincarnated? No, there were dozens of those Irish proverb books on the market. Heck, some of the witty sayings were even on coffee mugs. Elmer had probably seen them there.

"I do not want a man . . . prince or otherwise," she said emphatically. "So forget the matchmaker business. I'm not interested."

"But surely every woman wants to find her soulmate. Even you, who have lost your dreams. Admit it, lassie; it's a lonesome washing that has no man's shirt in it."

Cynthia glared, disbelieving, at the thickheaded fool. "If any man thinks I'm going to do his laundry, he's got another think coming."

"It was just a figure of speech, Cindy."

"Aaargh! Figure this. No man! No prince! No gift! No Cinderella! No fairies! I . . . am . . . not . . . interested."

"There, there." Elmer patted her hand. "He—the big godfather—was right in answering your grandma's prayers."

The dumbbell must have a head like a sieve. He didn't register a single thing I said.

"You need a fairy godfather real bad. Your heart's just cryin' out for a sprinkle of magic dust."

"Godfather?" Cynthia said tentatively. Why did Elmer keep harping on godfathers? "Oh, boy! I get it now. You're with the Mafia, aren't you? I've heard rumors that the Mafia is infiltrating Wall Street, but I never really believed it. What family are you with . . . Gotti, Gambino, Capone, Luciano—"

"Presley."

"Huh? I never heard of Presley in association with the Mafia. Is that a Nashville branch?"

"Geez! I'm not with any gang family, although there is the Memphis Mafia, of course . . . Elvis's old bodyguards. Unless . . . unless you consider seraphim a family."

Her body slumped with exhaustion, the events of the long day finally catching up with her. "My life is going to hell in a handbasket. First I get a corn. Then I lose my job. Now I'm to be rescued by a fairy godfather guardian angel."

"You *do* understand." Elmer puffed out his chest with satisfaction and put a comforting arm around her shoulder. "But I have to correct one little thing you said. I'm a fairy, not an angel. There is a difference."

"Do you really expect me to believe that you're a fairy reincarnated as Elvis? Come on!"

"Just think about it, darlin'. Fairies love music more than anything in the world. Elvis was the king of rock 'n' roll, the best music ever created."

"But why me?" Cynthia couldn't believe she'd actually asked the question, as if she gave credence to Elmer's ridiculous story.

"God had a plan for you, even before your grandma prodded him to get on with it. The corn was just the first step in the plan."

Cynthia started to laugh hysterically. Between laughs, she choked out, "God . . . I mean, the big godfather . . . gave me a corn . . . as sort of a celestial spur to make me believe in fairy tales again?"

"Exactly."

When she finally wiped the last tear from her eye, Cynthia cocked her head at the unsmiling show-biz caricature. "So where are your wings?" she asked derisively, suddenly frightened by Elmer's penetrating eyes, which seemed to see too much.

At first, he didn't answer. Then he relaxed and bobbed his eyebrows at her. "Why do you think Elvis wore a cape all the time?"

Sharks don't just disappear, do they? . . .

"She's vanished. Poof. Gone like the wind," Dick told P.T. two days later, sinking down into a chair before his office desk.

"Gone like a shark, you mean," P.T. concluded with a grimace. "She's just circling the body, waiting for the perfect moment to attack. . . ."

". . . when we let our guard down," Dick finished.

"Yep. This is a tactic, pure and simple, designed to drive us crazy."

"She's succeeding."

P.T. thought about all the mental anguish he'd gone through the past few days and had to agree. "I'll bet her lawyer is in on this. Another barracuda." P.T. tapped his Mont Blanc pen on the blotter, then stopped himself. The stupid thing was shamefully expensive—

equivalent to the down payment on his first car. "The picketing and threat of a lawsuit were deliberate teasers. They want us nervous and jittery. Just watch. The two of them are going to sashay in here, unannounced, any day now."

"And they're going to attempt to extort a pig-load of cash out of Ferrama." Dick pinched the bridge of his nose and sighed. He looked tired. Even his usual meticulous attire was rumpled. P.T. knew the stress of pulling off the stock offering, doing damage control on the picketing episode and searching for the Wall Street princess was taking its toll.

"*Attempt* is the key word, Dick. Let's try calling her home again." He pulled out her business card.

Dick put up a halting hand. "Give it up. There are fifty-eight message beeps on her answering machine, and fifty of those are from us."

"I even went over to her place last night," P.T. admitted. "She's not there, or else she's doing a good job of playing hide and seek."

P.T. decided not to mention how long he'd stood outside the Dakota, admiring the beauty of the famous block-long building with its eclectic Victorian facade of buff yellow brick and chocolate brown stone. Despite his admiration for the aged structure, which was accented by crenellations and an iron-gated archway leading to a central courtyard, it was not the kind of home he hoped to have one day. It was too . . . well, majestic. Nope, he was going to live in a regular neighborhood outside the city. Someplace with a name like Blue Falls or Oak Haven. Someplace where the rat race referred only to a species of rodents.

"So, we wait it out?"

P.T. shrugged. "It's not our standard M.O. I hate being on the defensive, but the witch has us by the balls. *For now.* But let's make sure we have all our ducks in a row before she finally comes in for the attack."

"Right." Dick tossed a folder onto the desk. "There's the P.I.'s report."

"Anything in her background?"

"Not much. Nothing criminal, anyway. But lots of interesting personality stuff that you might be able to use."

"Use? Me?" P.T. scowled at his friend. "Not the charm routine again?"

"Whatever works."

P.T. groaned.

"Hey, it doesn't matter how liberated women have become, they still dream of Prince Charming. And Cynthia Sullivan is no exception. The P.I. found out that she used to collect fairy-tale books when she was a kid." Dick smirked at him as if he'd just announced some monumental news.

"So what?"

"So, Cynthia Sullivan is a babe just waiting to be plucked off the vine. Like all the rest of womankind, she yearns, deep down, for a knight in shining armor. And guess what," he said, waving a hand in P.T.'s direction, "one prince coming up. Come on, *amigo*, do your magic."

"I already told you, she didn't fall for the looks."

Dick grinned. "I still say your version of the looks is too smooth. Women like a little edge to the game . . . an underlying rawness. I should give you lessons. All right, if you insist, I'll be the one to seduce the babe this time. Within a week, she'll be the first shark in history to purr."

"Screw you!" P.T. grumbled.

"No, screw *her* is what you mean. P.T., P.T., P.T.," he said, shaking his head, "you are still thinking about Cynthia Sullivan as a woman, not as the enemy. And that's dangerous. It's probably why your looks didn't melt her ice. In order for the looks to work, the seducer has to be cool, calm and uninvolved."

"You're pathetic."

"I know. Look, we're not accomplishing anything, sitting around here twiddling our thumbs. You wanna go grab a bite of lunch and drown our sorrows in three or four martinis? We can be pathetic together."

"Sounds like a plan. Can we go someplace where I don't have to be a prince?"

"Sure, as long as it's not McDonald's again. Besides, they don't serve alcohol."

As P.T. rose from his chair, the cover of the folder flipped open, and the face of Cynthia Sullivan peered up at him from a black-and-white photograph taken for her broker's license. She stared directly at the camera, unsmiling, but there was a twinkle of mischief in her Irish eyes, probably a reaction to something the photographer had said. "Damn, she's gorgeous."

"No, she's not," Dick asserted, looking sideways at him with concern as he attempted to whisk some wrinkles out of his slacks.

Coming around the desk, P.T. arched a brow.

"She's not bad looking, I'll concede that. But gorgeous? No way!"

"If a woman's appearance doesn't shout bimbo, you think she's less than a ten."

"She's hard, P.T. And foul-mouthed. Bette Midler with a Harvard MBA. Since when do you go for that type?"

"Unlike you, I never limited myself to types." He sidestepped the punch Dick attempted to deliver to his upper arm.

"Ha! She doesn't even have a great bod."

"Are you nuts? Those legs alone would drive a man to impure thoughts."

"I never knew you to be a leg man."

"I'm an everything man . . . when it comes to gorgeous women like Cynthia Sullivan."

"I am really worried about you."

"Don't be." He poked Dick in the arm as they walked out the door. "What can a goose do, a duck can't and a lawyer should?"

"Please. Your jokes are so old they aren't the least bit funny anymore."

"Stick his bill up his ass."

"See. Not funny. At all."

P.T. chortled anyhow, then asked, "Should we stop and see if Jake wants to join us?"

"Nah. He's down at the police station." Dick mumbled the last words.

"Why?" P.T. tensed, suddenly alert, and stopped in his tracks.

"I didn't want to worry you."

"Why stop now?"

"All right. If you must know, someone stole the limo."

"Oh, God!"

"And there are bullet holes in the elevator."

"What next? A stiff in the closet?"

"I sure hope not," Dick grumbled,

This "prison" was sort of a beauty spa. Sort of! . . .

Cynthia was bored stiff.

After two days of incarceration, she had indulged in five bubble baths using Priscilla's Perfumed Pellets. (Thank God her fifty-foot restraining chain extended to the adjoining bathroom.) She'd listened to every Elvis song ever recorded on an old-fashioned 45-rpm record player. (The first time Elmer had boasted that he had a forty-five collection, her heart had jumped, thinking he meant guns.) She had learned all she ever wanted to know (which wasn't much) about fairies, angels and rock 'n' roll from the flaky but kind-hearted Elmer. And she'd endured a mud mask, makeup demonstration, facial aerobics, color analysis, eyebrow waxing, manicure and pedicure from Ruth, who'd attended no less than five beauty schools where, Cynthia suspected, she'd been a less than superior student. Only brain-melting tedium had caused her to submit to the dingbat's ministrations.

No, that was mean-spirited, she immediately chastised herself. Ruth was a gentle, friendly woman who was trying her best to make Cynthia's confinement bearable. Unlike Naomi, who cared only about the castle and its unending renovations. Yesterday Cynthia had put a stranglehold on Ruth's neck, threatening to choke her to death if they didn't release her. Naomi had barely blinked an eye. "Go ahead," she had commented, walking blithely out of the room. "I've thought about it more than once myself."

In fairness, Cynthia conceded that Naomi might have known she'd never follow through. But then again, maybe not.

"I'm turning into a prune here," she called out to Ruth from her bubble bath. Through the open door, she could see Ruth sitting cross-legged on the bed, drying Cynthia's newly laundered panties and camisole with a blow-dryer. Naomi still wouldn't allow her any additional clothes, not even one of Ruth's gaudy bimbo outfits. The only way Cynthia could remove her underwear for washing was to pull the panties completely off both legs, then down the chain attached to her ankle—a ridiculous, convoluted procedure necessitated by Naomi's stubbornness.

"Just a sec," Ruth answered brightly.

"And this hot oil treatment . . . should it be congealing on my hair?"

Ruth bit her bottom lip. "Oops."

"Oops? Oops what?" Cynthia asked, emerging gingerly from the slippery tub. What she didn't need was another injury. Her toes were healing very nicely, thanks to the freedom of going barefoot and some Dr. Scholl's foot products Naomi had miraculously produced. Naomi was determined that when Cynthia was finally released, there would be no sign of the corn to produce in court. Little did she know that Cynthia's lawyer had already gotten all the photographic and medical documentation needed.

A half hour later, Cynthia was sitting on a chair by the bedroom window while Ruth used a diffuser on her long hair. Outside, birds sang melodiously, and fresh country air wafted in on a slight breeze.

"I am sick of hearing birds chirp merrily. Why do they have to be so merry all the time? And the air is too darn fresh here."

"Don't you like the smell of pine forests and wild flowers?"

"I can get that from a spray of Glade. Give me good ol' Manhattan any day, with horns blaring, venders hawking and life moving at a fast pace."

Ruth nodded and chewed gum at the same time. Watermelon flavor, she would guess. "Actually, I like cities, too. When I get my million dollars—that's what P.T. will give me after the stock sale, plus the trust fund—well, then Elmer and me are gonna buy a tour bus. He already has a band put together. And we're off to Las Vegas."

Viva Las Vegas! "Do you believe Elmer is . . . uh, a fairy?"

"A fairy!" Ruth exclaimed, then put the fingertips of one hand to her mouth and giggled. "Oh, Cynthia! You are such a kidder."

Yep, that's me. World-class kidder.

"Elmer is the sexiest man alive."

"He is?"

"Oh, yeah." Ruth rolled her eyes dramatically and picked up a funny-shaped comb with three long plastic prongs, which she was using to fluff out Cynthia's now dry hair. "My third husband, Chuck, was a Chippendale's dancer, and . . ."

Her third husband?

". . . Lordy, but Chuck did have the body of a Greek

god," Ruth told her, pausing with a slight smile of re-membrance. "I was out of luck, though, when it came time for Chuck to . . . well, you know. He was nothing in the sack compared to Elmer."

I do not need to know this. I do not want to picture Elmer doing . . . things. "I didn't mean that kind of fairy, Ruth. I mean the magical kind. You know, like Tinkerbell."

Ruth just gaped at her in confusion. Apparently, Cynthia was the only one to whom Elmer had given the fairy snow job.

"Just because Elmer is unique doesn't mean he's queer or *crazy*," Ruth told her defensively. "Elmer al-ways marched to the beat of a different drummer . . . uh, guitar."

Maybe he ought to march himself to the nearest psychiatrist, Cynthia thought, but she restrained her tongue, not wanting to hurt Ruth's feelings.

"There," Ruth said, stepping back to admire her handiwork. "You look much better. And your ends aren't dry at all now." She started to walk to the other side of the room. "Let me get a hand mirror so you can check out your new 'do."

"Just so it's not a beehive like you gave me yester-day. What I really want is my laptop with email access, a television with the stock channel and a telephone."

"We don't have cable or telephone connections here, Cindy." Ruth had taken to using Elmer's nick-name for her, despite Cynthia's repeated corrections. She was rummaging through her huge makeup car-ryall for a mirror.

"I'd also like to get my hands on your step-brother . . . Prince Ferrama."

Ruth glanced up, giving her a conspiratorial grin. "P.T. *is* good-looking, isn't he? You'll have to stand in line, though. Lots of women want him."

I'll bet they do. "That's not why I want him. I have no thoughts of unwrapping him, like the gift Elmer intends for me."

"Elmer plans to give you P.T.? For a gift?" The prospect seemed to stun Ruth. So that was another bit of info Elmer had shared only with her. "Well, if anyone can do it, Elmer can," Ruth concluded finally. She was now tossing every blessed thing out of her bag onto a dresser, in search of the elusive mirror.

"Yeah. Elmer says it's his mission in life to give me a Prince Charming . . . as a gift. In this case, Prince Peter. Gawd! It boggles the mind, doesn't it? Anyhow, I can't picture *unwrapping* a big box with the prince inside. But I do have this vision of *wrapping* him in about fifty yards of Naomi's duct tape and dropping him off the castle catwalk."

Ruth giggled.

She thinks I'm joking. "Or boiling him in oil."

Ruth giggled again. "The only oil in the castle is the one hundred percent virgin olive oil down in the kitchen."

"That'll do. Of course, I might just prefer stretching him on the rack, assuming this palace has a dungeon."

Ruth frowned. "Just a wine cellar."

"Perfect."

"Naomi was really mad when she saw what you did to P.T.'s oil painting." Ruth had finally found the hand mirror and was marching back toward Cynthia when her eyes shifted to the wall behind the bed.

They both glanced at the white-splotched portrait. Lacking darts, Cynthia had spent two hours yesterday, in between bubble baths, throwing wet dough balls, formed from rolled and dampened bread centers, at his portrait. He looked rather good with soggy splats on his full, unsmiling lips, which she refused to consider sensual, between his compelling dark eyes (black as Toal's cloak, her grandma would say, and deep as a maiden's well) and in the middle of his family crest, which adorned the gold pendant hanging from a ribbon around his neck (a neck she pictured circled by her squeezing fingertips).

Every time she mentioned the cad to her captors, they hedged and avoided direct answers. They wouldn't even tell her about his kingdom in the Canary Islands. She was convinced he was behind this madcap caper, and he was going to pay . . . with more than a stock settlement, too. Her price was going up by the minute. She only hoped her brain cells didn't atrophy during the next nineteen days. She'd need her wits about her when she cleaned his clock and that of Ferrama, Inc.

"Where's Naomi, by the way? I haven't heard her electric sander all morning." Cynthia didn't see much of Naomi, who held the key to her chains. Most of the time, Naomi was off sanding, drilling or painting.

"She had Elmer drive her to the hardware store in Red Hook. That's a little town about twenty-five miles from here." Ruth handed her the mirror and sat down on a chair beside her. "You'll be pleased to know that Elmer is gonna try to rent a TV and a DVD player. Not that we'd be able to get any television stations, but we can always watch movies."

"Of Elvis, no doubt," Cynthia muttered under her breath. Out loud, she asked, "Why is Naomi so obsessed with renovating this monstrosity?"

Ruth shrugged. "We all have our dreams, don't we?"

"But some of us know enough to make our dreams realistic. I assume she'll be using her million dollars to finish the job here. What a waste! I know a terrific mutual fund she could invest in that yields—"

Ruth made a tsk-ing cluck of the tongue and gazed at Cynthia with an expression bordering on pity. "Cindy, dreams aren't supposed to be realistic. What's the point of dreams if a person can't wish for the impossible?"

How did one argue with such logic?

"Naomi never had much of a social life, although I think she could be pretty if she'd only let me give her a makeover. And deep down I think she was affected by our mother's death even more than I. When Daddy married P.T.'s mother—I was only eleven then, and Naomi twelve—she began to dream of this grand home she would have someday where she would be totally in charge. You see, Daddy treated us like little princesses, never letting us make our own decisions. Then, when he died, P.T. took over and did the same thing. I never minded the domineering attitude of Daddy or P.T., but Naomi hated it . . . and still does. To her, having this castle represents a kind of . . . freedom."

It made an odd kind of sense to Cynthia. "So Peter is a prince through his mother's side of the family," she mused. "That must have been really exciting for you and Naomi when your dad remarried into royalty."

"Well, we were kinda young then. And P.T. started

bossing us around right from the start; so, it was hard to be impressed."

"I guess P.T.'s mother must have given up her right to the throne when she married for love, right?" Cynthia hardly suppressed her sigh at the romantic notion.

"Well, Eva did move to New Jersey with P.T." Ruth was looking everywhere but at Cynthia as she spoke. Their conversation must be dredging up painful memories.

"Eva Ferrama . . . what a beautiful name!"

"Oh, she was so-o-o beautiful, Cindy. Like a princess, she was . . . I mean, she was a princess and all that . . . but, well, you know what I mean. Let's talk about something else." Her face was red as a beet with discomfort.

"Just one last thing. Will Peter be willing to give up his castle to Naomi?"

"Hah! He hates this place."

"Oh? I guess that's why it's only fixed up in some places. Which reminds me . . . how come so much of it, like this bedroom, is only refurbished on one side?"

Ruth's eyes darted away, avoiding Cynthia's scrutiny. "Let's talk about something else," she suggested again. "Look," she said, pointing to the mirror in Cynthia's hand. "What do you think?"

Cynthia lifted the mirror and let out a little squeak of surprise. *Oh, my God, I have big hair. Really big hair. Really big curly hair. If ever there was a hair-do, this is a hair-don't.* She started to tell Ruth to comb it out immediately, then noticed her waiting expectantly for her response, a vulnerable look in her heavily mascaraed eyes.

"It's great," Cynthia lied.

Ruth let out a sigh of relief. "Oh, good. Maybe tomorrow we can do our nails again. I have Mango Madness and Red Hot Flame. Oooh, oooh, oooh, I know. Let's use the glow-in-the-dark Pink Passion."

"Super." Cynthia took another look at herself in the mirror. *I look like a Forty-second Street hooker. And now I'm going to glow, too. What next?*

From the open window, she heard a car door slam and Elmer's voice raised in song, as usual. "Someday her prince will come," he was belting out, off-key, to the background accompaniment of six hounds a-wailing, a thousand birds a-chirping and Naomi a-cursing. The only thing missing was the rattle of a pumpkin coach coming over the moat.

Did Cinderella have to put up with this crap? Cynthia wondered hysterically. Then she sighed in surrender. *Oh, hell, let the ball begin.*

Chapter Five

The you-know-what was going to hit the shark fan . . .

"Naomi and Ruth did what?" P.T. roared.

Jake and Dick cringed, their eyes darting around La Vida as diners' heads turned like dominoes in their direction. The two men had rushed into the popular restaurant moments before, interrupting his late-night engagement . . . a last minute tête-à-tête arranged in the futile hope of obliterating his concerns about the upcoming stock offering. Not to mention his annoying and escalating sexual fantasies about the missing Cynthia Sullivan.

When his mind had drifted this afternoon in the midst of an important conference call with his European distributors to visions of Cynthia Sullivan wearing an apron and nothing else, he'd known he had to find some way to divert his misdirected testosterone. An apron, for God's sake! The woman probably didn't even own an apron. Hell, he didn't even know if aprons existed outside the world of Andy Griffith's Aunt Bea.

"Go get laid," had been Dick's advice.

"That woman is spamming your circuits," Jake had agreed. "Yep, your hard drive needs a tune-up. Take care of your joystick, man."

As a result, he'd made a date with a model who had one of those single-word appellations that escaped his mind at the moment . . . Crystelle, that was it.

"P.T.," Dick said with an exasperated exhalation, jarring him back to the present. "Where the hell's your concentration?"

"In his joystick, would be my guess," Jake said with a grin.

"Joystick?" Crystelle stopped picking at her *foie gras en brioche* and blinked her hundred-thousand-dollar eyelashes at P.T. He knew the amount they were insured for because she'd told him so, repeatedly. He also suspected, though not yet from personal experience, that she would be an expert in handling a joystick.

The effect of the eyelid fluttering, intended to be alluring, was lost on his libido, which had an annoying habit—even facing the certain prospect of his hard drive being booted up by the end of the evening—of lingering on the fantasy of a pair of million-dollar Rockette legs. Dusted with flour. She would be baking him a cake. Chocolate, he hoped. Nude baking . . . now that had possibilities. Well, not really nude. There was that apron . . .

But he couldn't think about that now. Liz Smith,

seated at a conspicuous table in the tiny restaurant, was among those glancing in their direction. The woman, who was indeed ninety if she was a day, as he'd speculated days ago, flipped open her notebook with the speed of a carnivorous, gossip-smelling news-monger.

All this P.T. noticed in that split second that his befuddled brain registered the alarming news Jake and Dick had just delivered.

"Your stepsisters kidnapped the shark and are keeping her at the castle," Dick repeated in a hushed undertone.

"And Elmer Presley drove them there in *our* stolen limo," Jake added with indignation. Somehow, Jake had developed a personal attachment to the hunk of pretentious metal.

"I think they used my Bolgheri ties in the caper," Dick said, seething, as he shifted from foot to foot. "I swear, I'm going to wring Naomi's neck if there's even one wrinkle in them."

"Forget the ties," P.T. snapped.

"Easy for you to say," Dick grumbled.

"Elvis Presley stole a shark and is keeping it in a castle?" Crystelle made a little twittering sound as she asked her question, but her eyes sharpened with alertness. Crystelle was one bright cookie, despite her brainless bimbo affectation.

"No, no, no, *cara*," P.T. corrected, recognizing the danger. He couldn't take a chance that the publicity-hungry model would sell the story to the nearest tabloid. "Dick and Jake were just telling me that my stepsisters are trying out our new sharkskin shoes . . . the Elvis Presley blue suede shade. Against my orders,

I might add. Jake accidentally left the designer samples in the limo last night."

"Oh."

He put his fingertips to his lips, as if he'd revealed something he shouldn't have. "Of course, this is all top secret, sweetheart. Hush-hush. We wouldn't want the competition to steal our ideas." He flashed her an imploring look. Hey, two could play the eyelash batting game. Even Cynthia Sullivan had admired his eyclashes, he recalled with disturbing irrelevance.

"Of course, darling." Crystelle smiled sweetly at him.

P.T. would lay odds he would read all about this conversation in the fashion dailies tomorrow.

Suddenly, she straightened and threw back her overblown hair with dramatic effect, having just spotted Liz and a possible publicity op.

Oh, hell!

Dick made eye contact with him, motioning with a jerk of his head that he should slip away from his date. Crystelle's attention was divided now between her attempts to understand the nonverbal communication going on at her table and an attempt to gain the interest of the celebrity reporter.

One mention in Liz's column could up a model's asking price by thousands.

Or destroy a company. Especially when two of its major stockholders were engaged in a felony of monumental proportions.

"*Por favor*, would you excuse me for a moment, *querida?*" he inquired smoothly, pinning her with a smoldering expression that promised he would make it up to her later. A promise he now had no intention of honoring.

Crystelle practically swooned.

Hmpfh! At least with this babe his looks still worked. There was some balm to his bruised pride in knowing that.

As he followed Jake and Dick to the bar, he saw Liz rise from her seat and make her way toward his table. Now Liz and Crystelle were exchanging little air-kissing gestures on each of their cheeks in greeting. Women were so predictable.

Except for his wicked stepsisters.

The fantasy prince was having one hell of a fantasy . . .

It was four A.M. before P.T. was ready to leave for the Catskills.

P.T. had put Crystelle in a cab with promises he'd call her the next day. Then he had gone to his penthouse apartment—another showcase prop he would unload with his prince persona in a few short months. There, Dick and Jake had brought him up to date on the developments they'd uncovered in the past few hours.

Apparently, Naomi and Ruth had learned of Cynthia Sullivan's threats to sue Ferrama. Fearing that their windfall was going to fall through the cracks, they'd taken matters into their own imbecile hands and kidnapped the woman. *Santo Infierno!* Why the two dingbats didn't trust him to handle the situation himself he didn't know. He'd been taking care of their interests very well since Mort's death more than ten years earlier. Not only had he tripled the company's assets, but he'd upped his stepsisters' income significantly. But it was never enough.

"I should be back by this afternoon," P.T. said, having decided not to pack an overnight bag. "I want you two to carry on as usual."

Both men nodded.

"Dick, you've been handling most of the road shows anyhow, but in case I don't get back in time, you can pick up the presentation at Merrill Lynch, right?"

"Sure thing."

"Jake, you'll go over to the plant in Jersey and check on the patterns for the new design? It's important that Snake Magic be ready to hit the distribution outlets the same day our stock goes public. A double whammy to boost sales."

"Right. The foreman said the cutters are having a problem with the ankle strap, but I'm sure the machines just need to be recalibrated for those Brazilian leathers."

"And, Dick, I want you to take over my other appointments. The ad agency will be here at ten to pitch the new print campaign. We need all the good ink we can get from the press conference to be held on the twentieth. Make sure Claudia Vasquez, that new assistant in our promotions department, sits in on the meeting. I was really impressed with her ideas for the MTV market."

Dick smiled.

"Don't even think of hitting on Claudia. She's married."

Dick's smile melted. "What a spoilsport!"

"Also, Dick, that animal rights group will be here at one. They're concerned about the ostrich leather we're using on Sassy. Make sure you emphasize that Ferrama has a policy of adhering to endangered species laws, and that the only ostrich skins we use are from animals that have died of natural causes. That's why that shoe model is so rare and highly priced. We could sell a ton of those high heels if we were exploiting the animals."

"I know all this stuff, P.T. Don't worry," Dick assured him. "You take care of Naomi and Ruth . . . and that Elmer Presley dude. *Dios*, where does Ruth pick up these characters?"

"I have no idea." P.T. snorted with disgust. "She's like a flake magnet. Do you know what Elmer told me one time? He said he's my fairy godfather."

Dick and Jake both chuckled.

"Fairy?" Dick remarked then. "Geez! Did you give him one of your looks?"

"Not that kind of fairy," P.T. said huffily. "The other kind."

"What other kind?" Jake asked. He was leaning back in a Biedermeier chair solving, over and over, one of those impossible to solve chain loop desk games.

"The Cinderella kind."

"Huh? I thought that was a fairy godmother." Dick raked his fingers through his hair and redid the rubber band at his nape. It had been a long day and night for them all.

"Fairy godmother. Fairy godfather. Big difference, I guess. Anyhow, Elmer has delusions that he was sent to help me find a perfect princess."

Dick let out a hoot of derision. "It's women who fantasize about Prince Charming. Not men. Have you ever heard a guy talk about wanting to find his Princess Charming?"

"More like Bimbo for a Night," Jake offered.

They all concurred with that.

Or jackhammer sex on a flour-covered kitchen floor.

P.T. remembered something else. "When I scoffed at him, Elmer said something really weird. He gazed at me with those sad eyes of his and said, 'Any man can lose his hat in a fairy wind.'"

"If you ask me, Elmer sounds like a psycho," Dick continued.

"Do you think he's dangerous?" Jake inquired.

P.T. shrugged. "I didn't think so before, but, yeah, he's dangerous. All three of them are. Kidnapping, for God's sake! How will we ever undo this mess?"

"You're going to have to convince the woman that it was a harmless joke," Dick advised. "Then charm her like you've never charmed a woman before. Do you recall the Spanish heiress who refused to sell you that empty factory in Lisbon? She was one stubborn lady, but she came around. Even sold it to you at less than market value."

P.T. smiled in recollection. Dolores Lopez had indeed been adamant about holding on to the family facility that had been critical in Ferrama's European expansion plans. Damn, he had been good. But that was five years ago, and P.T. wondered if he still had the fire in his blood to pull off such a coup again. Especially with a Wall Street shark.

Well, he had to. There was no other recourse. Still, he resisted. "I told you, Dick, the looks don't work with her."

"Then try the touches. Hell, pull out all the stops and nail her upside down and sideways . . . till her teeth melt. I don't care how you handle her. Just don't come back till you've got her under control."

P.T. groaned. Lack of confidence had never been one of his problems, but for the first time in his life he wondered if he had the talent for the chase. And for the first time in his life, he cared on a personal level about the outcome. That was probably what was weakening his self-assurance, and he didn't like it one bit.

"Are you two talking about seducing Cynthia Sullivan into being on our side?" Jake asked incredulously. At the sheepish look on their faces, Jake burst out laughing. "God, I'd like to be a fly on the wall when that happens. Or doesn't happen."

P.T. flashed a scowl at Jake, who continued to chortle. Really, he was getting damn sick of people— Naomi, Ruth and now Jake—not trusting in his talents. He'd show them all.

He hoped.

"Take my Beamer," Dick said as they flicked off his apartment lights and moved toward the elevators. "It'll be more comfortable on the long drive."

"Nah, I'm taking the pickup," P.T. insisted. "Those back roads are a killer on a low-riding vehicle."

"I still say you're crazy for buying a truck. Okay, so you're tired of being a prince, but do you have to turn into a redneck? And orange . . . what ever possessed you to buy an orange truck?"

"It's not orange. It's Burnished Umber."

"In other words . . . orange," Jake stated.

Jake was getting a real smart mouth on him. He must be hanging around Dick too much.

"And that rustic cabin in the Poconos!" Dick continued. "Who are you kidding? Despite all your protests, you're accustomed to the finer things in life, not outside toilets." Dick pretended to shudder with horror.

"I'll adapt." P.T. smiled at Dick and pressed the ground-floor elevator button. "I plan to take off for a month or two after the stock hoopla dies down. I need to step back and think about what I want to do next. I'll do a little fishing. Relax. Regroup."

"Do you even know how to fish?" Jake asked.

"What's to know?" P.T. bristled. "Put a worm on a hook and toss the line in a stream. I bought a fishing video from L.L.Bean, and a whole bunch of equipment. I'm gonna be a regular guy . . . for once in my life."

"Oh, God!" Dick exclaimed. "Next you'll be scouting out a June Cleaver kind of wife and settling down in Beaver-Cleaver-picket-fence hometown America."

"Maybe I will," P.T. said defensively.

"I think I'm gonna puke." Dick was staring at him with horror. "I'm off to Cancún myself. A little sun, sand and frolicking. That's what you need, P.T., more frolicking in your life. Not this 'finding yourself' crap."

"You're not thinking about selling Ferrama, are you?" Jake's voice rose with alarm.

"Nah. But we've all been working under tremendous pressure these past five years." He shrugged. "I don't know what I want to do next."

"You need a new challenge," Dick concluded.

"Maybe," P.T. said hesitantly. Thoughts of Cynthia Sullivan popped into his head. Now, why did he think of her in the same category as challenge? Then he breathed a sigh of relief. So, that was all she was to him . . . a challenge. Hey, he could handle that.

And another fantasy popped into his head, involving remote cabins and campfires. And nude fishing. Oh, yeah! Nude fishing with the slow stretch-and-reach motion of perfectly sculpted bodies, male and female, casting rod and reel onto smooth waters and—

"Make sure you bring back the limo," Jake reminded him just before they entered the parking garage.

Sex in a limo. Nude bodies. Leather seats.
I'm losin' it here . . . bigtime.

Even so, P.T. found himself wondering if Cynthia knew how to fish. No matter! They would watch the fishing videos together, in the nude. Then bop into the limo for a little . . . bopping.

"And my ties," Dick added. "All twelve of them, especially the blue and yellow dragon one."

P.T. shook his head at the two of them. And saw a picture in his head of a campfire and toasting marshmallows on long sticks and nude campers, a male and a female.

"P.T., where the hell are you?" Dick's elbow nudged him back to the present.

"I have a sudden craving for marshmallows," he blurted out.

"I'm really worried about you," Dick said.

Seeing the concern in Dick's eyes, P.T. pulled himself together and tossed out, "How many lawyers does it take to screw in a lightbulb?"

"One," Jake answered for Dick. "A lawyer will screw anything."

Yeah, and maybe a prince shoemaker would, too.

Honey, I'm home . . .

P.T. was not in a good mood by the time he arrived at the castle five hours later. Not that his mood had been anything to write home about before that.

He'd barely left Manhattan when the pounding rains began. Twice, he'd been forced to pull off to the side of the interstate because of nonexistent visibility. Another time he'd stopped at a rest stop to take a short catnap. The metronomic click-click of the windshield wipers had been hypnotizing him to sleep. Finally, he'd reached the five-mile dirt road—now mud—which led up to the castle. His rear felt like ground beef from the poor shocks in the bouncing pickup truck.

Pulling to a stop, he waited for the rain to let up, staring morosely at the castle before him. Every time he saw the monstrosity—which wasn't often—he shuddered with distaste.

Five years ago, when he'd decided to turn Morton Friedman's cut-rate shoe empire into an upscale supplier to the rich and famous, he'd needed a palace as a backdrop for his royal persona. Dick had purchased the Spanish title for him, along with the deserted island "empire." But no way was P.T. going to build even a bamboo hut on that volcanic paradise that resembled some sci-fi lunar landscape. On his one and only visit, P.T. had seen more snakes than any person should see in a lifetime. Some of them had made their way into Ferrama shoe creations.

But the news media had been, and still were, curious about the new prince of leather. P.T. had suggested to Dick that they rent some villa or mini-castle in Europe for a week or so and take some photographs of him in his supposed home. But Dick had nixed the idea, and rightly so, pointing out that the European paparazzi were vultures when it came to sniffing out the truth. Besides, they probably had pictures on file of every bloody castle ever created.

So he'd bought this crumbling heap in the Catskills and done only enough renovations to have professional photographs taken of him lounging about his palace. No way would he let the press know of its existence. In fact, his zeal for privacy and insistence that the tabloids accept only his photographs of his castle residence had only enhanced his mysterious aura . . . and upped Ferrama's attractiveness in the marketplace.

P.T. had purchased the castle, built more than a hundred years before by railroad tycoon Henry Fowler, and its surrounding one hundred acres for a song . . . a mere five hundred thousand dollars, including the remaining dilapidated furnishings. Of course, the structure itself wasn't worth the cost of hauling the stone away. That was why it had stood vacant and unsold for so long. He'd always figured that the land represented a potential long-term profit if it could be subdivided at some point. But Naomi had fallen in love with the place—Naomi always had been a little half-baked—and insisted that it be included as part of her buyout settlement.

Never once had P.T. doubted the wisdom of the prince scam, though it could hardly be called that, since they'd done nothing illegal. It had worked, putting Ferrama, Inc., in the forefront of the fashion industry in record time, along with Calvin Klein, Ralph Lauren and the other biggies. And he didn't doubt for one minute that Calvin or Ralph would have employed the same tactics if they'd thought of them first.

Well, good riddance to both the castle and Naomi. Which reminded him of the purpose of this visit. Naomi wasn't going to have to worry about renovating this heap by the time he was done with her. She was going to be buried under it.

Seeing that the rain was coming down even harder now, accompanied by claps of thunder, P.T. decided to make a dash for the castle. Opening his door, he was immediately surrounded by a half-dozen yelping guard dogs on retractable chains. They looked like glue factory rejects. *Do dogs go to glue factories, like horses? Hell if I know!*

Snapping at his immediately sodden Gucci loafers and hanging onto the hem of his Fendi slacks, the hounds continued to yip and yap, slowing his progress across the moat bridge. Swiping at the water that blinded his eyes, he wasn't able to watch his step, and he slipped on a rotting board that broke under his weight. He landed face-first in a muddy trench along with the dogs, who frolicked over him with wagging tails and lolling tongues, obviously thinking he'd gone mud bathing deliberately. It wasn't quite the kind of frolicking Dick had had in mind, P.T. was sure.

He crawled out of the moat and made his way to the open door, where he noticed Naomi for the first time. She was standing with hands planted on the hips of her baggy denim coveralls, glaring at him. Naomi always glared at him.

"What the hell are you doing here?"

"Well, welcome to you, too," he snapped, brushing

past her into the ostentatious foyer. He didn't care if he did get mud on her chic denim outfit.

"Aaargh!" she shrieked. "You're getting mud on the Italian marble, you lout."

"Well, big deal, Naomi," he said, cutting her with an icy stare. Then he deliberately shook himself like one of the miserable mutts that wailed outside the door. Mud splattered everywhere, including Naomi's livid face.

"Go back to New York and take care of the company," she demanded. "You're not wanted or needed here."

"Where is she?"

"Who?"

"Cynthia Sullivan, that's who. What would ever possess you to try such a crazy stunt? Are you having a nervous breakdown or something, Naomi? Or early menopause?"

"Menopause? Menopause?" she sputtered, her face turning even redder with rage. "Women don't go into menopause when they're thirty-four years old, you jackass."

God, it was just like a female to fixate on the least important thing he'd said. "Where are you keeping her? Oh, no . . . please, don't tell me this place has a dungeon."

"Give me a break," Naomi snarled, her eyes unconsciously shifting upward.

"Cyn-thi-a," he screamed and made for the wide staircase, taking the steps three at a time. "Where are you? Cyn-thi-a!"

"Stop!" Naomi yelled after him. "She's safe, and her corn's almost healed, and this is the best plan. Really.

She won't be able to affect the stock offering if we keep her here for eighteen more days."

When he got to the first landing, P.T. glanced down at his stepsister. "And what are you going to do when she files criminal charges against us? And a civil lawsuit?"

Naomi shifted uncomfortably. "We're working on that."

"How?"

"Look, she's fine here. Oh, she grumbles a lot, but Elmer and Ruth are taking care of her. In fact, Ruth just got done doing her fingernails, and—"

"Her fingernails!" Oh, Lord, they wouldn't torture her, would they? Of course they would. Hadn't Naomi just said that Ruth was up there pulling out Cynthia's fingernails? Ruth . . . the gentle sister who wouldn't swat a fly when they were kids? Ruth . . . the warm-hearted teenage girl who dated every butt-ugly loser in the county when they were growing up because she didn't want to hurt anyone's feelings?

"You can't take that woman back, P.T. You'll ruin everything. I want my money to fix up the castle. I mean it. No one—not you, and not that foul-mouthed shark—is going to stop me."

As greedy as Naomi had been in the past, P.T. never would have believed her capable of deliberate physical cruelty. He gaped at her for a long moment, then told her where she could stick this blasted castle.

Not waiting for a response, he practically flew up the steps, continuing to shout, *"Cyn-thi-a!"* From somewhere in the higher regions—probably the fifth or sixth floor—he heard music playing. He followed the sound.

Moments later he charged madly through the open

doorway of a sixth-floor suite and came to a screeching halt. His jaw dropped open with surprise.

Cynthia Sullivan was sitting in the center of a huge platform bed. Her hair . . . her *big* hair . . . stood out from her head in a wavy, strawberry-blond cloud . . . a *big* cloud . . . and she wore nothing but the little lacy camisole she'd been wearing under her business suit three days ago. No, he corrected himself, she was wearing a pair of white silk briefs as well. It was no wonder he'd missed them, with the sight of all those miles of bare legs stretching out before him. At the bottom of the bed, Ruth sat painting Cynthia's nails a bright neon pink, even the three toes that were still covered with a light gauze. From one of those legs, a long chain extended from the ankle to the wall.

"No blood," he muttered with a heart-swelling sigh of relief. Slowly, the facts registered. Ruth wasn't torturing Cynthia; she was giving her a pedicure.

"Huh?" Cynthia said, gazing at him with equal amazement. He must look pretty . . . well, amazing himself, with his face and hair and clothing dripping rainwater and mud about him.

"You're just in time for the video," a voice said behind him.

He turned to see Elmer Presley standing next to a TV with a DVD player on top. On the screen the opening credits of a cartoon began to play. Cinderella. Elmer fiddled with the knobs a little before turning to P.T. "It's about time you got here."

"Oh, God, the fairy dwarf, too," P.T. observed, taking in Elmer's short frame wrapped, like a sausage, in a tight white jumpsuit studded with rhinestones. A huge belt with a clasp the size of a Frisbee bisected his midsection. On his feet were high blue suede boots, also studded with rhinestones. The same person must have done his big hair as Cynthia's.

"Don't call him that," Cynthia and Ruth chastised P.T. at the same time.

"I . . . am . . . not . . . short," Elmer asserted. "Why does everyone keep saying that?"

"Go ahead and put a spell on him, Elmer. For that insult, you ought to turn him into a . . . a toad. But then, he's already a toad," Cynthia commented. Although her remark was terse and to the point, he could tell by the spark in her blue eyes that she had a lot more to tell him. *A helluva lot more.*

From the corner of his eye he saw Naomi creep through the door and pick up Elmer's guitar. But his attention was diverted to the TV screen, where some nitwit began to belt out, "Someday my prince will come. . . ."

Just before his head burst with a shattering headache and his mind went blank, he thought he heard himself murmur, "I'm coming, I'm coming. . . ."

Chapter Six

Wake up, Prince Sleepyhead. Cinderella has a bone to pick with you . . .

It was hard to maintain anger at a blood-boiling temperature when the object of your rage was lying in bed beside you, chained to the wall, unconscious . . . wearing nothing but a pair of cute white boxers imprinted with green shamrocks.

Peter Ferrama was all dark skin and lean muscle from the top of his raven black hair to the bottom of his narrow, sexy feet. In repose, his sinfully long eyelashes were spread out like thick sable fans accenting a face of aristocratic Spanish features—high cheekbones, prominent nose, full lips, proud jaw. His arms were thrown over his head, relaxed, calling attention to patches of black hair in his armpits and on his well-honed chest, leading in a vee to the low-riding band of his shorts, then resuming on the trek down his long sinewy legs.

His was not the pumped-up body of a yuppie weightlifter, but the result of good genes and years of some vigorous physical activity. Polo or riding to the hounds or jousting or some such princely pursuit, she supposed. Or running from women who fashioned themselves royal groupies, she added as an afterthought.

"Handsome is as handsome does," the right side of her brain kept reminding the left side of her brain, which was locked in yum-yum mode.

Three hours had passed since Naomi had bopped him over the head with Elmer's guitar. He'd been too busy ogling Cynthia to fend off his stepsister's blow. What a scene had ensued then as Ferrama had sunk, wide-eyed with shock, to the floor!

Elmer had flown into a rage at Naomi's misuse of his precious instrument, which luckily survived without damage, despite Ferrama's hard head. "My guitar! My guitar!" Elmer had cried, caressing it like a baby. "May the seven terriers of hell sit on the spool of your breast and bark at your hardened soul."

Ruth had stormed at her sister then for employing such brutal tactics. "You could've killed P.T.! How could you? How could you? Put another curse on her, Elmer. Go ahead."

"May there be no butter on your milk, nor on your ducks a web."

"Huh?" she and Ruth had both exclaimed.

Elmer was giving Naomi the evil eye, except that his evil eye resembled a nervous twitch.

Naomi had pooh-poohed Ruth's recriminations and Elmer's curses. "If I'd wanted to kill him, I would have used my gun." Naomi had then pulled out her handy drill and another retractable chain, anchoring Ferrama to the wall in a similar fashion to Cynthia, but on the opposite side of the bed. Before she'd wrapped the chain around his gauze-bound ankle, she'd removed all his clothes, except for the boxers. The only reason she hadn't taken them, too, Cynthia suspected, was that she'd been squeamish about seeing her stepbrother in the buff.

Cynthia had urged Naomi to leave his clothing on. "He doesn't strike me as the shy type. Do you really think your stepbrother would care if he was naked, running along the interstate, if it meant he could escape?"

"Yeah, he'd worry about what the press would think," Naomi had responded with a sneer. "A prince wouldn't do such an uncouth thing."

Maybe she was right.

"Then put him in another bedroom," Cynthia had suggested. The idea of being confined in close proximity to the prince was a daunting prospect. She was afraid she'd break his bones. Or, worse yet, jump his bones.

"Nope! It's easier to watch you two in one place. Besides," Naomi said, her eyes narrowing craftily, "P.T. can keep an eye on you . . . for the family good."

"That would be like putting the fox to mind the goose," Cynthia had argued.

"Precisely." With that enigmatic comment, Naomi had gone off to plaster a wall or something. After assuring themselves that Ferrama was not seriously injured, Ruth and Elmer had prepared breakfast, then made excuses of some busywork that needed to be done. They obviously wanted to avoid Cynthia's nonstop complaints.

Elmer's parting shot of advice to her had been, "When the apple is ripe, it will fall."

Yeah, well, the only fruit in this room is wearing blue suede boots. "A person might as well whistle jigs to a milestone as tell her troubles to you," she'd called after the maddening little man.

He'd laughed with glee. "The Irish wolf ever did bark at her own shadow."

Her answering snarl had been lost in his departing footsteps.

The prince moaned and moved restlessly now. He was just beginning to awaken. She couldn't wait. Because she intended to bop him once or twice herself.

Cynthia watched as he gradually became aware of his predicament. At first, he cracked only one eyelid, putting a hand to his presumably aching head. Then he blinked with amazement and raised himself onto his elbows, gaping first at his nearly nude body, then at the chain running from his ankle to the wall, at the Cinderella disk playing on the TV set across the room and finally at Cynthia, in her scanty attire and matching chain.

"His and her chains!" he muttered, rubbing the fingers of one hand across his furrowed brow. "This is crazy."

"Yep." Cynthia was demonstrating incredible restraint in issuing the terse reply when what she wanted to do was berate him in an unending stream for causing this entire fiasco. In time, she promised herself. *In good time.* But she couldn't stop herself from remarking, "There must have been a whole lot of inbreeding in your family tree, 'cause you're all half-witted . . . you, Naomi, Ruth."

"I'm going to kill Naomi," he said in a seething tone.

"You'll have to stand in line."

Ferrama sat up, giving her his full attention. "Are you all right?"

"No, I'm not all right," she snapped. "Do I look like I'm all right?"

His midnight blue eyes swept over her, real slow, from the big hair she hadn't had a chance to tame down yet to her glow-in-the-dark pink toenails. "Yeah, you look all right," he said huskily.

God, that voice alone must snag women by the dozens. She decided to turn the tables on him, not wanting to feel intimidated by all that oozing virility. "You don't look much like a prince now." *Well, Einstein, that was a really bright observation!*

"Oh?" His lips twitched with amusement.

His half-grin really jerked her chain . . . so to speak. She hated it when he looked down his blue-blooded nose at her, one of the awkward common folks. "Without a crown, a prince is apparently just a man," she taunted. "As my grandma always said, 'You can't tell what's in the pot, girlie, till the lid is lifted.' "

He groaned, probably because he disliked her Irish proverbs. Most men did, since the best of the witticisms from the ol' sod cut straight to the heart of universal male blarney.

"Honey, you don't know me well enough to lift my . . . uh, lid. Besides, I may not have a crown, but I still have my scepter," he pointed out, bobbing his eyebrows at her.

"Huh?" When she realized what he meant, her face colored with embarrassment. "Oh, that was so . . . so gauche!"

He shrugged. "So, sue me."

"I intend to," she vowed. "When I'm done dragging your sorry ass through the court system, you won't have a crown jewel to your name." She'd deliberately used the crude term *sorry ass* because she sensed her earthiness made him uncomfortable. And she was not in the mood to please him in any way whatsoever.

"Wanna bet? You're not touching my *crown jewels* unless I let you." He thought a minute, then chuckled. "Oh, all right. My crown jewels are all yours, *querida*."

Cynthia's face grew hotter. This conversation was taking a decidedly suggestive route she didn't like at all. "Great shorts, by the way. Where'd you buy them? The royal Wal-Mart?"

"They were a gift," he answered distractedly as he searched under the heavy brocade bedspread folded at the bottom of the mattress, discovering the alarming fact that there were no bed linens. It was alarming to her, anyhow. She saw the minute understanding dawned as to the implications of the lack of sheets or pillowcases. His eyes went slowly from her near-nude body to his near-nude body, with nary a cover in sight. Then he smiled.

He smiled! The troll!

"Can I assume body heat is the only option in the

event of a sudden cold spell?" He was clearly enjoying himself. And hoping for a North Wind.

"A gift?" she said derisively, choosing to ignore his reference to body heat and take the discussion back to his boxers. Not that his underwear was really a better subject. "From some Irish lass with a shamrock fetish?"

He laughed. "No, they were a Christmas gift from Elmer. Don't you like them?"

"I couldn't care less. I just thought that a prince would be wearing the family crest on his skivvies, not some good luck charm."

"Oh, I've had lots of luck in my boxers, with or without the four-leafed clover," he boasted silkily. "As to the royal crest, it's imprinted on the inside of the boxers, on the reverse design of the shamrocks." He gave her a long moment to digest that news before adding, "Wanna see?"

"Stop kidding around. This is a serious situation."

"Who's kidding? I'm damn serious. Do you think I show my . . . uh, crest to just anyone?"

"Keep your peter in your pants, Peter," she snarled, though she couldn't hold back the tantalizing image of how he might look without his shorts.

He winced. "Someday I'm going to cure you of that foul language."

"It's a fine day when the fox turns preacher."

"Admit it, Cynthia, that Peter remark was a bad pun, even for you."

Cynthia's face was beginning to feel like an inferno. He was right. Long years of habit in a tough environment and climbing through the male trenches had left their mark on her. She'd never admit regretting the coarse words. But, damn, he was so disconcertingly attractive that he made her wish she was different. Really, how did a business executive with a desk job stay so fit? Before Cynthia could bite her tongue, she blurted out, "Do you fence?"

He frowned with confusion. "TVs and car stereos?"

"No, you idiot. Swordplay. Like épée, foil, saber."

"Oh." Now it was his turn to blush.

"Do you like to joust?"

"*Like* would be too strong a word." His eyes glittered with amusement at some private joke.

"What's that smirk supposed to mean?"

"Nothing, sweetheart. *Nada*. How did we get from you checking out my . . . uh, crest to swords? Oh, I get it . . . swords, scepters, phallic symbols."

"Do you have a death wish?"

He grinned at her, and Cynthia's sensory system went kaplooey, turning every erogenous zone in her body—even ones she never knew existed—on full red alert. How did he do that with just a slow, lazy twitch of the lips? More important, was it a deliberate ploy to divert her from her rightful anger? "Did you and Tricky Dick and the designer-chauffeur-geek plan this whole thing? Did you figure I would be more amenable to negotiating in a bed half-naked with you, rather than across a courtroom? Did you think my major fantasy in life was to get laid by Prince Charming? Do you have any idea how much trouble you are in, big boy?"

Ferrama was lying on one side. His left elbow, braced

on the pillow, supported his head. He was staring at her in the oddest way.

"Stop it," she demanded.

"Stop what?"

"Stop looking at me as if I was one of your island tarts."

"What island?"

"Your island . . . your principality."

"Oh, *that* island." He smiled and reached out a hand to finger one of the curls in her big hair. "There aren't any tarts on my island."

She slapped his hand away. "Oh, so you limit your princely philandering to women outside your realm. Good idea."

"Princely philandering? Where do you get these ideas?"

"I get these ideas from those smoldering looks you keep giving me. And you and I both know that a prince like you wouldn't be the least bit attracted to a woman like me. Therefore, it's a natural conclusion that you must do a lot of meaningless philandering."

He crossed his eyes and shook his head like a shaggy dog. "Would you care to explain that bit of logic?"

"Listen, I've seen pictures of you in the society pages. You've always got some glamorous babe on your arm with a Riviera suntan and a spa-toned, pencil-thin body."

"And?"

"And, even if I baked myself on a beach for days, I would still have white skin and—"

"Creamy," he corrected, running a forefinger along

the bare skin of her forearm. He pulled his hand back quickly before she could slap it away again. "Your skin is deliciously creamy, not white."

Boy, he is really good. If I weren't as sharp as I am, I might even be pulled in by his snow job. "And I could jog till I dropped and I'll never be anything but soft and curvy. Oh, don't give me that look. Ultra-thin and ultra-hard bodies are in vogue today, don't even try to deny it."

"How many men do you know who read *Vogue*? Or care what some wacko French designer tells them is beautiful." He let out a long sigh. "Ah, Cynthia, you have to know that I was attracted to you from the first minute I saw you picketing my building. Ask Dick. He's been teasing me about my infatuation ever since." He shrugged helplessly. "You are so damn beautiful."

Me? Beautiful? "Don't try that seduction routine on me, buster. You are such a frog."

He winked. "Yeah, but if you kiss me hard enough, I turn into a prince."

"Hah! I've kissed a few frogs in my time and, believe me, not a single one turned into a prince."

"Try me," he challenged.

Boy, was she tempted! "Give it up, Romeo. I'm on to you and all your slick *ri-bet* charm."

He gave her a long, doleful look before confessing, "I've been looking for you my entire life, *querida*."

Now that was a real low blow. The words every woman wanted to hear. And men knew that women wanted to hear them, so they spouted the magic words as if doling out candy. Cynthia couldn't allow herself to succumb to the practiced words of a born-to-please womanizer. She put her hands to her ears and closed her eyes.

Once she felt herself under control, Cynthia, with eyes still closed, stormed at him, "Enough of this b.s. You are responsible for my kidnapping, whether directly or indirectly. What are you going to do about this situation? Don't you think it's time to cut your losses? There's no shame in a man being thrown by a mare, you know. It's better to be turned back in the middle of the ford than to be buried in the flood. So, what do you say? Shall we call an end to this charade?"

Silence.

With trepidation, she slowly opened her eyes. To her horror, she saw the prince's eyes glued to her chest, where her breasts were arched outward under the revealing lace camisole, due to her upraised hands clamped over her ears. Instantly, she lowered her arms and crossed them over her offending bosom. "Did you hear what I said?" she squeaked out.

"No."

"Why are you looking at me like that?" *Dumb question. I practically invited the lech to ogle me with that stupid pose.*

"You don't want to know." His eyes danced merrily before he blurted out, "How do you feel about aprons?"

"How do you feel about Lorena Bobbitt?"

The thing about fantasies is there's always a new one . . .

"Ouch!" P.T. grumbled as he tripped over his chain for about the twentieth time.

"If you'd stop pacing, you wouldn't trip over your own feet," Cynthia observed.

"What the hell else is there to do?" For the past two hours he'd examined every inch of the Frick Suite (which he'd quickly nicknamed the Frickin' Suite)—as far as his retractable chain would go . . . into the bathroom, as far as the door leading to the corridor, over to the window, in front of the DVD player where, to his disgust, he found only Cinderella and Elvis Presley movies.

Earlier, he'd tried to chisel at the bolt securing his chain to the wall with a butter knife. He'd soon learned that his multitalented stepsister had installed an eight-inch toggle bolt into a secure-as-cement wall stud. Even worse, the bolt had some kind of wing unit on it that sprang free once the screw went all the way through the stud wall, thus ensuring that the fastener couldn't be unscrewed or pulled out. It would take a stick of dynamite to break it loose.

"Testy, are we?" Cynthia remarked cheerily. "If the cat scratches you, don't beat the dog."

"I swear, one more Irish proverb and I'll not only beat the dog, I'll throw it out the window to join those other howling creatures down in the courtyard." He gave Cynthia a piercing glower to let her know which dog he had in mind.

"If you think this is boring, wait till you're here a few days. You might even let Ruth give you a makeover."

"Not in this lifetime!" He cast her another glower. She sat at a round empire card table painting her fingernails to match her toes . . . a bright neon, glow-in-the-dark pink. Glow in the dark! That's all he needed . . . another fantasy to add to his repertoire.

He could just picture the scene. Oh, Lordy, could he picture the scene!

A pitch-dark bedroom. Him sprawled on his back, naked as a jaybird. And ten luminescent ovals moving over his body like a bloody grand piano. *Oh, yeah!*

The erotic light show would start at his shoulders, pause at his flat male nipples, spend a second or two examining his navel and his flat stomach—his flat stomach was one of his best assets, if he did say so himself. He sucked said belly in, just thinking about how those fingertips would feel.

Man, oh, man, this is the best non-sex I've ever had.

Okay, the little miniature flashlights were stalled at his midsection. Should they bypass the main event and trail on down his legs to the bottom of his very sensitive feet? It would give new meaning to "Happy Trails," that was for sure.

Nah! This was a male fantasy. Who needed all that foreplay when the organ was pumped and ready to play?

So, where was he? Oh, yeah, the ten dots of light were arranged around a column. Like a piccolo, not an organ, he decided—*Geez, this prince persona must be going to my head if I'm being refined in my daydreams, using nicey-nice musical euphemisms, like organ and piccolo for my good ol' Peter.* Drawing himself back to the ten little lights positioned on Peter . . . uh, the piccolo, he decided they would resemble fireflies, moving up and down in a rhythmic, fluttery fashion like a lava lamp.

Oooh, oooh, oooh! Stop the action! Rewind the fantasy tape. He'd thought of something else. Something much, much better.

How about if she stopped touching him and, instead, straddled his body? She'd be naked, too, of course. He would know she was there because of the slight pressure of her buttocks on his upper thighs. And his engorged erection could actually feel the warmth coming from between her legs, even though they weren't touching there . . . yet. He'd be able to see nothing . . . except for the ten lightning bugs making two increasingly smaller circles on her own upper body.

Oh, God! She's touching her own breasts. For me. My own personal illuminated lap dance.

Now the lights were moving lower. A slow, sensuous journey intended to tease and tantalize before reaching the ultimate destination . . . the minuscule space separating him from her.

P.T. could think of about fifty different possibilities as to what would happen next . . . all of them excruciatingly hot and exciting. He smiled when his overworked brain settled on a particularly naughty one.

"What are you doing?"

Uh-oh! The voice that broke through P.T.'s reverie was sharp and cool, not hot and excited. Luckily, it came from behind him.

"Checking out the music selection," he replied in a strangled voice.

"Let me see," she said. "Is there something I missed?"

Oh, yeah! Not in a million years was P.T. about to turn around now. Instead he clicked off the DVD player and grabbed a stack of 45 records at random from a nearby pile. Soon Elvis was belting out one of his torch songs, something about a hunk of burning love.

P.T. understood perfectly.

So did Peter.

Chapter Seven

She held all the cards, or so she thought...

"It's all your fault," he said.

"It's all your fault," she said.

"You could end this now," he persisted.

"So could you."

"I'm offering you a sweetheart deal, sweetheart. Take it or leave it."

"More like sweet 'n' sour, *sweetheart*," she shot back. "And a little heavy on the sour for my taste."

Pretending to stop and study the cards in their hands, they both took deep breaths to calm their tempers. Three hours had passed since Ferrama had awakened. After alternating between rage and disbelief over their predicament, the prince had finally settled down to a slow simmer, waiting for Naomi to show her face again . . . which she'd wisely chosen not to do. That was no surprise to Cynthia, who'd grown accustomed to the wily witch's evasive tactics. He'd suggested a game of two-handed rummy to pass the time. They were now in the midst of their third game, seated at the small empire card table near the window.

She could see his patience was wearing thin at her resistance to his feeble offers, as evidenced by the slight twitch in his clenched jaw and the pulsing vein in his forehead.

"All you'd have to do is sign my settlement offer, agree not to sue or file a criminal complaint, and we'd be back in Manhattan by dinnertime," he advised in a surprisingly calm voice.

"Oh, is that all!" she said scornfully.

"Be reasonable, Cynthia."

"Reasonable?" she retorted. "Number one, I wouldn't sign a settlement offer now for twice my original demand. Secondly, someone's going to jail for my kidnapping. And third, think O.J. when it comes to the size of the civil action you'll be facing."

"You can't seriously consider this a real kidnapping," he argued, rearranging the cards in his hands. He probably had another full house. She was working with a lousy pair of fives.

"It feels real to me." She rearranged her cards, too, but no matter how she rearranged them, they were still bad. Her eyes kept going back to his lips as he spoke. He had really, really nice lips. Lips that gave a normally intelligent woman some really dumb ideas.

"I agree that Naomi has gone overboard, but Elmer and Ruth are harmless accomplices," Ferrama continued. "Actually, this is more like a . . . well, a forced vacation."

"Vacation? In chains?" she scoffed, then added, "You and Naomi ought to contact one of those national travel agencies. You'd make a mint. Bondage Vacations 'R' Us."

"Sounds good to me."

Seething, she thought for a moment about his defending Naomi and Elmer and came to a logical conclusion. "Aha! So, you admit it finally? You were in on this kidnapping scheme?"

He tossed out his discard and slanted her a disgusted scowl across the small table. "Are you *loco?* Would I willingly have myself knocked out and chained to a wall? Would I break the law in such a flagrant manner just before my company's about to go public? Would I lock myself up with a"—he gave her a condescending onceover—"shark?"

That last barb really stung. And it was going to cost him. "Desperate situations make desperate men."

"Desperate? Lady, I came here to rescue you. The least you could do is show a little appreciation."

"Some rescue!" She glanced meaningfully around their strange prison.

He lifted his chin, affronted. "How was I to know Naomi had such a sadistic streak?"

"I still say you're the mastermind of this moronic plot. Elmer told me he was giving you to me . . . as a gift. He said this was part of some grand plan."

Ferrama's hand stopped midway in its reach toward the deck. "He did?" Then his lips turned up in a slow smile. "I kind of like the idea of being your gift. But the least Elmer could have done was tell me ahead of time. I would have wrapped myself in a bow." He continued the card game, chuckling now.

And she just knew he was imagining where he would have put that bow. "I think Elmer had visions of you being a knight in shining armor," she said derisively, "charging up to the castle doors to save his lady love."

"That makes sense."

"It does?"

"Well, I *am* a prince." He batted his princely lashes at her.

He didn't fool her. The dolt still thought he could seduce her into an easy settlement with one of those sultry looks of his.

Well, she was unseduceable.

She hoped.

"A prince who fell in the moat," she reminded him mockingly.

"That could happen to any knight. Perils of the profession."

"A prince whose white destrier is an orange truck. Now I ask you, what kind of prince drives an orange truck?" She'd seen it earlier, when she'd leaned out the window to get a breath of fresh air while he'd been conked out.

"It's burnished-damn-umber," he grumbled.

"No way. Some car salesman sure saw you coming. Umber is yellowish brown. That redneck heap is either rusting badly or it's orange. I saw it parked in the bailey."

"The bay leaf?" he asked, homing in on the most irrelevant part of her remark. Probably a diversionary tactic to deflect her attention from his stupidity.

"Not bay leaf, you numskull. *Bailey*. That's what Naomi calls the courtyard."

"Aaargh! This conversation has veered so far off

course, I can't remember where it started." He glared at her as if she'd committed said crime deliberately. "Hell, consider my truck a pumpkin coach, for all I care. Maybe Elmer threw fairy dust on me to addle my brain so I'd buy a vehicle that fit in with his delusional machinations."

"Hmmm. You might have something there. If Elmer could give me a corn, why not a pumpkin pickup for you?"

"Elmer gave you the corn?" he asked incredulously.

"Uh-huh. And he told me he was my fairy godfather. Like Cinderella."

"You? Cinderella?" He made a most insulting snort of disbelief.

"Hey, Prince Less-Than-Charming, watch where you cast stones."

He grinned.

And that made her even madder.

"Now that I think about it, the whole picture is beginning to fit," he mused. "I'm a prince. You're a princess . . . well, a Wall Street princess. There are two wicked stepsisters. And a fairy godfather." The grin turned into a full-blown smirk. "It works for me." He paused a moment before adding, "When do we get to the good part?"

"And that would be what . . . the ball?" She tossed back her crisis-de-coiffure hair, feigning a lack of offense at his teasing. *Wall Street Princess, indeed!*

"Nah! I say we skip the costume dance and move this show to the nitty-gritty." He paused dramatically before announcing, "I vote for Prince Charming doing the deed with Cinderella."

"Ferrama, you need to go back to royal charm

school." She ought to be angry, but laughter bubbled to the surface at his outrageous nerve.

He pretended to be insulted, but then he burst out laughing, too.

Finally, she wiped tears of mirth from her eyes with a tissue. "Admit you planned this fiasco. Come on. I might give you a few points for honesty."

"Carramba!" He exhaled loudly with exasperation. "The first I heard about this kidn . . . uh, incident was last night. As I've told you innumerable times now, my midnight dinner date at La Vida was interrupted by the unfortunate news of your . . . um, trip to the Catskills."

"Trip? You can put any spin you want on this, buster, but kidnapping is kidnapping." She picked up a card from the deck, studied her rotten hand, then discarded, not even bothering to bluff. "La Vida, huh? Who was your date, some princess?" Cynthia had agreed to play cards with Ferrama in the hope she could wheedle some information out of him. Normally, she was a pretty good card player, but it was rather difficult to play cards or carry on a normal discussion when there was nowhere to look except at a big canvas of dark masculine skin and muscle. At least that was the excuse she gave herself for her poor gambling skills today.

"Who was your date, some princess?" he mimicked. "No, my date was not a princess. Or a queen. Your constant jabs about my royal connections or royal pursuits are becoming tiresome. I'm a businessman now. Pure and simple. Could we just forget that I'm a . . . ah, prince?"

"Hard to forget when you keep rubbing it in my face." On the other hand, he did blush in the oddest way every time she mentioned his being a prince,

Cynthia realized. Maybe he'd abdicated or something. Or maybe he didn't like being different from the common folk. Or maybe she was seeing things that weren't there. But she was fascinated by his background of nobility and the niggling contradictions in his personality. One minute his language was heavily accented with silky Spanish words and the next he was spitting out Americanized phrases like a born-and-bred New Yorker. "Did you ever meet Kate Middleton?"

He hesitated, deliberately not meeting her eyes. "Of course." And, yes, that *was* a blush.

"Did you ever make it with any princesses?"

"Cynthia!" He did look at her now, and his eyes were wide with consternation. "You can't possibly think I'd answer such a question."

She shrugged. He probably thought she was an ill-mannered Ugly American type who didn't know anything about polite conversation. Actually, the question had just slipped out. "So, if your date wasn't a princess, then who? A movie star? Didn't I read somewhere that you were dating Julia Roberts?"

"Crystelle."

"Crystal what? I don't see what crystal has to do with Julia Roberts." *There I go again. I give up. Just let all the personal questions spew out. Make a fool of myself. Take a mental hiatus. Let this beefcake bozo take advantage of me.* "Oooh, I'll bet you're coming out with a new crystal-like, high-heeled shoe—sort of a Cinderella glass slipper—and Julia Roberts is going to be the spokesperson. Great choice!"

"You're amazing. That runaway imagination must come in handy on Wall Street." Then he mumbled, "Not Crystelle *what*, just Crystelle."

Cynthia furrowed her brow and watched with fascination as his darkly tanned face took on a delicious pink undertone. Suddenly, understanding bloomed. "Oh. You mean the model, Crystelle."

He nodded and threw his fanned-out cards on the table. "Gin."

"Again?"

He beamed at his ace-high straight.

She tossed her cards on the table as well, still with only a pair of fives. That was three games in a row he'd won. Enough was enough.

"What are you writing?" she asked. He'd picked up the notepad on which they'd been keeping score and was scrawling out some message that she couldn't read upside down. Two of the words were heavily underlined.

He turned the pad so she could read, "Tell Jake. *Glass slipper.* Great idea for new shoe design." Smiling, he gave her a little salute. "Thanks for the idea."

"Do I get a percentage of the profits?"

"Is that all you think about? Money?"

"Yeah," she said. *Hardly*, she thought, gazing at his magnificent chest and sinewed arms and very nice hands, with fingers she'd bet were extremely talented. Not for the first time she wondered what it would be like to make love with a prince. Would he be elegant and refined in his moves, or would he be demanding, as befitted his rank? Would he treat her like a princess in the bedroom, or a diversion to be discarded come morning? Tantalizing food for thought.

"I'm hungry," he said, yawning, as he stretched his arms wide. The posture caused his stomach to flatten even more, his abs to become prominent and his shoulder and upper arm muscles to bunch. Mid-yawn, he caught her appreciative stare and winked.

Her heart stopped for an exaggerated second, then jumpstarted into a faster beat. *Criminey! Can a wink cause heart failure?*

Sometimes she had a sneaky suspicion that he deliberately posed his body—bending over to pick up a pencil, reaching across her line of vision to fluff a pillow, hunkering down to fiddle with the TV dials— just so she would be tempted. Could it all be part of some harebrained seduction plot?

Not that she was tempted. At all. Nope.

Oh, God, think of something else. He mentioned being hungry, didn't he? "You already ate three of Elmer's fried peanut butter and banana sandwiches for breakfast."

"That was hours ago. And I didn't get to finish my red caviar omelet last night. Or the unopened bottle of Mouton Rothschild 1975 I left on the table."

"Treat yourself nice, do you, Ferrama?" Caviar and vintage wines were undoubtedly nightly fare for the prince. He'd probably never stopped at a McDonald's drive-through in his pampered life . . . although he had scarfed down those plebeian sandwiches of Elmer's with remarkable gusto.

"At four hundred dollars a bottle, I at least expected to sniff the cork." He lifted his shoulders indifferently, then tossed in, "Call me P.T."

"I can't. It sounds too much like Petie, a little boy's name. I don't see you as a little boy."

"I hope not." He threw back his shoulders as if to demonstrate.

Cynthia didn't need any convincing, as evidenced by her heart, which did another one of those stop-start maneuvers. "I guess I'll just have to call you Peter."

Back to pacing again, he stopped and glanced at her in a funny way. "Never mind. I can live with Ferrama." Then he resumed pacing.

The insufferable man even paced with elegance. *Darn it!* Back and forth across the room, chain dragging noisily, his long legs strode with the inborn grace of a cougar. With all that natural grace, he must be a great dancer. "Can you flamenco?" she blurted out, hitting on the only Spanish dance she could think of.

He stopped pacing and gaped at her. Then he poised himself on one foot, with the other leg raised at the knee. Head bobbing like a pink lawn ornament, he inquired with a chuckle, "Like this?"

"Flamenco, you idiot. Not flamingo."

"It was a joke, Cynthia," he grumbled. "Even princes are permitted a sense of humor." Then he resumed his aimless pacing.

She understood his misery and frustration, having two days' headstart on him. She decided to take pity on him. "Listen, why don't you go take a bubble bath? By then, our guards should bring us some lunch. Believe me, it helps pass the time."

"A bubble bath? Me? In that ancient tub?"

"Sorry, we're fresh out of gold-plated spas, your highness. But you do get to choose between lilac or musk essence . . . from the Priscilla and Elvis bath lines."

He sniffed with disdain. "I much prefer my Dior toiletries, but I'll take the musk, of course."

What a self-indulgent narcissist! "Of course."

"I don't suppose . . ." He gave her one of those slow, sweeping looks of his that she was now convinced was an affected ploy, but which nevertheless made her warm and ill at ease and jittery.

"No, I'm not going to scrub your back."

"Tsk-tsk," he said, wagging a forefinger at her. "That's not what I was going to say."

"Oh?" *I wish I could sink into the floor. But wait, he might have had something even worse in mind.* "Well, I'm not joining you."

"Tsk-tsk," he chided again.

I wonder if my face is as red as it feels.

"Would you draw my bath?"

"Get a life!"

He laughed softly. "Dare I hope that the bath towels are heated?"

"What bath towels?"

That stopped him in his tracks. "No bath towels?"

"Nope. Naomi is afraid we'll escape wrapped in a towel. So all we have to dry off with are those little guest hand towels," she informed him with relish.

"Naomi is nuts. I'd run down the highway naked if I could escape from this nuthouse . . . uh, nut-castle."

"That's what I told her. 'The prince has absolutely no modesty. He'd run naked in the New York Marathon if it would save his company.' "

"And did you tell her you would run with me?" he inquired, his eyes sparkling merrily. "Naked?"

"Get a life!" she repeated.

But that was not what she was thinking.

They weren't expecting company, but whoo-boy! . . .

"We have company," Ferrama announced later that afternoon. He was sticking his head out of the side window, straining to peer at something toward the front of the castle.

"It's probably one of Naomi's workmen," Cynthia commented idly. She was sitting on the bed giving her toenails a second coat. It was either that or continue to ogle the prince in his shamrock shorts, something she'd been doing entirely too much of for the past eight hours. Much more and her hormone generator was going to explode.

"I . . . don't . . . think . . . so."

"Contractors come and go all the time—electricians, painters, plumbers, landscapers. I think she's making arrangements for a massive renovation project to begin the minute she gets her cash from the stock settlement."

"Nope. This guy is driving a fifty-thousand-dollar black Cadillac Seville."

"How can you tell from this distance?"

"I have good eyesight. And it's hard to miss the lines of that luxury vehicle. Believe me, this is no plumber."

"Hah! Have you heard what plumbers charge these days? I have one client from Staten Island with a $1.2 million portfolio, all earned from toilets."

"Come over here. Quick. You have to see this."

"In a sec. I want to finish painting my toenails."

"Enough with the nail polish! You're giving me impure thoughts."

She glanced up to see if he was serious.

He was.

She could see his erotic appreciation in the flare of his aristocratic nostrils, in the lingering sweep of the tip of his tongue over presumably dry lips, in the slight rise of one of the shamrocks.

Oh, boy!

She set the polish aside and shimmied off the bed, sashaying over to the window. She was testing just what a shamrock could do with a little incitement.

He watched her the whole time with a smoldering, dangerous gleam in his dark blue eyes.

When she got to his side, she asked, "Nail polish gives you impure thoughts, huh? Are you a pervert?"

"Maybe."

She tilted her head.

"Picture a pitch-black bedroom, two naked bodies, preferably male and female, and ten glow-in-the-dark fingers performing . . . magic tricks."

She got the picture. "You *are* a pervert." She tried to laugh as she spoke, but it came out a squeak.

He grinned at her. She hated when he grinned at her as if he could have her anytime he wanted with a snap of his elegant fingers. He probably could, but that was beside the point. She refused to let him get the upper hand in these mental games they played with each other.

"Would you like me to paint your nails later?" she offered saucily.

He blinked with surprise. And interest. "Pink nail polish? Not on your life!"

"Oh, but didn't you know? It comes in Clear Night-Glow, too." She stared at his manicured fingers with their transparent enamel. The fact that he polished his nails still stopped her short, even though she knew many men did.

The grin he gave her then was slow and sexy and full of wicked promise.

She shifted uncomfortably, aware of the heat his body threw off—or was it hers?—and Elvis in the background appropriately belting out the seductive lyrics to "Loving You." It was a double-whammy assault on her senses, which she fought to control.

"What did you want to show me?" she demanded testily.

He hesitated, as if reluctant to break the electrifying mood. Then he put one arm on her shoulder, urging her to lean out the window with him, and pointed.

Cynthia tried to ignore the weight of his arm or the smell of his Elvis musk. Eventually, after a heart-stopping moment, she looked where he was pointing and saw what did indeed appear to be an odd sight.

One man in a dark suit, presumably the driver, emerged from the front of the sleek black car and opened the back door for another dark-suited man. The hounds were yipping and yapping like crazy, pulling against the limits of their retractable dog chains. Elmer restrained them during the daylight hours, freeing them to guard the palace grounds at night.

One of the animals had almost reached the driver and was attempting to nip at his pant leg. To her horror, the man reached under his suit jacket, pulled out a pistol and shot into the air. That poor dog and the other hounds went wild, barking and leaping futilely against their chains.

Cynthia screamed.

Ferrama shouted, "Hey! You can't do that!"

But no one heard them. There had to be at least two hundred feet and six stories separating them, not to mention a buffer of fake banana trees.

Naomi came rushing out of the castle then, waving her arms and no doubt giving them a tongue lashing. Good thing Elmer and Ruth had gone grocery shopping. Elvis might possibly be dead again since Elmer would never have stood for the stranger shooting deadly weapons around any one of his precious dogs.

Amazingly, another dark-suited man emerged from the back of the car, and everyone turned to him. He must have weighed about three hundred pounds, had a shiny bald head and a pet snake draped around his massive shoulders. He reached out a fat hand and, to their amazement, Naomi shook it in welcome.

"Sammy 'The Snake' Caputo," she and Ferrama said at the same time, recognizing the renowned underworld figure. "The Mafia!"

Chapter Eight

*D*um, dum, dee, dum, or was that dumb, dumb, the dumb? . . .

"The Mafia!" Naomi scoffed a short time later.

She was standing in the hallway, beyond the reach of his hands, which ached to get a grasp on her skinny neck. He'd wring it like a chicken's, given the chance. But, unbelievable as it was, his crazy stepsister was aiming a pistol at a point midway between his heart and his other favorite organ. He decided to forestall the pleasure, for now.

"We saw you talking to Sammy Caputo. We both did." He inclined his head toward the bed, where Cynthia was taking a little afternoon nap. "Don't deny it."

"Sammy Caputo?" Her eyes widened with what appeared to be surprise, but who knew with Naomi.

"Yeah, the guy with the bald head and the snake wrapped around his neck."

Naomi gave a little twittering laugh. "That was a silk scarf, not a snake."

The idea of the Cosa Nostra dropping by his estate to chat with Naomi had been preposterous to begin with. Was it possible that he and Cynthia had been mistaken? Hah! His life was one big mistake of late. "Who the hell were they, then?"

Naomi shrugged. "Businessmen. They said they're thinking about opening an Italian restaurant in the Catskills, and they made a wrong turn for Indian Mountain."

"That was a helluva wrong turn!" *She is lying through her teeth.*

"Whatever."

"Businessmen who carry guns?" he persisted. He couldn't give up the notion that something had been strange about the Cadillac trio. And Naomi had seemed to be shaking hands with one of them.

"They're from the Bronx. Everyone carries a weapon in the Big Apple. Even I own a handgun."

"I noticed. But even you don't shoot at helpless dogs." *You kidnap people but spare animals. A real paragon of virtue.*

Her shoulders sagged at that horrifying reminder, but then stiffened immediately. "He only shot in self-defense. He thought the dogs were going to attack him." She gulped several times, as if the words gagged her. Then she added, "We could have been sued, you know? Elmer should be more careful with those mutts."

"We're already about to be raked through the courts. What's one more lawsuit?"

Her upper lip curled into a sneer.

Uh-oh! Best not to rile her . . . too much, anyway.

"Why'd you call me up here? I have work to do," Naomi snarled, shifting from foot to foot in her ridiculous work boots. By the splatters on the steel-reinforced toes, he'd guess she was laying concrete today. *Jeesh!*

"Naomi, put down the gun. We have to—"

"What'd you do to wipe out the shark?" she asked with a leer, cocking her head toward the bed where Cynthia still slept.

"Not what you think." *Not what I'd like.*

Elmer and Ruth had brought them back a late lunch, Kentucky Fried Chicken with the works . . . chicken, mashed potatoes and gravy, buttermilk biscuits. All that heavy food, with no exercise, was making him groggy, too.

Not that he'd remotely consider slipping into the sack with her. He'd had a hard enough time keeping his eyes off her for the past hour—the key word being *hard.*

He followed Naomi's gaze to where Cynthia lay on one side, curled into a ball, like a kitten. Her cheek rested on her two hands, which were folded in a prayer position on the pillow. From the back he could see more than she'd like him to see of her butt through the straining silk of her panties. Her big mop of strawberry blond hair was strewn all over the place, but even so, her shoulder blades were visible against the lace camisole.

She was sleeping so soundly that every once in a while a breathy sound would emerge from her parted lips, a combination mini-snore and purr. He thought it was incredibly sexy.

When he looked at those oddly vulnerable shoulder blades and Cynthia's childlike posture in sleep, and when he heard her feminine snore, P.T. felt a heavy, tugging sensation in his heart. It was probably indigestion from all that fatty junk food. He sure as hell hoped that was the explanation.

"You're gonna have to make love to her, you know," Naomi observed. "A lot."

"I . . . beg . . . your . . . pardon." He turned back to his stepsister, hands on hips. Why did everyone in the world think he or she had the right to interfere in his personal life?

"It's the only way to get her on our side . . . to protect the company."

"Screw the company."

"See. I knew I was right to take matters into my own hands. You used to put the company interests first. Now you've become soft . . . an easy mark for every bit of fluff that crosses your testosterone radar."

He gritted his teeth and willed himself to speak softly, with a patience that had run out days before. "Naomi, this has nothing to do with business tactics or my reputed overinterest in women. The police are probably on your tail, as we speak. You've committed an ass-backwards felony here."

"Felony, smellony!" She waved her gun in the air dismissively. He wished she wouldn't do that. "You can fix the police business."

"Me?" *You did the crime, you pay the time, sister dear. Not me.*

"Yeah, charm the pants off the woman. You've

been doing it to women forever; you should have the technique down pat by now."

"Forever?"

"Remember Brenda 'Breasts "R" Us' Bicarro."

He groaned. Well, he'd stepped into that one. "Brenda Bicarro. Brenda Bicarro. How many times are you going to remind me about her? I was fourteen years old, for God's sake!"

"That's just what I've been saying. You've had eighteen years of practice. Seducing Cynthia Sullivan over to our side should be a piece of cake."

Our side? Which side would that be? The loony bin side? The criminal side? The fairy-tale side? "Since when is seduction the answer to everything? *Mierda*, you and Dick have like minds."

Naomi's face went beet red. "Dick and I have nothing in common, and don't you dare say that we do."

P.T. lifted a brow at the vehemence of her response. Normally, he would have taken great pleasure in teasing her about her longtime crush on Dick, but he decided to back off this time. Naomi under normal circumstances had been known to whack him on the head when riled. Naomi with a pistol, under volatile circumstances, was an unknown. "You are aware that Dick will hightail it up here by tomorrow if I haven't returned?"

"No, he won't." Naomi flashed him a triumphant smile.

"Why?" he asked hesitantly. The fine hairs stood out on the back of his neck.

"Because I called him from the cell phone in your truck."

His neck hairs went ramrod stiff with intuitive warning. "And?"

"And I told him you took Ms. Sullivan to your hide-away in the Poconos, where you intend to nail her."

"Nail her?" he inquired dumbly. "In the legal sense?" He was stalling for time while his benumbed brain assimilated the consequences of Naomi's actions.

"Nail her, in the sexual sense, you moron. Criminey, when did you get so stupid?"

"When did you get so vicious?"

"You never knew me at all, P.T." She sliced each word out with icy contempt.

Maldito! There was a whole lot going on here besides money and a stock offering. "Naomi, put down the gun and unlock my chain. I can unravel this whole mess. Trust me."

"Trust you? Trust you? I'd rather trust . . . a snake."

Did she mean Sammy "The Snake" Caputo? "At least give us some clothes. This is . . . indecent."

She snickered.

Wringing her neck was becoming more and more appealing.

"Where's your renowned royal ego, *Prince* Ferrama? Don't you have as much self-confidence in your macho abilities without all the princely trappings?" she taunted. "And by the way, Sleeping Beauty doesn't know you're not a real prince. You can thank me for that later. I'd suggest you keep up the charade. Work the Prince Charming bit for all it's worth."

Somehow the persona, and the seduction, sounded sordid when they came from Naomi's lips.

"It's just not right, Naomi."

"Well, big fat deal! Was it right that Daddy married your mother and doted on you like a real son instead of giving all his attention to his daughters? Was it right that he trained you to run the factory? Was it right that his will split the estate three ways, giving you sixty percent and me and Ruth only twenty percent each? Was it right for you to give up ten percent of your shares to split between Enrique and Jake, without asking us? Was it right for Daddy to make you trustee of our money, forcing us to beg each month for what's rightfully ours? Was it right that you changed the name of Daddy's company to your name?"

Good Lord! P.T. had never realized that Naomi's grievances had been festering for so long, or so deeply. And some of them were legitimate gripes.

"Naomi, I'm perfectly willing to sit down with you and go over each of your concerns. Maybe we can come to a mutually satisfactory solution. But this isn't the time for such a discussion. We have more urgent problems."

"Yeah, like how fast you can charm a shark."

P.T. crossed his eyes and counted to ten. "Okay, Naomi, let's cut through the bullshit. Exactly what will it take for you to release Cynthia . . . and me?"

"A legal document signed by her stating that her corn and subsequent injuries weren't caused by our company. A promise not to sue the company, or any of its individual parties for any matter whatsoever, including her . . . uh, kidnapping."

"I already offered her a substantial settlement to do just that. She refused."

"Well, golly, P.T., no one said it would be easy. It's going to take a lot of work on your part to convince her to sign. That's where the charm part comes in. Have you kicked on your charm generator yet?" She smirked at him.

"Is that all?" he asked, seething.

"Hell no! Do you take me for a fool?"

Fool is too mild a word.

"That Wall Street witch would sign anything to escape. You would, too, for that matter. Nope, her signature alone would mean nothing."

"So?"

"I've been talking to Elmer, and we've come up with a plan. A safety net."

Uh-oh!

"We think there's one thing that will ensure that she's on our side," Naomi said, "besides your boinking her a few dozen times."

Boinking? When had Naomi developed such an earthy vocabulary? Maybe she was right. He didn't know her very well.

Her eyes refused to make direct contact with his.

Make that two uh-ohs. "And that one thing would be . . . ?"

"Marriage," Naomi announced airily.

That was the last thing P.T. had expected to hear. His jaw dropped and his eyes almost bugged out. "Marriage? To whom?"

"You."

P.T. was too stunned to speak.

"Now don't say no before you think the idea through. It's a perfect plan. We'll have the ceremony here. Elmer can supply the music. Ruth says she could make the wedding feast—a blend of Irish and Spanish foods."

"Have you seen a psychiatrist lately?"

"And guess what?" Naomi continued enthusiastically, as if he hadn't even spoken. "Elmer is an ordained minister in some denomination I've never heard of—Church of the Latter Day Goofballs, or some such thing. He says it would be legal in New York State, but I doubt that. The important thing is that Cynthia buy its legality. Later you could get an annulment or divorce. It's a perfect plan, P.T. Just think about it."

He put his face in his hands and whimpered. He was thinking about it, all right. And the conclusion he came up with was, *I've fallen into a freakin' fairy-tale nightmare. And they expect me, Prince Charming, to play stud to a bloomin' Cinderella.*

Even worse, he realized with alarm, raising his head to glance over at said sleeping Cinderella, *I like the plan.*

A lot.

A good businessman must take inventory . . .

After Naomi left, P.T. slung his chain over his shoulder and climbed up the steps to the massive bed. *Why would anyone feel the need to put a bed on a platform? Talk about delusions of grandeur! A guy could get a nosebleed up here.*

He gazed down at the delectable Goldilocks dozing away. *Am I gonna be the bad old bear who takes advantage of poor ol' Goldy? Or am I gonna be the weenie bear who gets suckered in by Goldy? In other words, can I actually set out deliberately to seduce this woman?*

Damn straight! I've done it before.

But that was in fun, when I was younger.

Hah! How about Countess Ariana? That was just last week.

That was different. Ariana is sophisticated. She knows the rules of the game. She was probably out to scam me, too.

Cynthia Sullivan is sophisticated. She knows the rules of the game. Hell, she's probably the biggest high-roller scam artist of them all.

But I like her.

No, no, no. I have no time for "like." My company's about to go down the tubes. Forget "like."

But I want her.

Forget lust, too.

I don't want to hurt her.

Jeesh! I really am a weenie. What makes me think I won't be the one hurt?

Good point!

This is actually a noble thing I'd be doing.

Even he had to snicker at that one. Philanthropic sex.

Seriously, instead of feeling guilty, I should be feeling good.

Give me a break!

Really. The new stockholders would thank me for saving the company's financial butt. The three hundred Ferrama employees would thank me for saving their jobs. Naomi would thank me for saving her castle. Ruth would thank me for saving her rock 'n' roll fairy's career. He thought for a moment, glanced down at shamrock city, and smiled. *Peter would thank me, too.*

Peter swelled his thankfulness.

Hmpfh! At least someone—rather, some thing—appreciates me.

P.T. eased himself onto the mattress, on the opposite

side from Cynthia. Carefully, he slid himself closer. But not too close. *Best to let sleeping sharks lie. No making waves. Don't rock the boat. Man, this is gonna be a piece of cake. Who says we city boys don't know how to fish? God! Cynthia's wacky proverbs must be contagious.*

It wouldn't do for his prickly fish to awaken yet, though. He had a lot of thinking to do. And planning.

Suddenly Cynthia made a soft snuffling sound, rolled over onto her back, threw her arms over her head on the pillow, and kept on sleeping.

P.T. froze . . . and not just because he didn't want Sleeping Beauty to awaken yet.

He'd suspected before, but now he knew for sure: Cynthia "The Shark" Sullivan was an absolute babe. With her inadvertently wanton pose, partially clothed as she was, she could be a *Playboy* centerfold any month. Or year. Or century. A twenty on a scale of ten. In his book, anyway.

In sleep, her face lost its customary cynical expression. Her mouth pouted, soft and rose-colored. He'd never noticed before, but she had Marilyn Monroe lips. Now that he'd noticed, he couldn't stop noticing.

He yearned to lean forward and press his mouth to hers. Soft at first, testing, shaping. Then harder.

Would she taste like berries, or minty toothpaste, or have her own distinctive flavor? He'd discovered over the years that every woman had a unique taste. Cynthia Sullivan's would no doubt be tart, he decided with a silent chuckle.

He shook his head to clear it of such impossible

fantasies. This was a serious inventory he was taking. Casing the joint, so to speak. At least, that's what he told himself. But, Lordy, her joints were mighty fine. In fact, he was developing an appreciation for a whole lot of her . . . inventory.

That first day in his office, she'd commented on the thickness of his eyelashes. Well, hers were thick, too, but light. The same strawberry blond as her hair. No bottle blonde here.

She was tall, long-waisted and long-limbed, at least five-eight or so. A good height to match his six-foot-one.

Good for what? he asked himself.

Good for you-know-damn-well what, he answered himself.

Peter gave him another nod of thanks. *Son of a gun! What a talented fellow!*

She'd been right in describing herself as soft. No en vogue thinness of a high-fashion model here, or hard-bodied toning of a female athlete. But she was a fool, as was the whole fashion industry, in not realizing that men prefer women with a curve or two in the right places.

P.T. couldn't resist touching her, but he limited himself to a feather-light pass of his fingertips down the creamy expanse of bare skin from her upper arm to her wrist. Goosebumps followed in his wake, and she arched her upper body slightly in the sensuous motion of a petted cat. In that brief nanosecond when her chest elevated, then relaxed, he watched as her breasts bloomed with hard, budlike nipples.

Blood drained from his head, then began churning

to all the erotic spots in his body . . . about two thousand of them.

Peter went ballistic.

And Cynthia slept on.

He bit his bottom lip to stifle a moan and clenched his fists to keep from grabbing for her. Carefully, he lay back on the pillow, eyes closed, and counted to fifty. Then he added another fifty for good measure.

When he was calm again—well, relatively calm, with his heart still knocking out about a hundred beats per minute—P.T. decided that he needed to handle Cynthia Sullivan like any other challenge in his past, business or personal. Study the problem thoroughly. Know everything about his adversary . . . background, likes, dislikes, dreams, disappointments, family, relationships, strong points, weaknesses.

He'd have to lure her into talking about herself. Hell, that shouldn't be too hard. They had nothing else to do . . . nothing she would countenance at this stage, anyway. When he knew everything about Cynthia Sullivan—the child, the woman, the stock trader—he would have a better idea how to approach his seduction campaign.

It was a simple, age-old philosophy: Know thine enemy.

He should feel guilty about these devious machinations, but he didn't. As Cynthia's grandma would have said if given the chance to comment on his moral dilemma, "If the fox runs into the hound's embrace, who's to blame?" To his amusement, P.T. had noticed that many of the same proverbs were claimed by numerous cultures. That fox hound proverb was one his mother used to quote all the time, except she'd been referring to the gamblers who hung out in the San Juan casinos.

And another thing—the only way he was going to be able to pull off this seduction scheme was to bank down his attraction to Cynthia. Detachment, that's what he needed.

As to the marriage business, well, he didn't know about that. He'd play it by ear.

So, that was the plan. Get to know the shark, lure her with his indifference, overwhelm her with the royalty role-playing, then snag her with his sexual charisma. Tie the knot with her to seal the bargain, if absolutely necessary.

More confident now, he opened his eyes and peeked over at his prey. He was cool. He was in control. He could handle this job. No problem!

Cynthia let out another one of those breathy snores. They probably taught it in shark school . . . a mating call.

Peter about popped his cork.

P.T. survived the assault, barely.

Within moments, employing a few mind exercises, which included crossing his eyes and thwapping his palm against the mindless Peter—*ouch!*—his body was soon humming with indifference.

Or was that humming noise coming from the small winged creature that flitted over them and out the window on a stream of sunlight? How did a butterfly get inside, and up this high?

And wasn't it strange how the dust motes in the air resembled gold on the flickering sunbeam? Like fairy dust.

He could have sworn Peter grinned.

There are business proposals, and there are romantic proposals, and this was the strangest proposal of them all...

Cynthia slowly emerged from the deepest sleep she'd had in ages. In fact, she couldn't remember the last time she'd indulged in the luxury of a nap in the middle of the day. Wasting time equated with wasting money in her supercharged schedule.

Eyes still closed, she stretched with feline satisfaction. Who knew there could be such pleasure in the little things of life, like a drawn-out, bone-crunching stretch or a lusty yawn?

A sudden image came to her of lazy summer afternoons sprawled on her cot in the one-bedroom project apartment, waiting for Grandma to come home from the factory.

She'd been an obsessive reader then—fairy tales in the early years, followed by romance novels, especial medieval romances full of brave knights, beautiful ladies, wizards and happily-ever-after—a far cry from the hopeless, dangerous world outside her window. She would read for hours on end in those days, then stretch with a dreamy sigh, yearning for a future when such magic would enter her own dreary life.

Unfortunately—or fortunately—Cynthia soon learned there was no magic in this world. And happily-ever-after came only through hard work and ambition.

Funny that she should think of all that now. Drowsily, she ruminated over the cause. It was probably all this forced proximity to the sexiest man alive, and a prince to boot. "Beauty won't make the pot boil,"

Cynthia kept repeating to herself, but Grandma's familiar admonition didn't cut any ice this time. Cynthia's pot was about to boil over.

Gradually, she recalled her circumstances and how she came to be sleeping in the middle of the afternoon. Reluctantly, her heavy eyelids fluttered open, then shot wide.

Ferrama was sitting cross-legged on the bed, within touching distance, watching her.

"Do you believe in magic?"

"What?" she squeaked. *Oh, God! Now the jerk is reading my mind, too. And, no, I do not believe in magic. No, no, no!*

He tilted his head in confusion, and she realized that the words had come from Elmer's record player sitting on the stand by the door. It had been the Lovin' Spoonful on one of those rock 'n' roll classics records, not Ferrama, who had asked the disturbing question, "Do you believe in magic?"

Whew! For a minute there I was beginning to believe in all this fairy-tale nonsense Elmer spouts.

Meanwhile, the prince continued to stare at her. How long had he been watching her like this? In her sleep, for heaven's sake! And why?

"What are you doing?" she demanded indignantly.

"Watching you snore."

"I do not snore."

"Oh, yes you do," he said with a strange rasp in his voice.

His wonderfully expressive eyes swept her body but kept coming back to her chest area, as if he couldn't help himself. Once, he ran the tip of his tongue over his mouth, wetting his lips.

She glanced down and could have died of mortification. Because her arms were still thrown over her head from stretching, her breasts were uplifted, her nipples clearly visible. Cynthia hated her breasts. Unlike the chic unisex models with flat chests and barely discernible nipples that most businesswomen emulated, Cynthia had full breasts and large nipples. Sometimes she even covered the tips with Band-Aids and wore de-enhancing bras. It wasn't that she wanted to deny her femininity; she just didn't want to share it with strangers.

And the "stranger" in her bed was gaping at her feminine assets like an overeager teenager. Correction: He was probably repulsed. In his jet-set circle, real breasts with real nipples would be unfashionably common . . . maybe even vulgar.

She sat up and folded her arms over her chest. Which only caused his eyes to shift to the long expanse of her bare legs.

His Adam's apple moved once, twice, three times, and he licked his lips again.

She felt each sweep right down to her toes. Her oversensitive nipples were probably the size of grapes by now. Much more of this visual torture and she'd be licking his lips for him. Or one of those damn shamrocks. There were twenty-seven of them, she could attest, to her chagrin. That was one of the reasons she'd decided to take a nap. Compulsive shamrock counting had been taking its toll. Unchecked, she might have given in to the temptation to tally up the family crests, too. Or the family jewels.

"Stop that. Stop it right now," she insisted.

"Stop what?" He blinked those ridiculously long lashes at her in puzzlement.

"Ogling me." Now that sounded dumb, even to her. But, really, was he doing it on purpose? Trying to turn her on, that is. What a ridiculous notion! As if any man would be stupid enough, or egotistical enough, to think that merely staring at a woman would make her hot and bothered. On the other hand . . .

"Oh." He turned his attention to the bedpost on her right. She thought she heard him mutter, "Peter made me do it."

"What did you say?"

"Nothing," he said to the bedpost. "You must not be offended by my staring at you, Cynthia. It means nothing."

Nothing? Looking at me means nothing? See. I was right.

"After all, I'm in the fashion industry. I often find myself examining the female form with thoughts of how to provide better products. Fat women, thin women, short, tall, buxom, boyish. I study them all the time—in airports, along city streets, while dining in restaurants. I make mental notes to discuss with Jake at a later time. It's the bane of my profession, I suppose." He was still talking to the bedpost.

Buxom? Why did he throw that word in there?

"It's a purely clinical observation, you see." His lips twitched, as if he was fighting a grin or, more likely, a sneer of revulsion.

Yeah, I see all right. I do repulse him. She sat up straighter and wrapped her arms around her upraised knees. "You can stop speaking to the bedpost. I'm decent now."

He looked at her and released a disbelieving snort. "Hardly."

She bristled. "What's that supposed to mean?"

"Just that our lack of attire is indecent. I spoke to Naomi about it a short time ago. I think she might relent and give us some clothing."

No more shamrock counting. "Thank goodness!" she said. *Darn it!*

"It's really so bourgeois of Naomi to put us in this unseemly situation," he elaborated, pursing his lips prissily.

She supposed princes did that a lot . . . pursed their lips prissily . . . in dealing with the less regal folk. He wasn't nearly as blood-boilingly attractive when he pursed his lips prissily. A definite hormone douser. She considered for an insane second asking him to do it more often.

"I mean, it's bad enough to be confined against one's will with a person of the opposite sex not of one's choosing. But it is tacky beyond belief to have no apparel. Or bed linens. Do you think this mattress cover is synthetic?" He was picking at the pill balls on the striped mattress, his nostrils flaring with distaste.

Oh, this is good. This is really good. Lip pursing and nostril flaring. Pretty soon I won't be attracted to the royal pain-in-the-ass at all.

But then he glanced up at her and licked his lips again.

Well, maybe not pretty soon.

"So, when you were talking to Naomi, did you knock some sense into her thick head?"

"Hah! I couldn't get that close."

"Well, you've got to do something. I can't stay here for another eighteen days. I just can't," she said.

"Neither can I. We've already started the road

shows to the brokerage firms participating in our stock offering. Dick can handle one or two of them, but if I don't show up soon, alarm bells are going to go off."

"I'm sure your sleezeball lawyer will come up with something. Besides, by the time a company files with the SEC, most of the groundwork is already done; so lighten up. Your biggest problem is not your stock offering, sweetheart. Your biggest problem is me . . . and my potential lawsuit."

"So I should sit around and do nothing?" he sniped.

"Hell, no! I'm the one who's got to get out of here. Even though I can't be on the trading floor till my foot heals, I have to keep in daily contact with my clients. In this business, a broker is only as valuable as his "book," his big accounts. At the first whiff that I'm out of touch, every trader worth his book will be hot on my accounts."

"Even ones in your own firm?"

"Especially ones in my firm." Cynthia didn't like the look of sympathy in Ferrama's eyes and quickly added, "Hey, the world's a rat race everywhere these days. Stab in the back, or be stabbed in the back. I don't imagine that it's any different in your line of work."

He seemed to consider her words before speaking. "You're probably right. Fashion is certainly competitive, and a company is only as attractive as its most recent profit-and-loss statement or last year's fashion coup. Still, we've been protected somewhat by being a family enterprise."

"That will all change in a few weeks."

"I suppose."

"Then make Naomi release us, dammit."

"You still think I'm in on this deal, don't you?" As an afterthought, he added, "Dammit."

"Whatever!" She waved a hand with unconcern. "Somehow you . . . I . . . hell, both of us . . . have got to convince Naomi that it's in her best interests to cut her losses right now. And don't give me that bull about signing my rights away as a means to that end. It won't happen."

"It wouldn't work anyway," he said, raking the fingers of both hands through his hair in frustration.

He had really nice hair, Cynthia noticed. Thick and jet black. And sexy . . . especially when he combed it back off his face and behind his ears, highlighting the one gold loop earring and the strong neck and . . . *geez, I'm pathetic.*

"Why wouldn't it work?" she asked, forcing herself to concentrate on the problem at hand . . . not the hunk at hand.

"Naomi doesn't trust either of us. She thinks you would sign anything, then later renege."

"She's right."

"And she thinks I'd help you escape, even if it meant jeopardizing the company's future."

"Is she nuts?"

He shrugged.

"So what do we do? Sit here and watch Elvis movies and Cinderella cartoons while our professional futures get flushed down the Hudson?" She cast him a sweeping glare of disgust at his inability to save the day. She hoped he felt really bad about it. Some knight in shining armor this prince was turning out to be.

"I wasn't going to mention this, but there is one possibility . . . no, forget I even brought it up."

"What? Tell me."

"No. You'd never agree."

"Try me."

That response brought a twitch, then a full-blown grin to his lips, which he quickly stifled. "Well, if you insist," he said with a deep sigh of resignation. "But remember, I didn't really want to make the suggestion."

"Aaargh!" she shrieked. "Suggest away."

He winced at the shrillness of her voice, gave her one of his overburdened princely looks of condescension, then licked his lips one last time. Holding her gaze, he said the last thing in the world she'd ever expected.

"Will you marry me?"

Chapter Nine

*I*t was seduction, all right, but the question was who seduced who? . . .

"Marry you? Marry you?" Cynthia launched herself forward like a rocket, propelled by sheer outrage, and knocked the prince backward on his royal patoot.

Somehow the creep must have discovered her old fantasy of a gallant prince galloping down Lake Shore Drive to rescue her from a life of abject loneliness and poverty. And his proposal was an attempt to use those long-dead dreams against her. The blue-blooded baboon!

Even worse, her not-so-chivalrous knight was laughing his royal ass off as he attempted to thwart her pummeling fists. "Can I take that as a no?" he chortled.

"You can take that as never, you egomaniac," she ground out as she aimed a punch for his smiling mouth.

He jerked his head at the last moment, and her fist landed on the mattress beside his head. But she was not above using her teeth or a well-placed knee. Every time his fingers immobilized one of her hands, she whacked him with the other.

"*Maldito!* Give it up, *chica*. It was just a proposal."

"*Just* a proposal! How many of those suckers have you tossed out to gullible women across the world? Ten? Twenty? A hundred?"

He tilted his head at the vehemence of her words. "None," he said softly.

"None?" At first, she wasn't sure she'd heard him right. Then she realized it was probably all part of some plot. Seduce the Wall Street pest, make her think she's special, toss in a phony marriage proposal, then, when she least expects it, snare her into signing away her legal rights. *As if!*

With a growl, she resumed her assault. She must resemble a madwoman . . . a shark on the attack. But she didn't care. No one, *no one*, made fun of her. Not the hoity-toity girls at St. Bridget's Academy, where Grandma had finagled her a scholarship. Not the Harvard boys who mistook her voluptuous form and gritty Chicago language for an easy lay. Not the Howard Sterns in Brooks Brothers suits on the exchange floor. Not the Prince of Fools who thought he could bamboozle her with a marriage proposal.

Finally, Ferrama stopped fighting off her siege and went still, glancing downward with horror. He'd just noticed the blood welling from a thin red welt one of her glow-in-the-dark pink fingernails had made across his chest. *Oh, geez! Did I really do that? I'm a maniac. The man has turned me into a maniac.* Ferrama's complexion was turning kind of green. Her brave knight apparently had a thing about blood. Some knight!

His laughing eyes grew stormy then, as he regarded her with consternation. Quick as lightning, he wrapped his arms around her squirming body, which was plastered all over the top of him, and rolled over swiftly. Before Cynthia had a chance to blink, she found herself flat on her back, with the prince plastered all over the top of her.

I will not allow myself to consider what a great plasterer he is.

He twined his fingers with hers and pressed them firmly against the mattress, high above her head.

I will not allow myself to consider how his chest hairs feel against my breasts.

Then he locked his legs around hers, further arresting her movements.

I absolutely, positively will not allow myself to consider how his bare legs feel against my bare legs.

"If you wanted to ravish me, princess," he said silkily, "all you had to do was ask."

Her only response was a low hissing sound.

He closed his eyes, sighed, then opened them again, impaling her with a glare. "All these sounds you make are enough to drive a sane man mad. Growls, snores, hisses. Are you deliberately trying to turn me on? Consider this fair warning, sweetheart, you'd better not purr or I won't be responsible for my actions. Chivalry goes only so far."

"What?" she shrieked. There he went again, making fun of her. As if growls and snores and hisses were feminine attributes to be desired! And she'd never purred in her life. And never would. Not ever. Really.

"Remember one thing," she raged. "Often the hound that was made fun of killed the deer."

The expression on his face changed as he stared at her, suddenly somber. With a raspy Spanish curse, he rearranged his hold on her by clasping both of her wrists in one hand, still pressed to the bed above her head. Then he moved his other hand to cup her chin, tipping her face up for better study.

"You're weeping," he accused, as if she was engaged in some unpardonable act, like cheating at cards.

"No, I'm not," she denied, even as she felt a fat tear slip out of her brimming eyes and begin a slow slide down her cheek. Cynthia never cried, but all the events of the past few days must be affecting her nerves. She never had been able to take teasing well, fearing someone would discover how very vulnerable she was inside. Because she'd perfected a hardened veneer, few people ever suspected her deep-seated insecurities. This was the last straw, though. Having a real prince make a fake proposal to her, and then laugh . . . well, a woman could take only so much.

At least, that was what Cynthia told herself.

Using a thumb to wipe away the tear, Ferrama did an unforgivable thing. He licked the tear off his thumb with an idle flick of the tongue.

"Don't," she whispered.

"Don't," he beseeched at the same time.

"Don't what?" she asked. Her brain felt fuzzy and disoriented at his nearness. And he was moving closer. Good thing her arms and legs were restrained! Who knew what she would do?

"Cry," he said tenderly.

She felt his breath against her mouth and barely stifled a sob. Instead, a tiny hiccough escaped.

He groaned.

She felt the pleasure of that sound all the way to her toes and out to every goosebump on her body. Who knew goosebumps were erotic zones?

"Those sounds you make are driving me up the wall," he confessed with a low masculine grumble.

His grumble was pretty sexy, too, she thought. Geesh, maybe they were both under the influence of Elmer's fairy dust.

He used a forefinger with infinite gentleness to wipe another tear from her face.

Why the hell am I crying?

"Do you always weep when men ask you to marry them?" he inquired.

"No one's ever asked before," she admitted before she had a chance to bite her tongue.

"Really?" He smiled widely at that news, though why she couldn't imagine. "Well, no one's ever asked me, either. Do you see me crying over it?"

"You're laughing at me again, aren't you?"

"If I don't laugh, I'll be doing something else."

"Like?" Normally Cynthia wouldn't have asked such an open-ended question, but this man was having the most astonishing effect on her. Every brain cell in her head seemed to be engaged in meltdown. Her heart was racing madly. And she really, really wanted to kiss those full, sensual lips that were hovering only a tantalizingly few inches from hers.

"Kissing." His breath was warm against her mouth as he moved an inch closer.

Huh? Is he reading my mind? Is he feeling sorry

for me because I let a measly tear or two slip out? Is he still trying to seduce me into a settlement?

Who cares?

I care. This is taboo territory. If I let the prince kiss me, next I'll let him do . . . well, other things. Then I'll be lost, lost, lost.

"No!"

He raised his somnolent eyes in question at her fierce protest. "It would be just a kiss," he coaxed. "A way to pass the time."

"Just a kiss!" she scoffed. "And what would that be pressing between my legs?" *That it, Cynthia, go for crude. Turn him off with your bluntness.*

"Oh." He glanced downward sheepishly. "That's Peter. Don't mind him. He has a mind of his own."

"You named your . . . your . . . ?" she choked out. "Oh, good grief! As in Peter and the Twins?"

But he never answered her. He was too busy brushing his lips across hers, real slow, as if he was savoring every infinitesimal millimeter of the journey. "You have the most delectable, erotic, hot-as-sin mouth in the world," he murmured against her parted lips, midway through his trek.

May the trek last forever! she thought with mind-melting pleasure.

"I'll try my best," he promised huskily.

Oh, damn, did I speak aloud? "Release my hands," she begged.

"Why?"

"So I can hold on."

"To what?"

"You."

He raised his head to look at her. His lips were

slack with arousal, and he hadn't even given her a real kiss yet.

"Because . . . because when you get around to *really* kissing me, not just these little sissy brush strokes . . . well, I figure I'm going to need to hold on for dear life."

"Sissy? Are you saying I sissy kiss?" His dark eyes lit up at the challenge. "Now you've done it, Cynthia. I'm probably going to regret this . . . you're probably going to regret this, but I have no choice now. Nope. Dare a prince and you dare the devil. *Qué será será.*"

P.T. had lost control of the seduction about a hiccough and a sob ago. He was acting purely on reflex now, and his reflexes were being fueled by two zillion pounds of raging testosterone.

A sissy kiss, huh? I'll show her. If there was one thing a Spaniard—well, okay, a Puerto Rican—knew how to do, it was kiss. He put his heart and soul into his kisses. He savored them, like fine wine and good sex.

He released her hands and advised in a husky voice he scarcely recognized, "Hold on tight, Cynthia."

Before she could ask what he meant, he spread his legs wide. Since they were entwined with hers, that meant her thighs went wide, too. Biting back a roar of triumph, P.T. insinuated himself with the precision of an F-14 pilot into the Irish channel, flush against the target.

She gasped, and her clear blue eyes went huge.

He would have gasped, as well, but his heart was beating so fast he could barely breathe. At the same time, his blood thickened, causing his limbs to feel heavy. His movements, even the slight tilt of his head, took on a sluggish, slow-motion sensuality.

He wished this moment could last forever. The sheer, unadulterated pleasure of allowing his body to rest against hers—heart to heart, belly to belly, sex to sex—was the most intensely wonderful sensation he'd ever experienced. So intense that he felt tears well in his eyes at the wonder of what could only be described as magic.

When he lowered his mouth to hers now, her lips were already parted in welcome. Holding her gaze, he braced his elbows on either side of her head and furrowed his fingers into her wild strawberry blond hair, grasping her scalp.

Never breaking eye contact, she reached up and did the same with her fingers in his hair. The light pressure against his scalp was almost his undoing. Her gesture was clearly a signal of surrender. At the same time, she was giving notice that she would be an equal partner in this kiss . . . and whatever followed.

With a low growl of his own masculine surrender, he kissed her then. A savage, hungry melding of mouths and tongues and slickness, his and hers.

The kiss went on and on and on. Perhaps he feared that if he stopped, even for a breath, it would break the spell. And so he shaped and pressed and plunged and softened and nibbled and devoured. And succumbed to the most glorious kiss of his life. Which was much more than a kiss. It was a statement of something so powerful, he couldn't begin to understand its meaning.

Meanwhile Cynthia "The Shark" Sullivan was shaping and pressing and plunging and softening and nibbling and devouring him in equal measure.

And Peter was screaming silently for attention, "Me, me, me!" But P.T. didn't dare move, down there, or this "kiss" would end far too soon, in a highly unsatisfactory manner.

Then Cynthia did the worst possible thing. She moved, down there. A slight arching of her hips. A little wiggle, side to side. A breathy moan. And all hell broke loose.

He rolled over so that she was on top, the kiss still unbroken. His hands roamed frantically over her shoulders and back and buttocks, especially her buttocks, which he massaged through her silk panties. When she began to undulate against him and pressed her sweet tongue inside his mouth, he saw stars behind his closed eyelids and rolled them over again.

Now he moved against her, rhythmically, and his tongue was in her mouth, where she sucked on it with a matching rhythm. He wanted to take this slow, to remove her clothing, inch by inch, to lick her breasts and other places. He satisfied himself with running his hands under her camisole and testing the weight and shape of her breasts in his hands; the nipples were large and hard against his palms.

She cried into his mouth then, and tried to break their kiss. He realized that her breasts, with the wonderfully large nipples, were her sweet spot . . . the most erotic, sensitive zone on her body, and he smiled exultantly against her lips, refusing to allow her escape.

He began to manipulate her hardened peaks, first with circular motions of his palms, then between his thumbs and forefingers. His lower body began to thrust, involuntarily. Hard, spasmlike motions. She raised her knees to cradle his hips and spread herself wider.

He should stop now. He really should. In fact, he broke the kiss, panting. And realized immediately that it was a mistake. Watching her just spurred him on farther, and faster. Her eyes were closed. She licked her lips dreamily. Her cheeks were flushed with passion.

Without thinking he pushed her camisole upward, exposing two of the most beautiful breasts he'd ever seen. They were full and tipped with engorged, rose-colored nipples. Exquisite.

"No," she whimpered. "Don't look at me."

But he was done looking. With a raw growl, he took one nipple into his mouth and began to suckle. The other breast got equal attention from his flicking fingertips.

She began to scream and he put his lips over hers again, taking her long, drawn-out scream into his mouth.

Her arms flailed wildly and her legs went rigid as she arched her hips off the mattress. Her orgasm was approaching at an uncontrollable pace, he knew that, but still he resumed suckling at her breasts, mercilessly. His erection felt hard as steel as it pounded against her slickness, which he could feel even through his shorts.

When she grabbed his shoulders and dug her nails into the skin and bucked against him in short, rapid convulsions, he arched his head back so that he could watch her coming. It was a glorious manifestation of woman at her sensual, powerful best. Giving all she had to give in the most elemental, earthy way, and taking from her mate in equal measure.

He lost control himself then and surrendered to the pounding, driving instincts of his sex. Finally, finally, he arched his neck backward and roared out his supreme satisfaction.

When he came to his senses a short time later, he found himself lying flat atop Cynthia, his face resting in the curve of her neck and shoulder. Their chains were hopelessly tangled.

He raised his head slightly.

She was smiling.

He lifted a brow.

"The next time you ask a woman to marry you, you should send an emissary . . . you know, like you royal princes always do."

"An emissary?" he asked cautiously.

"Yeah. A friend, maybe."

"A friend?"

"A *close* friend."

He was beginning to understand. "Like Peter?"

"A very talented fellow, that Peter," she remarked. Her eyes were twinkling merrily.

"I taught him everything he knows."

"I'll bet you did." She narrowed her eyes suspiciously. "Have I just been royally seduced?"

"Do you feel seduced?"

"That would be an understatement."

He grinned.

"Or maybe I just seduced you." She batted her reddish-blond lashes at him.

Was it possible? Had she turned the tables on him?

"Do you feel seduced?" she asked, tossing his question back at him.

Utterly. "I don't know. Maybe you'd better try again. Just to make sure."

"Good try, Prince. But the drawbridge is back up, and the battlements secured."

"We could negotiate a truce."

"I don't like your method of negotiating."

"You don't?"

"Well, actually I do. Too much. Stop smirking. Now that I know what you're up to, I can fight off your advances."

"I'm not *up* to anything right now."

Peter moved slightly, making a liar out of him.

Her eyes went wide. "Would you mind lifting yourself off me? Carefully."

Hey, he had more reason to be careful than she did. And now that his brain was returning to normal, he realized the really embarrassing situation he was in. Damp shorts. Less than spectacular holding power in the sexual prowess department. No prospects of a second chance to redeem himself. *Pathetic, that's what I am. A pathetic putz of a prince!*

Finally, they were both back on their respective sides of the bed, both beet red with embarrassment over the clumsy maneuvers necessitated by their enmeshed chains, their disheveled, damp clothing, and the lack of any distraction other than Elvis swivel-hipping away in *Blue Hawaii*. P.T. took a deep breath for courage. "So, are you gonna marry me or not?"

Cynthia began to laugh, and laugh, and laugh.

He was pretty sure that laughter wasn't a positive sign.

Lying is really hard work . . .

The sight before Cynthia's eyes was enough to boggle the mind. A real "Candid Camera" moment. If only she had a video recorder to preserve it for posterity!

Prince Ferrama was teaching Elmer Presley how to do a combined hip swivel and knee gyration to the tune of "Jailhouse Rock." And he was good. Really good.

To make the picture even more bizarre, Ferrama was wearing a gaudy Elvis suit. A wide belt cinched in the waist of a too-short pair of fire-engine-red bell bottoms studded with black sequins. The sides of the slacks had Velcro strips that adjusted, presumably as the King gained weight, which was convenient for P.T., with his not-so-convenient chain. Or maybe they belonged to an Elvis impersonator stripper. On top was a matching red, high-collared jacket with linebacker shoulder pads and a little shoulder cape. Unfortunately, he wore the jacket unbuttoned, exposing a tantalizing view of his chest hair, which continually drew her attention like a stud magnet . . . and not the carpentry kind.

Of course, she was in no position to sneer. She was decked out in a dress belonging to Ruth—a tank-top, one-piece, purple spandex dress worn over her short-sleeved lace camisole. If she had ever had any physical secrets, they were fully exposed now.

Elmer and his three-piece band, the Teddy Bears, whom Naomi refused to allow on the property for practice sessions, had apparently just signed on for a weekend gig at Leonard's Lounge in Poughkeepsie. Their big break, or so Elmer hoped. But Elmer was worried that he'd get fired on the spot if he didn't get the King's sexy body movements perfected. Personally, Cynthia thought he had a lot more to worry about with his voice.

Ferrama, exhibiting more negotiating acumen than he'd ever displayed with her, had talked Elmer into getting them some clothes in return for a few Elvis impersonation lessons. The need for clothing had become desperate. After their encounter on the bed this afternoon, the blushing prince had plopped himself into the bathtub and washed his own ignominiously damp boxers, muttering something about having given up "dry-run sex" when he was a teenager. He'd refused her offer to dry his shorts with a blow-dryer. Instead, he'd proceeded to walk around after his bath, cursing under his breath, with the nearly transparent, wet shamrock shorts hugging his narrow hips and tight buttocks. Not that she'd noticed.

She'd also bathed. In cold water, without bubbles. The necessity for icing down her raging hormones was paramount. How could she have succumbed to the obvious moves of a devious make-out expert?

Because he *is* an expert, that's why. And so damn gorgeous. And charming. Not to mention being a . . . *sigh* . . . prince. Geez! It appeared her dreams weren't quite as dead as she'd thought.

"Where did you ever learn about Elvis?" Cynthia asked Ferrama when there was a break in the song. Ruth had just walked in with a tray holding a frosted pitcher of lemonade and four tall glasses. A welcome treat on this humid July evening.

"*Everyone* has heard of Elvis," Elmer declared indignantly.

Cynthia chuckled. "I meant, how did a prince on the Canary Islands watch Elvis?"

"Haven't you ever heard of satellites?" Ferrama answered, walking over to turn down the volume on the tape player. "Besides, my mother remarried when I was ten and we moved to the States . . . Hoboken."

"Hoboken? New Jersey?" Somehow Cynthia just

could not picture Prince Ferrama in Hoboken, New Jersey. *The Prince of Hoboken*, she mouthed silently.

"Is there any other Hoboken?" he chortled. "Anyhow, Elvis died before I was born, but my mother was an Elvis fan. She had every one of his records ever made." The expression of disgust on his face was pure royal condescension.

"Oooh, oooh, oooh," Elmer exclaimed, practically salivating. "By any chance, do you still have the collection?"

Ferrama shrugged. "I suppose." He turned to Ruth. "Are all those boxes still in the attic at home?"

Cynthia was getting confused. "You have a home in Hoboken, too? Besides this castle? And the palace in the Canary Islands? I suppose you have a villa on the Riviera, too. And a little hideaway in Beverly Hills. Not to mention a Manhattan penthouse. Geesh!"

"Hey, I never said I had a palace on Isla de Serpientes," Ferrama protested. "I distinctly remember telling you that my province was in the Canary Islands, but I never said there was a palace there. Uh-uh!"

"Island of Serpents! That's the name of your province?" This prince was sounding more and more . . . strange.

Ferrama's right eyebrow twitched. Just once. But it was a definite twitch. In fact, Cynthia had noticed that every time the prince said something that appeared to stretch the truth a bit or seemed a mite devious, his eyebrow twitched. For instance, his eyebrow had practically done the rhumba when he'd asked her to marry him.

"Well, we have a bit of a reptile problem on my island," Ferrama explained. His eyebrow did a little twitch-twitch.

Elmer groaned and put his face in his hands. She thought she heard him mutter something like, "Dumbest damn prince in the universe!"

"Yeech! Snakes!" Ruth squealed with a visible shudder.

Something still wasn't right with this picture. "What kind of kingdom has no palace? Even Monaco, small as it is, has a palace."

"Volcanoes," Ferrama mumbled.

"I beg your pardon," Cynthia sputtered.

Elmer's eyes rolled heavenward. "Why me, God? Why me?"

"A volcano eruption wiped out the castle, and we haven't had a chance to rebuild. Yet." Ferrama's eyebrow did a neat triple twitch.

"There's a volcano on your island?" Cynthia inquired, more and more suspicious. "Oh, so that's why you haven't finished the renovation here. You need to pump all your extra cash back into the island's recovery."

"Volcanoes!" Ruth squealed, almost knocking over the glass of lemonade she was pouring. "Didja see that Tom Hanks volcano movie? I loo-oove Tom Hanks, except he's too skinny."

Elmer gave Ruth a little smile of appreciation, then shot Ferrama a disgusted scowl. "Volcanoes?" He threw his hands in the air. "To quote Cindy's grandma—"

"Oh, no!" It was Ferrama who put his face in his hands now.

"—empty bladders are loquacious."

"What the hell does that mean?"

"He means, 'A silent mouth is musical,'" Cynthia interpreted for Elmer.

Ferrama raked the fingers of both hands through his hair with frustration. "Aaargh! Would both of you chuck the proverbs and speak in plain English?"

"Shut up," Elmer said.

"What?"

"I'm telling you to shut up before you tie a knot with your tongue," Elmer advised with a weary shake of his head.

"Does everyone want lemonade?" Ruth asked brightly. Elmer made a big deal out of helping her pour each of the glasses and hand them out.

"Where's your father?" Cynthia was determined to get the missing pieces to the puzzle.

"My father went away when I was still in my mother's womb," Ferrama informed her stiffly as he sipped elegantly at his drink.

She, too, sipped at the sour beverage. Apparently, Ruth wasn't any better in the kitchen than in the salon. Still, she drank it down, studying Ferrama the whole time. So, his father had died before he was born. How sad! But did that mean the monarchy was a matriarchal one? Why wasn't he running his own country? There were still too many pieces missing in this puzzle. "Did the crown pass to you then?"

"Crown? What crown?" As Ferrama finished off his lemonade with a pinched mouth—his must have been overly tart, too—Elmer nudged him and whispered something under his breath. "Oh, *that* crown. Well, yes, you could say that, except that I have an uncle who's next in line before me . . . uh, Fred."

"Fred?" Cynthia, Elmer and Ruth all asked at once.

"Frederico de la Ferrama," he said breezily. "Yep, Uncle Fred. My mother's brother. When dear ol' dad flew the coop, Fred became king. Good thing, too, 'cause King Fred makes a much better monarch than I ever would." He was dabbing at his forehead with a towel; Cynthia couldn't see if he was twitching.

Flew the coop? Now that was an odd way to refer to his father's death. Hmmm. He was probably being flip to hide his emotions. Men were such dopes that way. But at least she had an explanation for why Ferrama was a prince, and not the king. "I suppose you're next in line, though."

"Could we please talk about something else? I'm bored with this subject."

"The wedding will be held on Monday, after I get back from Poughkeepsie," Elmer informed them as he began to pack up his guitar.

"No!" she and Ferrama said at the same time.

Elmer shrugged. "It's out of my hands. Orders from above."

"God talked to you?" Ruth asked in an awestruck voice.

"Yep. He always does, darlin'. And he's not too happy when he sees hanky-panky goin' on before the blessed vows." Elmer gave her and Ferrama a knowing glower of reproval. How could he know of their matinee? Was he a Peeping Tom? No, he and Naomi had been gone all afternoon. Hidden cameras? Nope. She'd examined every inch of the room. But somehow Elmer knew.

She and Ferrama both blushed.

"Listen up, you thick-headed fool!" Ferrama snapped. "I do not want to get married."

Boy, did you change your tune, buster. A little afternoon delight and you're reneging on your marriage proposal already? "Neither do I," Cynthia concurred. It was the only time she'd ever agreed with the prince. But they had to stand united on this point.

"You will," Elmer said enigmatically, staring pointedly at their empty glasses. "You will."

Chapter Ten

Twitching in the sheets is not the same as shaking the sheets . . .

"Do you feel anything yet?"

"Hell, no. Just these scratchy sheets," P.T. griped from his side of the mile-wide bed. He knew every irregular warp and woof of the bed linens intimately, having tossed and turned for the past two hours, trying to sleep. He'd probably worn a shine on his shamrocks.

"Used to satin, are you?"

Used to satin, are you? he mimicked silently. The woman's constant jabs were getting just as irritating as the damn sheets. But he knew it wasn't his creature comforts she referred to. His bed partner—what a joke that was!—was just as worried as he about Elmer's parting hint, and their verbal sparring had been going on incessantly ever since. "Only the bourgeoisie use satin sheets. I prefer Egyptian Pima cotton, never less than twelve hundred count."

Every once in a while P.T. made a halfhearted effort to reinforce his prince persona. Not that he knew diddly about thread counts. He'd overheard Dick talking to Maureen on the subject one day, though, when his secretary had been about to depart for a white sale at Macy's.

"Well, you should be thankful we have bed linens at all."

"No, Cynthia, *you* should be thankful. To me." In return for the sheets, he'd agreed to stop cursing Naomi nonstop—an activity he'd engaged in for over an hour, at the top of his lungs. That had been after Elmer's ominous insinuation. By the time his stepsister had relented, he'd been almost hoarse from trying to make himself heard over the bellowing dogs down in the courtyard who, no doubt, thought he was harmonizing with them. Besides that, he'd run out of creative swear words.

Naomi had brought the sheets around midnight. He had to admit she didn't look half bad, when awakened from her beauty sleep—hair rumpled, wearing a bed shirt that read I AM WOMAN, HEAR ME RIVET— even despite her perpetual scowl and pistol.

She'd also deposited some alarming news. "You can quit your bellyaching for the rest of the weekend. The only one hearing you will be the dogs," she'd informed him as she made a great show of putting on a pair of industrial strength ear protectors—the kind highway riveters used to block out sounds.

"Yeah, well, maybe I'll start breaking a certain Elvis record collection . . . one vinyl at a time. Betcha Elmer rock 'n' rolls himself up here so fast his blue suede boots leave skid marks on your parquet floors." Gee, why hadn't he thought of that threat earlier? Maybe he would be on his way back to Manhattan by now.

Naomi had just smirked at him as she sashayed out of the room, calling over her shoulder, "Elmer and Ruth decided to shuffle off to Buffalo . . . ah, Poughkeepsie. They won't be back till Sunday night. He left a message for you, though. The wedding will be on Monday at five . . . God, the saints, and two hardheaded fools be willing. I assume the hardheaded fools would be you and El Sharko." He'd heard her chuckling from down the dark hallway before she'd added, "Oh, and another thing. Elmer said to make sure and tell you, 'Listen to the magic.' "

"Yeah, well, if this is magic, it's bo-o-o-ring."

"Thank you," Cynthia said from the other side of the bed, jarring him back to the present. Her voice was soft with apology, and he recalled that he'd told her she should be thankful to him for getting the bed linens. But then she spoiled the effect by adding, "It's great that you got the sheets for us, but I still think you should sleep on the floor."

It was about the tenth time she'd made the suggestion. He knew why she harped on the subject. "Are you afraid to sleep in the same bed with me, princess? Afraid of what you might do . . . in the heat of the night?"

"Ha, ha, ha. As if! I don't feel a thing for you . . . certainly not heat. Elmer must have been playing a joke on us. Ha, ha, ha."

Yep, she was afraid. Hell, he was afraid, too. And a tad curious. Okay, a lot curious. "I don't feel anything for you, either," he lied.

P.T. wasn't sure whether he could sleep side by side with Cynthia, all night long, without touching her, or other things. And what if he had to do it for seventeen more nights? *Carramba!* He was only human, after all. Even a prince had his limits.

And where was his lofty plan for detachment? He should be aloof. Uninterested.

"Why don't *you* sleep on the floor? Wall Street traders are known for their tough hides; it shouldn't be uncomfortable for you. Besides, I grew up with a valet sleeping on a pallet at the foot of my bed. I'm entitled to the bed."

"Valet, huh? I bet your right eyebrow is twitching."

"What's that supposed to mean?"

"Every time you fib, your right eyebrow twitches."

"It does not," he asserted and put a hand up, just to check.

She laughed, turning toward him slightly. He could just see the smile on her face by the light of the full moon filtering through the window into the darkened room. More clear were the ten glow-in-the-dark fingernails resting on top of the sheet, but he couldn't think about that or he really would go nuts. "The twitch only happens in the midst of a lie, silly. Tell me another lie. You'll see."

"Hmpfh! I can't think of any lies." *She thinks I'm silly. Geesh! I told Dick I was burned out in the charm department. I'm pretty sure silly is not a good thing for a prince. And silly definitely doesn't cut ice in business negotiations.*

"Say . . . oh, tell me I'm the most beautiful woman you've ever met," she suggested.

"Cynthia, you are the most beautiful woman I've

ever met," he said in a deliberately low, raspy voice. Under his fingertips, his eyebrow didn't move even a fraction. "No twitch," he reported.

"Well, maybe you're just a selective twitcher," she declared huffily, "because, believe me, I saw twitches before. Plenty of them."

"I can make myself twitch . . . in other places," he boasted. *"On command."* Peter perked up with interest, twitched, then snuggled down again when it became apparent he wouldn't be called to duty.

"Me, too," she said on a wide yawn.

Peter was definitely interested now. "Me, too? What does that mean? Me, too?" Surely she didn't mean what he thought she did. The possibilities of all that mutual twitching could be . . . well, interesting.

"It means you've been checkmated, Ferrama. Go to sleep."

Telepathic sex? There's an idea! . . .

An hour later, Cynthia awakened from a sound sleep and jackknifed to a sitting position. To her right, still on the far side of the bed, Ferrama did the same thing.

"Touch me again and you're dead meat, mister."

"I didn't touch you," the prince said with affront. "You touched me."

They looked at each other and the wide expanse of mattress between them. "Elmer!" they both concluded at the same time.

"Am I still . . . uh, touching you?" he asked tentatively, exploring his lips with the fingertips of one hand.

She thought for a second, then groaned. "Yes, you're kissing me. Stop it."

"How?"

"Hmpfh! Isn't that just like a man! In the midst of a crisis, he asks how good he is."

He chuckled. "I meant, how do I stop?"

"Oh."

There was a short silence. "*Am* I a good kisser?"

"Superb. Darn it!" She let out a sigh. "Where'd you learn to do that little fluttery thing with your tongue?"

"Gene Simmons."

"The musician?"

"Yes. I met him years ago in Cannes at the film festival. You'd be surprised at what you can learn over a case of French wine. Did you know that Princess Caroline once . . . well, never mind."

She closed her eyes and arched her neck, attempting to understand the incredible pleasures stemming from her lips, where a hungry male mouth was pressed . . . but not really. A telepathic kiss? "Are you thinking about kissing me, and that's why I can feel it?"

"I'm thinking about a hell of a lot more than kissing," he choked out. "Especially with your hand clamped around my . . . oh, ooh, oooh!" He ground out the last word painfully.

"This is horrible," she cried out with mortification, trying very hard not to think about what she was not really doing.

"No, Cynthia, it is definitely not horrible," he informed her in a suffocated whisper. "The first thing I'm going to do when I get back to the office is call my broker."

"Why?" How could he think of business at a time like this? If she was doing what she suspected, her actions went way beyond sexual harassment. "Are you going to report me to the SEC?"

"Hell no. I want to buy stock in the company that makes that glow-in-the-dark nail polish."

An inordinate pleasure gushed through Cynthia at his half-baked compliment.

After an extended period—about a minute—during which the only sounds in the room were those of their soft breathing, she asked, "Are you by any chance twitching?" She wasn't referring to his eyebrow.

"To beat the band." He paused. "And you?"

"A little," she admitted. *A lot.*

He released a long male growl of erotic agony and fell back on the bed, arms thrown over his head. Panting, he writhed from side to side.

"What . . . what am I doing now?"

"You . . . you don't want to know," he ground out, rolling over onto his stomach and burying his face in the pillow.

Yes, I do.

His body was ramrod stiff, except for an occasional involuntary flexing of his hips. She could even hear the grinding of his teeth as he fought whatever it was she was doing to him. She felt guilty about causing him so much anguish, even though it wasn't her fault. Not really. "Can . . . can I help?"

At first she thought he hadn't heard her. But finally he raised his head and stared at her, a slow smile spreading across his lips.

"I thought you'd never ask, princess."

Was it a drug or fairy dust? . . .

"Ouch!"

Cynthia had been shimmying across the mattress so quickly, she probably had brush burns on her behind. Midway she'd run into the prince, who'd been equally enthusiastic in his rush toward her. In all the excitement . . . and there was a lot of it . . . her bruised toes had hit his shin. Even in the semidarkness, she saw bright stars.

"I'm sorry," he murmured, reaching for her. "Am I inside you already? Was I thrusting too hard? I'm not usually so lacking in savoir faire."

Savoir faire? Thrusting? How does a man thrust with savoir faire? She put up a halting hand to stop his embrace and squeaked out, "No! Stop!"

Ferrama flinched at the untimeliness of her change of heart, but he didn't push her. Instead, he dropped his extended arms and waited for an explanation.

Cynthia tried to understand her abrupt reversal. It was the words, *savoir faire.* Never in her life had she heard a man talk about making love with savoir faire. But this guy was a prince. How could she have forgotten that vital fact? Plus, he was her adversary in what could be the most important business deal of her life. And he was probably an accomplice in her kidnapping, too. Was she really prepared to make the mistake of her life for a fleeting moment of pleasure?

Maybe.

Ferrama tilted his head inquiringly a bare few inches from her. Although he respected her command not to touch her physically, mentally he was skimming his fingertips over her with loving concern . . .

the line of her jaw, her parted lips, the curve where her neck met her shoulder.

She groaned

"Ah, *querida*, perhaps if you tell me what I'm doing, I can match it with real actions and slow down the pace." He was already pulling off his shorts, probably thinking to ease himself between her widespread legs and into her—*Holy cow! When did I spread my legs?*—without any foreplay. *Hah! Any more foreplay and I'll set the sheets on fire.* With frenzied haste, he managed to push his boxers off his legs and down the chain.

"You're not inside me, you dolt." She gasped then as she got her first in-the-flesh gander at Peter. And it wasn't Peter, the prince, she was gaping at. It was Peter, the penis. *Lordy, Lordy! He does have a rather impressive . . . uh, royal scepter. No Peter Cottontail here.*

"I'm not?"

"Not what?"

"I'm not inside you?" Disappointment showed clearly in his voice and on his frowning face. He rested his head on his hand and stared at her, still not understanding. "But you cried out in pain."

"My broken toes hit your shin." But it wasn't his shin where Cynthia's traitorous eyes kept wandering. *Lordy, Lordy!*

"I'm sorry. I really am clumsy tonight. Shall I rub it for you?"

"Rub what?"

He regarded her with amusement, sensing the wayward direction of her imagination and her gaze. "Your injured foot."

Oh. "No, that won't be necessary," she started to say, but already he was there mentally, his wet tongue licking at the appendages, then taking them one at a time into the heat of his mouth. Closing her eyes, she saw stars again, but not from pain.

"Can I touch you now, Cynthia?" he asked hoarsely. "Really touch you?"

She shook her head, unable to speak.

He made a low growling sound of frustration, which was almost her undoing.

"Business and pleasure should never mix." *Who was the moron who came up with that warped philosophy?*

"Is that another Irish proverb?" he grumbled.

"No, it's the maxim of my life." *Moron extraordinaire.* She rotated her head on the pillow to give him mental access to her neck. The guy did sneak from one body part to another with incredible finesse.

"*Maldito*, I hope I'm having as much fun as you appear to be." He was watching her react to his invisible caresses.

She forced her heavy eyelids open. "Help me here, Ferrama. If we do this, we'll never be able to face each other in court."

"Court?" he said stupidly as if it was the first time she'd threatened him with a lawsuit. Or had he thought she'd dropped that notion in the heat of passion?

"Yes, court. Did you think I'd lose my brain as well as my inhibitions when you slipped a drug in my drink?"

"Me?" he inquired icily as he sat up and jerked his underwear back on. "You think I would use drugs to seduce you?"

"If the shoe fits." She shrugged, moving back to her own side of the bed.

He slid his body to his side of the bed, as well.

A long, angry silence ensued. Then, just before he turned on his side, facing away from her, he spoke in a tired voice. "If it was my intention to seduce you with drugs, why do I feel as if I'm the one who's been seduced?"

Chivalry sucks! . . .

Elmer had, indeed, put a spell on them.

P.T. recognized that unbelievable fact, even if Cynthia didn't, when a half hour later the mental foreplay started all over again. *A time-release spell?* Even though Cynthia lay fuming on the other side of the bed, her wet tongue was in his ear. Despite his fury at the woman's insult, he couldn't stop himself from grinning.

Whether it was a drug in their lemonade or fairy dust in the air or just plain woo-woo magic . . . the end result was the same. It was as if computer chips had been implanted in both their libidos and were being orchestrated by remote control . . . from heaven or from Poughkeepsie, he wasn't sure which.

"How you can possibly find anything humorous in this situation is beyond me," she chided, making a slapping motion in the vicinity of her breasts. He didn't think it was a pesky fly she was whisking away.

"You gotta laugh when you think about it. There you are, glowering at me like I'm the prince of frogs. And the whole time you're lapping me up with ear sex."

"Ear sex?"

"Yep. Tongue and groove tango. Are you sure you haven't met Gene Simmons, too? Oh, man! That wet-and-blow routine is a masterpiece." He paused to let his words sink in, then added, "Can you do it again?"

"You're making that up. I've never done anything like that in my . . . remove that finger immediately!"

He glanced over at her, then did a double take. "What are you doing . . . I mean, what am I doing to you . . ." Although she flashed him a glower of disgust, she couldn't seem to control the undulating of her elevated hips. He had a pretty good idea where his finger was now; Peter did, too.

After that, things got out of hand. Again. Within minutes, their passions were stimulated into a frenzy and they were moving toward each other with warp speed. Totally out of control, they practically babbled with incoherent moans.

At the last possible moment, P.T. pulled back with horror. It was as if he was having an out-of-body experience in which he could view their bodies from above. The picture was unbelievable, wildly erotic and beautiful. But not the way he wanted their first sexual encounter to be. "Call me crazy, but I can't do this," he choked out, drawing on reserves of chivalry he never knew he had.

"Please," she whimpered.

He gritted his teeth and prayed to Saint Lancelot for strength. At least he hoped Lancelot was a saint. "When we make love, Cynthia, I want it to be because we both want it. Not because Elmer or Naomi or whoever is calling the shots."

"It's because you don't really want me," she accused.

This was P.T.'s chance to show detachment at its ultimate best. A few shock treatments of princely disdain, followed by a dollop of charm, and he'd be able to pull the shark in like a minnow. His personal and business life could be back on track.

It was the hardest thing P.T. had ever done when he said with cool aplomb, "You're probably right."

Cynthia's little gasp was a slice to his heart.

Peter was probably crying.

P.T. felt like crying himself. Lancelot notwithstanding, chivalry wasn't all it was cracked up to be.

There's foreplay and then there's FOREPLAY . . .

Cynthia felt like crying.

After another bout of involuntary mental caresses had aroused them to fever pitch again, she'd thrown a pitcher of cold water on the fires, figuratively speaking, by inquiring whether he'd ever been in love. Where that question came from, she had no idea. She just thanked God that she hadn't asked if he'd ever been in love *before*.

Then, a half hour or so later, in the midst of another round of carnal activity—Cynthia felt as if she was on a sexual roller coaster—Ferrama had been the one to stop the action with an out-of-the-blue declaration: "I don't have any condoms. I wouldn't feel right about not protecting you." He'd looked as astonished as she'd felt by his sudden reservations.

These final countdown reversals seemed to pop into their heads, blocking their actions, forcing them to behave contrary to their raging hormones. Red flags from the beyond.

And now they were about to begin bout number

five. It was enough to make a grown woman cry with frustration. A half hour ago, she'd thought the telekinetic sexual torture couldn't get any worse.

She'd been wrong.

Ferrama was holding her hand, that's all, and it was the most incredibly sensual thing she'd ever experienced. Fingers laced, palm to palm. No movement.

"Are we holding hands?" he asked softly from his side of the bed.

She nodded.

"I thought so."

She didn't want to talk now. The strange bond connecting them where their hands were joined was too special. A clear denial of his earlier rejection. A speaking gesture of warmth and caring and promises too precious to analyze.

This clasping of hands was more arousing to Cynthia than the blatant, raw mental foreplay she'd withstood thus far. Slowly, by degrees, she felt her temperature rising. Need billowed out from her constricted chest, sensitizing her skin, making her yearn for completion. And somehow she sensed that the completion she sought was not just of a physical nature.

Dangerous, dangerous thoughts for a woman to have about a business adversary.

Impossible dreams for a gritty stock trader and an upper-crust prince.

"I lied, you know," the prince confessed. His pulse thrummed against hers as he spoke.

"You do that a lot."

He pressed his fingers tight, then released. "I lied about not wanting you," he elaborated. "I do want you. Desperately."

"I know." Cynthia startled herself with that response and realized that she had, in fact, known that he wanted her even without the telling twitch. They were both playing denial games with themselves.

"Let's make love," he entreated with a sigh of surrender.

Her heart beat madly against her chest walls, and excitement churned under her skin like a million fluttering hummingbirds. She could barely think. "It wouldn't be love. Lust, pure and simple, that's all it would be."

He shrugged. "Semantics."

"I've never had a meaningless sexual relationship in my life," Cynthia said. She couldn't believe she was putting up obstacles to an act she wanted with all her being. It didn't even sound like her voice when she continued, "I'd never respect myself if I started down that road now."

He nodded, to her surprise and disappointment. "It occurs to me that we're like two players in one of those open-ended video games. You know, the ones where the ending keeps changing."

"And the characters' actions are determined by the person with the remote control," she said, beginning to follow his train of thought.

"The game player wielding the clicker must have a bizarre sense of humor, though . . . or an unusual set of ethics."

"It makes a weird kind of sense," Cynthia agreed. "Hot foreplay is okay, but only of the nontactile type . . . and absolutely no consummation. Tantalizing torture."

He lifted an eyebrow. "My touch tantalizes you?"

"Your touch tortures me."

He smiled, choosing to put his own spin on her protest. "So you agree, it's like there's an invisible shield that keeps us from actually making love."

"A shield. Hmmm. I don't know about that. It's not like a plexiglass screen shoots up between us on the mattress. It's something much more ethereal."

"Conscience," he concluded.

She laughed.

"Think about it, Cynthia. Whoever's directing this outrageous game is using our consciences against us."

"Maybe," she said hesitantly. "And the goal would be?"

"Marriage," he said with disgust. "Elmer and Naomi have got it into their heads that we should be married. I told you that before."

"Well, celestial matchmaking aside, I have no desire to marry you."

"Likewise," he retorted. Then, "How come?"

"Number one, you're not my type."

"What's your type?"

"Not a prince, that's for sure."

"And?"

"My career is too important to me right now. Maybe later. Marriage wouldn't fit into my life at this point. No way."

"Is that all?"

She cast him a sideways look of disbelief. "You're my enemy. Not only are we on opposite sides of an upcoming legal battle, but you, or your family, kidnapped me. Not a good basis for marriage!" She watched him bite his bottom lip as he concentrated on her words. "What about you? Why wouldn't you be interested in marrying? Are you a confirmed bachelor?"

He shook his head. "I want to get married someday and have a family, a big family, I hope, but the time isn't right now. The company's stock offering, the launching of some new products, just too many things that would detract from the time I would want to give a new wife."

"Are you obliged to marry a princess?"

He favored her with a sudden arresting smile. "No, I'm not going to marry a princess. A royal chick wouldn't fit into the coop I have planned."

Cynthia hated the constriction she felt in her chest as he spoke about marriage to another woman. "Well, now that we know the purpose of the spell, or whatever it is, what do we do about it?"

"Hell if I know. I'm getting too old for sex games. Don't you have one of those granny wisdoms that would apply here?"

"Too old, huh? How about, 'The older the buck the harder the horn?' " she offered with a grin. Maybe the answer was to laugh at themselves. It was better than crying.

He grinned back at her. "Are you saying I'm horny?"

"No, I'm saying your horn is hard."

He shook his head at her coarse humor. "How can you be so sweet one minute and prickly the next?"

She shrugged, and tossed out another of her grandma's sayings. "Though honey is sweet, never lick it off a briar."

"I'd brave your briars for a few good licks, honey."

His quick retort drew an involuntary smile. Their hands were still linked and the warm feeling persisted. Not a roiling, whirling dervish of passion, but low-banked embers of arousal, just waiting to be stirred. "You don't really want me. It's just a momentary hunger." She brightened as another Irish maxim came to her. "Eaten bread is soon forgotten."

"Don't be so quick to make judgments, *cara mia* . . . until you've experienced my eating."

She groaned at the double entendre.

She felt as though he was lifting their clasped hands to his mouth and kissing the knuckles, one at a time. The whole time he held her eyes across the wide expanse of the bed. She felt the warmth of his breath and the nibbling bite of his firm lips, as if flesh was really meeting flesh.

"Tell me more, *querida*. Make me laugh, or get angry. Anything to forget the pain of my longing for you."

Her brain went blank. She tried to remember all the reasons she shouldn't care about this man. Just days ago she'd been carrying a picket sign proclaiming him a frog. She chuckled with inspiration. "Never pluck a frog," she pronounced cheerily.

"Oh, Cynthia," he said with a slow, wicked grin, "it's not plucking I have in mind."

Blushing, she watched him slide off the bed and stand. "Where are you going?"

"To take a bath . . . a cold one. Are there any ice cubes left?" He glanced toward the silver ice bucket on the chifforobe.

It was almost dawn—as if she needed reminding, about a million blasted birds were already beginning their wake-up routine—and the image of the prince, soaking in that seven-foot marvel of porcelain decadence, was enough to make her consider doing a swan dive into the frigid depths. Between the two of them, they'd probably set the world record for converting water into steam.

He started to stomp off toward the bathroom, dragging his chain behind him. But then he paused, as if sensing her prurient thoughts. "Wanna join me? I'll let you use the last of Priscilla's Passion bath oil. And I promise I'll behave."

"Your eyebrow is twitching."

"That's not a twitch, that's a waggle. Wanna see what else I can waggle? In fact . . ." His words trailed off and his eyes widened with accusation. *"Cyn-thi-a!"*

Before her very eyes, the waistband of his boxers pulled out and pinged back of its own accord.

She gave Elmer a mental high five.

Chapter Eleven

A wicked twist on the age-old fairy tale . . .

The prince had been in his royal bath for over an hour when Naomi arrived with breakfast.

And lunch.

And dinner.

And snacks.

Actually, what she brought was two heavily laden Sheffield trays of not-so-gourmet foods, which she set on an inlaid rosewood desk by the door. "This should do you two for the rest of the day," Naomi grumbled. "I'm priming the walls in the second parlor today and I can't stop once I start."

Cynthia hobbled over, discovering to her surprise that her toes barely hurt now. All that exposure to the air, she supposed, not to mention having no reason to put weight on her foot, had hastened the healing process.

"My goodness!" she said, barely stifling a giggle when she got closer to the trays. The feast included a loaf of white bread, jars of peanut butter and jelly, a huge carafe of hot coffee, several packets of sugar, a quart of two-percent milk and a six-pack of diet soda (at least Naomi was watching out for their weight), a box of Lucky Krisps cereal *(who knew they had corn flakes in the shape of four-leaf clovers?)*, a gallon-size zip-lock Baggie of ice cubes to fill their bucket, a basket of fruit and an assortment of potato chips and pretzels. Not a caviar egg or pretentious bottled water in sight!

The only utensils provided were of the plastic picnic variety, presumably so they wouldn't be able to use a butter knife or fork for a weapon. There were also cups, saucers and soup bowls of what appeared to be fine Meissen china. The irony of disposable flatware combined with museum-quality dinnerware didn't escape her.

Most important, there was a folded newspaper. Cynthia couldn't wait to get at the stock pages. The market might very well have collapsed in the past three days, for all she knew.

"I'm off then," Naomi announced, blushing brightly. Cynthia wasn't sure if she was embarrassed over her food offering or the kidnapping itself.

"Wait! Stay and have a cup of coffee with me," she urged hastily. "I suspect your stepbrother has fallen asleep in the tub, and I'd like the company." Cynthia wasn't surprised at Ferrama dozing off. Now that the effects of Elmer's spell appeared to have worn off, she felt drained of energy, too. She didn't believe it was a spell, though. More like some illegal drug. "Come on, just for a minute. I can sit over there, out of reach." She pointed to a nearby banquette—a long upholstered sofa with one roll-over arm.

"Well," Naomi said hesitantly, "I suppose I could have one cup."

Quickly, before she changed her mind, Cynthia poured them each a cup of black coffee, taking note of Naomi's halting hand when she was about to reach for sugar and milk. Cynthia backed up and sat down gingerly, making sure she didn't trip over her chain.

Naomi plopped down into a straight-backed chair and, with a long sigh, idly examined the watermarks and worm holes on the inlay of the desktop. Her shoulder-length brown hair was pulled back and tucked under a painter's cap. She wore a clean pair of paint-spattered coveralls over a white tank shirt. Cynthia re-alized as the woman crossed one leg over a knee and leaned back that she had a nice shape. In fact, her fresh-scrubbed face, marked by clear skin and straight fea-tures, and smelling faintly of Ivory soap, was really very attractive. When she wasn't frowning, that is.

Ivory soap. I haven't thought of that in years. It was Grandma's favorite . . . mainly because it was the cheapest brand on the market. Cynthia decided to buy some Ivory soap when she got home.

"Why're you smiling? Do you think I'm funny?"

Cynthia jolted to attention and saw that Naomi was back to frowning again. "No, it was the smell of your Ivory soap."

"What's wrong with Ivory soap? Not every woman

feels the need to pamper herself with overpriced personal products. I have better things to do with my money." She sniffed, affronted.

Boy, talk about a chip on the shoulder! "Naomi, my grandma always used Ivory soap. I was smiling because your scent reminded me of . . . of someone I loved very much." Her voice cracked with emotion. Really, during the last few days her emotional control had developed more fractures than a linebacker's knee. Not a good thing for a stock trader.

"Oh. Sorry if I sniped at you. I've been doing that a lot lately."

So, Naomi was a woman who guarded her emotions well, too. And she was stressed out by their situation, just as Cynthia was. It was not a comfortable realization, recognizing that she and Naomi were alike in some ways.

"No problem," Cynthia conceded and sipped at her coffee. A companionable silence settled between them. Finally, she remarked, "This is a monumental task you've taken on . . . the castle renovations, I mean."

Naomi nodded wearily, and Cynthia noticed the fine lines bracketing her eyes and lips. Was she exhausted because of her awesome restoration project, or because of her heinous role in a felony? Probably both.

"Why is it so important to you?"

Naomi sliced her a quick look, obviously suspicious of the motive behind her question. "Why do you want to know?"

She shrugged. "I understand strong women wanting . . . things. I entered a male dominated profession, after all. I've set unthinkable, unfeminine, short-term goals for myself—making money. Even worse, I aspire to long-term goals that some would consider laughable for a former ghetto girl from Chicago." She paused only for a second before confiding, "I want a seat on the New York Stock Exchange someday." *Now, why did I reveal that?*

Naomi smiled with understanding. It was the first time she'd seen Naomi smile, Cynthia realized, and the wide grin made her genuinely attractive. A little makeup, a wardrobe change, and a personality overhaul would do wonders.

"Despite all that, I don't grasp your vision here," Cynthia said.

"My mother died when I was five years old and Ruth was four," Naomi began. "Daddy hired one live-in housekeeper after another. They never stayed for long. I guess Ruth and I were a little, ah, difficult." She grinned sheepishly at that last revelation. "The bottom line is that we never had much of a home. Oh, we always had a nice house, but not a home. Daddy was a workaholic, gone from early morning before we awakened to late at night after our bedtime. I remember one time, it was my ninth birthday . . . well, never mind." She turned away from Cynthia and poured herself another cup of coffee.

"But didn't that change when your father married Eva Ferrama? I know she came from a royal family and all that, but then you had a traditional home life, right?"

"Wrong."

Cynthia's head shot up.

"Eva was nice enough, but she was a flake. A beautiful, useless ornament. That's where Ruth got all her warped ideas. I had to show Eva how to empty a vacuum cleaner bin, sort laundry, close the flue on the fireplace. If you're picturing 'The Brady Bunch,' forget it. Eva didn't even know how to bake a pie. Geesh! Besides, she and Daddy went out a lot . . . to the country club and stuff."

Cynthia's childhood had been nothing like Naomi's, but she could empathize with the loneliness that permeated her words. And she supposed Eva's lack of knowledge about such domestic matters was understandable. Being a queen, or former queen, Eva probably hadn't been taught to do such plebeian tasks.

"Did Eva have a tiara?" *Oh, gosh, where did that question come from? Darn, darn, darn! I know exactly where. In those fairy tales I devoured as a child, the queens and princesses always wore a diamond crown . . . a tiara.* In fact, Cynthia suddenly remembered a dime-store rhinestone tiara her grandma had bought her one Christmas. She used to float around their dingy apartment in her nightgown and tiara, dreaming impossible dreams. She wondered what had ever happened to that precious keepsake of her girlhood. *But those were long-ago fancies. How stupid of me to imagine a queen in Hoboken, New Jersey, wearing a crown!*

"Actually, yes," Naomi said, to her surprise. "The silly twit wore it every New Year's Eve to the Charity Ball."

Cynthia put the fingertips of one hand to her furrowed brow and rubbed, thinking. "What does all this have to do with your renovation project?"

"Everything. Daddy loved me and Ruth, but he was old-fashioned. He treated us like dolls. Can you imagine me as a doll?"

How about a Martha Stewart Barbie?

"Daddy never talked business with us, even when we were growing up. Said that was man's work. He believed it was all right for a woman to have a career, as a hobby, but just till she got married and had babies."

"Incredible!"

"Yeah. He even tried to push me toward marrying one of P.T.'s friends who he brought home from Rutgers. An arranged marriage . . . can you imagine that?"

"Your stepbrother went to Rutgers?"

"Well, just for a year. Daddy died suddenly, and P.T. had to quit school and take over the company. I was a junior at Cornell then, and Ruth was in her second year of her first beauty school. Thanks to Daddy's overprotection, we didn't know a thing about manufacturing shoes."

"You went to Cornell? I'm impressed, Naomi."

"Why? Do you think you're the only intelligent woman in the universe?"

"Ouch! That was warranted, I suppose. It's just that you project this image of—" She waved a hand in the direction of Naomi's coveralls.

"You'd think that a savvy stock trader would know better than to judge people by their exterior trappings."

"Double ouch!" Cynthia was seeing Naomi with new eyes and finding her much more complex than she'd imagined. "What did you study?"

"Teaching," she said with disgust. "Daddy insisted. But I took every architectural course I could fit in on the side."

"Let's backtrack a bit here. Your father was an Archie Bunker when it came to his view of feminism. And he tried to fix you up with some guy. What's wrong with that? Successful women have been working around obstacles like that for centuries." Cynthia was trying hard to find the link between this personal history and Naomi's need for a castle.

"I suspect, but I'm not certain, that Daddy might have even offered Enrique money, like a dowry. The most mortifying thing is that he refused. Not that I didn't refuse, too, but the louse refused first. I hate him, I really do."

"Enrique? You mean Dick Alvarez?" *Good grief! Naomi and the Hispanic stud lawyer?*

"The one and only. After P.T. dropped out of college, they stayed friends. Then, when Enrique graduated from law school, he joined Friedman's Wholesale Shoes, too. A little later they hired Jake. And the three of them conspired to steal the company."

"P.T. stole your family business?" Now this was information Cynthia might be able to use in her lawsuit.

"Not legally, but in all other ways, yes. P.T. changed the name of Daddy's company. He changed the whole product line. He gave it his stupid royal prince imprint. Never once did he consult me or Ruth. He . . ." Naomi's words trailed off as she realized how much she was revealing with her angry tirade. Darting a quick glance at Cynthia, she straightened, and her face closed over.

"Let me get this straight. Your father bequeathed his entire company to his stepson and left his two blood daughters out of the will?"

"Of course not. Daddy gave us the house and a trust fund and twenty percent each of the company. The other sixty percent went to P.T., ten percent of which he later divvied between Enrique and Jake."

"All because he thought a man would be better able to run a company," she concluded for Naomi.

"Right."

"Once again, what does this castle and your renovation plan have to do with all that?"

"When P.T. bought this castle five years ago—"

"He does take his royal duties seriously then," she interjected with unwarranted enthusiasm. "Your stepbrother said his uncle was king, but he must have wanted to establish a palace for himself until the crown passes to him."

Naomi just gaped at her.

"His mother must have been so pleased. And those banana trees . . . now I understand. They were added to remind him and his mother of their island homeland."

Naomi's gaping mouth clicked shut. "P.T.'s mother died when he was fifteen . . . of cancer."

"Oh." Her heart went out to P.T. then, when she thought of him as a young prince, alone in a foreign country. "All the more reason for him to be sentimental about having his very own palace. He told me there was no castle on his island, but I knew he had to be kidding."

"Yeah. A great kidder, that P.T." Naomi was looking at her as if she was two turrets short of a full castle.

"So, your stepbrother bought this place and started to renovate it. Why did he stop?"

Naomi shrugged. "It was costing too much money. He had his penthouse in the city. He was busy playing prince playboy. Taking the fashion industry by storm was much more fun. He had no vision of what this castle could be."

"Unlike you."

"Unlike me," Naomi agreed. "The minute I saw this place I was a goner. Oh, Cynthia, didn't you ever dream when you were a little girl of a fairy-tale castle and Prince Charming and all those things that would fill your life with magic and love?"

"Nope," Cynthia lied. *This is too, too weird. Naomi the Terminator and I have way too much in common.* "I prefer to live in my high-rise apartment building, thank you very much."

"Do you live in Manhattan?"

"Uh-huh. Upper West Side. I just bought a co-op apartment in the Dakota."

"The Dakota!" Naomi hooted. "That's as close to a castle as it gets in the city. You phony, you! You're a dreamer just like me. You just hide it behind those shark teeth."

"Like you?" Cynthia arched a brow. But what she was thinking was, *No, no, no! It can't be true. I'm not a dreamer at all. I purchased that apartment because it was a good investment. It had nothing to do with its palatial exterior. Oh, God! It can't be true. I can't have subconsciously bought into the fairy-tale fantasy. Surely I left those unrealistic yearnings behind me long ago.*

Naomi was grinning like a Cheshire cat.

Time to change the subject . . . turn it back to Naomi and her foolish dreams. Not my foolish dreams . . . not that I have any dreams. Uh-uh! "Forget about me. There's something missing in your fairy tale, Naomi. This castle is a dump, and there's not a *charming* prince in sight."

"Hah! Who needs a prince? I'm disappointed that a money maven like you doesn't see the possibilities."

"Possibilities?" Cynthia repeated.

"Yep. I'm gonna open the biggest, poshest bed-and-breakfast in the world. The Castle."

"A bed-and-breakfast? In a palace?" Cynthia laughed, but not with derision. "You might just have an idea there. Sort of a Mira Lago of the North, sans Donald Trump. Sky-high prices. Exclusive clientele."

"There you go!" Naomi smiled at her warmly . . . well with as much warmth as Naomi was capable of showing.

"The only thing missing in this equation is the capital to finance the venture. I don't want to be unkind, Naomi, but the million-dollar cut you expect to get from the stock transfer won't be nearly enough. Not that you yahoos are going to have all that much profit after I'm done dragging you through the courts. And I sincerely doubt whether you'll be able to dip into a trust fund for the added cash."

"I'm not a total dunce, you know. I have my own plans." Naomi's face took on a crafty, secretive expression. "Besides, do you have any idea what the furniture in this place is worth?"

The price of hauling it away?

"Millions."

"Naomi! Most of it's damaged junk."

Naomi shook her head vehemently. "Even with the deplorable damage, these are valuable antiques. There are Philadelphia Queen Anne chairs in the dining room that would bring a hundred thousand each at Christie's."

Cynthia straightened with interest.

"Some of the paintings were done by world-famous artists. Do you know, there's even a Winslow Homer landscape in the billiard room?" Naomi preened with pride on imparting that information.

Cynthia wondered why Naomi would tell her these things when she knew a law-suit was pending. *Because she doesn't believe it will ever happen. She really thinks I'll marry her stepbrother and drop all my complaints. All-in-the-family logic.* Not in a million years would she marry Ferrama, not even to gain a fairy-tale prince. But no need to rile Naomi with that news now.

"Have you brought in appraisers?" Cynthia inquired.

Naomi nodded. "But I've only shown them a few pieces. I wouldn't ever consider selling off all the furnishings. That would destroy the historical character of the castle. But a few items wouldn't hurt."

"Oh, is that who those men were yesterday? Appraisers? You told your stepbrother they were businessmen who'd lost their way, but I'll bet you didn't want to alert him to these hidden treasures. Good idea."

A rosy tint crept up Naomi's neck. "Yeah, that's what they were . . . appraisers." Standing abruptly, she announced, "Well, I've got to go." Instead of leaving, though, she shifted from foot to foot. "There is one thing I wanted to ask you . . . a bit of professional advice."

"About stocks?" Now that was a surprise. A kidnapper seeking hot stock tips from the kidnapee.

"I just had a general kind of question. It involves a friend of mine."

Yeah, right.

"If a person was selling off a large block of stock,

would the other members of the corporation know about it ahead of time?"

Little alarm bells went off in Cynthia's head. What was Naomi up to now? The devious glint was back in her hazel eyes.

"Well, Rule 144 of the SEC might apply here. Are you on the board of directors of Ferrama?"

"No."

"Do you have a position of influence in the corporation? By that I mean, do you have a say in important decision-making procedures?"

"Hah!"

"I'll take that as a 'no.' Well, in that case, keeping your anonymity may be possible, but I'd have to know more details."

"How about trust funds? Can they be broken?"

Cynthia shrugged. "Once again, it depends . . . whether they're irrevocable, or not . . . whether all parties were agreeable to the conditions. There are lots of considerations. A good trust lawyer could address those points in a sec."

Naomi seemed to be pondering her advice.

"You know, Naomi, if you'd release me, I could help you get the best deal for your stock, or give you the names of some reliable attorneys."

"Hah! I'd rather trust the Mafia."

"The Mafia?"

"It was just an expression. Geesh! You and P.T. have this Mafia fixation. Besides, I only wanted the information for my friend."

Cynthia's shoulders slumped as it became apparent that Naomi was not going to release her, under any circumstances.

"Did you really think I'd let you go just because we shared a coffee klatch?"

Cynthia sighed. "Naomi, it's imperative that I get back to work. Let's put our cards on the table here, woman to woman. What will it take for you to unlock this chain?"

"You already know the answer." Naomi made busywork of adjusting some loose strands of hair under her cap. She must have left her pistol downstairs, but that didn't matter, since she was out of Cynthia's reach. "In a way, you've got the key."

It took only a second for Cynthia to understand. "Marriage? Marriage is the key? Give me a break. You can't possibly think I'd marry your stepbrother just to escape. And, besides, what's to stop me from suing you once I'm free? Promises made under duress count for zip in the courts."

"I figure a few nights of honeymooning with P.T. and you'll agree to just about anything. Has he popped the big question yet?" She inclined her head, waiting for an answer. When none came, she whooped, "He has! I can tell by your blush."

"Naomi, just think about how you felt when your father tried to force you into a marriage you didn't want. How can you do the same thing to me?"

"This is different. I have better motives. Besides, you'll enjoy being married to P.T. In fact, it looks like he worked you over pretty good already. And I mean that in the nicest possible way."

Heat infused Cynthia's face and, without thinking, she put the fingertips of one hand to her lips, which still felt bruised, deliciously so. Peering downward, she confirmed what she'd already suspected . . . the nipples of her stimulated breasts were clearly delineated by the spandex dress.

Folding her arms across her chest, she was about to deny Naomi's allegation because, after all, none of that love play had actually taken place, but she gave up with a loud sigh of resignation. "Okay, I'll admit it. I'm attracted to the jerk. I wouldn't mind having him around my apartment for a day or two"—she rolled her eyes at a grinning Naomi—"or twenty. You know, a personal boy toy. Someone to do the laundry. Fetch me bonbons. Fresh-squeeze my orange juice. Serve my meals . . ."

"And other things," Naomi finished for her.

"Yep." She returned Naomi's grin.

"In the buff?"

"Absolutely! My personal buff puff."

Naomi let out a snort of laughter. "See? It's not so bad. It's like a modern-day fairy tale."

"The X-rated version?"

"Triple X. But in this rendition, the princess could kick the prince out on his royal tush once he's served his purpose. Hell, there are lots more knights in the palace pool, anxious to come forth with ready sword and shield . . . well, with ready *sword*, anyhow."

"You are bad, Naomi." Cynthia couldn't help joining in Naomi's laughter.

"Yeah, well, a wicked stepsister has got to do what she's got to do. It's a big bad world out there, Cinderella."

"Well, this Cinderella is *not* going to marry the prince, no matter what."

"Never say never, honey. Maybe this marriage is your destiny, like Elmer keeps saying."

"I don't care what kind of crazy crap you and Elmer pull. I can wait you out if I have to. I've got the patience of Job. As for destiny, my grandma always said, 'Patience can conquer destiny.' "

"Ah, I do love those Irish proverbs of yours, Cynthia. But there's an old Hebrew saying I like better." Naomi flashed her a triumphant smirk. "By degrees are castles built."

"There is not a tree in heaven higher than the tree of patience," she countered with a *hmpfh* of one-upmanship.

"Tsk-tsk, didn't you ever hear the adage: 'Time and patience would bring the snail to Jerusalem'?" She chalked an imaginary one in the air. "To my way of thinking, you could substitute shark for snail and the moral of the maxim would remain the same."

"Arrggh! Read my lips, Naomi. There'll be white blackbirds in a purple sky before I marry that shoe cobbler Casanova stepbrother of yours."

"White blackbirds, huh? Never underestimate the power of genetic science. And who knows what'll happen to the sky's color when the ozone layer finally bites the dust?"

Cynthia made a face at Naomi's back as she walked toward the door. Naomi was already in the corridor when she paused, then turned. "Oh, by the way, I forgot to give you another message from Elmer. He is the strangest fellow, don't you think? For the life of me, I don't know what Ruth sees in him, but—"

"Na-om-i! Get to the point. What message?"

"Beware the second phase."

I'll show you mine if you show me yours . . .

"I am not a boy," P.T. asserted irritably when he reentered the bedroom a short time later, making reference to Cynthia's boy-toy remark, which he'd overheard from the bathroom.

"Oh, boy!" she squealed from behind the newspaper she'd been reading. She was sitting on the other side of the room at the card table, eating a bowl of dried cereal and blueberries swimming in milk while she perused *The New York Times*.

"I'm a man." He put his hands on his hips, feeling the need to set the woman straight, although his stomach growled with anticipation at the sight of food.

He put aside his hunger for the moment, though, and glared at the infuriating woman. She had some nerve, making sexist, demeaning comments about him while he was out of the room. Especially when he'd been chivalrous enough to remove himself from her torturous bed and immerse himself in a frigid bath till the spell wore off . . . and his you-know-what almost fell off, too. "I'm not a boy to be toyed with," he repeated through gritted teeth. "I . . . am . . . a . . . man."

"Man, oh, man!" She gaped at him over the newspaper, which she'd lowered only as far as her nose.

When he began to stomp toward her, dragging his blasted chain behind him, she stood with a gasp, dropping the newspaper to the floor. "Put some clothes on," she demanded in a shrill, panicky voice.

Her words passed right over his poleaxed brain as he stopped dead in his tracks, his jaw dropping. Between the frigid bath and now *this*, P.T. wasn't sure how much more his battered libido could take.

Standing before him, chin raised indignantly, eyes glittering with blue flames of fury, was a strawberry blond goddess. And she was strawberry blond *all over*. He knew that because the sputtering harridan was totally, gloriously naked.

Talk about a welcome party! And for breakfast, yet! It must be true what they say about breakfast being the most important meal of the day, he thought with immense appreciation.

Peter was appreciative, too.

Forget breakfast. I've got another repast in mind, babe.

I'm up for that, Peter concurred with silent, universal male body language.

"Put some clothes on right now, mister, or I'm going to cut off your royal scepter with a plastic butter knife." She put her hands on her hips, mirroring his posture, and he grabbed for the bedpost to keep his suddenly rubbery legs from buckling.

"Wh-what?" He couldn't stop staring. Not that he tried.

Cynthia had been right yesterday when she'd stated, self-consciously, that she had curves. She did. A lot of them. All alabaster slopes and swells of luminescent skin, not quite ivory and not quite cream, but an enticing mixture surely blended by the gods to drive a mortal man mad. In the midst of that visual feast were two large, raspberry-hued buds that ignited P.T.'s hunger into a raw, raging appetite.

In that instant he realized that he'd been ravenous for a long, long time.

But then her words filtered into his testosterone-flooded brain. "I *do* have clothes on," he maintained, "but, believe me, I never would have bothered with these Elvis stripper pants if I'd known you were going to welcome me in your birthday suit." He looked down pointedly at the neon red bell-bottoms he wore.

She made a small gurgling sound of disbelief, her eyes fixed on his lower extremities, where he was demonstrating with a little flourish of the hand that he was, indeed, clothed. Geesh, you'd think he was mooning her, or something equally objectionable, by the way she was practically hyperventilating.

"Birthday suit?" she shrieked. "I know Ruth's obscene spandex number doesn't leave much to the imagination, but at least I'm covered." She waved a hand to encompass her body from chest to thigh. "See."

He saw.

"What kind of seduction game are you trying now? What's up, Ferrama?" Her face immediately turned raspberry red to match certain other parts of her body as her gaze snagged on his midsection. *And lower.* "I mean, what's with the nudist bit? It's rather unsubtle for a prince with your suave reputation." Her voice dripped with sarcasm.

"I'm not nude. You are," he informed her haughtily.

They both jerked to attention as understanding hit them like a bolt of lightning.

"The second phase!" they said simultaneously.

"I'm going to kill Elmer, I swear I am," she stormed, reaching down to grasp the newspaper, then slapping it in front of her body.

"Me, too," he said ingratiatingly, but what he really thought was, *Thank you very much.*

They were becoming a little bit fruity . . .

An hour later, Cynthia peeked out from under the bed sheet, which she'd drawn up to her chin. Yep, the prince was still naked. The second phase of the spell was still in force.

He sat at the card table, buck naked, reading the newspaper with an infuriating nonchalance, crunching away on what must be his third bowl of cereal. She would have thought his tastes would run more to *pâté de foie gras* or some fancy-schmancy Spanish omelet on a bed of truffles.

Crunch, crunch, crunch!

She pulled the sheet over her head. You'd think she'd be able to sleep after her sleepless night. No way! Her nerves were shot.

Crunch, crunch, crunch!

Meanwhile, Ferrama was so darn blasé about this mortifying turn of events that she wanted to shake him.

Crunch, crunch, crunch!

Or stuff the box of Lucky Krisps down his throat.

Crunch, crunch, crunch!

She was not a person used to sitting by idly, waiting for things to happen. It frustrated her to no end that she'd lost control of her life. She remembered one time when a guy took her sailing on a date. It was the most miserable day of her life, wasting an entire afternoon waiting for the wind to push the boat. If she could have, she would have jumped into the lake and pushed the boat herself.

Crunch, crunch, crunch!

She sat up abruptly, sheet shoulder high, to glare at him. "Do something, dammit!"

Surprised, he jerked his head to look at her, taking in her modest pose with the sheet. A slow grin crept across his lips, and she knew . . . she just knew . . . the sheet was invisible to his twinkling eyes. With a groan of dismay, she drew her knees up to her chest.

"Were you talking to me?" he asked politely. *Were you watching me?*

"No, I wasn't watching you." *Damn, they should outlaw that grin of his. It's a lethal weapon.*

At first, he cocked his head in confusion. Then he grinned wider, almost as if he could read her mind. She could have sworn he murmured, "Bang-bang."

"Don't just sit there," she snapped, annoyed as much at herself and her straying eyes as at his failure to do anything to solve their dilemma.

"You want me to stand?" he asked. *That's the first intelligent suggestion she's made today. And, man, am I glad to oblige. What do you say, Peter?*

"No, I don't want you to stand, you dolt," she said in a rush. "I want you to stop chomping on that cereal. I want you to come up with a plan. I want you to get us out of this madhouse." *I want you.*

His eyes went wide, then slowly seemed to turn from midnight blue to smoldering black. "I want you, too, baby." *Rev up the engines, Peter. It looks like we're off to the strawberry patch after all.*

"The only fruit you're going to eat is those blasted blueberries."

"I like blueberries," he said defensively. *I like raspberries even better, though. What I'd like to suck are those raspberry nipples of yours. Come on, baby, flash me again. Let's make horizontal fruit salad*

"I do not have raspberry . . . body parts." Her face flushed hotly. *I knew it. My nipples are too big. He noticed. I wish I could melt into the mattress and disappear.*

"Raspberry . . . ?" He frowned with puzzlement. "Hey, I didn't say that out loud. Are you reading my mind?" Before she had a chance to react to that astounding accusation, he added, "And you know damn well your breasts are gorgeous."

"I never said anything about . . . I mean, I never said anything *out loud* about—"

It hit them both at the same time. "The third phase!"

After that, their thoughts went haywire, ripping back and forth with total abandon.

I want to make love with her so bad.

I've never wanted a man like I want him.

She is so damn beautiful. If she only knew what effect she has on me, she'd sure as hell use it against me.

His eyelashes are so incredibly long and silky for a man. I get aroused just looking at his eyelashes. Amazing!

Her breasts are magnificent. I'd like to lick those hard peaks till she screams. And screams. And screams.

Look at his lips. No, don't look. They're full and sensual and firm. I wonder if he'd like to kiss for a really long time. Kiss, that's all.

I would.

In the end, it was Cynthia who this time opted for

a cold bath. As she clanked off to the bathroom, sheet wrapped around her, mummy-style, she heard the prince think.

Great ass!

Life didn't get any worse than this.

Chapter Twelve

Getting to know you ...

By Sunday afternoon, he and Cynthia had been through more phases than the moon in all its lunar cycles. They were both feeling a little loony.

Well, Elmer should be back by this evening, and the rock 'n' roll matchmaker was going to get a resounding welcome into the twilight zone. The interfering fairy was going to see stars—and he didn't mean music celebrity stars.

Cynthia thought the worst of the phases had been seeing each other naked, but he disagreed. He'd gotten a whole lot of enjoyment out of that one. Who knew a woman could blush on so many body parts? Or that there were fifty ways to view a swaying butt?

Nope, in P.T.'s opinion the worst of the phases had been the one where he kept blurting out Elvis love songs, serenading Cynthia like a lovestruck idiot. Not that he hadn't been good. Hell, he'd impressed even himself with the authenticity of his husky croon, accompanied by a cute grin that was uptilted on one side (with a little practice, he might even add it to his look repertoire in the future), and, of course, a few Elvis bumps and grinds. His pièce de résistance (although Cynthia was still resisting) was a down-on-the-knees, arms outstretched wail of burning love. At one point he'd seriously contemplated, *out loud, for God's sake*, the possibility of growing sideburns. *Geesh!*

He would have been mortified except for one thing. At the same time he'd been belting out "Stuck on You" while he ate a peanut butter and banana sandwich, or urging Cynthia to "Please Surrender" as he chain-danced her around the room, or proclaiming with alarming crudity "It's Now or Never" to a tone-deaf Peter, Cynthia had been making an equally ludicrous display of herself.

She'd turned into the sexpot Ann-Margret . . . a regular dynamo of dancing, flirting energy. Flicking her wild strawberry-blond mane over her shoulder movie starlet style, she'd given him sultry, half-lidded, come-hither looks, and danced up a storm in showgirl fashion straight from the movie *Viva Las Vegas*.

He'd gotten to see a whole lot more of her magnificent figure during that phase *(Thank you, God!)* while she'd bent and contorted and flung her body about in Ruth's spandex dress. For some reason, she hadn't appreciated his observation that she'd make a good stripper if she lost her Wall Street job for good.

P.T. made a mental note to suggest to advertising that in one of the print layouts for "Naughty or Nice," a red stiletto heel, the shoe should be worn with a bimbo dress just like this. Or maybe with nothing at all. Hmmm. For certain, he was going to insist that the model have strawberry blond hair.

He glanced over to the bed where Cynthia was curled up, kitten-style, and decided to share that thought with her. "You know what would look good on you?"

She was just awakening from a nap. They did a lot of napping in between phases of Elmer's spells. There was nothing else to do but sleep, if you didn't count watching Elvis and Cinderella movies or listening to Elvis and Cinderella music or taking bubble baths or reading *The New York Times* for the twentieth time or skimming Ruth's beauty magazines (although that one article on the correlation between frequent sex and good complexions was rather interesting).

Well, actually, there was one other thing they could do, but when he'd suggested it to Cynthia, she'd advised him to do that very thing to himself. Boy, did she have a foul mouth on her!

"What did you say?" Cynthia asked sleepily as she sat up and stretched.

"Huh?" He was too busy watching her stretch . . . an exercise in feline sensuality. His own personal sex kitten! She must have learned that pose from Ann-Margret. Or was that the way sharks got out the kinks? Frankly, he kind of liked her being kinky. "Oh, uhmm, I said, 'Do you know what would look good on you?' "

"You?" she scoffed, taking note of his undue interest in her stretch.

Yep, the woman did have a tendency to zap him at every turn with her razor-sharp tongue. He'd like to ping the elastic in her latex a few dozen times to cure her of that habit. In fact, he'd like to ping her elastic *period* . . . all over.

"No, not me," he said, making a deliberate effort to plaster a grin on his face. He knew his grin had an effect on her; so he was grinning a whole lot. He'd become a regular grinning prince. "Red stiletto high heels would look good on you . . . the ones we launched this year, called 'Naughty or Nice.' With your legs, they'd look sensational." He put up a halting hand at the indignant expression that flashed onto her face. "No, no, no! Don't go feminist on me, getting all bent out of shape just because I commented on your legs. That wasn't meant as sexual harassment. It was a good old-fashioned compliment."

"Well, thank you then," she said meekly. Too meekly.

He glanced up sharply from the card table where he'd been working on the *Times*'s crossword puzzle on and off all day long. He prided himself on getting a grand total of two words thus far.

"Oh, great! You're crying," he accused. He could take her foul mouth and her abrasive personality—they were part and parcel of her strange appeal to him—but weeping? No way!

"I am *not* crying. I never cry." A fat tear escaped one eye and slid down her flushed cheek.

He got up from the table and shuffled over to the bed, climbing up beside her. Fluffing the pillows behind them, he wrapped an arm around her shoulder and tugged her against his side. It was a sign of her weakened state that she didn't slug him. "Everyone cries sometimes," he told her.

"Do you?"

He tried to think of the last time he'd cried. Suddenly, he pictured himself at his mother's hospital bed . . . seventeen years ago. He blinked rapidly to fight back the sorrow generated by that alarming realization. *Seventeen years!* Had he frozen himself emotionally?

"Well, do you?" She leaned her head away slightly to get a better view of him.

"Not much," he confessed. "But *you* have good reason to let loose. You've been through a lot this weekend."

She nodded. "So have you." Then she raised a fingertip and touched the edge of his eyelashes. "Did your mother have such long eyelashes, too?"

That shook his composure. Were they back to reading each other's minds? A quick perusal of her features assured him that it was just an idle observation. "Yes. Yes, she did," he admitted in a raspy voice. "In fact, her eyes were the first thing you noticed about her, now that I think about it. She never wore mascara or eyeliner like other ladies. It would have been overkill with those thick, thick lashes surrounding eyes of a startling shade of . . ."

". . . midnight blue."

He darted her a surprised glance.

"Like yours."

His throat tightened then and he closed his eyes, fearing he might actually be tearing up.

She used the opportunity to caress the lashes of both his eyes. "Do you mind?"

He shook his head, eyes still closed, and allowed her to run the pads of her fingertips over the hairs, little feathery brushes, back and forth.

"They *are* silky, just like I thought," she murmured.

"Is silky good?"

"Silky is *very* good."

The tightness in his throat eased, and his lips turned up slightly. "What else do you like about me?"

She chuckled at his obvious bid for compliments.

He rolled onto his back, keeping his arm around her shoulder so that she was leaning over him. Then he folded his hands under his head. He kept his eyes shuttered, wanting to prolong the rare peace between them.

"You have a strong nose." She sketched its contour from bridge to upper lip.

"Strong doesn't sound attractive. Cyrano had a strong nose—"

"So did Pinocchio."

"Are you saying my nose is too big?" *Or that I'm a liar?*

"Your nose is just right, Ferrama," she assured him, giving the tip of his nose a playful tap. "Your ears, on the other hand, are a mite oversized."

"They are?" He cracked his eyes open a slit to find her face hovering close to his, *very close*, as she examined the sensitive whorls of first one, then the other ear. His heart slammed against his chest walls in excitement, then began a steady, accelerated beat.

"Just kidding," she said, biting her bottom lip in concentration as she continued her wonderfully torturous investigation.

He bit his bottom lip, too, but not because he was concentrating. He was afraid he might rear up and inspect her ears, tit for tat. With his teeth.

Exercising remarkable restraint—at least he thought

it was remarkable—he closed his eyes again. Fortunately, she'd moved back to his face with her tactile exploration.

"Your Spanish heritage is evident in your high cheekbones and black hair," she noted, tracing the bones under his eyes with the fingers of both hands, then raking them quickly through his hair at the sides.

In order to have freedom of movement for both hands, she'd allowed her upper body to rest against his chest. Chivalrous knight that he was, he didn't even look where they were joined. But he wanted to.

"Your whiskers are prickly, though. Do you have to shave twice a day?"

"Sometimes." He didn't elaborate, wanting her to guess when that sometimes might be. Wanting her to know he would shave again for her, if she wanted him to.

"Even the hair under your arms appears silky," she said in a breathy voice, and stroked him there.

He almost shot up off the bed. Instead, he clenched his clasped hands into fists behind his head and gritted his teeth. But a low moan escaped anyway.

"Shhhh," she soothed. Apparently she knew the effect she was having on him. And still she continued.

Am I about to get lucky? Man, oh, man, that ton of Lucky Clover cereal I inhaled this weekend must be working. Or was it Krispy Clover?

Or is my seductive charm more potent than I'd thought?

Hell, who cares? One doesn't look a gift-horse . . . uh, shark, in the mouth. He relaxed as much as possible with testosterone pumping through his bloodstream like a wildcat gusher.

Correction: The marvelous feeling flooding his body wasn't exactly arousal . . . not of a raw sexual nature, anyhow. It was more like a squeezing, then release of something deep inside him, resulting in this odd swelling sensation. He couldn't explain. All he knew was that it felt damn good.

"Do you know what your best body part is?" she asked, interrupting his disturbing thoughts.

He grinned. Opening his eyes fully now, he saw that she was propped on one elbow, gazing down at him.

"Not that," she said, pinching his shoulder. "It's your lips."

She was so close he could feel her breath fanning his parted lips, could feel her heart beating against his, could see the dark rings surrounding the clear blue irises of her eyes.

"Would you like me to kiss you, Cynthia?" His voice was so low and raspy he barely recognized it.

She cocked her head, considering. Then she sighed. "I guess not."

His body, which had stiffened with tense anticipation, slumped now with disappointment.

She rolled over on her back, and they reversed positions. She folded her arms behind her neck (causing the spandex to do incredible things across her chest . . . not that he was looking), and he leaned over her, braced on an elbow.

"Why?" he asked, trailing a fingertip over her puffy, bruised-rose lips. Her lips were one of her best features, too.

"Why what?" she whispered.

"Why don't you want me to kiss you?"

"Oh, I want you to kiss me, all right, but . . ."

That strange swelling in his heart grew and grew, like billowing clouds.

". . . but it's a road we can't travel. It would be a dead-end street for me." She let out a little breathy sigh of regret.

Her breath felt hot and wonderfully erotic against his fingertips. His fuzzy brain fought to understand her logic, but it was full of sensual clouds. "Why?" he choked out.

"Because you're a prince, and I'm a . . . commoner. It isn't done. You have to marry well for the sake of your people."

He had to laugh at that. "Cynthia, this is America. There are no class separations here." Briefly, he thought about telling her the truth, that he wasn't really a prince, but he didn't. For one thing, he was reluctant to shatter this incredible bond building between them. Plus, behind all the clouds fogging his thought processes, he still worried about his company and the danger this woman posed to its well-being.

"Yeah, but you're a *Spanish* prince. Don't deny that you're expected to marry some royal princess. *Noblesse oblige*, or some such thing."

"That's French."

"Same difference."

"I'll marry whomever I want," he informed her testily. When had this conversation steered its way to matrimony? Kissing was one thing, the big "I do" was another thing all together.

"Well, at the very least you'll be in the market for a trophy wife," she babbled on. "And foul-mouthed, materialistic, far-from-blue-blooded stock traders hardly qualify."

"I kind of like your foul mouth." He bobbed his eyebrows at her, trying to lighten the mood.

She ignored him. "I'll bet your uncle, the king, already has some European princess lined up for you. Are there any unmarried princesses in Maraco these days?"

"Cynthia," he reprimanded, "I'm not going to marry a freakin' princess."

"You have a pretty wicked mouth on you, too, Ferrama."

"Yeah," he agreed, with a grin that said there were some advantages to having a wicked mouth.

She tsk-tsked him, but the way she was staring at his mouth was very unsettling. Nice unsettling, not bad unsettling. *Oh, man, I better steer this conversation to safer ground.* He was still wary of her questions about marriage.

"Tell me why you never cry," he urged, taking a strand of her hair between thumb and forefinger and rubbing the satiny threads with sensuous appreciation. He even raised it to his nose to inhale the faint flowery scent left by her shampoo.

At first she didn't answer, seemingly enthralled by his fascination with her hair. Finally, she said, "My mother abandoned me when I was a baby. She was really young . . . only sixteen . . . and unmarried. Grandma had raised eight other children back in the old country . . . that's what she called Ireland . . . but Siobhan . . . my mother . . . was what she always termed 'the child of my old age, the child of my heart.' Grandpa died in the peat works before Siobhan was born."

P.T. put a closed fist to his mouth, studying Cynthia, whose eyes had gone misty blue with remembrance. His heart, which had been swelling with emotion a short time before, now constricted in empathy with her pain. He understood all too well how it felt to lose a parent at a young age. Hell, his father had blown the family nest before he'd even hatched. "Your father?" he inquired.

She shook her head. "I never knew my father. He was an American exchange student at the University of Dublin. Presumably he promised to marry my mother. That's why she went off with him to Chicago, but"— she shrugged—"he never did."

"Go on," he encouraged, skimming the palm of his hand up and down the smooth skin of her arm, from the edge of the short sleeve to the wrist, over and over, in comfort.

"Grandma followed Siobhan nine months later when she got a telegram telling of my birth. My mother was living in a shelter for the homeless at the time."

"Oh, Cynthia." What an ugly way to enter the world! And he'd thought his life in Puerto Rico had been bad.

Her chin jutted out with pride. "We survived, that's the most important thing. Anyhow, as soon as Grandma arrived and got us an apartment in one of the projects, Siobhan dumped all her responsibilities on Grandma. She had no job. Just welfare. That little bit she spent on clothes and parties. If it weren't for the food stamps, we probably would have starved. Finally, Siobhan just skipped off with a new boyfriend, this time a motor-cycle guy who was riding around the country, trying to find his soul." She gave him a rueful look. "He found it in Albuquerque, where he and my mother overdosed and died. I was two years old at the time."

Her voice was so devoid of emotion when she spoke of her mother's death that he wondered if she hadn't walled off all her anger and resentment and hurt. Like him? Hadn't he realized just a short time ago that he hadn't succumbed to tears for seventeen years? How long had it been since Cynthia had wept?

"Did your grandmother take you back to Ireland?"

"No. At first she stayed in Chicago, hoping my mother would get her act together. Later, she waited, expecting my mother to come home for me. By the time my mother died, Grandma was already working in a sewing factory, and she'd started a new life here. All her children . . . my aunts and uncles . . . were grown, with their own families back in Ireland. It was easier just to stay."

"Your grandmother must have been a strong woman."

Her somber face broke into a wide smile. "That would be an understatement. Picture Attila the Irish Hun."

He smiled back at her. "So, you grew up in the projects. What made you decide to go into finance?"

"Money."

He arched a questioning brow.

"You grew up with wealth; you wouldn't understand what it's like to be poor . . . to always yearn for better things . . . to feel like you don't belong."

Me? Not understand poverty? Hey, sweetheart, you're talking to the shoeshine kid here. This is P.T., world-class yearner. "Did you work when you were young?"

"No. It was too dangerous in our neighborhood. Grandma wouldn't even allow me to go out of our apartment. I used to read all the time . . . fairy tales. Oh, wipe that smirk off your face, Ferrama. I was a little girl then. Cut me some slack."

"So you were living in this ivory tower high-rise, dreaming of Prince Charming," he teased. A strangely alarming thought occurred to him. "Were there lots of princes in your life?"

She slanted him a disbelieving scowl. "No, but there were lots of toads." The unspoken implication was that he was one of the warty group. "Actually, I never dated much. Reading all those books paid off. When I was thirteen, Grandma talked a local priest into getting me a scholarship to a ritzy private girls' school in the suburbs . . . St. Bridget's Academy."

"You don't seem too happy about that."

"It was hell." Her face turned stormy. "If I felt like Little Orphan Annie pressing my face against the candy store window when I was a kid, I felt like I was pressing my nose to the country club gate at St. B's. You have no idea how cruel adolescent girls can be. There was never any question that I was the token poor person in the academy. And from day one it was hammered into me that I was inferior in breeding, gauche in manners, brassy in appearance"—she rolled her shoulders as if it didn't matter, although it clearly did—"a misfit."

And you're still trying to meet those impossible standards, he realized with sudden insight. *Brazen and aggressive on the outside, insecure and needy inside.*

"It wasn't any better at Harvard, where I got a scholarship. Believe me, money speaks everywhere.

So, taking a cue from the little girl who buried her face in fairy tales, I immersed myself in other books and became the best damn student in the world."

P.T. couldn't blame her for her hardened attitude. Though his motives were different, he was equally obsessed with amassing enough wealth to chuck the whole rat race. The difference was that she wanted to stay in the rat race . . . to be the mother of all rats herself.

"The girls at St. B's made me cry, but no one's been able to since then," Cynthia continued, summing up her rambling answer to his question about why she never cried. "Nope, I learned my lesson well. Make enough money so that no one will ever be able to look down on me again. Stop dreaming about fairy-tale happy endings and make my own dreams come true."

"Ah, *querida*, it won't work, you know."

"Why not?" she snapped, raising her chin defensively.

He chucked her playfully on the jaw in remonstrance. "Using financial success to measure your worth doesn't work. Believe me. I've been spinning that wheel for years. Don't get me wrong, I intend to make a ton of money with this stock offering. But I plan to use it as a means to another end."

"Charity?" Her eyes went wide with surprise. "You're going to give it away?"

He laughed. "Not quite. No, I'm going to use the profits to de-prince myself. I've learned that if you have enough wealth, you're free to be whoever you want."

"Why are you criticizing me, then? We both agree that money is the key to acceptance."

"Yes, but you want enough cash to fit into a certain strata of society. I want enough cash to escape its stranglehold."

"I don't understand."

"I just want to be a regular guy. Joe Schmoe, living in a small town, with a wife and two or three kids. Little League baseball. Pot roast. A minivan."

"Prince Beaver Cleaver," she scoffed.

"What's wrong with that?"

"Get real, Ferrama. You're caviar, not pot roast."

"I could be."

"God, what a pair we make! The would-be Wall Street princess and the prince who would rather abdicate."

With a smile, he leaned down and, without thinking, brushed his lips against hers. It was barely a kiss, so fleeting was the pressure, but his blood rushed like a river undammed.

She whimpered. "Don't."

"I must," he murmured against her mouth, compelled beyond all reason to connect with her. This time he settled his mouth more firmly over hers, moving his head from side to side, shaping her warm lips into pliancy.

She groaned into his open mouth.

He groaned back.

He kissed her for a long time, and she kissed him back. It was a gentle, unbroken movement of flesh against flesh, but so much more than that. With a wild roaring in his ears, he recognized that something wonderfully monumental was happening to him.

For the first time in seventeen years, he wanted to cry . . . with joy.

Finally, he pulled back and gazed at her. Tears brimmed in her eyes and she repeated in a soft whisper, "Don't."

"What?" He wanted to kiss her again, and hug her, and make love to her. But more than that. He wanted her in his bed and his life. He wanted . . . so many things. He settled for cupping her cheek with a gentle caress.

"Don't make me believe in dreams again."

His heart stopped, then jump-started again. "I want to make your dreams come true."

"Is that a line?"

"Is my eyebrow twitching?"

She examined his right eye for the telltale sign. "No."

"Well, then."

"But I think your nose is growing."

He smiled down at her and gave her smart mouth a quick nip of his teeth.

She inhaled sharply. She must be equally affected by this strange chemistry between them.

"It's not a line, Cynthia. It's the honest truth. And I don't understand it any more than you do."

"I'm scared."

"A scared shark?" he joked. *I'm scared, too, sweetheart. Real scared.*

"Do you think this is another phase of Elmer's spells?"

He frowned. He hadn't thought of that. "I don't know. Maybe. Actually, I don't care."

"What's happening to us?"

He was blindsided then with sudden understanding. *Oh, no! Oh, no, no, no!* "I think . . . *Dios mio!* . . . I think I'm falling in love with you."

Instead of sneering, or laughing, or making one of her crude remarks, Cynthia sighed. "I think I love you, too."

They both stared at each other in wonder. And alarm.

"This is horrible," she cried.

"Yes," he agreed, though it didn't feel horrible. He inhaled deeply with resignation and asked the only thing he could. "Will you marry me?"

A tear slid from the welling eyes of the woman who claimed she never wept. "Yes."

Chapter Thirteen

I love you . . . for now . . .

Less than twenty-four hours later, Cynthia Kathleen Sullivan and Prince Pedro Tomas de la Ferrama stood before the Reverend Elmer Presley, about to be married. They were waiting for Naomi and Ruth to arrive.

She glanced over at Ferrama, decked out in a double-breasted gold lamé wedding suit, with no shirt. The bell-bottom slacks sported a clasp the size of a brass hubcap and had Velcro sides, like the red ones. Sometimes she really wondered about Elmer. Or were these leftovers from Ruth's Chippendales ex-husband?

Cynthia complemented Ferrama perfectly in a gold lamé wedding sheath—a form-fitting, ankle-length, bimbo confection with a neckline cut down to her navel and a slit up the side from ankle to mid-thigh. On Jennifer Lawrence it would have looked great. She was not Jennifer Lawrence.

Her bridegroom was still arguing with Elmer over the whole spell business. Under normal circumstances, she would have been offended at his anger, but she understood the conflicting emotions that assailed her soon-to-be-husband. She shared them.

"I'm tellin' ya, laddie, the big godfather works in mysterious ways."

"*Mierda!* Enough with the godfather garbage. It was a spell, dammit."

Elmer winced at his sacrilegious language. Then he raised a hand to rub the black eye swelling one side of his face. It had been a gift from Ferrama the night before when Elmer had returned from his remarkably successful gig in Poughkeepsie.

"I'm tellin' ya, there was no spell. No drugs in your lemonade. No magic dust. Fairies don't work that way," Elmer said indignantly. Then he softened, addressing them both. "Miracles are a gift from God, my children. Never question a miracle."

"The only miracle is that I didn't kill you when I had the chance."

"You made us fall in love," Cynthia added. "That was a really underhanded trick."

Elmer gazed at her fondly, his good eye misting over with emotion. "Ah, Cindy, love is the greatest miracle of them all, not a trick. Your grandma is so pleased."

"Hmpfh!" He was probably right. Her grandma must be dancing a heavenly jig over her finally biting the marriage bullet. Not that this would be a real marriage. "Tell me again, Elmer, in what church were you ordained?"

"Church of The King," he answered without hesitation.

She and Ferrama exchanged a look that said clearly, "Bogus." Which was what they wanted, of course. As long as Elmer and Ruth and Naomi believed the marriage was legitimate, that was the most important thing. By tomorrow, Cynthia fully expected to be on her way back to Manhattan. The spell would be broken. No more love complications. She would be free to sue the hell out of the bunch of them.

But first she was going to have a wedding night. She deserved that much for all her pain and suffering. And being in love with Prince Ferrama was a real pain.

"Are you sure it's not the Presleyterian Church?" Ferrama snickered. "I recall hearing about that denomination during the hoopla a few years back commemorating the twentieth anniversary of Elvis's death. Or how about the Church of the Latter Day Elvis?"

Elmer drew his short body up with affront. He was wearing a black-sequinned cassock with a mini cape. A white rhinestone-studded clerical collar stood up in exaggerated Elvis fashion. "Elvis was the King," Elmer asserted fiercely, "but there is only one King of Kings. Best you remember not to profane Him or His holy sacrament, lest the wrath of the Almighty come down on you in just punishment."

"I think he's already punished me. I'm about to get married, aren't I?" Ferrama quipped.

Cynthia recoiled inside at the bitter words of the

man about to become her husband. It was okay for her to be using him in this marriage farce, but she didn't like the idea of his lack of enthusiasm. Not one bit. After all, he'd been the one who asked her.

Well, okay, the proposal had come under duress. A spell counted as duress, didn't it? And no way was she buying Elmer's contention that he hadn't zapped them with something. She couldn't have imagined that skin-tingling virtual foreplay, or their transformation into Elvis and Ann-Margret clones, or seeing Ferrama naked—*Lordy, Lordy!* Could she?

"Furthermore, you insolent pup," Elmer went on, "it's only the Lord who can make a racehorse out of a jackass. Don't tempt him to reverse the process."

"Are you saying I've got no pedigree?"

"No, I'm saying you're behaving like a jackass," Elmer snapped. "I didn't put a spell on you, boy, but I wouldn't be above slapping a curse or two on your ungrateful hide."

"I'm shivering in my boots," Ferrama retorted. "Or I would be if someone had given me a pair of shoes to wear." He glanced down pointedly at his bare feet.

"You should be fearful. I have some powerful curses at my disposal."

"Such as?" Ferrama scoffed.

"May the devil swallow you sideways. May there be no cream on your porridge nor on your cat a tail. May the flame be bigger and wider which will go through your soul than the Connemara mountains if they were afire. May you be afflicted with the itch and have no nails to scratch with. May a mountainslide land upon you. May you have a pig's snout on you and the mouth of a sheep."

"Enough already!" Ferrama said, holding up both hands in laughing surrender.

Irritated, Elmer stomped over to the doorway to see what was holding up Naomi and Ruth.

"We need to talk in private," Ferrama said suddenly, drawing her over to the side. She hobbled along beside him, using one crutch as a cane. With all the standing today, her toes were beginning to ache. Her feet were bare, too.

Easing down to a settee with his help—it was hard enough to stand in the tight sheath, let alone sit— Cynthia tried to adjust the slit that revealed all of one leg. Eventually, she gave up with disgust. To her even greater disgust, she turned to notice Ferrama's eyes glued to said leg with what could only be described as hunger.

Intense hunger.

She should have been angry. She should have let loose a crude, cut-to-the-bone insult. She should have done something . . . anything . . . to halt the hot ache of yearning his nearness engendered.

But, gol-ly, it was a heady, heady sensation being wanted by a man like him . . . a prince, for heaven's sake!

If it was only this childish prince fixation that attracted her to him, Cynthia could accept that. If it was only his sinfully enticing good looks, Cynthia could accept that, too. But there was a dangerous bond growing between them, its silken threads connecting and wrapping around them like a tender cocoon. If this was love, Cynthia feared she might never escape . . . even when the spell was long broken.

Deep in concentration, as if he was searching for

the right words, Ferrama took her one hand in both of his.

And her pulse skittered.

At sight of the fresh coat of neon pink nail polish Ruth had given her this afternoon, a flicker of a wicked smile tilted up one corner of his mouth, Elvis-style, revealing a tiny dimple.

And she remembered what he'd said one day— teasing, no doubt—about how he'd like to make love in the dark with those glowing nails traveling all over his body. Her temperature rose about ten degrees.

But then his expression became serious as he tipped up her chin with one finger so she was staring directly into his eyes. The fingers of his other hand laced with hers.

For a long moment, their gazes held, and awareness swirled around them like fairy dust.

He made a rough sound deep in his throat.

She whimpered.

"We don't have to do this," he said, giving her a last-minute chance for escape. From the marriage, anyhow.

"Yes, we do." Cynthia tried to pull her hand from his clasp, but he held tight. "Naomi will never let us go. This is our only shot. If you want an out, don't look to me for an excuse."

"I don't want out, Cynthia," he said in a husky voice. "More than anything in the world right now, I want in."

Her face heated under that suggestive double entendre. "That's lust speaking, and Elmer's spell."

"Undoubtedly." He didn't seem at all concerned.

"Don't you care?" she cried.

"I care too much, that's the problem."

Oh, he is such a snake-oil charmer! It's a line he's probably used a thousand times before. But I wish . . . oh, God, how I wish . . . "This is no way to get married."

"No, it's not," he agreed. "If things could be different, though, I think I would still want . . . well, this isn't the time for that." He seemed to have trouble swallowing.

What had he been about to say? Cynthia's heart hammered at all the possibilities. Impossibilities, really. But her foolish heart was beyond reason.

"I always imagined that when I got married, it would be in a church filled with family and friends," he confessed sheepishly. "There would be organ music and tons of flowers and my bride coming down the aisle in a white wedding gown."

Her jaw dropped at the idea of a man harboring the typical female dream. Not her, of course, because she refused to be typical. And she'd lost her dreams long ago. "I never imagined getting married at all." *Except back when I was a little girl and still believed in dreams-come-true.*

"Oh, Cynthia," he murmured, patting her shoulder in sympathy.

She slapped his hand away. A pity bride? That she couldn't countenance. "And as to the bride-in-white business, honey, well, if you're expecting a pure-as-undriven-snow virgin, forget it. I've been through the slush a time or two."

He let out a hoot of laughter and shook his head at her. "You never let me down, sweetheart. Always have to get in the last word, don't you? And better yet, a coarse one, guaranteed to shock."

"Whatever." She glared at him for a moment, barely restraining herself from blurting out that, despite her crude boast, she wasn't all that experienced. Instead, she pointed out, "It won't be a valid marriage." It was more a question than a statement.

He nodded. "When we get back to the city, you'll be able to unsaddle me faster than an Irish Thorough-bred."

She had to smile at that analogy, especially since Elmer had implied he was more a jackass. "Which of us would be the horse and which the saddle?"

He smiled back, and her heart skipped a beat. He was so damn gorgeous. "We could take turns," he offered, wagging his eyebrows at her.

"I give a rough ride," she countered, to her horror. It was especially horrifying because she never engaged in this kind of provocative flirtation. He must be repulsed by her vulgarity. She was.

Instead, Ferrama tugged her closer and breathed in her ear. "Ah, *querida*, I never expected any less from you."

Tears smarted her eyes, and she attempted to avert her gaze.

Cupping her chin, he forced her to look at him again. "Don't you dare go self-conscious on me now. I have big plans. And expectations."

Big plans? What kind of plans? Oh, my! And expectations? Of me? Oh, my! Behind them, Cynthia heard Ruth and Naomi talking as they entered the room. Elmer put a record on the machine, Elvis's rendition of

"It's Now or Never," presumably the wedding march. Panic rose up in her.

"Are we going to do the deed, Cynthia?"

Despite her misgivings, despite all reason, despite her fears, she didn't even hesitate. "Yes."

Suddenly, she knew. It didn't matter if this marriage lasted for an hour or a decade. She wanted it . . . more than escape, even.

He drew her to her feet and handed her the crutch. Standing close, he whispered, "I love you, Cynthia."

"For now," she emphasized, seeking to dampen the wild emotion his precious words ignited.

He shrugged, and she didn't know if that meant he concurred or he didn't care.

"I love you, too," she declared. It was only fair that she return his sentiment.

"For now?" Oddly, he wasn't smiling as he asked the question.

"For now," she said. But inside, an unsettling voice insisted, *For always.*

It was short and sweet . . .

The wedding was over in a remarkably short period of time.

Naomi, who'd stood out of chain's reach in the doorway, had brought two bottles of aged wine from the cellar.

Ruth had prepared a nuptial feast of Spanish paella and Irish soda bread. And, of course, fried peanut butter and banana finger sandwiches.

No longer angry at Ferrama, Elmer had slipped

him a special gift—protection against a particular "curse." Cynthia didn't have the heart to tell the little Elvis, although she did confide it to her new husband later, that she was already protected and had no need for what appeared to be a gross of condoms.

Elmer had outdone himself in performing what certainly had all the rituals of a traditional marriage ceremony, except for his closing remarks. To Cynthia, he'd said, "An Irishwoman carries her heart in her hand. Praise the Lord!" To her new husband, he'd advised, placing her hand in Ferrama's, "Cherish the gift divine destiny has given you."

Then he'd raised his eyes heavenward and prayed, "May the Lord keep you in his hand and never close his fist too tight."

As a final clincher, he'd concluded, "In the eyes of God and all the heavenly hosts, including Elvis, I now pronounce you, Pedro, and you, Cindy, to be man and wife . . . prince and princess for all time."

He loved her not-so-tender . . .

They were finally alone.

P.T. took one last sip of wine and set the crystal glass aside. He didn't require any more booze to fuel the buzz in his head . . . a buzz caused more by his rising arousal than alcohol.

On the other side of the room, nervously twirling the stem of her own empty wineglass, was his blushing bride. And she *was* blushing, all the way down her exposed cleavage and all the way up her side slit.

He crooked his finger at her.

She set her glass on the card table and crooked her finger back at him.

Well, you outrageous thing, you! I guess you showed me. Only belatedly did he realize that she had interpreted the gesture as an overbearing, presumptuous order . . . an imperial summons . . . not the seductive lure he'd intended it to be.

But what the hell . . . go for it. He smiled. His lazy, I-can-do-things-you-can't-imagine smile.

She looked as if she'd like to bolt through the open window. Or upchuck.

He was betting on the former, and his legendary charm. With deliberate slowness, he unbuttoned his garish jacket and shrugged it off, dropping it to the floor.

She licked her lips, watching.

So far, so good. The buzz in his head intensified. Holding her eyes, he undid the clasp on his belt and let it slip from his fingers. Unfortunately, it clunked to the floor . . . not the best mood enhancer.

She blinked, putting a hand over her heart. And she licked her lips again. Apparently she'd missed the clunk.

Slow down, slow down, slow down, he cautioned himself. A losing battle.

Maybe I should reconsider this whole marriage business. Maybe some guidelines are needed before we go any farther. Maybe Cynthia and I should sit down and talk.

Yeah, right!

With trembling fingers, he fumbled with the Velcro fastening on his stripper slacks and let them pool at his feet. There was something to be said for stripper slacks, he thought with utter irrelevance. He wore only his shamrock shorts now. But only for a second. He shucked those, too.

She made a soft, mewling moan.

Only then did he crook his finger at her again.

She raised her chin, about to balk, and flashed him one of those "as-if!" looks she did so well. But then she seemed to reconsider. With mischievous eyes dancing, she gathered her gold gown in two fists, thigh high, and began to bunch the filmy fabric so the hem rose inch by inch. She stopped at the knee. *No, no, no!* Then she took one step toward him. Only one. *Yes, yes, yes!*

Heart hammering, he matched her one step. But it was a big one.

Her lips turned up slightly in a Mona Lisa smile of mystery. While inching her gown up to mid-thigh, she took another hip-swaying step toward him.

P.T. loved her legs, all five hundred miles of them. He really did. And he was seeing a whole lot of them right now. More than anything, he wanted to lunge at her. But he was a prince. Princes didn't behave in such an uncouth manner. They had a reputation to uphold. *Hell!* With monumental restraint, he took only one more step. But his stride was so wide it probably resembled a split.

Was that a giggle he heard from her? No, sharks didn't giggle. He'd forgotten to crook his finger this time.

And still the hem was rising. In the background, Elvis was working himself into a feverish pitch, something about "temperature's rising." As Cynthia's hem rose, so did Elvis's voice, and P.T.'s body heat. Fever, to be sure.

Enough was enough! With a hiss of pure male

frustration, he closed the distance between them, taking the teasing witch into his tight embrace. He had no idea what those disjointed words were that he was murmuring against her mouth, into the sweet shell of her ear, along the curve of her shoulder. He was pretty sure, though, that the soft purring sounds she was making indicated pleasure. That and her squirming body, which was helping to accommodate his overeager hands as they clutched the sleekness of her gown from the back, shoving it higher and higher. With a triumphant cry, he maneuvered it over her head. It flew over his shoulders and landed with a whoosh.

For a long moment he did nothing but savor the delicious sensation of her naked body pressed against his naked body. Eyes squeezed tightly shut, he nudged her closer.

She raised her arms and burrowed her fingers in his hair.

He put one hand on the small of her back, the other on her nape, under her luxuriant hair. She was a tall woman—at least five-foot-eight—and their body heights conformed to each other well. Very well. His erection pressed against her lower belly, its tip nudging the curls at her vee.

Myriad emotions swirled over and through him, like a sensory mist. There was bone-melting arousal, of course, but equally potent was the humbling need he had to not only make love to this woman, but to love her. She was his now . . . *his*, and he didn't care if the marriage was valid or not.

There was no doubt that soon he would give her pleasure and receive pleasure in return, but his heart unfurled with a desire to keep her at his side, to protect her, to cherish her, to fulfill her dreams, to give her children, to share her secrets, and his, and maybe even cry with her some day, if necessary. In effect, he wanted to slay all her dragons, to be her knight and live happily ever after in whatever magic castle she chose. Even on the Upper West Side.

With that whimsical thought, he put his hands on her forearms and stepped back a pace to get his first good look at his mate. His senses reeled. "Gorgeous," he sighed.

"No, I'm not," she started to demur.

He put a fingertip to her lips. "Yes, you are. You're gorgeous and you're mine."

"I'm not—"

"Shhh. You're mine," he repeated.

She stood still, arms at her sides, as he examined her from blushing cheeks to blushing breasts to blushing belly to blushing thighs, even to blushing toes. He brushed the backs of his fingers over her nipples, which were large as berries, and hard.

She bowed her back and keened, a low, wanton plea.

He cupped the mounds from underneath and lifted so the points stabbed his palms.

She whimpered.

He placed a hand on the slight swell of her stomach. The muscles lurched against his skin.

He considered touching her elsewhere but bridled the impulse. For now.

Raising his eyes back to her face, he saw that her lips were parted and she was breathing erratically. He skimmed the pad of his thumb over her mouth, and she nipped at him.

She put her hands on his forearms then, forcing his hands to his sides. And she began her own visual exploration.

"You're the one who's gorgeous," she said in a breathy whisper. "And you're mine."

More than you know, honey. More than you know. He felt her eyes, like a caress, as they moved from his face to his flat nipples, which he wished she would touch.

She did.

His penis hardened and lengthened with just that passing of fingernails over sensitive nubs.

He groaned.

She did it again.

"Cynthia," he warned.

She chuckled with satisfaction. And moved lower. Using the knuckles of one hand, she traced the path of his chest hairs, over his abs, his navel and—*oh, my God!*—along the rock-hard length of him.

His mind went blank then and a buzzing roar erupted in his ears. With a triumphant howl that could be described only as a battle cry, he grabbed her by the waist and lifted her high against his body. To the pounding rhythm of Elvis belting out "I want you, I need you, I love you," he walked her to the bed. He was only dimly aware of her nipples rubbing his, her stomach flush against his, her arms wrapped around his shoulders, her legs around his hips, her cleft aligned with his shaft.

He tossed her onto the bed and followed her down.

In one fluid motion, he nudged her legs apart and entered her hot wetness, to the hilt. He penetrated so deep . . . to the heart of her . . . and then swelled even more. A perfect fit. A perfect, perfect, perfect fit.

He didn't move. He couldn't.

"Wait!" he heard through the haze of his overpowering excitement.

Wait? Oh, no! Please, God, no nonconsummation spells now. He braced himself on extended arms and raised his head slightly to peer down at her. "Cynthia, you couldn't possibly expect me to stop now. Chivalry goes only so far."

She giggled, an incongruous girlish reaction whose ripples could be felt all along the length of him. "Your watch is caught in my hair. That's all I meant."

"Oh." Within seconds the strand was free, and he was braced on his arms again, staring down at her.

"I don't want you to stop," she said softly.

"Good. Because I can't."

Her lips parted with a slight smile as she widened her thighs and drew her knees closer to her chest.

And, unbelievably, he thickened and elongated even more, stretching and filling her molten folds.

Her eyes went huge with wonder.

He would have given himself a pat on the back for being so wonderful if he weren't paralyzed with arousal. In some remote, idiot portion of his head, brain-shocked by bliss, he tucked away a good name for a new shoe, "Ecstasy."

He groaned and lowered his open mouth over hers, murmuring against her lips. "I'm . . . out . . . of . . . control . . . here . . . babe."

"Good," she breathed, nibbling his bottom lip.

He felt himself pulse inside her.

And she pulsed back.

He gritted his teeth and arched his neck to withstand the sheer ecstasy.

Raising her bottom off the bed, she rolled her hips from side to side, once, twice, in encouragement.

What little self-control he still maintained shattered then. "This won't be sweet and gentle," he warned, moving them higher on the mattress and guiding her hands upward to grasp the head rails of the bed. "I'm sorry."

"Don't be sorry." She was panting as heavily as he was.

"Jack-hammer sex," he elaborated, wanting to be sure she understood, "isn't the way a man should take the woman he loves for the first time."

She blinked several times against the misting in her eyes. "Any way you want me, love. I'm yours."

With a guttural male growl of exultant surrender, he pulled out of her, then slammed back in.

Fierce shudders rocked her, and she screamed her pleasure.

Long, *excruciatingly long* strokes soon shortened as he rode her hard, barely aware of her convulsing around him in repeated orgasms while he palmed her bottom, elevating her higher, or laved a deliciously pebbled nipple, or placed a hand between their slickness, strumming her to wailing heights of urgency.

"I love you, love you, love you," he shouted thickly as he surged into her one last time, shooting his essence clear to her womb as her body pumped him with continuous, nonstop spasms.

Only dimly was he aware, as blood drained from his head and he sensed himself drifting into instant sleep, or a coma, that it was the best damn lovemaking he'd ever experienced. He smiled to himself, thinking that shark sex had to be the world's best-kept secret.

Or maybe love made all the difference.

Chapter Fourteen

And then he turned into a hunka, hunka burning love, or she did, or they both did. Whatever. It was hot . . .

"Wake up, Sleeping Beauty. Your prince has come."

Cynthia must have drifted off. She heard the soft words through a vapor of floating sensations . . . satiation, drowsiness, amazement and, most of all, a new, gently unfurling love, so intense it took her breath away.

She opened her eyes to find her husband braced on one elbow staring down at her. "Boy, did my prince come!" she murmured sleepily.

He tweaked her playfully on the chin. "That's not what I meant. Your prince has come to take you away from your mundane world to a land of fantasy, where all your dreams come true."

Fantasy? Dreams? I have no dreams, she thought in a panic. But what she said was, "Who says my world's mundane?"

"Anything will seem mundane after tonight, my princess," he boasted with silky promise.

"You're not short on ego are you, Lancelot?"

"Just call me Lance." He grinned. "Seriously, a knight must be ever confident if he is to go about storming castles."

"How many castles were you planning on storming?"

"Just one," he drawled, placing his fingertips against the pulse in her throat and lowering his lips toward hers. Before he sealed the kiss, he said thickly, "I give you fair warning, my lady, it's going to take a long time."

"A slow assault?" she managed to get out as she tunneled her fingers through his thick hair, pulling him closer.

"*Very* slow."

"Woe is me."

He smiled against her parted mouth. "Woe is we."

"The spell might fade away any minute," she reminded him.

"Then you'll be back to thinking me a toad."

"You're a toad, regardless."

He nipped her bottom lip. "You better like toads, then, because we're going to take advantage of every minute of this honeymoon while the mood lasts."

"The slow assault?"

"The *very* slow assault."

The prince was true to his promise. This time his lovemaking was a prolonged, muted arousal. If their first coming together had resembled the eye of a hurricane, now they were caught in a summer storm . . . slow building but equally powerful in its force.

"Love Me Tender" wasn't just a song title; it became her lover's credo.

Kisses. At first there were only kisses. Endless, drugging kisses that went on and on. Supremely, agonizingly tender. A woman's dream come true.

Her mouth. "Can you taste how much I want you?" he murmured mid-kiss.

Yes, yes, yes, yes, yes, yes.

Her ears. "Can you hear me panting for you?"

I thought it was me.

Her arching throat. "I can feel your heartbeat racing, love. Slow down. Slow down."

How does one slow a runaway train? Or an out-of-control fantasy?

Her palms and wrists, the insides of her elbows. "So soft! You're so damned soft."

Oh, my! Who knew? Who knew?

Her breasts—oh, Lord, her breasts! How he kissed her taut nipples! But only the lightest skimming of warm lips over turgid flesh. And the delicate undersides. "Beautiful, beautiful, beautiful."

I . . . can't . . . stand . . . much . . . more . . . of . . . this. She wanted him to linger there. She told him so, "Please," and gripped his head, trying to hold him in place. To no avail.

"Too soon, *mí corazón*, too soon." Ignoring her breasts, which swelled and ached unbearably for kneading fingers and deep suckling, he resumed his tantalizing trail of kisses. He had his own map and his own driving agenda.

Her stomach got his attention next. A warm kiss brushing over the sensitive palette, with only the flicker of a tongue inside her navel. Her muscles clenched and unclenched in response. Couldn't he see that her defenses were falling brick by erogenous brick? Surely it was time to cross the moat.

When he kissed her inner thighs, she parted for him. But he bypassed that intimate invitation. Instead, he traced his lips down one leg, over her toes, then up the other leg, rasping barely coherent words of appreciation the entire time.

Then . . . oh, then . . . he nudged her legs wide with his knees and kissed her *there*. He settled his lips over that secret part of her and shifted his kiss from side to side. Once, twice, that's all. But it was like hot oil poured over crumbling battlements. More fuel on already ignited embers.

To her dismay, the rogue knight retreated and sat back on his heels. He watched her expectantly.

Suddenly, without warning, she came. A fluttery orgasm of progressively more intense spasms accompanied by involuntary short jerks of her hips.

And still she mewled for more, reaching out her arms for him.

He shook his head with a soft smile and commenced the second phase of his assault. Touching. Wonderfully expert, torturous touching.

"Your hands are magic," she said.

"No, love, I just bring out the magic in you."

He explored her face with fingertips so light that the downy hairs on her skin rose to meet them, like sensory magnets. Her eyelids, the outline of her mouth, the fine bones of her cheek and jaw. And all along he whispered low, velvety words of wonder, punctuated by the refrain, "And you are mine."

When he grazed her collarbone and the vulnerable curve of her neck with the knuckles of one hand, she felt something long buried inside her break free. How could such a nonsexual caress create such erotic havoc? This was sex at its best, and yet it was so much more than mere sex. It was a celebration of all that was good between a man and a woman.

Through a glaze of excitement, she watched her husband . . . her lover . . . her prince . . . as he bent over her. His ebony hair took on gilded shades of brilliance from the many candles Ruth had lit around the room. The tiny gold loop earring glittered in his right ear. Flickering flames created enticing planes of light and shadow on the dark skin of his lean body.

And you are mine, she thought, mimicking the poignant vow he'd been repeating to her in an endless litany.

When he came to her breasts this time, he stayed. For a long time.

With loving care, he pleasured and worshiped her there. As if sensing her oversensitivity, his hands and mouth, even his teeth, were gentle to the point of agony. No matter if he was pushing her breasts high from underneath, or teasing the mounds with feathery fingertips, or kissing the hard, hard nipples, always his tongue came back to lave the tips with wetness. When he took a nipple into his mouth, deeply, aureole and all, his suckling had a gentle, soul-reaching rhythm.

And the phrases he used to pay homage to her femininity were wickedly outrageous, enough to make a fair maiden blush. Good thing she wasn't a maiden, she thought irrelevantly at one stage, though the candle glow on her ivory skin did turn her fair . . . fairer and more beautiful than she'd ever been before.

Not surprisingly, she came again.

And, not surprisingly, he would not come into her.

"It's too much," she whimpered, reaching out for him. "Too much."

"It's not enough, *querida*," he said. "Not nearly enough." All this, despite the fact that his breathing was erratic, his hands trembled with restraint and his erection stood out with rampant need.

Parting her curls with one deft hand, he stroked her slickness, then entered her depths with one, two, three long fingers, pumping her to yet another climax. He had to hold the other hand flat against her breastbone to keep her from bolting up off the bed.

To her frustration, he moved on to her legs, the backs of her knees, her toes, the soles of her feet. She'd never dreamed a lover's hands could be so hot and tender at the same time. She'd never dreamed there were so many erogenous zones on a woman's body. She'd never dreamed she could love a man as much as she loved him. She'd never dreamed, period . . . at least, not for a very long time.

Then, when she thought he would at last join with her, he rolled over onto his back and guided her hands to him, urging her to explore his body in like fashion.

"This power you exert over me . . . it frightens me," she confessed.

"Ah, sweetheart, the only power I have is what you give me."

With hushed words and sighs and gasps, he showed her all the ways she could pleasure and torture him, as well. And, without words, he showed her how her surrendering to his masterful seduction had rendered her the conqueror.

When at last she'd touched and admired and kissed and, yes, even bitten, almost every part of him, she circled his hard, ridged maleness with both hands.

Releasing a roar of capitulation at her unrelenting persuasion, he lifted her by the waist and eased her down onto the steely length and breadth of him.

For an instant, neither of them could breathe, or move, as she pulsed around him.

And then, still imbedded in her, he rolled her over onto her back, braced himself on extended arms and, with neck thrown back in corded torment, he stroked and stroked and stroked her, in and out, flooding her body with a neverending flow of love and rising urgency. Finally, through the blinding light of her own shattering explosion, she heard herself scream and him cry out, hurtling them both into a new place where wild passion and pure love mingled and became one.

It was a slice out of time. One of those special gifts the gods sometimes deign to grant humans. No matter what else happened, she would cherish this miracle forever.

"I love you, Cynthia," he murmured against her damp neck.

"I love you, too," she whispered, pressing a soft kiss to the top of his head.

And somewhere from her memory came an old reminder of her grandma's, "What the winds of God bring, the rains of God can wash away."

Surely God would not be so cruel.

For the first time in many, many years, Cynthia said a little prayer. And added in an undertone, "Take a hike, Grandma."

She thought she heard a distant voice croon, "Fairy tales can come true, it can happen to you . . ." followed by the tinkle of laughter. She wondered for one insane moment if it was an answer to her prayer, accompanied by Grandma's mirthful reaction to her advice. But, no, it was probably Elmer playing one of his records in the distant reaches of the castle and Ruth laughing at one of his miserable riddles.

Or was it?

Her husband raised his head to gaze at her with what could only be described as adoration.

God, I can't believe this gorgeous man is really my husband. I mean, he's not really my husband in the legal sense, of course, but still the thought makes me humble.

"What's that song you're singing?" he asked drowsily. *Song? He'd heard the song, too?*

"Nothing," she replied with a smile.

Cynthia realized then that she'd never lost her dreams, not totally. She'd just been waiting for her prince to come.

Company's coming! . . .

Unfortunately, the honeymoon didn't last long.

At ten o'clock the next morning, P.T. half-reclined in the sybaritically long and deep antique tub, taking a bubble bath with his new wife, who half-reclined at the opposite end.

He'd picked her up and carried her into the bathroom a short time earlier when it became apparent she was going to play that universal female morning-after game. Analysis and Second Thoughts.

"I shouldn't have done this," she'd moaned.

Yeah, right.

"It was a mistake."

Not in my book.

"Don't look at me. I'm naked."

Trust me, babe, I've seen all your secrets.

"Did you seduce me?"

His answer was a grin, which prompted her to punch him in the stomach—his cue to take a break.

The water was deliberately hot to ease muscles aching from a long night of deliciously energetic lovemaking. Now that she'd lost her shyness once again—*thank you, God!*—they were feeding each other strawberries dipped in champagne, which a surprisingly considerate Naomi must have left after the wedding ceremony.

He stretched out his legs, ignoring the creaking of his abused knees, and poked his big toe against one of Cynthia's sweet spots. She had lots of them, he'd discovered through their endless wedding night. He anticipated the chore of locating more. *Chore? Ah, a man's work is never done.*

Cynthia arched a brow at him and stretched out one of her own long legs, tweaking him in one of his own sweet spots. His favorite, actually.

Peter perked up.

That was when all hell broke loose.

"The Mafia's coming! The Mafia's coming!" Naomi shrieked, running into the bedroom. She stopped dead in her construction worker boots and let out a squeal of embarrassment at viewing them in the tub through the open bathroom door.

"Go away," he ordered.

A beet-red Cynthia sunk deeper into the bubbles.

Naomi turned her back on them but didn't budge. "Get out of the tub, P.T., and forget about your damn libido for once."

"I'm going to kill you, Naomi, I swear I am."

"You'll have to stand in line, big boy. The Mafia has first dibs."

The Mafia?

He and Cynthia exchanged a puzzled frown and rose as one, like two dolphins, sloshing water over the side. Unfortunately, they had only little hand towels with which to dry themselves.

Ever practical, Cynthia stomped proudly into the bedroom, a buck-naked goddess. She trailed a stream of water in her wake right in front of Naomi, whose gasp could be heard all the way into the bathroom.

"You'd better be careful you don't stain that Oriental carpet," Naomi griped to her back. "It's worth—"

He spat out a really foul expletive that shut his stepsister up . . . for the moment, at least.

Angrily, Cynthia pulled the top sheet off the rumpled bed, quickly dried herself with it, then stomped back to the bathroom to hand the damp linen to him. He started to suggest that she go back and get a dry pillowcase or two, got one glimpse of her clenched jaw and changed his mind.

Fifteen minutes later he was dressed in the red Elvis suit with black sequins and Cynthia was wearing the purple spandex bimbo dress while Naomi fumbled to unlock their chains. They were finally going to escape the castle, but not in any way he'd ever imagined.

They had exactly two hours to flee the castle before the Cosa Nostra arrived.

To his amazement and consternation (anger would come later), Naomi had tried to negotiate her own deal for the stock offering . . . with the Mafia, of all things! Then she'd changed her mind. Apparently one didn't change one's mind with the Mafia. This had to be the dumbest, most dangerous thing Naomi had ever done.

"Naomi, this is the dumbest, most dangerous thing you've ever done."

She clamped her lips tight and said nothing—a clear sign of how scared she was. He was beginning to get a little scared himself.

The metal links of the dog collar that had been wrapped around his ankle clanked to the floor. He took the key from Naomi's trembling hands and proceeded to release Cynthia's manacle, as well.

"Tell me again, how do you know that they're coming after you? Could it be a joke? Maybe you misunderstood. Are you sure they're the Mafia?" he demanded.

"They probably sent her a horse's head," Cynthia quipped.

He shot her a scowl of reproval. She was not taking this situation seriously enough.

"There was a telegram delivered this morning," Naomi replied. "I checked all the rooms, and there was no horse's head."

Gawd! She has to be kidding. "You checked all

one hundred and three rooms in this crumbling heap? For a horse's head?"

"Yes, I checked every room in this *castle*, you creep. Can you think of anyone else who would have been willing to do it for me?"

When no one answered, Naomi went on, "The telegram said: 'Deliver signed stocks. Noon. Alternative: Sleeping with fishes.'"

"How does a good girl from Hoboken get involved with the Mafia?" Cynthia asked, continuing to shake her head with confusion.

Naomi shrugged. "They approached me."

"Where?" P.T. snapped.

"At the hardware store in Newark."

He groaned and raked his fingers through his hair. "Why would the Mafia be interested in a shoe company?"

"Actually, the Mafia has been attempting to infiltrate a lot of companies lately, even brokerage firms," Cynthia informed him. "Money laundering, drug fronts . . . that kind of thing."

"Now you tell me," he growled.

"I told you to let me handle this for you," Cynthia scolded Naomi, who was, unbelievably, making the bed, muttering something about not wanting to leave her castle in disarray.

"You knew about this?" He straightened to glare at the strawberry-blond traitor.

"Well, Naomi hinted that she was going to sell off a large block of stock to break some trust fund, and I advised her—"

"How could you, Cynthia? Behind my back?"

"Now wait a minute, I'm not the guilty party here. I just—"

"Your own husband? You would stab your own husband in the back?"

"You weren't my husband at the time. Hell, you're not my husband now, either—"

"Don't be so sure about that," Naomi yelled from the bathroom. She was draining the water from the tub and picking up the damp towels and the sheet. With a snort of disgust, she regarded the puddles on the tiled floor.

"Don't be so sure about what?" he and Cynthia asked at the same time.

"The marriage."

"Huh?" he and Cynthia said, like twin parrots.

"Elmer showed me some legal documents last night. I think . . . now don't get all shook up . . . I think he might be an honest-to-God, licensed preacher."

"A *real* marriage?" he and Cynthia exclaimed, instantly recognizing the implications. They glanced at each other with horror. At least she appeared horrified. He was feeling a little thrum of pleasure that he was actually married to the woman he loved. And, yes, he was still in love with the Wall Street shark. Elmer's love spell hadn't worn off yet, and he was beginning to hope it never did.

"You swore he wasn't a legitimate minister," he accused Naomi, who was done with her housewifely chores and approached them rather hesitantly. "You said it would be a sham."

He immediately wished he could bite back the incriminating words.

"When did you two discuss this potentially bogus

marriage?" Cynthia asked, her eyes narrowing suspiciously.

"Now, honey—"

She socked him in the stomach . . . for the second time that day. And it wasn't even ten-thirty.

"Don't you honey me, you . . . you rat! You planned this marriage all along, didn't you . . . long before Elmer's spell? Last night was all a setup."

Though she hadn't really hurt him, he hunched over at the waist and moaned, giving himself time to regroup. That was a buzz word Dick used a lot for creative lying. "It was not . . . I did not," he protested, going for the wounded, hangdog expression.

He could tell she didn't buy it. His eyebrow was probably twitching.

"It's the truth," Naomi said, surprising P.T. by coming to his defense. He reminded himself to mark this red-letter day on his calendar when he got back to the city. "I told P.T. that marriage would be a good idea, a way to bring you over to our side, but he said I should see a psychiatrist."

Cynthia turned wounded eyes on him.

"Thanks a lot, Naomi," he grumbled.

"Well, is everyone ready to rock 'n' roll out of here? It's TCB time," Elmer announced brightly as he ambled into the room in a shocking pink pearl-studded jumpsuit, teetering on his high-heeled blue suede boots. Ruth followed him in a matching pink spandex jumpsuit, teetering on a pair of glittery gold Ferrama stiletto heels, appropriately named Midas Madness.

P.T. crossed his eyes, feeling on the verge of madness himself.

"Isn't this exciting?" Ruth chirped, scooting over to Cynthia with the little birdlike steps necessitated by her high heels. She gave his wife a hug. "The Mafia! Just imagine. I bet we'll be on CNN, or something."

"Have you got your dream back, Cindy girl?" Elmer slanted Cynthia a sly, knowing wink.

She blushed.

P.T. tried to catch her eye to see just what that blush signified, but she deliberately averted her gaze. Meanwhile, Elmer and Ruth dropped to the floor and began to put old 45 rpm records in a cardboard suitcase.

"What are you doing?" In the midst of a presumably dangerous situation, these two dingbats were packing away records.

"I'm not leaving without my record collection," Elmer asserted. "And my guitar."

"I already packed your costumes in tissue and put them in the back of the limo," Ruth informed him.

Elmer smiled his approval at her.

"And I've got to get the Winslow Homer," Naomi said, heading for the door.

"Who's Winston Homely?" P.T. asked. "You've got some guy stashed here? Where? And his name is Winston? Geesh!"

Naomi gave Cynthia a look that said "See?"

He didn't see, at all.

"I'm taking the dining room chairs with me, too. No way am I leaving behind my Philadelphia Queen Anne chairs. And—"

"Have you ever thought about getting a real life, Naomi?" he snarled with exasperation.

"Have you ever thought about taking a good golly gander at your own life, brother dear?" Naomi snarled back. She addressed the remainder of her remarks to Cynthia. "Who knows what destruction those hoodlums might inflict on my priceless chairs!"

"Winslow Homer is a famous artist," Cynthia explained to P.T. "His paintings are worth a fortune. And the dining room chairs are presumably valued at a hundred thousand dollars each."

P.T. gaped at Cynthia and then at that sneaky Naomi, who hadn't bothered to tell him that *his* castle housed such treasures.

"Well, we don't have the time or the space for that crap," he decided, "worthless or otherwise."

"We can take that orange truck of yours and the limo," Naomi insisted.

"It . . . is . . . not . . . orange," he said through gritted teeth.

"You could always let the dogs loose to guard the palace," Cynthia offered as a compromise to Naomi.

If he didn't already love Cynthia, he would now. What a doll!

"Uh-uh. No way!" Elmer said, straightening to his full five-foot-five. "Wherever I go, my hound dogs go."

As they left the castle a short time later, each of them carrying a dining room chair, he made the mistake of tossing out a teasing comment to Cynthia. "Do you think we'll tell our grandchildren about this one day?"

That was when she gave him his third sucker punch of the day.

A Graceland road trip . . .

The pickup truck was loaded high with bungee-strapped dining room chairs, not one but five paintings, a suitcase of records and a guitar. The driver was a short guy in a pink Elvis suit with his left elbow leaning on the window and his right arm wrapped around his big-haired sweetie in a matching Vegas-chic outfit. The two goofballs, oblivious to the danger surrounding them, were harmonizing—if it could be called that—on one Elvis tune after another.

In the lead of this two-vehicle caravan was a limo driven by a Spanish prince in a red Elvis suit, complete with wide lapels, black sequins, huge shoulder pads, mini-cape and an industrial-sized belt. His fuming princess sat beside him, wearing a purple spandex dress that would cause the royal guard in any kingdom to revolt. (She was still mad over the presumed marriage plot; but then, he was mad that she hadn't told him Naomi was about to stab him in the back.) In the back seat, Naomi was trying her best to ignore the six smelly, wailing hound dogs shedding their mangy fur all over her. P.T. suspected the yip-yip-yipping dogs had some extra sense that tuned into Elmer's singing behind them, like dogs hearing a high-pitched squeal that no human could.

When P.T. pulled over to a roadside gas station to fill up, one customer after another did a double take on seeing his gang emerge from their vehicles like a troupe of carnival freaks. He would have laughed if it wasn't for the sobering fact that on the far side of the interstate he saw a black Cadillac whiz by in the opposite direction. He couldn't tell through the tinted windows if the passengers had seen him, but since the car didn't slow down, he figured they were safe. For now.

He paid for the gas and the package of crackers and can of diet soda Cynthia slammed on the counter in front of him. It would serve her right if her crackers crumbled. They were about to walk out the gas station door when the pimply faced attendant observed, "Do you guys know that you're not wearing shoes?"

He and Cynthia looked at each other, looked down, then back up at the gape-mouthed kid. "No. Really?" they said simultaneously.

Their sarcasm was lost on the dimwit who replied, "Really."

The final insult came when a gum-chewing woman with a grating Brooklyn accent came up to him. "Yo, sweet hips, whaddaya say ta givin' a fellow New Yawkah yer autograph?"

"You don't want my autograph, lady."

"Yeah, I do. I collect Elvis impersonator autographs."

"Nobody collects Elvis *impersonator* autographs."

She puffed out her chest with pride. "I have seven hundred and seventy-six, including Elmer's." She waved to the beaming jerk, who was over at a roadside vendor's buying six velvet Elvis paintings, along with one of those dashboard wiggly Elvis figures, all of which he proceeded to stuff into the already overloaded pickup. "Elmer said ya do the best Elvis hip swivel in da world. Will ya show it ta me, huh? That would be so soup-ah cool. I kin have Harvey haul out da video recorder." Noticing his glower, she added, "Oh, never mind 'bout da video recorder, if it's ax-in too much, but how 'bout da autograph." She shoved a ballpoint pen and a map into his hand.

Elmer had already signed, "Elvis Lives. Long live the King. Elmer Presley."

While P.T. scribbled his own moronic message, after discarding the notion of writing "Screw Elvis," the woman cracked her gum loudly and glanced idly over at the limo. A smirking Cynthia was leaning against the hood, drinking her soda and eating a cracker.

"Nice dress, hon," the woman remarked, "but yer nipples are showin'."

Yeeesss! There is justice in this world, after all.

They were a sight for sore eyes . . . any eyes, actually . . .

The apartment doorbell rang persistently. A long, uninterrupted buzz.

Enrique Alvarez had just emerged from the shower and was combing back his wet hair in front of the bathroom mirror. With a curse, he pulled a pair of black sweat pants up over his naked body and stalked toward the door.

It was only three in the afternoon, but he'd come home after a round of roadshow meetings with the antsy underwriters, who were insisting on the prince being available for the last few presentations. He was planning on heading up to the Catskills this evening to see what the hell had happened to P.T. It wasn't like him to disappear for so long without calling. Even though Naomi had called him days ago claiming P.T.

had gone to the Poconos with the shark, he figured the castle was as good a place as any to start tracking down his boss.

"Open the freakin' door, Dick, or I'm going to kick it down."

"Speak of the devil," Enrique mumbled as he flicked the various deadbolts, pleased to know he wouldn't have to leave the city after all. He thought he heard dogs barking on the other side of the door. For one insane second he wondered if P.T. had brought some dogs back with him, but then dismissed the thought. It must be that pet walker Mrs. Livingston had hired to exercise her poodles.

The door swung open, and Dick's eyes almost popped out.

The first one to enter was a raging, barefooted P.T. in a red Elvis suit.

"Damn, you look good, boss."

Luckily, he was able to duck at the last minute and avoid the punch to his smiling mouth.

Cynthia "The Shark" Sullivan walked in next, face flushed, chin held high. She was also barefooted, looking like sin-on-the-hoof in a dress, or almost dress, that could only be described as Forty-second Street haute couture. He also noted that she was not using crutches. *Hallelujah!*

"Say one word, Alvarez, and you are toast," she gnashed out.

He couldn't have spoken if he'd wanted to.

But he had no time to dwell on her or what circumstances had prompted her arrival here with P.T. in their Vegas Strip attire. Elmer-the-loonybird-Elvis and his Bobbsey Twin girlfriend Ruth, in matching pink jumpsuits, were being dragged inside by six leashed hound dogs.

"No, don't release those mutts on my new—"

Too late. Elmer and Ruth dropped their leashes.

"—white carpet."

Six yipping dogs went wild.

"Meet Aron and Priscilla and Lisa Marie, The Colonel, Gladys and Grace," Elmer said proudly.

One made a flying leap . . . or as much of a flying leap as such a decrepit creature could make . . . for Enrique's black leather Heidellsen sofa, fur and fleas flying in its wake. Another dog was taking a leak in the middle of the aforementioned white long-haired Turkish carpet. A third dog, obviously thirsty, headed down the hallway toward the bathroom, where a loud slurping noise ensued. The fourth was chewing on the leg of his baby grand piano, which had come with the apartment. A fifth lay down on a cushioned window seat and fell asleep . . . or died. A sixth had developed an intimate affection for his leg.

He was too stunned to be outraged. That would come later. Or sooner. Just not yet.

The only one left was Naomi, who stood out in the corridor, reluctant to enter. She was probably afraid that he would tease her, which he always did. It was one of the greatest joys of his pathetic life. Hell, he'd been doing it for a dozen years, ever since her father had practically offered her to him on a silver matrimonial platter. Dumb shit that he'd been (and still was, of course), he'd declined.

And Naomi had been in a wrath ever since. She never had recognized that his teasing was his dumb-man way of trying to make peace. He absolutely refused to consider the possibility that it might mean he wanted a piece of her. Not Naomi. Never.

She looked ridiculous, as usual . . . and adorable, as usual. Today she wore paint-spattered white workman's coveralls over a short-sleeved white T-shirt. On her feet were heavy leather boots that could probably crush concrete.

"Hi-i-i-i, Na-o-mi," he drawled, crooking his finger for her to come in.

She gave him the finger.

He grinned.

She glared.

It was a game they'd been playing for a dozen years or more.

He continued to grin and added a look.

Her face went from pink to red as she stomped through the doorway, stopping directly in front of him. Then she pulled out a pistol, causing his heart to drop about three feet. That was just before she stomped on his bare foot, hard . . . really hard.

"Owwwww!" Through the haze of pain, he realized that she wasn't waltzing victoriously into the living room. He hoped she wasn't planning on using that gun, especially since it was aimed at a really special place on his body, one he hoped to keep for a while longer. She waited till his vision cleared. *Uh-oh!*

As in one of those slow-motion film clips, he noticed that everyone in the room had turned to them. Only then did Naomi let loose with a through-the-teeth whistle that would pierce the eardrum, causing all the hounds to rush to her.

Holding his gaze, she put her weapon aside and reached into a large carryall looped over her shoulder.

"I figured I'd give the sweet things their doggie treats," she explained with some hidden meaning. Then she tossed out a dozen dog-eared Bolgheri ties for their chewing pleasure.

"Don't push me, Enrique," she warned, sashaying past him with all the aplomb of a Mack truck. "I've been taking shark lessons."

Chapter Fifteen

Welcome to my humble abode...

"I love the Dakota," Cynthia said with a weary sigh. "It feels almost human to me—a living entity with arms wide, welcoming me home."

"Hmpfh! It looks like a dreary fortress," Ferrama grumbled as their cab pulled up in front of the imposing building near midnight. The taxi driver parked, waiting for the other cab with Naomi and two FBI agents to arrive.

Startled, Cynthia spun away from him on the seat and tried to hide her hurt by examining the famous landmark. The original jonquil yellow brick and reddish brown cornerstones of the huge eight-story cube had long since darkened with years of New York grime. But its eclectic architecture—heavy on ledges, balconies, decorative iron railings, bay windows and

ornate gables—gave it a fanciful character, like a castle. "It does resemble a fortress . . . a *majestic* fortress,"
she conceded.

"It's a castle, dammit. You're living in a castle and
loving it."

His vehemence shocked her.

"My dream is to escape the whole prince/palace/
royals carnival," he tried to explain, "and you're aching
to jump on the calliope. What you don't understand is
that, despite the gilt and pretty music, a wooden horse
is just a wooden horse."

"Huh? Are we talking about the Dakota or something else? It's only an apartment building, for heav-
en's sake."

"No, Cynthia, it's much more than that. It's a
dream . . . the difference between your dreams and
mine. It's about souls connecting and drifting apart
and . . ." He raked his fingers through his hair, as if
amazed at his own words. "Go ahead and laugh. I
have no idea where the hell that poetical 'souls drifting' crap came from. Probably Elmer. *Mierda!* I can't
believe I'm spouting this stuff now, when I should be
concentrating on the stock offering and Naomi's Mafia
shenanigans."

Puzzled, she put the fingertips of one hand to her
furrowed brow. "My soul isn't drifting, it's just tired.
And this tired soul considers the Dakota a haven tonight, whether a stronghold or a palace. Be honest;
can't you see its ageless sense of security . . . its unspoken assurance that if it could withstand the barrage of
time, we humans can survive our crises, too?"

His face, which had been in a perpetual frown the
past hour, softened. "Are you in crisis, *cara?*" With

one arm draped over her shoulder, he cupped her face, turning her to him.

"I'm in crisis, all right. No doubt about that."

"Ah, let me take care of all your problems, sweetheart."

"Are you demented?" she sputtered. "You *are* the problem."

"Me?"

"After the past five hours of meetings in Alvarez's apartment with police, FBI agents, underwriters and your company officials, as well as phone calls to my own distraught boss and clients, not to mention the past week of emotional battering since I first met you . . . well, call me a whiner, but personally I think it's no wonder my nerves are strained to the limit. The only thing not hurting on me are my broken toes which, amazingly, seemed to have healed." She took a deep breath, then continued, "And don't look so jubilant; it doesn't mean I'm not going to sue your gorgeous butt."

He grinned, whether at her long-winded reply or the "gorgeous butt" reference, she wasn't sure. Either way, the grin was a further prod to her anger.

"And while I'm thinking about it, I don't appreciate at all your allowing those agents to assume I'm your babe du jour."

"Not a wild assumption when you consider that babe outfit," he remarked, giving the edge of her cleavage a little snap.

She slapped his hand away.

He laughed and told her to sit tight while he stepped outside the taxi to see if he could see the other cab coming.

Left alone for the moment, Cynthia had to admit that she was as upset with herself as she was with Ferrama. Never once that day, even when surrounded by law enforcement officials, had she brought up her kidnapping. Or contacted her lawyer, Marcia Connor. Not because anyone had demanded or even asked it of her. The time hadn't seemed right. Yet.

Also surprising, and dismaying, was the fact that neither she nor Ferrama, or the dingbat gang, had mentioned the marriage ceremony. Even if it had been fake, you'd think someone would have considered it of importance.

She was still suspicious of Ferrama. They hadn't had a chance to talk in private since she'd gotten the alarming news this morning that the marriage had been plotted by him and Naomi long before she'd consented.

Was Ferrama equally confused? Was that the reason for his ornery mood? Was that why, throughout the day and evening, no matter what he'd been doing, or whom he'd been speaking with, his gaze kept coming back to her? When he'd passed by, on his way to pick up the phone or find a document, he'd invariably touched her shoulder or trailed a finger longingly over her bare arm.

The questions, and promises, and so much more in his midnight eyes gave her hope. A dangerous, dangerous thing hope was, in Cynthia's opinion. Did she dare surrender to its seductive lure?

At the same time she wanted this whole nightmare over, she wished with all her heart that she could go back to last night . . . her wonderful wedding night . . . and freeze time, barring the intrusion of reality. What a ridiculous notion! Comparable to living in a dream world.

"One swallow never made a summer," her grandma had taught her. *And one night of lovemaking does not a marriage make*, she added now.

"Ah, lassie, do not be breaking your shin over a stool that's not in the way," she heard Grandma counter in her head.

"Deception is a *big* stool, Grandma."

"There're two tellings to every story, Cindy girl."

Since when did Grandma refer to me as Cindy? That's Elmer's misplaced nickname for me. I must be going over the edge if I'm having mental conversations with my long-dead grandmother. I know what it is. I'm afraid. For the first time in ages, I'm afraid.

"Desire conquers fear, sweet one," Grandma advised softly.

How can an imaginary voice be soft?

"What do you really want? What is your heart's desire?"

Prince Ferrama, she replied without hesitation.

Then immediately changed her mind. *No, no, no, no!* She was just so confused.

How could she be in love with a man she'd met only a week before?

Had Elmer really zapped them with a spell, and would the love they now shared fade with the waning of the mystical ties?

Did she want to lose this marvelous love?

Was she truly married? To a prince?

How did her "husband" feel about all this? Was it an amusing lark to him? Or a deliberately planned scam, as she suspected?

Regardless, would her life ever be the same?

As if sensing her inner turmoil, Ferrama abruptly opened the cab door for her, pulled her out and tucked her close to his side, kissing the top of her head with unsettling gentleness. "Everything will work out, *querida*," he assured her. "Trust me."

As much as she yearned to lean on him, she pushed him away. She saw the flicker of hurt in his eyes, but she couldn't stop herself. Self-reliance was the safer route.

Where does he see our relationship going from here? Cynthia wondered. She was afraid to ask.

More important, if I were to offer to drop my lawsuit, would he drop me like the Prince-ess of Fools?

Too many questions. Too few answers.

She craved time alone . . . to sleep and think and regain her old objectivity, if that was possible. "Go back to your own apartment, Ferrama," she said tiredly. "I'm okay now."

He slanted her a disbelieving look as he finished paying the taxi driver. "No, you're not okay. And neither am I."

She tilted her head to get a better view of him. The man had to be as bone weary as she was, and still he looked gorgeous. Darn it!

"Your grandma's been talking to me in my head," he admitted with a wry grimace.

"You're kidding!"

He shrugged. "It's either that or my conscience has an Irish accent." A little half-smile tugged at his lips. "She likes me, by the way."

"Oh, my God!" she exclaimed.

"Oh, my God!" a female voice echoed behind her.

Cynthia jumped with surprise and turned to see Naomi gaping at the Dakota as if she'd fallen down Alice in Wonderland's garden hole and landed in a magic kingdom. "It's . . . spectacular."

Cynthia hadn't noticed Naomi's arrival, so fuzzy was her brain with exhaustion and the chaos of her bewildered thoughts. The two agents accompanying her walked off and took up almost invisible posts in the building's shadowy alcoves.

That was another thing bothering Cynthia. The FBI had recommended that Naomi lay low and find a good hiding place till they'd apprehended Sammy Caputo and his Mafia cohorts. Naomi had declined the federal agents' offer of a safe house, pleading instead for Cynthia, presumably an unknown to the bad guys, to shelter her temporarily.

Decline would be too soft a word to describe how Naomi had reacted to Alvarez's offer that she stay with him. It could be because the slick lawyer's offer had been accompanied by a wink and what had to be the wickedest grin on the face of the earth. Oddly, Alvarez did a lot of that wicked grinning around Naomi.

To her astonishment, Cynthia had found herself consenting to harbor her own kidnapper. The FBI guaranteed that agents would be guarding her apartment 'round the clock.

Alvarez had been given the honor of playing host to Elmer and Ruth, though he'd advised them that the hounds would be in a kennel come morning. "And no Elvis music!" Alvarez had ordered. He preferred highbrow classical jazz. Luckily, Jake had shown up and agreed to take the animals to his mother's house in Long Island. "Don't Be Cruel" had been blaring from

Alvarez's state-of-the-art stereo system by that time. So much for the lawyer's admonitions!

Cynthia couldn't wait to see if Ruth would give the shifty rogue a makeover . . . not that he needed one, physically anyhow.

"Let's go inside," Ferrama suggested, now that Naomi had arrived.

"Miss Sullivan, it's good to have you back with us again." The words came from the stone-faced doorman standing before the Dakota's arched gateway entrance, once used by carriages depositing their passengers in the inner courtyard. The doorman waved her and her companions through. A single blink of his widened eyes was the only sign that he'd noticed their bizarre appearance, even after a darting perusal of their bare feet.

Heck, he must have seen lots worse over the years, considering the eccentric inhabitants of this landmark dwelling. In fact, Roberta Flack and an entourage of loudly chattering musicians, carrying instrument cases, were exiting now . . . all dressed in garish theatrical attire.

"Cynthia, you missed my party," Roberta reprimanded with a wagging forefinger as she was about to pass by in a cloud of expensive perfume. Pausing only for a second, her quick glance also took in Ferrama and Naomi, then went back to Ferrama. She winked at Cynthia then. "You go, girl!"

They were already into the building's corridor when Roberta called after them in a laughing voice, "Yo, Elvis! You ever need a job, just call me."

Ferrama said a foul word and punched the elevator button for the eighth floor.

The usually tight-lipped Naomi was babbling on incessantly about each aspect of their surroundings. "Don't you just love the mahogany woodwork and doors? P.T., look at those antique elevators. They're just like our castle. . . . I swear I've seen side tables and gilt mirrors like these at Wintherthur. . . . Do you think there are craftsmen who could duplicate those carved plaster ceiling medallions? Oooh, oooh, oooh, I want some etched glass light fixtures like those."

Cynthia was pleased at Naomi's admiring comments, but it was Ferrama at whom she kept gazing. For some reason, she yearned for his approval of her good taste in picking the Dakota for her home.

He said nothing, just stared at her with a fierce, unreadable intensity.

Her heart sank with an ominous foreboding. She'd been right to be fearful, after all.

When they finally entered her apartment and Cynthia snapped on the soft lighting, she tried to see her home through his eyes. It was not a large apartment, nor was it luxurious by Dakota standards. Some units had up to eighteen rooms, an equal number of fireplaces and massive drawing rooms accented with Baccarat crystal chandeliers. Hers was only two bedrooms, two baths, a living room, a loft study, a kitchen and a pantry. But they were spectacular, in her opinion, especially with their floor-to-ceiling windows overlooking Central Park. She wanted Ferrama to share her enthusiasm.

P.T. hated Cynthia's apartment.

Oh, it was just as magnificent as Cynthia had declared it to be. And that view of Central Park had to be worth a million bucks in itself. But the living room—or drawing room, as it must once have been classified before being divided in half—had lofty, fifteen-foot ceilings decorated with fancy pastel-tinted medallions and cornices, like a birthday cake.

Why couldn't there be cozy rafters and warm paneled walls?

The windows were framed with what appeared to be festoons of flowing silk in a trompe l'oeil effect, Cynthia was explaining to Naomi. Actually they weren't drapes at all, but hand-carved and painted wood.

Why can't she have real curtains like ordinary people?

He berated himself for his irrational attitude, but her apartment was elegant, dammit. *Elegant!* The kind of place a prince and princess might buy for a little New York getaway flat, not too large that a permanent staff would be required, but not too small for sophisticated parties.

All day P.T. had sensed a distance growing between himself and Cynthia. He felt a desperate need to get her alone and do something to close the gap before it became a chasm.

This apartment just accentuated their problem. It represented everything he was trying to escape. If this apartment and Cynthia's dreams were synonymous, then what chance did they have for a future together? Especially when Cynthia found out he wasn't really a prince . . . a little tidbit of information he'd neglected to disclose to her yet.

"Naomi, why don't you go to bed?" he suggested with the subtlety of a weedwhacker in a hair salon.

The two of them gaped at him as if he'd lost a few

more screws, then turned their backs on him, resuming their tour.

"Paul Segal, an architect who lived in the Dakota, came up with the idea of dividing some of the rooms horizontally. If a room had fifteen-foot ceilings, why not build a loft with stairs leading up at one end, thus creating another room? The historical preservation purists went nuts, but it didn't stop Segal. Some people use them for sleeping lofts. Mine is a home office."

"Do you have any Scotch?" he asked, ambling over to what appeared to be a fully stocked bar in an ornate niche near the fireplace. *I could use a belt or two, or five.*

"Yes. I think there's some Dewar's and Cutty," Cynthia answered.

"I only drink Laphroaig. Straight up. Do you have that?" It had been a long time since he'd remembered to employ his prissy prince personality. He was in a surly enough mood to engage it now.

Cynthia stopped midway up the short flight of stairs leading to her study, where she was continuing her tour with Naomi. The blush that bloomed on her cheeks was a clear indication that he'd rattled her old insecurities. "No, I don't have Laphroaig."

"Why don't you have a beer, P.T.?" Naomi interjected. "Better yet, why don't *you* go to bed and sleep off this mean mood you're in."

He thought about telling Naomi what she should do, explicitly, but instead stomped off to the kitchen, where he leaned against the open refrigerator door. There wasn't much there that wasn't moldy or dried out. He took out the milk and sniffed to see if it was okay. Then, checking furtively to see if anyone was looking, he chugged down half a quart straight from the carton. Definitely un-princely. And supremely satisfying.

He tried to belch as an added touch but couldn't. Too many years of savoir faire, he supposed with a rueful grin. Maybe later he'd scratch his armpits. Or watch professional wrestling, even though he hated it. Did this showplace even have a TV?

How had he made such a mess of his life? He felt his dreams crumbling around him, like that stupid castle in the Catskills, and he didn't know what to do about rebuilding. It seemed a monumental, almost hopeless task.

A voice with an Irish lilt commented dryly in his head, "Handfuls make a load, boy."

"Huh?"

"The only cure for spilled milk is to lick the pitcher."

Suddenly inspired, he gave Grandma a mental high five, then set out a carton of eggs, a stick of butter, some cheddar, a half-used onion and the remaining milk. Next he checked the cabinets, where he found a small can of jalapeño peppers and a jar of salsa. When Cynthia and Naomi returned to the kitchen from their world tour, he had a bodacious Spanish omelet sizzling on the gas range, buttered toast in the warming oven and a pot of coffee brewing in a yuppie gourmet contraption. He was swigging down his second can of Bud Light, feeling mighty pleased with himself.

"You did this? By yourself?" Cynthia asked, slack-jawed with surprise.

"No, the maid bopped in."

"You're drinking beer? But I thought—"

"Well, sometimes when there's no Laphroaig available, I don't mind slumming with a beer. It makes me feel like one of the common folks."

Naomi guffawed.

Cynthia narrowed her eyes. "Your eyebrow is twitching."

With a laugh, he tweaked Cynthia's chin, then took her by the shoulders, steering her to the table, where he proceeded to serve her a much-needed midnight meal.

Naomi just surveyed him with her usual all-knowing smirk. He ignored her. If she wasn't going to bed, as he'd suggested, then he would pretend she wasn't there. Undaunted, Naomi helped herself to a heaping plate of *his* omelet and plopped her butt down between him and Cynthia, who was savoring his offering as if it was a royal feast. The little sounds of appreciation she made were warming the cockles of his heart. And some other cockles, too.

Maybe things would turn out okay, after all.

The princess threw down the gauntlet . . .

Finally, finally, finally, Naomi went off for a bath and then beddie-bye.

He propped his chin on his cupped hands, his elbows braced on the table. He inhaled deeply, taking in the still lingering scent of strong coffee and the more seductive scent of his wife. "Can I tuck you in, Mrs. Ferrama?" he asked with a cute little bobble of his eyebrows. At least, *he* thought the affectation cute. It was one of his lesser looks, one he was still perfecting.

Her head jerked up from where she'd been studying her empty coffee mug. He wasn't sure if her alarm was due to the reference to tucking or to her being Mrs. Ferrama. Whatever. He was in too good a mood to be daunted by trivialities.

Life was good. He had hope. He was about to get laid.

"I really think you should go home," she said nervously. "It's not a good idea for you to stay here."

What? Where did that come from? He scooted his chair closer and took both her hands in his. "I'm not leaving you till this danger passes."

"It's Naomi who's in danger, not me," she argued.

"You *might* be, and I won't take that risk. Besides, there's a more important reason. Will you look at me, please?"

Her eyes had shifted, as if she was having difficulty facing his direct gaze. That was a good sign, in his opinion. When she raised her chin, he saw fear and insecurity in her misty blue eyes. Not such a good sign.

"I love you, Cynthia, and you love me. Isn't that the most important thing?"

"But what if it's only a spell?"

He squeezed her hand, trying to convey how strongly he felt. "I'm beginning to think there never was a spell . . . that Elmer just planted the idea in our heads and we ran away with it."

"Is that possible?" The tinge of hope in her voice was like a blast of adrenaline to his ego. Not to mention his cockles.

"Yes. Yes, I think it is. But even if there were some spell or something, who's to say it isn't like a seed? Once it germinates, does it matter how it got planted in the first place?" *Man, am I on a roll. I oughtta start a new company and bottle this stuff.*

A tiny smile tugged at her luscious lips. "You do have a way with words, Ferrama. But I have so many questions. You're like a puzzle I can't quite figure out. Some of the pieces are missing."

"We both have questions and lots of unresolved issues, I agree, but I just don't think now is the time to hash them out. There's less than two weeks till the stock offering, and I was wondering . . . well, I have an idea for you and me. A sort of deal."

"Uh-oh," she said warily. "Do I need a lawyer?"

"Not that kind of deal. This is what I'm thinking. Since you can't go back to work yet, and the feds want you to stay put with Naomi, why don't you help me in the interim? Be my personal stock consultant."

"Absolutely not. Legally, I'm not permitted to get involved in your stock operation. Besides, your underwriters would have a fit. And my boss would fire me on the spot . . . for good, this time. Not to mention losing my SEC license."

"No, no, no. I meant advise me as a friend and wife and lover." When she didn't go all purple and ballistic over the lover bit, he went on. "After the stock goes public, I swear to you on my mother's soul, we will make a financial settlement regarding your injury and the kidnapping that will be more than acceptable to you. I'll work with you privately or through your lawyer, whatever you want. And as to the missing pieces of my puzzle, I'll give all of those to you then, I promise. Just bear with me a little while longer, babe. Trust me."

"Boy, that's a lot of promises, Ferrama. And you're asking for a tremendous leap of faith . . . to trust a rogue like you."

"Well?" His heart was lodged in his throat as he waited for an answer.

"It's a deal. Two weeks. Then all bets are off."

He leaned forward and gave her a quick kiss of thanks for her vote of confidence. "You won't be sorry, *querida*."

"Just don't let me down, Ferrama. Trust doesn't come easy for me, and I'm giving up my pride to cut you this slack."

He tilted his head to the side, as if listening to a distant voice.

"What?"

"Your grandma just said to tell you that pride is a hook well lost to catch a salmon."

"You lying fish you, that motto is on one of the Irish coffee mugs on that shelf above the sink," she accused with a laugh.

"Well, I knew I heard it somewhere." He grinned unabashedly.

"There's just one condition to the deal. You get a two-week reprieve from full-puzzle disclosure, as long as you consent to . . ." She paused deliberately.

His body stiffened, and the fine hairs stood out on the back of his neck. "Conditions?"

She nodded, then smiled enigmatically. "No sex."

"No sex?" He let out a hoot of laughter, figuring she must be kidding.

She didn't return his laughter. In fact, she folded

her arms across her chest and waited out his laughter with a solemn, stubborn expression on her face.

He frowned with puzzlement, trying to figure out her game.

This woman who made love with me all night long with uninhibited enthusiasm is saying "No sex?" This woman who echoed my refrain, "You are mine," and meant it, is now saying "No sex?" This woman who is caught in the same love web as me is saying "No sex?"

"This is our honeymoon, in case you've forgotten, wife," he pointed out with amusement and tried to pull her close for another kiss.

She resisted. "No sex or no deal."

He tilted his head in question. "Why?"

"Sex muddies the waters. When we get involved again . . . if we do . . . I want to have no doubts at all."

"I love you. Don't think I take those words lightly when I say them, Cynthia. I thought you loved me, too."

"I do. And believe me, I take the words a lot more seriously than you do. I've never said them to another man. Tell me truthfully, Ferrama, can you say the same?"

He felt his face heat and considered lying, but only briefly. His eyebrow would probably give him away anyhow. "No, but I never meant those words before."

She threw her hands up in a "See!" attitude.

He thought for a moment. No way was he going to accept her terms, but he understood her caution. "How about a counteroffer? This is a bargaining table, right?" He pounded a fist on the kitchen table for emphasis.

"Sure. Why not?" She smiled sweetly.

Well, you overconfident shark, you! You still think

you can beat me in a business deal. "I get a two-week reprieve. You get two weeks of no sex . . . *unless* you beg for it."

She burst out laughing. "I'll never do that."

"Never say never, sweetheart." He matched her sweet smile, and raised her with a wink.

"Never." She stretched her sweet smile, winked back and added a haughty toss of her magnificent hair.

God, I love her. "Never challenge a Spanish prince, especially when he's pulling out his armor," he cautioned, "or you may be hoisted on your own petard."

"You're the one with a petard, oh knight."

He grinned. "You noticed."

"You are outrageous." As they shook hands to seal the deal, she repeated, "Never, I tell you. Never, never, never."

And then the royal kinkiness began . . .

Never lasted about thirty-five minutes.

Cynthia had just finished tidying up her kitchen and was standing at the sink, dead on her feet. She was about to go up to the study, where she planned to sack out on the soft upholstered sofa, alone, and sleep for at least ten straight hours.

"Are you ready?" Ferrama asked behind her.

She jumped with surprise at his silent approach. She'd heard the water from the shower stop running fifteen minutes earlier and assumed he was already in her bed for the night.

"Ready for what?" she inquired tentatively as she turned with foreboding. Then she gasped.

Her husband stood before her, looking like a regal Spanish prince. His shimmering black hair was combed wetly off his recently shaved face. Beads of water his towel had missed lay like diamonds on the dark skin of his collarbone, on some chest hairs, on his flat stomach.

The impossible man was totally naked, except for one tiny gold hoop earring in his right ear.

"You promised," she accused. "No sex, remember. We made the deal. Is this how you keep your word?"

"Tsk-tsk, Cynthia. Did I mention sex? I merely asked if you were ready. Which do you prefer, by the way?" She noticed, then, that in one hand he held a bottle of baby oil and in the other a jar of Albolene cream.

Her face blazed with embarrassment at having misunderstood. He must have a skin rash and was seeking her advice. Perhaps from shaving. Or maybe his ankle was chafed from the chain. She refused to look any lower than his waist, though. "I use the baby oil for removing eye makeup, but it's a good generic lubricant. The cream was Grandma's old standby cure for dry skin."

He grinned.

So, the rogue didn't have a rash. She should have known. "Which part of 'No sex' didn't you understand, Ferrama? Listen, I'm too tired for games tonight. Joke's over. Ha, ha, ha."

"That's precisely the point. You're tired."

"Get to the point and cover yourself, for heaven's sake."

"Oh, I forgot I was naked," he lied. And she didn't need to see a twitch as proof. "But you shouldn't mind. We're married, after all."

She crossed her eyes with frustration.

"You look kind of cute when you do that."

"Aaargh! I'm exhausted beyond belief, Ferrama. Can't you see that?"

"Precisely," he said, stepping forward. "Actually, I prefer the baby oil." He set the jar of cream on the counter. "So, come, sweetheart. It's time to put yourself in expert hands."

"Keep those expert hands to yourself, you louse." Her shoulders slumped wearily. "I'm really disappointed in you. You said I could trust you. You said—"

"—no sex," he agreed.

"Huh?"

He dangled the baby oil bottle by its neck with the fingers of one hand, while the fingers of the other hand laced with hers, coaxing her from the kitchen. "Do you prefer Swedish or sensual?"

"Is that a trick question?"

"Massage, darling. I'm talking massage."

"Whose massage?"

"Yours."

There are only two people in this hallway. Me and the naked god. If I'm to be massaged, then the masseur has to be . . . oh, no! Her befuddled brain finally cleared.

"No!" she asserted, coming to a halt and digging in her heels, even when he tugged on her hand.

"Yes. I insist."

"You have no right to insist."

"Ah, that's where you're wrong, *querida*. As your husband, it's my role to protect you and see to your needs. Right now, your aching, exhausted body needs my ministrations. You will have a massage, make no mistake about that."

"Listen to me, you blockhead, there will be *no sex.*"

"I know that, sweetie." He paused, his eyes glittering with a fiery gleam. "Unless you beg for it."

So that was his game plan. Torture till capitulation. "No."

"Yes."

"You can't make me."

He arched a brow with amusement. "You either walk or I carry you. Which will it be?"

He carried her, over his shoulder, squealing and pounding on his back, into the master bathroom, where, to her dismay, she saw, once he set her on her feet, that he already had several large bath towels laid out on the tiled floor. Even more shocking were the objects he'd arrayed beside the towels. A silk scarf. A pair of fuzzy mittens. A peacock feather from the hall vase. A buff puff. A powder puff. A braided cord belt with beaded tassel ends. What a busy bee the prince had been!

Her eyes shot to his in alarm. He was leaning against the closed door, waiting. His posture said "lazy." His coiled muscles and tight jaw said "ready to pounce." The click of the lock said "danger."

"Are you a pervert?"

That surprised him, and his expression relaxed into a slow smile. "Define pervert."

"I find it really difficult to carry on a conversation with you when you're wearing no clothing. Put on that robe." She pointed to the oversized terry-cloth robe hanging on a wall hook.

"I prefer to give my massages in the nude. Less messy."

Whoa! What mess? "Given a lot of nude massages, have you, lover boy?" she inquired snidely, hating the rush of jealousy those images provoked.

"Thousands." She couldn't tell if he was serious or not. "And there will be no conversation, by the way. I have rules for my massages. No talking from the massagee. Just one-word responses, when necessary."

Massage rules? He really must be into kinky stuff. What have I gotten myself into? "Like?"

"Please. Don't. Tingles. Hot. Stud. Yeeess."

"You're incredible." She shook her head at his outrageous nerve.

"I know. Take off your dress."

"Not on your life."

He shrugged. "Your way. My way. Little difference."

She licked her lips nervously and backed up slightly as he unfolded himself from the door and began to approach. "Why are you doing this?" she cried out, her back against the wall.

"Because you need it. And because I want to. Take off your dress, Cynthia. I want you to shower first."

"Oh, so now there's a shower involved, too. No sex, but two naked people in a shower together, lathering each other up? Give me a break."

"I wasn't planning on joining you in the shower, silly girl. Unless you *beg* me to. I have only so much endurance."

In the end, she took off her dress while he watched. And she showered alone in the glass cubicle, a modern exception to the old-fashioned bathroom with its ball-and-claw tub, while he watched. And she dried herself while he watched. And she combed her hair before the mirror, arms held high, breasts rising and falling with her actions, while he watched.

She was aroused.

He was aroused. That was apparent from his parted lips and dilated pupils, not to mention an impressive erection.

He indicated with a motion of his head that she was to lie on the towel.

She did, facedown.

A slight rustling and the feel of his body heat close by indicated that he'd dropped to his knees. Taking her arms, which had been folded under her face, he arranged them above her head. Before she realized what he was about, he tied the silk scarf around her eyes.

"No," she protested in a panic, trying to rise up. It was bad enough being naked, but being blind, as well, rendered her totally vulnerable to whatever he wanted to do.

"Shhh," he said, pressing a hand to her shoulder blades. "Trust me."

Strangely, she did. "No sex," she repeated, though.

He chuckled. "Unless you beg."

From the instant he began to lay his expert hands on her, Cynthia understood that this was going to be much more than a massage.

"You must remain totally passive, Cynthia. Do nothing unless I tell you. Submit to everything." As he spoke in a low, silky voice, he was warming baby oil in his hands and slathering it over every inch of her skin, from the nape of her neck, down to her toes and out to her fingers. "Place yourself *totally* in my hands, *querida*. Can you do that for me . . . your husband?"

A little thrill of danger rippled through her body. "I don't know if I want—"

He slapped her lightly on a buttock with the tasseled beads. "Shhhh. One-word answers, remember?"

"Why?" He was giving her orders, as if he was the royal majesty and she a mere subject. An uncomfortable image.

Before she could voice her outrage, he spoke again. "In submitting yourself to my will by passively receiving pleasure, you open yourself to the flow of energy coming from my body to yours. The fingertips and hands and mouth and teeth are the conductors, but the message they carry won't be a physical one. It will be one of love, *cara mia*. If you are open to it."

Lovemaking without making love? His words were magical caresses to her battered emotions. Still, a part of her held back. "And you've done all this, and said all those loving things, to thousands of other women?"

"Well, maybe not thousands," he admitted with a husky laugh. "And that was more than one word, naughty girl. I'm keeping a list of all your transgressions, for which you will have to suffer dire punishment later."

"A punishment which will, no doubt, involve much moaning, I suppose."

"Absolutely. And you now have two check marks on your transgression list."

She recalled then that he'd said he hadn't performed this special massage for thousands of women. "How many? Other women, I mean?"

He hesitated. "None."

None? Cynthia's heart sang at the news, improbable as it was. "Hah! I'll bet your eyebrow is twitching."

"No, it's not, my suspicious wife. And you have four check marks, in case you're interested."

"Then how do you know all this massage stuff?"

"Five transgressions! Geesh, are you a glutton for punishment? If you must know, I read a book. No, don't snicker. Really, I did. But I never tried it on anyone else. I think . . . I think I was waiting for you."

Waiting for me? Oh, if only that were true!

A throbbing silence followed in which Cynthia decided, for once in her life, to take a chance. Go against the tried and true. She would give up her will to another, and prayed to God that he would live up to her trust.

For an hour and more, he worshipped her body by stroking his palms over the slick surfaces of her skin. Wide sweeping caresses. Circles. Short skimming strokes over sensitized flesh. Then he moved to kneading the large muscles in her back and arms and legs, even the insteps of her feet.

After that was friction—delicious exercises in how textures affect the body's senses. The soft but firm press of skin against skin. Feathery tracing of curves, followed by the harsher abrasion of the buff puff, then back to the whispery tendrils of a powder puff. A soft brush, a fuzzy mitten. And if that wasn't enough, he began percussion—the gentle pounding of her body surface.

All this he did, then flipped her over on her back and started over again.

Never once did he touch her breasts or genital areas. He didn't need to.

The entire time he whispered soft praise for her individual body parts and wicked, wicked words of what he intended to do to those body parts someday . . .

but not today, because he'd promised her no sex . . . unless she begged. And in the end he punished her, as he'd promised, for not adhering to his rules, and she moaned as he'd promised, and she wished she'd never made him promise to honor her conditions.

When he was done, having reduced her to a boneless, mewling repository for his flow of sweet love energy, only then did he sit back on his knees, straddling her thighs, and release her scarf. And she saw that he was very, very aroused.

"I love you," he whispered.

She thought she said the same, but perhaps not. Her body was so eroticized, she felt disoriented. Holding her arms open for him, she did what he'd probably planned all along.

"Please," she begged.

But he shook his head slowly from side to side, and leaned forward to press a soft kiss to her lips. "Not now, my love. Not like this." In one fluid movement, he stood, lifted her into his arms and carried her into the bedroom.

Tucking her into the cool sheets on her side, he slid in behind her and wrapped his arms around her, enfolding her in his spoonlike embrace. As they began to drift off, he kissed the oily satin of her bare shoulder and murmured sleepily, "We will work things out, *querida*. I promise. Sweet dreams."

Okay, so Cinderella was a little bit kinky, too . . .

Sweet dreams awakened P.T. in the middle of the night.

Well, actually, they weren't sweet at all. They were hot. Very hot . . . and raw . . . and sinfully carnal . . . a man's fantasy.

He smiled against a pair of warm lips that were kissing him, openmouthed and wet. A pointed tongue delved into his mouth, like an invader staking territory. Not that he was fighting back. Hell, no.

But there was more . . . *much more* action going on.

The woman was elevating herself over him on all fours, breasts swinging in a tantalizing arc across his chest hairs. Before he could grasp what she was about, she eased herself down onto his erection—*Peter is in great form tonight.*

This was pure heaven. God must be rewarding him for his earlier chivalry in foregoing sex with his wife after driving himself practically up the wall and back again with his masochistic massage.

The woman just sat there, impaled, waiting, watching him. Then, when she sensed she had his full attention—*when had that ever been in doubt?*—then she raised herself up to a sitting position. He moved even deeper inside her, filling and stretching her to the limit and then some. Arching his neck, he gritted his teeth against the overwhelming waves of pleasure washing over him. Peter was in penis paradise.

When he made love to a woman from the top position, he savored the intense, concentrated feeling of her body clasping him, like hot, lubricated fingers. But when the woman sat astride, like his dream lover was now, oh, it was so much more subtle. Then, a man had to concentrate to prolong the lapping and stroking, almost licking sensation of her inner folds on his organ.

But P.T. couldn't concentrate. And he sure as hell wasn't going to be prolonging the main event for very long at this rate, even though the woman hadn't begun her strokes.

"Are you ready to beg?" a silky voice asked.

Huh? Since when do dream lovers talk? A sneaky suspicion crept into P.T.'s testosterone-dazed brain. He cracked open one eyelid. Then both eyes flew wide open. *Holy hell!* Cynthia was sitting on him like some princess on a throne, grinning like the cat that swallowed the milk.

"Cynthia?" he cried out, reaching up to lift her off him.

"Oh, no!" She laughed and rocked her hips around in a perfect circle. Then reversed the movement. *Oh, God! She's playing hula hoop with Peter.* Then she stopped. She just stopped and smiled at him, a teasing, exultant, I've-got-you-by-the-balls expression of challenge.

"What are you up to, Cynthia?" he ground out.

She leaned forward and tweaked him on the chin. "I'm not the one who's up. You are. I'm waiting for you to beg, Prince Peter. Remember, no sex till the begging begins."

"That was supposed to be you, Cynthia. Move, dammit, before I explode." He tried to grasp her hips and make her begin the strokes that would bring him release.

She knocked his hands aside. "I already begged . . . hours ago. Now it's your turn." Meanwhile, she was doing something really interesting with a strand of her hair, brushing it back and forth across one of his nipples. He wasn't usually sensitive there, but now he swore there was a direct electrical current to the pulsing rod imbedded in her circuit walls.

Wrapping her fingers around his forearms, she extended her arms so that her upper body bowed backward, then spread her legs flat, parallel to his, and let herself spasm around him. He couldn't tell if she was climaxing or making her inner muscles work. Either way, he was impressed.

Her posture gave him access to her breasts, which she probably didn't realize. He raised his head and took one nipple into his mouth. It was big and hard and incredibly sweet. With his first suckle, she let out a primitive, needy wail. *Now* she was climaxing, and he was trying to buck up against her to begin the strokes that would start his climax, too. But the stubborn witch wrapped her legs around his and refused to move, even when she was unraveling around him.

"Sonofabitch!" he growled in surrender. "Please. I'm begging. Please, please, please, please, please!"

Only then, with sobs and panting noises, did she begin to move on him, a slow, unsteady lifting and easing down. Too slow, too damn slow! He flipped her over on her back, still inside her, and laced his fingers with hers. Then he began the long, hard, pummeling strokes that were essential to ease this building firestorm. He had no idea what words he was uttering as he kissed her lips, laved her nipples, nibbled at her ears . . . the whole time pummeling her against the mattress. She bent her knees to cradle his hips, but he was out of control. Long strokes became shorter and rougher and still he was like a piston, driving, driving, driving toward . . .

Finally, with a roar of exultation, he reached his

climax, shooting his semen into her wildly convulsing sheath.

When his heart slowed down from its heart attack speed and blood no longer roared in his ears, he raised his head to look down at his amazing wife.

She smiled up at him shyly. *How can she look shy after practically blowing my head off?* "My prince!" She sighed.

He rolled over on his side, taking her with him, and began to laugh with pure, soul-swelling joy. "The ball has barely begun, princess."

Chapter Sixteen

All's well that ends well . . .

Cynthia's fairy tale did come true . . . for the next week, at least.

Although Naomi was always hovering in the background, she'd become engrossed in the Dakota's history and was reading everything Cynthia had in her library. Plus, the lady next door, an architectural historian, had lent Naomi dozens of books on restoration supplies. Naomi was in DYI heaven.

P.T. was as devoted a husband as Cynthia could have wished for, although she still didn't know if the marriage was legal. P.T. said they'd get married again if it wasn't legit, and she'd agreed, without hesitation.

P.T. had to go out on some of the road show presentations with Alvarez to the underwriting firms, but mostly he stayed with her and worked from the apartment. She was able to get caught up on her client calls when he was gone and had made arrangements with her boss to enter orders through another trader, who would share commissions.

Life was good, and Cynthia was hopeful.

The only problem was her husband's increasing nervousness. Something was drastically wrong, and he wouldn't discuss it with her. Sometimes when she'd glance up suddenly, she saw fear in his eyes. When she asked what was the matter, he always closed up and said, "We'll discuss it when the stock offering is over." And then he'd make her forget her questions with endless, inventive lovemaking. One time, though, he'd hugged her tightly and whispered urgently, "Don't ever leave. No matter what, remember that I love you."

That "no matter what" kept niggling at Cynthia's almost perfect euphoria.

This morning they were in the kitchen having a cup of fresh ground coffee when the doorbell rang. It was nine o'clock and P.T. had nothing on his agenda for the day; they both looked up quizzically.

"Stay here," he commanded. Picking up Naomi's pistol, he headed cautiously for the front door, wearing only a pair of old gray sweatpants.

Her apartment was littered with his clothing and personal items, more and more of which arrived and stayed each time he went out and came back. She'd always been meticulous about the tidiness of her personal space, but she didn't mind now. She was totally, gloriously, in love.

"Go back," P.T. said in a hushed voice from the

entryway when he noticed that she'd followed him. He directed his gaze meaningfully at the mid-thigh-length nightshirt she was wearing . . . a gift he'd bought for her on a whim yesterday when passing a novelty shop. Imprinted on the front was: MY PRINCE IS A FROG, BUT HE CAN RIBET ME ANY DAY.

"See who it is first," she said, sotto voce, pointing to the peephole in the door.

He glowered in exasperation at her defiance but did as she'd suggested anyway. "Damn!" he exclaimed. Setting the gun on a hall table, he began to undo the dead bolts. "There go my plans for the morning."

Cynthia already knew what those plans had been. She'd blushed when he'd told her a half hour ago in the shower, and she didn't blush easily these days. So it wasn't surprising that she echoed his expletive with a "Damn!" of her own.

When he stepped back from the open door, Elmer, Ruth and Alvarez rushed in, all talking at once. Alvarez rolled his eyes at P.T. in a they-made-me-do-it silent message.

It was the first she'd seen Ruth and Elmer since they'd arrived in Manhattan, and they hugged her warmly. Elmer was wearing his favorite aqua-sequinned jumpsuit with the blue suede boots. Naomi was a cotton candy confection in pale pink tank top with matching pencil-slim jeans and high heels. Both of their hairdos were so poufy they must have spent hours creating the effect, not to mention a gallon of hair spray.

As they moved into the living room, Elmer and Ruth were oohing and aahing over her apartment.

Alvarez sauntered up to her, gave a meaningful smirk at her nightshirt and leaned forward to kiss her cheek. Near her ear, he whispered, "You have a hickey on your neck. Looks great with the whisker burns on your legs."

She could feel her face turning hot. The jerk! "How are lawyers like sperm?" she asked coolly.

Alvarez groaned, but P.T. grinned.

"Only one in three ever works."

"Very funny!" Alvarez commented dryly. To P.T. he said, "Now I know where you've been getting all those hickeys you can't hide under your shirt collar. She's a bloodsucker."

"Chill out, Dick," P.T. warned.

They were all walking toward the kitchen, lured by the smell of coffee. P.T. put his arm around her shoulder and pulled her close. He probably thought she was offended by Alvarez, but she wasn't. She knew Alvarez was only kidding.

"Come on, darlin'," Elmer encouraged Ruth. "Let's make these folks a batch of good southern cookin' for breakfast."

P.T. exchanged a resigned grimace with Cynthia. It appeared the gang was hunkering in for several hours.

"What are you doing here, anyway?" P.T. asked Alvarez.

"I have some papers for you to sign. Besides, one more minute in my apartment with those two fruit-cakes and I was going to slice my wrists with a guitar pick . . . or Naomi's nail file. Did you know that women actually curl their eyelashes, P.T.? There's this crazy contraption they slip their eyelashes into and then squeeze. And I'm starting to hear Elvis songs in my sleep. I wouldn't admit this to anyone else, but I now know all the lyrics to 'Heartbreak Hotel.' Where's Naomi? I haven't had a good tease in ages. I think of her every time I trip over one of her blasted dining room chairs."

She and P.T. stared openmouthed at Alvarez's long-winded diatribe.

"Hey, this cabin fever is affecting me, too."

"Is it safe for you to have brought Elmer and Ruth here? The Mafia might be tailing Ruth for a clue to Naomi's whereabouts."

Alvarez shrugged. "One of the two agents guarding my place came with us, and he took a really circuitous route. So far, the feds haven't noticed any activity near my place or yours, though the house in Hoboken was trashed pretty bad a few days ago. Don't worry, we've been careful. Guess I'll go wake up Naomi. How do you figure she'd feel about my slipping into her bed, naked?"

"Do you have a death wish, Dick?" Cynthia wondered aloud.

A short time later, they sat at the kitchen table, sipping coffee, waiting for the biscuits to finish baking. A pig load of scrambled eggs, sausage, hotcakes, hash browns and various other cholesterol-laden items sat in the warming oven.

Elmer beamed at the sight of her hand linked with P.T.'s on the table. "It looks like my work here is almost done."

"Almost?" P.T. arched an eyebrow with amusement.

"Well, there is that old triad," Elmer said with a twinkle in his eye.

Uh-oh!

"What's a triad? Another of those Irish bullshit sayings?" Alvarez asked.

Elmer frowned at him, wagging a finger. "I may have to make you my next assignment."

Everyone laughed at that, except Alvarez. "I think I'll go wake up Naomi."

"No!" they all hollered.

"What triad, Elmer?" she inquired. He'd said his work was *almost* done with her and P.T.

"The three loveliest things to see are a garden of white potatoes, a ship under sail and a wife after giving birth."

A baby? Is he talking about a baby? And me? Cynthia went white with horror and P.T. began choking on his coffee. Alvarez was hooting with laughter.

Elmer speared Alvarez with one of his I-could-turn-you-into-a-slug looks. "Beware of your misplaced mirth, boy. No man ever wore a tie as nice as his own child's arms around his neck. You may be appreciating that fact sooner than any in this room."

"Huh? Me? No way!" Alvarez blustered, clearly disconcerted.

"Perhaps you should go wake up Naomi, after all," Elmer insinuated with a wily wink at the others seated at the table.

"Naomi? Are you suggesting that Naomi and I . . ." He shook his head, hard, at the staggering notion.

"If a cat sits long enough at the hole, she'll catch the mouse."

"Stop talking in riddles, dammit," Alvarez sputtered. "For your information, Naomi has never come sniffing around my cheese. She'd rather turn the mouse-trap on me and spring the trap on one of my favorite body parts."

"Methinks you do protest too much," Cynthia commented.

"Are you serious?" P.T. asked her. "Naomi and Alvarez?"

"Never!" Alvarez asserted, slamming his coffee mug on the table. It had to be the first time in his life that he'd blushed. "Since when did I become your target, Elmer? Seems to me you have all the work you can handle already. Leave me be."

"He that is born to be hanged shouldn't fear water," Elmer said. "There's no fightin' fate, boy."

"Screw fate. And if you think for one minute that I'm going to screw Naomi, you've got another think—"

"Are you talking about me, Enrique?" Naomi asked icily.

Everyone turned, their jaws dropping open.

Naomi was leaning against the doorjamb, glaring at Alvarez. She wore an ankle-length robe of Cynthia's of shimmery cream silk, belted at the waist. Her hair was a sleep-mussed mass of gold-highlighted chestnut tangles. Most surprising was her knock-me-dead *Playboy* centerfold figure, revealed by the clinging garment. *Who knew? Who knew?*

Alvarez was the first to speak. "Will you marry me, Naomi?" He immediately turned shocked eyes on Elmer. "I didn't say those words. Did you put those words in my head?"

"Who me?" Elmer batted his eyes with mock innocence.

"Yes," Naomi said, to everyone's amazement. Especially her own. "I didn't say that. Honest, I didn't even speak. That wasn't me speaking. Stop it, Elmer, stop it right now." Tears welled in her eyes and she fled from the room.

"What the hell is going on?" Alvarez moaned, face in hands. "Now I'm hearing voices in my head."

"Do they have an Irish accent?" P.T. smiled widely. He was probably pleased to have the fairy spirits directing their attention away from him.

"Yes." Alvarez peered at P.T. with alarm.

"What do the voices say?" an awestruck Ruth wanted to know.

"There never was a scabby sheep in a flock that didn't like to have a comrade," Alvarez disclosed with another moan.

"See," Elmer said with a nod of satisfaction. "I was right."

"I assume you're the scabby sheep," Cynthia commented drolly to Alvarez.

"What does it mean?" The dapper lawyer, who prided himself on his well-cultivated suntan, looked rather green. Elmer did have that effect sometimes.

"It means you're about to have your fleece sheared," P.T. observed, grinning.

"By Naomi?" Alvarez's face went even more green.

Alvarez never got his answer because a loud shot rang out, followed by two more. They came from the vicinity of the outside corridor . . . exactly where Naomi had fled a moment earlier.

Oh, God, she wouldn't attempt suicide at the prospect

of a relationship with Alvarez, would she? Cynthia wondered.

Everyone rushed toward the open front door, where two men lay on the floor with gunshot wounds to the shoulder and leg. Armed FBI agents and uniformed police were swarming all over them. A stunned Naomi stood terrified against a far wall, whimpering. Alvarez went to her without hesitation, wrapped an arm around her shoulder and led her away from the scene. She must have witnessed the whole thing. In fact, she'd probably run from the apartment after the incident in the kitchen and been attacked by Mafia guys, one of whom Cynthia recognized. An agent was holding a writhing snake by its tail with distaste . . . Sammy Caputo's trademark.

Another one bites the dust . . .

Ruth and Elmer's visit to the Dakota turned out to be a deliberate ploy. The agents had allowed Alvarez to bring them there, knowing the Mafia would trail after them. But at least the danger was over now. Apparently, Sammy Caputo was a small-time Mafia rogue. With him in custody, the feds didn't see any need for Naomi to stay in hiding any longer.

It was only noon now . . . hard to believe so much had happened in the past three hours. Ruth and Elmer had already left for Hoboken to start tidying up the mess there. Alvarez was helping Naomi pack her things so he could take her to Hoboken, too.

Cynthia and P.T. surveyed the mess in the kitchen . . .

enough food to feed an army left uneaten. With a sigh, Cynthia walked over to turn off the warming oven. Slanting a sideways glance at her husband, she suggested, "What do you say we go back to bed?"

"Have I told you lately that I love you?" was P.T.'s response.

"Not enough. Not nearly enough." She winked at him. "Maybe you'd better show me."

On the way, in an open bedroom door, they saw Alvarez and Naomi in a wicked embrace. Naomi was pinned against the wall by the lawyer's insinuating body. Or was it Naomi who had Alvarez in a bear hug? They were kissing each other hungrily.

Cynthia looked at P.T. He looked at her.

"Amazing!" they both said at the same time.

But Cynthia thought, as she had often during the past week, that fairy tales really could come true.

And thus do dreams shatter . . .

"Congratulations, Prince Ferrama," the president of Donaldson & Donaldson said, shaking P.T.'s hand warmly. "We certainly hit the street with a bang."

Feeling a slight buzz from the glass of champagne she'd drunk, Cynthia braced herself against a paneled wall of the boardroom at Ferrama, Inc., where a celebratory party was just breaking up. She watched with admiration as P.T. worked the room smoothly, all decked out in a sharp Ermenegildo Zegna black pinstriped suit with a crisp Ralph Lauren white shirt and red-patterned Bolgheri tie, a gift from Alvarez. Yep, her husband was a born huckster with a promoter's instinct. The man was so slick he could skin a louse and send the hide and fat to market before the louse realized it had even been snared. Not a bad attribute for surviving in the rat race of high finance, she had to admit.

And, yes, it appeared the prince really was her husband. Elmer had surprised them all with a bona fide ministerial license. Cynthia had bagged herself an honest-to-God prince. But this was a day for acknowledging P.T.'s triumph, not hers.

The stock offering had exploded onto the market with resounding success. Not only was the issue oversubscribed—more demand than shares available—but those who got in on the initial offering at five dollars saw it get an immediate two-dollar premium. The five-dollars-per-share stock was already worth fifteen dollars a share. All that translated into several million dollars more for the Ferrama and Friedman pockets, plus a sizable amount for Jake and Dick.

Cynthia had a cashier's check for a cool million in her own purse, P.T.'s settlement offer for all her pain and suffering. She wasn't sure if she was going to accept it yet, but she might.

P.T. caught her eye across the room, as he had throughout the evening, and she recognized the unspoken communication. *Our celebration will be held in private. Soon.* Cynthia couldn't wait.

She marveled at all that had happened to her in the past three weeks. How could she be so blessed? What lucky clover had she plucked to bring her this good fortune?

Good luck comes in slender currents, misfortune comes in rolling torrents.

Cynthia recoiled at the dire warning that had just flitted through her mind. Was it Grandma or instinct at work now? Or perhaps just the fear that if she was too happy she might make the gods jealous.

"How's it goin', toots?" Alvarez drawled, coming up to lean against the wall beside her. He looked half-crocked, but he was probably only dazed, as he had been the past week, ever since Elmer had zapped him with a Naomi love potion. At least, that was how everyone chose to view the outlandish notion of the womanizing Alvarez head over heels in love with the overbearing Naomi.

"Pretty good. How about you?"

P.T. glanced over at her and winked. She winked back.

Alvarez witnessed the exchange and grinned. "I forgot to congratulate you. Naomi just told me that you and the boss got hitched at the castle. Does that mean the lawsuit is kaput? Man, that P.T. is something when he sets his sights on a quarry. Who would have believed he'd get nailed in the process, too?" He chuckled to himself at some private joke.

She turned to study him uneasily. "Why would you say that?"

"You know . . . the whole seduction scheme. You fell for it hook, line and sinker."

"Yeah, I guess I did. What a sucker I was, huh?"

"Nah, don't beat yourself up over it. It happens to women with P.T. all the time. And you got the last laugh, babe, don't forget that. You bagged and gagged him, good and proper."

Cynthia's heart felt like a lead weight in her chest.

It was all a setup. I knew it. My mind told me so . . . a million times. But I let myself hope. I let myself dream again. Oh, God!

"I never thought you'd fall for the prince routine, though—"

"Prince routine?

"Yeah. At what point did you realize he wasn't a real prince?"

Is he saying P.T. is only pretending to be a prince? Oh, no! He promised me. He said, "Trust me." If he lied about that, how many other lies did he tell me? Did he lie when he said he loved me? Was that the biggest scam of all?

"A sharp cookie like you surely caught on from the beginning." Alvarez gazed at her benevolently. To him, *smart cookie* was a compliment, even in this context. She couldn't be angry with the jerk. He wasn't being cruel. He just didn't see that, with every word, he was slicing her heart into pieces.

Putting a blank expression on her face, Cynthia inquired nonchalantly, "I never did understand the need for that whole charade."

"Are you kidding me? When we came up with that campaign to change the direction of Friedman's shoes to Ferrama five years ago, the royalty connection was an inspiration. It gave us an instant P.R. bonanza. I'm not sure we would have succeeded in this competitive business without it."

The missing puzzle pieces fell together for Cynthia. Unfortunately, she was discovering that when the puzzle was completed, there was no room for her in the picture.

Stricken, she searched the room through the blur of welling tears and finally located Ferrama—*plain old Peter Ferrama. Dammit. Not a prince. Not my husband. Not my lover. Not my anything.* He was standing in a group of office employees, including Maureen, when he became aware of her scrutiny.

Like a slow-motion video, she saw the instant he realized that his game was up. At first, he just tilted his head in question. Then he glanced at Alvarez, still lounging against the wall beside her, then back to her. His dark skin paled visibly, as he silently mouthed, "No!"

She didn't know what happened next because she spun on her heel and ran from the room. He caught up with her as she was about to enter the elevator.

"Go away," she sobbed.

"No. Never." He wedged a shoulder into the closing doors and came up beside her, trying to take her into his arms.

She shrugged him away.

"Let me explain."

She raised her chin angrily. "Did you come up to the castle with a slimeball scheme to seduce me into a quick settlement?"

"No . . . yes . . . it's not like it seems, *querida.*"

"Oh, how is it, then?" she stormed. "Is it that you came up to seduce me but fell madly in love? Is it that there never was a love spell? Is it that you and Elmer and your stepsisters have been in cahoots all along? Is it that you set out to catch a shark and I've been the centerpiece of a world-class fish fry?"

"It's not like that at all, Cynthia. Just calm down and I'll explain everything. Be sensible."

"Sensible? I'll give you sensible," she shrieked. Forcing herself to take several deep breaths, she said in a flat voice, "One more question. Are you a real prince?"

"Technically, yes."

She let out a loud exhalation of disgust. "Technically?"

"Dick bought a title for me, and a vacant volcanic island in the Spanish Canaries. But to answer your question . . . am I a prince? Hell, no."

"Where are you from?"

"Puerto Rico."

She put a fist to her trembling lips to stifle a cry.

"Ah, Cynthia, what difference does it make?"

"You fool! If you can't see the difference, then you know nothing at all about dreams and hope and, most of all, trust."

The elevator doors swished open and she started to exit, head held high. She wasn't sure how long she could hold out before her shaky legs gave way under the duress of her breaking heart.

To her back, she heard him whisper, "I love you."

It should have been enough—that precious declaration—but it wasn't. Not in the real world, where dreams and hopes were dead . . . where fairy tales did not come true.

The princess found a cause . . .

Cynthia was miserable.

For the first time in a week, she'd left her apartment. She was sitting now on a bench in Central Park, watching the children feeding the ducks, lovers walking by arm in arm, police patrolling the area . . . in essence, life continuing around her while she felt dead inside.

She would never be able to forgive Ferrama for restoring her hopes and dreams only to tear them apart again. She'd refused all visits and telephone calls from the wretch, had even changed her phone number so she would be able to take business calls without hearing his phony professions of love on her answering machine. If she didn't know him for the con artist he was, she could swear there had been tears in his voice. Hah! From the man who professed never to weep!

Elmer, Ruth, Naomi, even a fiercely apologetic Alvarez, had also tried repeatedly to storm her barricades, but she'd been adamant in refusing any contact from the enemy camp. And they were her enemies, no doubt about it.

"Like the sun on the hill and the thistle on the hearth," Cynthia murmured with a sigh, "that's how fleeting a man's affections are."

It would be hard to forget Ferrama. She tried to tell herself that the other old triad was true, too. "Three things there are that leave no trace: a bird on a branch, a ship on the sea and a man on a woman." But she feared it wasn't true in her case. Ferrama's trace would always be on her. Always.

On Monday, Cynthia would return to work. She hoped life would regain some semblance of normalcy. She would survive. Sharks always did. But it would be a different Cynthia Sullivan who hit the exchange now. A wiser one, who'd learned well from her harsh lesson: never trust; take the offense; harden the emotions; never, ever believe in dreams again.

"Is that a fairy castle?"

Cynthia was jolted out of her morbid reverie by the sound of a child's voice.

A little girl of about four, dressed in faded denim coveralls, had sidled up on the bench beside her and was staring off in the distance at the barely discernible outline of the Dakota. To a small child, she supposed it would appear to be a palace.

"Yes, sweetie, you could say it is."

"I'm gonna be a princess someday," the girl told her, swinging her tiny legs over the edge of the seat. Her blond hair was braided neatly into two pigtails, tied with ratty red ribbons. She was an absolute doll, but clearly from a poor family if her holey sneakers and mended clothing were any indication.

"I'm sure you will, sweetheart. Where's your mommy? She must be worried about you."

The child pointed to a group of children near the edge of the pond, supervised by two overworked women. "Thass Miss Penny. She's from the center. She reads me Cinderella every day."

"Well, that's nice. You like fairy tales, do you?"

The girl nodded. "But we don't have any, 'sides Cinderella. Miss Penny's gonna buy some more . . . someday. But first . . ."

The young woman—Miss Penny, Cynthia presumed—ran up to them. "Diana, you have to stop running off like this. You know the rules. No wandering." She turned to Cynthia. "I'm sorry if she was bothering you. It's just that we're so understaffed at the project's day-care center. We try to keep tabs on the children for this one field trip a month, but . . ." She shrugged helplessly.

"Diana was no problem. In fact, I enjoyed talking with her," Cynthia said, but all she could think of was that Diana lived in the projects. Just as Cynthia had.

On her walk back to the Dakota, a teenager on a bicycle, boom box blasting, almost ran her over, so deep in contemplation was she. Ironically, the song blaring out at about a hundred decibels was, "I'm So Lonesome I Could Cry." For some reason, Cynthia didn't feel like crying now.

The minute she got home, she rooted through some old boxes till she found what she'd been searching for—her childhood collection of tattered and well-read fairy-tale books. She tightened her jaw with determination. Never underestimate the power of an Irishwoman with a mission.

I might not have any fairy-tale endings in my life, but I sure as hell can make them happen for other children. Princess Diana, I'm about to make your dreams come true.

He was so lonesome he could cry . . .

P.T. was so lonesome he could cry.

A week after his stock offering . . . the day his world had fallen apart . . . a box of his clothing and personal items was delivered to the Ferrama offices by special courier. Inside was a terse note, formally addressed to Peter Ferrama on business stationery:

Don't call or try to contact me anymore. If you ever cared for me at all, respect that wish.
                                    Cynthia Sullivan

He'd thought it telling that she'd used her maiden name. And even more soul-crushing had been the note she'd scribbled on the back of the uncashed million-dollar check she'd enclosed:

You won. Congratulations. Is there any heat greater than that of shame?

He'd honored her request to be left alone, grudgingly, but as a last-ditch effort to win her back, he went on one of the morning TV talk shows for an exclusive interview. In that excruciating twenty minutes, he disclosed the entire prince charade, why he'd pulled it off and what he'd lost in the process. He hadn't used Cynthia's name, but he hoped she'd see the show and his remorse. He prayed she would forgive him.

Unfortunately, the interview backfired.

The next day Ferrama stock shot up another two points. His face was plastered on every tabloid in the country, along with speculation on who the mystery woman might be. Old photos of him in compromising poses were dredged up. Some Internet scandal blog claimed to have some European historian with documents showing he really was a prince, after all . . . that his absentee father had been a renegade Spanish prince.

Cynthia would probably believe that he'd done the TV interview for self-serving purposes. For money and ambition and the betterment of his company . . . as he always had in the past.

As an indication of how desperate he was, P.T. finally went to Elmer for advice. He was performing a gig in

Jersey City at the Colonel's Lounge—the opening act for Francine, The Double-Jointed Stripper.

Between sets, P.T. tried to talk to Elmer over the sound of the loud bump 'n' grind music and raucous male catcalls. "What should I do, Elmer? You should have some answers. I love her. She loves me . . . I think. I just don't understand."

"Ah, laddie, did ye not know there are three kinds of men who fail to understand women: young men, old men and middle-aged men."

"You're a lot of help."

"What is got badly, goes badly. Your remorse is worth cuckoo spit without action."

"Would you stop talking in those damn riddles?"

"The effects of an evil act are long felt, boy, so don't be expecting easy solutions."

"Should I get rid of the company? Wear sackcloth? Beg her on hands and knees?"

"Words will not free the friars, nor a heartsick maid. Think with your heart, not your mind. What is it that the lassie wants, deep in her heart of hearts?"

P.T. had no idea. Well, yes, he did. "A prince?"

"You've crushed her dream. Now give it back to her."

P.T. wasn't sure if he was up to the task, but he was determined to try. He was going to be the best damn prince that rode down the New Jersey Turnpike. He was going to be so courageous, she'd fear for his life. He was going to be so chivalrous, she would swoon. He was going to be so knock-your-socks-off charming, she wouldn't be able to resist him. He was going to put every prince before him to shame.

But first, he was going to pray.

And finally the frog became a prince . . .

Cynthia had been back at work for a month . . . a different person than she'd been a few short weeks before. Harder. Coarser in her language. Driven by ambition. Colder with her friends and acquaintances.

Except for the one day a week she volunteered at the Blue Bird Day-Care Center in the projects.

Thanks to her hard-nosed experience in sales, Cynthia had managed to coax fifty thousand dollars in contributions from her bosses, business associates, clients, anyone who listened to her or failed to escape her path in time. As a result, the Blue Bird now had a complete library of children's books, including every fairy tale ever written. Stereo and video equipment. A children's computer system. The walls of the drab center had been painted in bright shades of blue and yellow and green. Playground equipment was on order. Volunteers had come out of the woodwork.

Little Princess Diana, wearing a twenty-five-year-old tarnished tiara that had belonged to another little girl in another ghetto long ago, was half-reclining now on a huge beanbag chair with Cynthia. The hard-as-tacks stock trader was reading Cinderella to her for the fifth time that day when the blare of trumpets resounded throughout the building. Everyone sat up straight and glanced at one another with puzzlement— the three dozen children, the half dozen adults, including volunteers, even the janitor.

The director, Penny Wilkins, stepped up behind Cynthia and asked, "Did you plan this as a treat for the children, Cynthia?"

The trumpets blared again, sounding almost like the

ones she'd heard outside Buckingham Palace one time on an A&E special, announcing the arrival of a royal party. In fact, she'd watched a rerun of it with her husband one night during their short honeymoon in her Dakota apartment. They'd been in bed at the time, and . . .

Every fine hair stood out on her body in sudden suspicion.

He wouldn't.

Would he?

This time the blare of trumpets was accompanied by the stern-faced arrival of two lines of imperial guards, attired in what resembled uniforms that might have been worn by palace courtiers in days of old. The contingent stopped and raised swords to form an arch. The loud monotone voice of one of the men announced, "Prince Pedro Tomas de la Ferrama."

Penny twittered behind her, and Diana sighed.

Through the saber canopy strolled the most outrageous sight Cynthia had ever witnessed in all her days. The Frog Prince . . . the Prince of Trolls . . . the Prince of Broken Dreams. Her husband.

Diana let out a wistful "ooooh" of delight. People started to clap. And Cynthia put her face in her hands. When she looked up again, he was still there, and approaching her with the regal grace of a born-to-the-manor nobleman.

He was wearing some kind of velveteen suit with tight leggings tucked in low leather boots, a hiplength, long-sleeved tunic, belted at the waist and over it all a floor-length fur robe that trailed behind him. A huge gilt crown sat on his head, tilted slightly askew.

He looked ridiculous.

So, why is my heart thundering? Why are tears welling in my eyes? Why do I care that there are tears in his eyes?

Cynthia tried to sit up, but Penny put firm hands on her shoulders. "Don't spoil this for the children," she pleaded.

Cynthia swallowed hard over the lump in her throat and hissed at her husband, who had dropped to one knee before her. "You look like an idiot."

"Yes, m'lady wife," he agreed. Under his breath, he remarked, "Good thing I ditched the codpiece."

"He's your husband?" Penny whispered. "Holy cow!"

"Holy Cow" just about sums it up. "What kind of pathetic stunt is this, P.T.? Are there TV cameras outside? Will this boost your stock sales?"

P.T. raised his chin haughtily and pulled a scroll from his belt. "I have come to read you a proclamation, oh shrewish lady." He whipped open the scroll, undaunted when it failed to flourish the first time, "Cheap scroll makers," he mumbled.

Cynthia put a palm to her mouth to hide a grin. *I am not going to be amused by him. I'm not.*

"Let it be known by one and all . . . Prince Pedro Tomas de la Ferrama loves his wife, Princess Cynthia Kathleen Sullivan Ferrama, with all his heart and soul."

Cynthia made a snickering sound.

He flashed her a dark look and continued. "Throughout time, men have been known to transgress, but women have forgiven them."

"Not this woman!"

"This I do pledge . . . never for the rest of my days will I lie to my beloved wife."

"How about anyone else?"

"Don't push it, babe," he muttered, and tipped up his unruly crown, which kept slipping down on his forehead. It must belong to someone with a really big head, though P.T.'s was plenty big enough. "This, too, do I pledge . . . to give up all my worldly assets into her hands."

"So, you want me to handle your portfolio, huh? Too late, bozo. I handle only a select clientele."

"And verily do I promise to take her to my royal principality, where she may view our holdings." Under his breath, he added, "Volcanoes, snakes and all."

Cynthia did giggle then. She couldn't help herself.

His face relaxed like magic at what he must consider a sign of her softening. She tried to glare at him but failed.

"Let it be written in all the annals, whenever Princess Ferrama so deems it, she may order her husband to don absurd royal garb . . . though subjects from far and wide may laugh at him, though women no longer find him irresistible, though men smirk and TV comedians rule him fair game, though pigeons drop—"

"Enough 'thoughs' already. I get the point."

"Petitions have I here signed by myriad subjects, attesting to the pain one Prince Ferrama hath suffered these many weeks. Long is his sorrow and deep the hole left in his life by the absence of his soulmate."

Cynthia's mouth dropped open. "I'm impressed. Who wrote this drivel? Elmer?" She didn't really consider it drivel, but if she acknowledged how deeply touched she was, he'd take advantage; she knew he would.

He tossed back his head, affronted . . . and almost lost his crown. "I did, and many a nub did I break on my quill seeking the perfect words."

"Well, then, I suppose they're satisfactory."

He flashed her a smoldering glance. "This final pledge do I make to my lady wife. Let all hear it said . . . I, Prince Pedro Tomas de la Ferrama, do love thee, Princess Cynthia Kathleen Ferrama, with all my heart and soul. If thou wouldst give this cur another chance, I wouldst make thee the happiest woman in all the kingdoms of the world. And I wouldst make a home for thee . . . thou . . . whatever . . . in the Dakota or the Poconos or the suburbs or Camelot, whate'er be thy whim. And we wouldst drive pickup trucks or BMWs or limos or horses if thou choose. We will dance Irish jigs, or *flamingoes*"—he grinned at that misspeak—"or line dances. Yeah we may listen to Elvis music till the cows come home, or the record player breaks. Just know"— his voice cracked—"just know that I cannot live without my fairy princess."

Cynthia couldn't speak.

He stared at her, silence resounding in the air like cymbals, fear and vulnerability apparent in his dark eyes, despite his absurd, touching words. When she didn't react, he jerked his head for one of his guards to approach. "Bring forth the coup de grâce." Under his breath, he added, "I hope."

He handed her a silk-wrapped gift. "For you, my lady love, the latest creation of Ferrama."

Tentatively, Cynthia unfolded the scarlet fabric

and saw inside two glass slippers . . . well, they were some synthetic material designed to replicate glass. She raised her eyes in question.

"'Tis called Cindy's Dream. I thought about calling it Cinderella, but this name seemed more appropriate." He took one of the pumps from her hand, removed a loafer from her foot and slipped the shoe on with ease. It was probably a size nine, as the lout had once pronounced her size to be, not her real size, seven and a half. Whatever.

With one hand around her ankle and the other clapped over his heart, he pleaded, "Will you be my Cinderella?"

"Yes," she whispered. How could she say anything else? How could she not forgive a man who would risk making a perfect fool of himself to win back his love? How could she face the rest of her life without this rogue in it? "Yes," she repeated, louder now.

"Yes? Did you say 'yes'?" He closed his eyes, as if saying a silent prayer. "Thank God!" he whooped, rising creakily. "My knee is killing me." He pulled her into his arms with a jubilant laugh, his crown falling to the floor with a clunk.

His face turned somber as he regarded her. "You will never regret . . ." he started to say, but had trouble continuing as tears filled his beautiful eyes. He pressed a palm to his mouth and closed his eyes, fighting for control. When he opened his eyes, he told her in a raw voice, "I am so sorry for hurting you."

"I know that," she whispered. And she did.

Realizing that they had a huge audience witnessing this touching scene, she pulled him into a storage room.

"If I could be a real prince for you, Cynthia, I

would," he swore between soul-searing kisses and breath-stopping hugs.

"You are such a fool, Ferrama," she said. "Don't you know you are my prince? For always."

Epilogue

Elvis lives! . . .

Prince and Princess Pedro Tomas de la Ferrama lived a happy life amid their various kingdoms in the Upper West Side and the Poconos.

The prince learned to fish, and his princess wore an apron on certain occasions.

Their creative shoe designs ended up in museum collections. And they amassed great wealth from a pumice stone industry located on their island homeland, where volcanoes flourished, to their great fortune.

They had two children. Tom took over the shoe company and added a line of millinery, for which he was credited with single-handedly bringing back into fashion upscale women's hats. Siobhan gained fame as an Irish folk dancer.

Enrique Alvarez and Naomi Friedman were married on Valentine's Day. He gave up lawyering and together they restored and operated the Castle Bed 'n' Breakfast. The waiting list for reservations ran two years' long. Their five children grew up to help with the vastly popular establishment. Everyone who met the couple swore they were made for each other . . . a match made in heaven.

Elmer Presley and Ruth Friedman headed off to Memphis, where Elmer gave up his singing career for a highly lucrative Elvis memorabilia store. Ruth did glow-in-the-dark manicures in the back.

Some say that Elvis died on August 16, 1977, but his fans know there was an everlasting magic in the King. Some even say they catch a glimpse of Elvis here and there.

For those who believe, the legend lives on.

And for those who believe, fairy tales surely can come true.

Can't get enough of *USA Today* and
New York Times bestselling
author Sandra Hill?
Turn the page for glimpses of her amazing
books. From cowboys to Vikings, Navy
SEALs to Southern bad boys, every one
of Sandra's books has her unique blend of
passion, creativity, and unparalleled wit.

Welcome to the World of Sandra Hill!

The Viking Takes a Knight

⊗

For John of Hawks' Lair, the unexpected appearance of a beautiful woman at his door is always welcome. Yet the arrival of this alluring Viking woman, Ingrith Sigrundottir—with her enchanting smile and inviting curves—is different . . . for she comes accompanied by a herd of unruly orphans. And Ingrith needs more than the legendary knight's hospitality; she needs protection. For among her charges is a small boy with a claim to the throne—a dangerous distinction when murderous King Edgar is out hunting for Viking blood.

A man of passion, John will keep them safe—but in exchange, he wants something very dear indeed: Ingrith's heart, to be taken with the very first meeting of their lips . . .

Viking in Love

☙

*C*aedmon of Larkspur *was the most loathsome lout*
Breanne had ever encountered. When she
arrived at his castle with her sisters, they were
greeted by an estate gone wild, while Caedmon
laid abed after a night of ale. But Breanne must
endure, as they are desperately in need of protection . . . and he is quite handsome.

After nine long months in the king's service, all
Caedmon wanted was peace, not five Viking princesses running about his keep. And the fiery redhead who burst into his chamber was the worst of
them all. He should kick her out, but he has a far
better plan for Breanne of Stoneheim—one that
will leave her a Viking in lust.

The Reluctant Viking

⊗

The self-motivation tape was supposed to help Ruby Jordan solve her problems, not create new ones. Instead, she was lulled into an era of hard-bodied warriors and fair maidens. But the world ten centuries in the past didn't prove to be all mead and mirth. Even as Ruby tried to update medieval times, she had to deal with a Norseman whose view of women was stuck in the Dark Ages. And what was worse, brawny Thork had her husband's face, habits, and desire to avoid Ruby. Determined not to lose the same man twice, Ruby planned a bold seduction that would conquer the reluctant Viking—and make him an eager captive of her love.

The Outlaw Viking ·

☬

As tall and striking as the Valkyries of legend, Dr. Rain Jordan was proud of her Norse ancestors despite their warlike ways. But she can't believe it when she finds herself on a nightmarish battlefield, forced to save the barbarian of her dreams.

He was a wild-eyed warrior whose deadly sword could slay a dozen Saxons with a single swing, yet Selik couldn't control the saucy wench from the future. If Selik wasn't careful, the stunning siren was sure to capture his heart and make a warrior of love out of **The Outlaw Viking**.

The Tarnished Lady

*B*anished from polite society, Lady Eadyth of Hawks' Lair spent her days hidden under a voluminous veil, tending her bees. But when her lands are threatened, Lady Eadyth sought a husband to offer her the protection of his name.

Notorious for loving—and leaving—the most beautiful damsels in the land, Eirik of Ravenshire was England's most virile bachelor. Yet when the mysterious lady offered him a vow of chaste matrimony in exchange for revenge against his most hated enemy, Eirik couldn't refuse. But the lusty knight's plans went awry when he succumbed to the sweet sting of the tarnished lady's love.

The Bewitched Viking

Even fierce Norse warriors have bad days. 'Twas enough to drive a sane Viking mad, the things Tykir Thorksson was forced to do—capturing a red-headed virago, putting up with the flock of sheep that follows her everywhere, chasing off her bumbling brothers. But what could a man expect from the sorceress who had put a kink in the King of Norway's most precious body part? If that wasn't bad enough, Tykir was beginning to realize he wasn't at all immune to the enchantment of brash red hair and freckles. Perhaps he could reverse the spell and hold her captive, not with his mighty sword, but with a Viking man's greatest magic: a wink and smile.

The Blue Viking

⟡

*F*or Rurik the Viking, life has not been worth living since he left Maire of the Moors. Oh, it's not that he misses her fiery red tresses or kissable lips. Nay, it's the embarrassing blue zigzag tattoo she put on his face after their one wild night of loving. For a fierce warrior who prides himself on his immense height, his expertise in bedsport, and his well-toned muscles, this blue streak is the last straw. In the end, he'll bring the witch to heel, or die trying. Mayhap he'll even beg her to wed . . . so long as she can promise he'll no longer be . . . **The Blue Viking.**

The Viking's Captive
(originally titled MY FAIR VIKING)

❧

yra, Warrior Princess. She is too tall, too loud, too fierce to be a good catch. But her ailing father has decreed that her four younger sisters—delicate, mild-mannered, and beautiful—cannot be wed 'til Tyra consents to take a husband. And then a journey to save her father's life brings Tyra face to face with Adam the Healer. A god in human form, he's tall, muscled, perfectly proportioned. Too bad Adam refuses to fall in with her plans—so what's a lady to do but truss him up, toss him over her shoulder, and sail off into the sunset to live happily ever after.

A Tale of Two Vikings

⊗

*T*oste and Vagn Ivarsson are identical Viking twins, about to face Valhalla together, following a tragic battle, or maybe something even more tragic: being separated for the first time in their thirty and one years. Alas, even the bravest Viking must eventually leave his best buddy behind and do battle with that most fearsome of all opponents—the love of his life. And what if that love was Helga the Homely, or Lady Esme, the world's oldest novice nun?

A Tale of Two Vikings will give you twice the tears, twice the sizzle, and twice the laughter . . . and make you wish for your very own Viking.

The Last Viking

*H*e was six feet, four inches of pure, unadulterated male. He wore nothing but a leather tunic, and he was standing in Professor Meredith Foster's living room. The medieval historian told herself he was part of a practical joke, but with his wide gold belt, ancient language, and callused hands, the brawny stranger seemed so . . . authentic. And as he helped her fulfill her grandfather's dream of re-creating a Viking ship, he awakened her to dreams of her own. Until she wondered if the hand of fate had thrust her into the loving arms of . . . **The Last Viking**.

Truly, Madly Viking

⊗

A *Viking named Joe? Jorund Ericsson is a tenth-century Viking* warrior who lands in a modern mental hospital. Maggie McBride is the lucky psychologist who gets to "treat" the gorgeous Norseman, whom she mistakenly calls Joe.

You've heard of *One Flew Over the Cuckoo's Nest*. But how about *A Viking Flew Over the Cuckoo's Nest*? The question is: Who's the cuckoo in this nest? And why is everyone laughing?

The Very Virile Viking

Magnus Ericsson is a simple man. He loves the smell of fresh-turned dirt after springtime plowing. He loves the feel of a soft woman under him in the bed furs. He loves the heft of a good sword in his fighting arm.

But, Holy Thor, what he does not relish is the bothersome brood of children he's been saddled with. Or the mysterious happenstance that strands him in a strange new land—the kingdom of *Holly Wood*. Here is a place where the folks think he is an *act-whore* (whatever that is), and the woman of his dreams—a winemaker of all things—fails to accept that he is her soul mate . . . a man of exceptional talents, not to mention . . . **A Very Virile Viking.**

Wet & Wild

✧

W/hat do you get when you cross a Viking with a Navy SEAL? A warrior with the fierce instincts of the past and the rigorous training of America's most elite fighting corps? A totally buff hero-in-the-making who hasn't had a woman in roughly a thousand years? A dyed-in-the-wool romantic with a hopeless crush? Whatever you get, women everywhere can't wait to meet him, and his story is guaranteed to be . . . **Wet & Wild**.

Hot & Heavy

In and out, that's the goal as Lt. Ian MacLean prepares for his special ops mission. He leads a team of highly trained Navy SEALs, the toughest, buffest fighting men in the world and he has nothing to lose. Madrene comes from a time a thousand years before he was born, and she has no idea she's landed in the future. After tying him up, the beautiful shrew gives him a tongue-lashing that makes a drill sergeant sound like a kindergarten teacher. Then she lets him know she has her own special way of dealing with over-confident males, and things get . . . **Hot & Heavy**.

Frankly, My Dear . . .

&

*L*ost in the Bayou . . . *Selene had three great passions:* men, food, and *Gone With the Wind*. But the glamorous model always found herself starving—for both nourishment and affection. Weary of the petty world of high fashion, she headed to New Orleans for one last job before she began a new life. Little did she know that her new life would include a brand-new time—about 160 years ago! Selene can't get her fill of the food—or an alarmingly handsome man. Dark and brooding, James Baptiste was the only lover she gave a damn about. And with God as her witness, she vowed never to go without the man she loved again.

Sweeter Savage Love

❧

The stroke of surprisingly gentle hands, the flash of fathomless blue eyes, the scorch of white-hot kisses . . . Once again, Dr. Harriet Ginoza was swept away into rapturous fantasy. The modern psychologist knew the object of her desire was all she should despise, yet time after time, she lost herself in visions of a dangerously hand-some rogue straight out of a historical romance. Harriet never believed that her dream lover would cause her any trouble, but then a twist of fate cast her back to the Old South and she met him in the flesh. To her disappointment, Etienne Baptiste refused to fulfill any of her secret wishes. If Harriet had any hope of making her amorous dreams become passionate reality, she'd have to seduce this charmer with a sweeter savage love than she'd imagined possible . . . and savor every minute of it.

The Love Potion

⊗

Fame and fortune are surely only a swallow away when Dr. Sylvie Fontaine discovers a chemical formula guaranteed to attract the opposite sex. Though her own love life is purely hypothetical, the shy chemist's professional future is assured . . . as soon as she can find a human guinea pig. But bad boy Lucien LeDeux—best known as the Swamp Lawyer—is more than she can handle even before he accidentally swallowed a love potion disguised in a jelly bean. When the dust settles, Luc and Sylvie have the answers to some burning questions—can a man die of testosterone overload? Can a straight-laced female lose every single one of her inhibitions?—and they learn that old-fashioned romance is still the best catalyst for love.

Love Me Tender

&

Once upon a time, in a magic kingdom, there lived a handsome prince. Prince Charming, he was called by one and all. And to this land came a gentle princess. You could say she was Cinderella . . . Wall Street Cinderella. Okay, if you're going to be a stickler for accuracy, in this fairy tale the kingdom is Manhattan. But there's magic in the Big Apple, isn't there? And maybe he can be Prince Not-So-Charming at times, and "gentle" isn't the first word that comes to mind when thinking of this princess. But they're looking for happily ever after just the same—and they're going to get it.

Desperado

☙

Mistaken for a notorious bandit and his infamously scandalous mistress, L.A. lawyer Rafe Santiago and Major Helen Prescott found themselves on the wrong side of the law. In a time and place where rules had no meaning, Helen found Rafe's hard, bronzed body strangely comforting, and his piercing blue eyes left her all too willing to share his bedroll. His teasing remarks made her feel all woman, and she was ready to throw caution to the wind if she could spend every night in the arms of her very own . . . **Desperado**.

*G*ive in to your Impulses!

These unforgettable stories only take a second to buy and give you hours of reading pleasure!

Go to *www.AvonImpulse.com* and see what we have to offer.
Available wherever e-books are sold.

AVONIMPULSE